To

Dear Eileen,

Enjoy.

With much love

Mo

X

THE ROUGH AND THE SMOOTH

THE ROUGH AND THE SMOOTH

Mo Barker

Book Guild Publishing
Sussex, England

For my mother

First published in Great Britain in 2006 by
The Book Guild Ltd,
25 High Street,
Lewes, East Sussex
BN7 2LU

Copyright © Mo Barker 2006

The right of Mo Barker to be identified as the author of
this work has been asserted by her in accordance with the
Copyright, Designs and Patents Act 1988.

All rights reserved. No part of this publication may be reproduced,
transmitted, or stored in a retrieval system, in any form or by any means,
without permission in writing from the publisher, nor be otherwise
circulated in any form of binding or cover other than that in which it is
published and without a similar condition being imposed on the
subsequent purchaser.

All characters in this publication are fictitious and any resemblance to
real people, alive or dead, is purely coincidental.

Typesetting in Times by
IML Typographers, Birkenhead, Merseyside

Printed in Great Britain by
CPI Bath

A catalogue record for this book is available from
The British Library.

ISBN 1 84624 011 5

Contents

Chapter 1	1
Chapter 2	19
Chapter 3	37
Chapter 4	51
Chapter 5	69
Chapter 6	111
Chapter 7	133
Chapter 8	159
Chapter 9	189
Chapter 10	229
Chapter 11	257
Chapter 12	273
Epilogue	295

1

September 1985.

A lull in trading afforded Susy the time for a quick cup of coffee and a cigarette. Inhaling deeply, she leant back against the stall and stared fixedly over the rooftops of the dowdy buildings in the Mile End Road and into a clear blue sky. The forecast was stormy: thunder and lightning, coupled with a tropical downpour. They got it wrong again. Prone to bouts of day-dreaming, the buzz of the market traders selling their wares all but disappeared as Susy closed her eyes and escaped the humdrum routine of everyday life. A sharp prod in the ribs brought her right back to reality. 'Dreamin again, eh? What you need, luvvy, is a real job. Do you no good 'anging around 'ere, you're going no place, do you 'ear me, don't want to end up like an old bag o'nothing.' Katie left a startled Susy to serve a customer and returned to her stall, '—yes darlin', two pounds of sprouts and five pounds o'Edwards.'

Katie looked 80, but if the truth be known she was much younger. A market trader all her life, if you could call it a life, more like an endurance test. She meant well and always found time for Susy, especially since her mum died, leaving her to run the stall single-handed. Katie turned again, plying the cigarette from her mouth, and waved a bony finger under Susy's nose. 'Get away from 'ere darlin'. What's stoppin' you? Go up West, make somethin' of yourself, eh? Good-lookin' gal like you could 'ave anythin' she pleased.'

'Good-looking,' the old girl's words rang in Susy's ears. Katie must be boss-eyed, she thought, for on a good day, in a bad light, maybe she could have anything or anybody she liked. Anyone, that is, who could get past the cast-iron grip of her dad, Eddy. For when he was not chasing a bit of skirt, he was preaching the ten commandments to her. A good Catholic upbringing had taught her that what lay ahead was marriage and a baby every two years for the next 15 years. Whatever happened to fun and the good times? How had she managed to reach the age of 25 and still be a virgin? Katie was right, she had to get away and soon.

The market was always frantic on a Saturday and Susy reluctantly returned to her customers. It was almost a year since her mother had died and life was not the same without her: she missed her desperately. Always so full of fun and laughter, she did not believe the doctors when they told her she had only six months to live. How did they know? Was there nothing they could do to stop the cancer ravaging her already frail body? Keep her alive, make her whole again?

At the end of the day's trading, Susy piled the last few boxes in the back of the transit van, hopped up behind the wheel and pulled away from the market. The sky was beginning to grow dark. 'Nite, Katie.'

'Get lost,' she yelled back.

Susy headed off home, travelling east along the Mile End Road towards Leytonstone. Rain began to fall heavily and traffic started to build up. The old transit van did not take kindly to heavy traffic, but on a straight run with her foot down, she would undoubtedly reach the destination. Anxious not to break down and cause a tailback to the city, Susy kept revving the engine. 'Come on Tulip, baby, you've got to make it,' but no words of encouragement helped and at the next junction Tulip died. Susy turned the ignition again and again, but nothing, not even a cough. 'Oh, bloody hell,' she screamed, banging the dashboard with the palm of her hand, as a flash of lightning lit up the sky, followed by a rumble of thunder in the distance. Torrential rain began to fall. Susy hung over the steering wheel gazing vacantly into space. She was stranded and, glancing at her watch, realised that Eddy would not be home yet. She despaired, but just maybe he would still be at Dave's café. Traffic started to move slowly past the broken-down van, with angry-looking occupants mouthing unheard obscenities through closed windows. Nobody stopped to help. Susy tugged on her jacket, slid the door of the van open and jumped out. Somewhere there would be a telephone box and pulling her jacket collar up and her head down she ran until, soaking wet, she located a call box. She tapped in the café's telephone number and waited.

''ello, Dave's Diner.'

'Dave, it's Susy. Put dad on the line.'

''e's not 'ere, Princess.'

Susy sighed. 'What time did he leave?'

''aven't seen 'im all day, babe. Anything wrong? You sound a bit funny.'

'Where can I find 'im Dave? I've broken down.'

'Search me, darlin'. Maybe 'e's at Norma's. Where are you?'

'Norma. What's 'e doin' with that old sow's ear?' Susy replied angrily.

'Ow, don't get upset, babe, she's OK is Norma, a bit of a laugh, you know what I mean. Your dad, since your mum passed on, he needs, well, you know, he needs a bit of recreation.'

'Recreation! She's not called the Stepney steeplejack for nothin', Dave. My mum would turn in her grave if she knew.'

Just the name of Norma Randle was like waving a red rag to a bull, for Susy had always thought Eddy was fooling around with Norma long before her mother died. 'I'm in the Mile End R–' The pips went and the line cut off. Susy fumbled in her jeans for another coin without luck.

She stumbled out of the telephone box in a rage and headed back towards the van, with great rivers of water pouring down her face as the wind and rain continued to rage. God, what a night, she thought, wiping water from her face with the sleeve of her jacket before she noticed somebody sitting behind the wheel of the van.

"'Ay! What the hell are you doing?' But as she drew closer her scowl turned into a broad grin.

'Billy, my saviour! Am I glad to see you darlin'.'

'Broken down, have we? I thought it was you. 'Bout time you changed this tin can, sweetheart.'

'How did you know it was me, Billy?'

'How did I know?' he shrugged. 'Take a good look, Susy, frigging canary yellow. They could pick this one up by satellite.'

'A joker,' she laughed. 'Just get me home quick. Do you think you can get her going?'

Billy was already outside with the bonnet up. 'You got a torch?' Susy shook her head and sank back into the passenger seat. She never carried anything in the van except fruit and veg. Then Billy almost disappeared under the bonnet, making a few cursory remarks as the rain continued to pour. Finally he surfaced. 'The carburettor's had it, babe, there's no way she'll start. I'll have to tow you.' Banging closed the bonnet and sliding back the van door he asked, 'Don't suppose you got a tow rope, have you? – Na, didn't think so,' then disappeared around the back of the van.

Susy smiled to herself. Billy O'Brian was a carpet layer, lived near Walthamstow, quite handsome in a craggy sort of way, but he had a bad reputation with the girls. With his dark hair and blue eyes he had played havoc with many hearts, dating three or four girls at a time, if he got the chance. Maybe that was why he stopped, she mused, the dirty devil.

Billy drove his pickup around the front of Susy's van and hooked her up to the back of his vehicle. 'OK, let's go. You still living in the same place?'

Susy was back behind the wheel, 'Yeah, ready when you are.'

Billy shouted instructions through the half-open car window, 'Now, when I brake you brake, OK darlin'? Don't want you trying to overtake me now, do we?'

That smile was certainly getting to Susy. She had not had a date for months, maybe longer and she allowed her imagination to drift, wondering what he had harnessed inside those blue jeans.

Should the opportunity present itself, she was certain he would allow her a peek, quite possibly a fully-fledged exposure.

They were off to a jumpy start and cornering was a nightmare, but finally they got a steady pace going and eventually pulled up outside Susy's home. The lights were on, Eddy was in and Susy had completely forgotten about Norma. Her thoughts were with Billy, hoping he would ask her out. Sure, she would take her chances with the others, competition was healthy. At last the rain had stopped as they walked up to the house together and Susy was angling for more time. 'Don't know what I would 'ave done if you 'adn't come along.' She laughed nervously. 'Still be thumbing it, I guess.'

'Think nothin' of it, darlin', I would 'ave done it for anyone.' I bet he would, she thought. ''Ow 'bout a drink sometime, catch up on old times, eh?'

Not wanting to sound too eager, Susy began to conjure up a full diary of forthcoming events, when the front door flew open and Eddy, larger than life, stood shadowing the doorway, his silhouette physically heaving.

'And what time do you call this then?' Susy shrank back at his bark. 'Market shut hours ago, where've you bin?' he glanced fiercely at Billy.

Susy butted in, 'I broke down, you weren't 'ere or at Dave's. I did phone.' An all too frequent interrogation was about to begin and she knew that it could go on for hours.

'Who's this then?' he roared.

'It's Billy, 'e gave me a tow. I'd still be there if it wasn't for 'im.'

Eddy was raging, 'Billy who?'

Billy politely interrupted; getting angry was not going to solve anything. 'Er, Billy O'Brian, Mr Stevens.'

'Get inside,' Eddy bellowed at Susy,

'But Eddy.'

'Susy, get inside, I'll handle this.'

Susy ran into the house not daring to look back and rushed upstairs. When Eddy Stevens was angry everyone did as he said.

'You're Harry O'Brian's boy, aren't you?' Billy nodded. 'Got a bit of a reputation with the ladies, I 'ear.' Eddy took a pace closer to Billy and raised his fist, 'Just let me tell you once, sonny boy. Now you go fuck the other girlies and stay away from my princess, she's not for you – I don't 'ave to warn you again now, do I?' Eddy grasped at Billy's collar.

'OK, Mr Stevens, I 'ear you loud and clear.' Billy spun around and vanished into the night, leaving Eddy growling quietly to himself, before walking back into the house.

'Susy, come down 'ere.'

After peeling off her wet clothes, Susy entered the lounge buttoning up her dressing gown. He was a force to be reckoned with, was Eddy Stevens. His home was his castle and his family his subjects. That is the way it had always been and would always be. Under his roof was under his rules and Susy was on the carpet again. She was going to get the same shit whether she had done something or not, might as well do it and be damned she thought, and have a whale of a time. Eddy was calmer, 'Sit down, babe and let's 'ave a little chat.' Susy obediently sat down opposite Eddy and waited for the blast, but he was different somehow, as she watched with curiosity the corners of his mouth turn up into a half smile. He spoke softly. 'Now, sweetheart, I don't want you mixing with crap like that Billy O'Brian. You're worth more than that and I didn't bring you into this world to end up with the likes of 'im. You're a little lady and you're goin' to find a prince charming to look after you, just like I do.' He was going soft in the head, Susy thought. There was something amiss and she could sense it. What was he up to? She knew Eddy inside out and this was a different angle. She waited and listened. 'Some day, babe, you'll know when the right one comes along and then everything will fall into place.' Susy searched the face for a sign and still said nothing, for he had not yet finished. 'Like when I met your mum,' he smiled. 'We were young, 'bout your age and for the first time we fell in love.' Bullshit, Susy thought, he'd been through the whole of Bethnal Green and she was six months pregnant. He continued.

'Then we got married and you came along, making everything sweet, and that's what I want for you, the best. Haven't I always given you everything you wanted?' Susy was silent, words failed her, for Eddy had given her what he could readily lay his hands on. Could this gentle approach mean that the time had come when he wanted something in return?

'Yeah,' she finally said, not quite sure what she was agreeing to.

'So I want you to think 'bout what I 'ave said, you'll see, it makes sense.' He got up and walked out of the room, while Susy remained seated, staring blankly into space. Billy O'Brian had had nothing at all to do with that conversation. What was Eddy up to? What did he want?

Susy questioned his motives. He's looking pretty racy tonight, she noted. She did not remember seeing him in that suit before and what was that smell, aftershave? Phew! She got up and followed him into the kitchen.

'Going out?' she queried.

'Yeah, think I'll go out for a bit.'

Susy turned to face Eddy. 'Where're you goin' then?'

'Think I'll go up The Stow. Frank and Dave said they were goin', seein' that it's Saturday night and all that.'

'Oh yeah! They wearing new whistles, too?' she teased.

Eddy turned to admire himself in the reflection of the window, 'Like it, babe? Frankie had a job lot in, I got one in blue, too.'

Susy circled Eddy, watching his every move. 'Still duckin' and divin', our Frankie, then?' She knew she was getting the upper hand.

Eddy chuckled, pinching her hard on the side of the cheek. 'Don't you be a cheeky princess. Now, be a good girl while daddy goes out to play.' He pulled on his coat and with a nod and a wink he was out of the front door.

Thankful for the peace and quiet, after what had been a hectic day, Susy could indulge herself. A hot bath to soothe the aching body, followed by a large scotch on the rocks to relax the mind, she felt cosy and comfortable. As sleep overcame her, she climbed wearily into bed and switched off the light.

Susy turned over in bed disturbed by a faint knocking and banging, only to sink straight back into a deep sleep. Again, only louder, the same noise woke her, when she tossed over in bed and made a grab for the clock: 3.20 a.m. She groaned, flopped back on to the pillow and soon drifted back to sleep again. A crash and soft laughter filtered through the house as Susy, now wide awake, swung her legs out of bed and over to the bedroom door. All was quiet as she opened the door and peered along the landing to Eddy's bedroom, where his door was wide open. Hearing only the beat of her heart, Susy tiptoed out on to the landing. Eddy was not home and yet she distinctly heard the sound of voices. She crept back to her room and climbed back into bed. Tomorrow she would remind Eddy to get a dog. She snuggled back under the warm duvet. Tomorrow was Sunday, she could sleep until noon, breakfast in bed with the papers. A high-pitched scream and a woman's voice brought Susy quickly out on to the landing again. Slowly she sneaked down the stairs to where the faint sounds of voices could be heard emanating from the living room where the lights were on. Susy crept closer, hardly breathing, so as to catch every word.

'No, Eddy – stop it!' As a hand slapped across bare flesh.

Susy lined her back up against the wall outside the living room door, which was ajar and listened. She could hear Eddy moaning. 'Shush babe – gimme a kiss, go on, just a little one.'

Susy waited for Norma's muffled reply, 'You're insatiable, you are, Eddy Stevens. Get off, will ya.'

There was another loud slap and suppressed laughter. 'Norma, sweetheart, I think I love you.'

Susy gently inched the door open and looked inside, to see Eddy's bum, whiter than a pound of lard, pants hanging around his thighs and riding high over Norma's half dressed body, his rough hands pawing at her breasts. Susy was repulsed as she banged the door and marched back to her room.

'Norma bleeding Randle!' she said out loud, 'The cow.'

Susy threw herself back on to the bed and recalled the conversation she had had with Eddy earlier. He had never brought a girlfriend back to the house before when she was there. What did it all mean? What was it he had said. 'When the right one comes along you'll know.' Norma Randle, was she what it was all about? Susy did not sleep another wink that night, knowing what she had to face in the morning. In fact, she was up at eight and breakfast was long over, when Eddy strolled into the kitchen like a lion after a kill. 'Morning, babe.' Susy glanced up from the paper but did not answer. She noted the blue silk dressing gown and velvet slippers. Eddy certainly did not deprive himself of life's little luxuries. The gold cross and chain, a Christmas gift from her mother two years previously flagrantly hung around his neck. Had he no respect?

'Morning, babe,' he said again, 'bin up long?'

'Couldn't sleep,' she replied. 'Have any luck at the dogs?'

'Na, waste of time. Frank and Dave didn't show, so I pushed off down The Swan.'

Susy watched him rustle up some coffee and as he opened the kitchen cupboard and took down two cups and saucers, she pretended not to notice. A tray! Norma was still around. Eddy sensed some tension, 'Got anything on today, sweetheart?'

'Johnnie's bringing over another van and taking Tulip back to the garage.'

'Ah good, good – ace mechanic is Johnnie, a little gem. Be sweet to 'im babe, I don't want to lose 'im.'

Susy watched Eddy sidle past her with tray in hand and make his way upstairs again, his huge frame bouncing along like an adolescent.

Eventually Norma had to put in an appearance, for the only way out of the house was through the front door. Susy bided her time. Johnnie was late and it was getting very close to lunchtime. The commotion above stairs alerted Susy to a possible sighting and moving into the hall, she folded her arms in front of her and leant against the wall in anticipation. Eddy was first, followed by

Norma, her emaciated body topped by the biggest pair of knockers this side of the Blackwall Tunnel. Eddy certainly had his hands full. He smiled broadly, ushering Norma forward towards Susy, 'Norma, Susy.'

'I know,' Susy said flatly, eyeing her up and down.

'Good-looker your Susy, Eddy, all that lovely red hair.' Norma screwed her face into a toothy grin.

Susy transferred her attention to Eddy, 'What's she doin 'ere, sleeping in my mum's bed?'

'That's enough of your lip, my girl,' Eddy said, grabbing his jacket and bustling Norma towards the front door, avoiding any further confrontation.

'So where're you goin'?' Susy yelled after them.

'None of your business,' Eddy bellowed. 'And I'll speak to you later.' Slamming the door behind him, the sound reverberated down the hall. She stood there until the sound of Eddy's Jaguar disappeared down the street, then returned to the kitchen.

Susy sat down hard on a kitchen chair, cupping her head with her hands. She felt trapped and despairing. Where was life leading her? What was she going to do? She worked, ate and slept according to Eddy. He knew her every move, every moment of her life. A wave of panic came over her as she could foresee the future. Norma would inch her way into Eddy's life and before too long into his home, their home. She was already fetching and carrying, keeping house. Susy had no friends, no boyfriends – he forbade it. There was always a good reason to say no. 'The family, babe, think of the family.' Susy let out an earth-shattering scream, 'Mum, where are you, you'd know what to do.' Tears streamed down her face. 'This God-awful life I'm leading, please somebody help me.'

'Aye, anybody in?' A loud rapping on the window made Susy turn around. 'Susy, is that you in there? You all right, sweetheart?' Susy wiped the tears away with the sleeve of her sweater; she had forgotten about Johnnie. She shuffled to the door and opened it, then shuffled back towards the kitchen. Johnnie was close on her heels, overtook her in the hall and, grabbing her by the shoulders, shook her. 'OK, where is he, which way did he go, darlin'?' Johnnie glanced nervously out of the kitchen window and into the back garden.

'No, no, Johnnie, you've got it all wrong.'

'I'll 'ave the bastard darlin'.' He flung open the kitchen door.

'No stupid. Aye come back 'ere,' Susy said, trying to grab Johnnie's arm. He was prancing around the garden like a bloodhound. 'What'd he get, babe?' Susy stood in the doorway and could not believe what she was seeing. 'Nothin', Johnnie, honest, there's nobody 'ere.'

'Don't give me that, Susy, I heard that scream.'

Johnnie continued to dodge shadows, turning over everything in the garden shed. Satisfied that there was not an intruder he walked slowly back to the house, sweat pouring from his brow, thankful he did not have to put up a fight. Johnnie's sparring days were long over, as his beer gut suggested.

Susy's tears had turned to laughter as she explained to Johnnie that there was no intruder and that she was just reflecting her lot in life, letting off steam, having a blast.

'Johhnie, my mum's barely cold and 'ere's that tart Norma Randle moving in on me and Eddy. I've got to get out of 'ere, but I don't know 'ow I'm goin to do it. I've only ever known the market. Eddy always gave me everything when I was a kid, but I'm a big girl now. What do I do?'

Johnnie was flattered that Susy should value his opinion, want his advice. His wife never did, so he said. He was sterile. 'Shame,' Susy said, 'you'd make a great dad.' Johnnie was the salt of the earth, help anybody out if he could. He sat for a while gazing into his beer.

'Well, my sister Gill manages a fashion shop up West, might be worth a try darlin'. Want me to give her a bell?'

'Anythin', Johnnie, I got to make a start somewhere.'

'OK, sweetheart, I'll do it first thing tomorrow.'

Almost forgetting the reason for being there, Johnnie threw Susy the van keys as he left and drove off with Tulip on tow.

* * *

Another working day was beginning as market traders were setting up for a busy day. Susy always arranged her stall artistically, placing rows of the best produce on display with neat little cards strategically placed. Begrudgingly, she served the early punter who interrupted her masterpiece. Should have been a sculptor or a painter, she thought, standing back and admiring her work. Maybe there was still time to learn. Fired by the prospect of a new life, a new start away from the market, anything was possible. All she had to do was get off her backside and move on.

'Morning darlin'. It's lookin' good today.'

Susy swung around. 'Morning, Mary. How's it goin', good weekend?'

'Lovely, sweetheart, christened the little one this weekend. Seems it's the only time the family gets together at dos like that, then all they do is fight. Can't win, eh!'

Susy put the finishing touch to her display, 'Yeah, tell me about it.'

'Where's Katie?' Mary asked.

'Shouldn't be far away,' Susy replied, glancing at her watch, 'She's late this morning. Probably had one too many again last night.'

'Ah to be sure, she like a tipple, does Katie, but she's never late.'

The market was busy, with not a moment to spare. Susy's regular punters seemed to converge on her at the same time, but Katie's stall remained empty. The morning flew by with traders bouncing bawdy remarks at one another across the market and Susy was hopping from one leg to the other. 'Mary, cover for me, I've got to have a pee. Quick, else I'll wet me knickers.'

'All right now, but don't be long.' Mary turned to serve the next customer as Susy grabbed her cigarettes and ran. After the blessed relief of emptying her bladder, she stopped for a coffee and as she lit up, her thoughts turned to Katie. In all the years she had been at the market, Katie never missed a day unless there was a wedding or funeral to attend. 'Oh no, I gotta phone,' she mumbled to herself.

The telephone rang for what seemed like an hour, but no reply and placing the telephone back on the hook, Susy doubled back to the stall. Mary was waving her hands furiously in the air. 'Jesus, Mary and Joseph, how long does it take to have a pee darlin'?'

'Leave it out, Mary, I was only five minutes.'

'Sure you were. Time for a quickie I'll not be mistaken.'

'Gimme a chance, just gimme a chance.' Susy's grimace betrayed her anxiety.

'What's happened, luvvy, is somethin' wrong?' After explaining the telephone call, Mary placed her arm around Susy's shoulder. 'Katie, she's as strong as an ox. She probably took a day off and forgot to tell you, silly girl. Now get back to work, just look at that queue.'

There was not a let up in the day's trading, never had she seen the market so busy. Good for business, but not so good for her back. All that lifting and heaving of box after box of produce was damaging her health and she was glad to drive out of the market that afternoon. Straightening up, she put her foot down and headed east yet again, but this time she would check on Katie.

Left into Globe Road, past the Horn of Plenty, she knew the road turned off to the right, but which one? Past Alderney Road, Massingham Road, nothing looked familiar. At Bancroft Road she turned right and parked, got out of the van and began walking. She remembered the stuffed cat on the window ledge, her precious Queenie, long gone to the cattery in the sky. And the hideous Toby jug, won in a Christmas raffle, the only thing in life that she did not have to work for, took prime position next to Queenie in the front window, and there they were. Susy banged on the door and listened, there was no sound coming from within. She banged again harder and shouted Katie's name. Peering through the letterbox, Susy could see past the hallway and through into the kitchen, where piles of dirty crockery were stacked up on the drainer. Feeling distressed, she had to try one more time. Crashing the door knocker hard against the door she yelled, 'Katie, open up, it's me, Susy.' A face appeared at the window of the house next door beckoning Susy forward. The little old lady ushered Susy to her front door which she clicked open gently, inviting her inside.

The frail old lady in her wraparound apron and pom-pom slippers tottered badly towards the kitchen, with Susy close behind. She sank heavily into a chair and, taking a deep breath, told Susy how she had not seen Katie for several days and she did not have a telephone to call anybody for help. Susy listened intently, whilst popping the kettle on for a cup of tea. Susy began to pace up and down. 'I've got to get in there somehow.' Maybe there was access through the back. No sooner had she said the words, Susy climbed over the garden fence and was trying Katie's back door, which was locked. There was nothing else to do but to break in. On retrieving a brick from the garden she took aim and shattered the glass, flicked the latch to open up the window and clambered in.

Susy felt a cold sweat break out over her body. She was intruding, but she had to go on. 'Where are you, old girl?' she whispered as she slowly crossed the kitchen floor. The washing up had been there for days, unemptied ashtrays lay everywhere. She placed her hand on the kettle as she passed, which was cold, and there was not a sound, except the drip-drip of the kitchen tap. Susy left the kitchen and took several unsteady steps towards the living room, quickly glancing towards the stairs on her way. The room was sparsely furnished. A two-seater Draylon-covered settee stood facing the fireplace, flanked by matching armchairs. A standard lamp positioned in a dark corner of the room under which Susy's gaze fell on the unfinished knitting sticking out of the workbasket. The television, now quiet, that gave Katie her only form of entertainment grandly showed off the wedding photograph of Katie and her soldier husband, lost too many years ago. Susy took a step forward, striking her toe on something hard. She looked down to find an empty Johnnie Walker bottle at her feet. As she bent down to pick the bottle up, she also noticed an empty whisky tumbler on the floor, but to her horror what she suspected and prayed she would not find, but she did, was Katie face down on the hearthrug. Susy felt for a pulse, not expecting to find any, rose from the scene, found the phone and dialled the police.

There were no suspicious circumstances; Katie had died from a heart attack, she was 68 years old. There were no children from her short wartime marriage and the few friends she had were market people. Susy left the funeral arrangements to the lads from the market. She could not cope with any more grief, attending the service at the church in Roman Road, along with the other traders. All through the sermon she could hear Katie's words to her the week before, echoing over and over again. 'Get away from here darlin' – get away – make something of yourself.'

Life got back to normal quickly as though nothing had happened. Katie's stall was snapped up immediately by some flashy upstart who Susy took an instant dislike to. Listening to his daily helping of carnal knowledge only added fuel to the fire of change that she desperately needed. She had not heard a word from Johnnie in three weeks. When she finally caught up with him he was full of apologies. 'Sorry, sweetheart, I'll phone Gill tonight, promise. Eddy's had me working like a dog, straight up. Ain't 'ad a minute to myself.' Susy believed him, she knew what a hard taskmaster Eddy was, but he paid well and if Johnnie lived long enough, Eddy would make him a rich man. True to his word, Johnnie telephoned Susy that very same evening and arranged for her to meet his sister the following Monday.

Gill managed a fashion shop in Covent Garden and could never find a good girl who would stay. The interview with Susy, a girl from her home turf, might prove to be successful.

Much to Susy's surprise Eddy approved, seeing that it was 'family' and not wishing to rock his own apple cart, gave her his blessing.

Sunday was spent in the bathroom. Eddy was out for the entire day and there was nothing to stop Susy pampering herself. After all, this was the beginning of the rest of her life and she had to look gorgeous, come what may. Up came the Lean Cuisine from the kitchen, coffee pot and cigarettes on a tray, which she placed precariously on the bidet, then stood back and took one good hard look at herself in the mirror. 'Today you look like an old crow, but tomorrow you'll glow like a bloomin' rose.'

The Body Shop shares must have soared when Susy staggered out of the shop and now surrounded by her purchases, she began the full service needed to transform her into a beautiful swan. This is not going to be easy, she thought, as she lay back in the tub examining her anatomy. With razor in hand she attacked the legs, careful not to make any incisions while doing so. The neglected body was at least a stone overweight. The hands were rough with stubby nails and the rarely-to-be-seen-legs needed a major overhaul. Then a steaming hot bowl of henna lay patiently waiting for the Honey and Oatmeal mask to be removed. When applied to the thick shoulder-length hair, the concoction would be piled high and strapped inside a polythene bag and allowed to fester until the desired effect was reached. Time for a pause, another pot of coffee, a cigarette and the Sunday newspapers. The day progressed steadily with a pedicure, manicure, exfoliating, creaming and general streamlining of Susy the slave into Susy the siren. Satisfied that she had done her best, and leaving the mudslick of a bathroom that had been her haven for the day, she pottered back into the bedroom. She selected a dark-green suit, with a nipped-in waist and knee-length skirt: the finishing touch for the morning.

The underground was the easiest route and Susy quickly found herself above ground, making her way towards the covered market. At the bottom of James Street she stopped in her tracks. 'Cor, it's changed! I don't believe it.' She walked on, 'It's terrific! I like it.'

Covent Garden, reopened in 1980, was a labyrinth of boutiques, cafés and craft shops. Susy almost danced along, eyes darting everywhere. Gone was the old fruit and veg market that she used to visit with her mum when she was a child. The bustle and noise of the familiar market traders was replaced by the quieter hum of beautiful people busy starting their day. As she entered the central market the smell of fresh coffee reached her nostrils, but no time to linger over a freshly filtered coffee, or indeed sit and just gaze at the world walking by. Susy had to locate the boutique and, desperately trying to keep her eyes above shop window level, she hurried along one row of shops and then another. She could hardly miss the freshly painted white façade **CRAWFORDS** in bold black lettering. She pushed open the door and stepped inside. The boutique was set on two levels, with woodblock floor and plain white walls with racks of neatly-hung clothes. Her presence was not noticed. In her very best voice Susy said, 'Hello?' directing the sound down the stairwell to the basement. Immediately, there was a clip-clop of heels on the stairs, and a tall, leggy blonde appeared, dressed in plum-coloured silk trousers and tunic.

'Can I help you, Madam?' she enquired politely.

'I have an interview at eleven. My name's Susy.' A flash of disapproval crossed the assistant's face.

'Ah yes, take a seat.' She ushered Susy to a chair with a wave of her hand. 'Gill will be with you in a minute.' The apparition then floated down to the basement level, leaving Susy alone and a little apprehensive.

Susy caught a glimpse of herself in a mirror, stood up, swivelled around and back again. She ruffled her hair, checked her teeth for lipstick smears and her tights for unseen ladders. Tugging the jacket sharply down on her waist, smoothing the skirt with the same movement, everything seemed all right. Then the door swung open and Gill breezed in. She was a female version of Johnnie, slimmer of course, about 35: there was no mistaking the likeness. Beautifully dressed in brown suede trousers and cream silk shirt, impeccable makeup and shiny dark hair that swung off her shoulders. 'Hello, you must be Susy,' she said, breathless. 'Sorry I kept you waiting, darlin'.' Sounding flustered, she bellowed down the stairs, 'Trudy, can you come upstairs?' She turned to Susy and smiled sweetly, 'We'll go downstairs for a chat. Fancy a coffee?' Susy warmed to Gill immediately, she felt that she was a good egg. 'Leave what you're doing, Trudy, it will wait, darlin',' Gill turned again to Susy and raised her eyebrows. 'Lights are on, but there's nobody in.' Trudy glided up the stairs passing a half smile at them both as they waited. 'Stay up here, sweetheart, until I tell you otherwise. You got that?'

The boutique was chic, upmarket French and Italian clothes. Gill travelled to the Continent several times a year and needed a responsible girl to hold the fort and run the business while she was away. They had to be good with people, conscientious and hard working. Susy certainly fitted the bill. 'Look what I get,' she said, gesturing upstairs, 'beautiful, but brainless.' The shop opened at ten and closed late, three weeks' holiday to start, plus a substantial clothes allowance at cost. Susy felt her insides dance with delight. A lifetime of lie-ins, start at ten. She had usually done four hours hard graft by that time and a clothes allowance, too. Whoopee! She really wanted this job. Gill could not have been more frank. Susy had to be groomed, she had all the basic qualities required, but she needed a lot of style and the accent needed toning down a bit. 'Remember,' she said, 'you can't sell a Flora Kung creation the same way you sell five pounds of King Edwards.' Gill was prepared to give Susy the opportunity to prove herself, if Susy was also prepared to give the job her best. She had until the end of the week to make up her mind.

As Susy left the boutique she mingled with the midday shoppers, under a bright sunny October sky, with a chill of winter in the air. The cafés were filling up, wonderful smells of lunches being prepared wafted around her. She resisted the temptation to stop for a pastry, remembering the weight she had to shed to become svelte and beautiful. Ambling around the market, she marvelled at the transformation of the old market, parts of it almost unrecognisable, except the pubs, where people were spilling out on to the pavements. The atmosphere was happy, carefree, fun and she wanted so much to become part of this young person's metropolis. Susy did not need a week to decide what she wanted, this was exactly what she wanted. At the underground, she found a telephone. Her new life was beginning a week on Monday.

2

'Oh Richard, darling, why is Vanessa always so late when the Bonningtons are coming for dinner?' Lady Caroline searched in vain for her daughter Vanessa's arrival through the bedroom window. 'They are always so punctual and Jeremy is such a lovely young man, so right for her. It would be so nice.'

'Caroline,' Sir Richard interrupted, 'I think you know the answer. All this confounded matchmaking. First it was the Wilson boy, what was his name? Simon. Then that gangly oaf Rufus Fielding. Vanessa's still young, plenty of time for marriage and babies. Don't suffocate her Caroline, let her live her life.'

Seven o'clock, Sir Richard Baron and his wife Caroline were having a small dinner party at home for nine people, black tie. The Bonningtons were their close friends for many years and both gentlemen were Lloyd's names. Jeremy Bonnington, their only son, a bespeckled academic of 23, was totally unsuitable for Vanessa, a year older, but Lady Caroline continued to push for a union between the two families.

Vanessa was tall, blonde, slim and extrovert. She looked every inch the beauty her mother had been, but with the forceful personality of her father. Vanessa had been out on a hack and was in no particular hurry to return home, but it was getting dark and reluctantly thought she should put in an appearance at the dinner party, if only for daddy's sake. After stabling her horse and with half an hour to go before the deadline, she sped upstairs and climbed under a hot shower. The water felt good and after a full ten minutes she climbed out reaching for white towelling robe to be greeted by her mother.

'Vanessa. Oh good, you're back, darling. Now do hurry, they will be here any moment and promise me please, you will be nice to Jeremy.'

'Yes, mummy.' Vanessa tugged at her wet shoulder-length hair, exasperated at her mother's neurosis. She was getting worse as she was getting older and she could only put the attitude down to that time of life.

'He's such a fine young man, Vanessa, a good match. Daddy and I would be delighted if you both would start seeing one another.' Vanessa turned to face her mother, her large blue eyes shimmering with anger. 'Mummy, he's a moron, he probably still masturbates into a hanky. How could you possibly think that I would consider him?'

'Oh dear,' Lady Caroline steadied herself against the dressing table. 'How could you use such words, Vanessa? If your father heard.'

'If daddy heard, he would probably applaud me, mummy. Jeremy is a jerk!'

Lady Caroline went white for lack of oxygen, anger welling up only to be interrupted by the arrival of the Bonningtons. Saved by the bell, Vanessa thought, as she watched her mother turn on her heel and storm out of the bedroom, slamming the door behind her.

Vanessa arrived as dinner was being served, making an entrance a film star would be proud of. She swept into the oak-panelled dining room in an ivory silk evening dress that caressed her body as she moved, her hair simply pinned back into a French pleat. Sir Richard rose immediately to greet her.

'Vanessa, Vanessa,' he kissed her on the cheek, then stood back to admire his favourite child, 'just beautiful.'

'Daddy, so sorry I'm late,' she glanced at her mother, there was no response. 'Mr and Mrs Bonnington, good evening and Jeremy, how nice to see you again.'

Vanessa was seated, as expected, between Jeremy and her brother Rupert, who always found these occasions entertaining to watch. The other two guests at their table were David Fielding and his wife, Veronica. Mercifully their son Rufus was now engaged to an art dealer specialising in the Renaissance at Sothebys, which undoubtedly pleased the Fieldings, their passion being fourteenth to sixteenth century art.

The evening progressed with the usual politeness. Lady Caroline had found her composure and was being the perfect hostess. Not once did her eyes meet Vanessa's, although Jeremy had more than a fair share of her attention. The meal was sumptuous as ever, accompanied by fine wines from Sir Richard's extensive cellar.

Jeremy was drinking more than usual and his wandering left leg was rubbing eagerly against Vanessa's thigh. Dessert had just been presented, a huge ice cream bombe was placed centre table, with swirls of meringue delicately decorated with crystallised violets and rose petals. Exclamations of 'Oo' and 'Ah' circled the table, before the sugary mound was whisked off for dissection. Jeremy squeezed Vanessa's thigh with his left hand. She immediately pushed him away, glaring into his glazed alcoholic eyes. Undeterred, his hand gripped her thigh once again.

'Rupert,' Vanessa whispered to her brother, 'I need a diversion.'

'What?'

'A diversion, damn it. I need a diversion. Think of something, will you?'

Jeremy's arm slipped around Vanessa's shoulder and down the back of her dress. Rupert noticed her dilemma and quickly rose to his feet.

'Rupert, my boy, not leaving are you?' enquired Sir Richard.

'No, father, no, er, what I wanted to tell you was,' Rupert edged away from the table, 'what I really wanted to say was–'

'Yes, well we're all listening.'

Rupert had reached the fireplace, bouncing up and down on the balls of his feet searching for words that would not come, when he caught Vanessa's eye.

'Go on,' she mouthed, with Jeremy's chin resting on her shoulder, 'get on with it.'

'I'm thinking of going to America,' he said quickly.

'Oh no!' Lady Caroline exclaimed.

'Yes, that's it, America. New York, to be precise.' Rupert had their attention; whatever he said now was irrelevant. Vanessa saw her chance and scooping up a handful of the frozen desert, thrust her hand hard into Jeremy's crotch, rigorously rubbing the exposed appendage. Jeremy did not know whether to be shocked, or delighted, if he felt anything at all.

'There,' she said, her voice getting louder, 'that's the nearest you'll ever get to an orgasm!'

Silence fell as the party turned around, with Lady Caroline totally horrified at another outburst of bad behaviour from her daughter, while Jeremy just hung languidly in the chair, covered in ice cream. Vanessa rose ladylike from the table and excused herself, saying that she had a very full day tomorrow and needed an early night.

'Hump! Yes, well, gentlemen, shall we retire to the lounge for a night cap?' Sir Richard led the way out of the dining room, trying to maintain the flow of the evening, and was followed like a line of ducks into the lounge.

The following morning Vanessa was up early, after hearing Rupert's Lotus roar out of the drive at 7.30. Piers, her younger brother, was not due back from France until later that evening. She was meeting Stephen for lunch at the Compleat Angler in Marlow, but had time to mount Charger and go for a ride. The sun was glistening on the early morning dew, but there was a chill in the air, summer was definitely over.

The house stood in an elevated position, almost hidden from the tiny brick and flint village of Hambledon, where Vanessa had lived all her life. As she approached the sleeping cottages she slowed down, bearing around by St Mary's Church past the village Post Office, over the humpback bridge and headed for the Hambledon Valley. On a perfect morning to be out riding, she broke into a canter, then veered Charger around Mill End Marina. There she dismounted and tethered the horse to a fence. With her helmet and crop under her arm she peeled off her gloves and made her way towards the weir. She could hear the roar of the water as she approached. Boats of all shapes and sizes moored silently to her right as she strode out along the causeway fringed by swaying reeds, and the roar of the water got louder. She paused mid stream, the cool breeze lightly striking her warm skin and noticed a lone fisherman, who could be seen almost mummified on the far bank. Maybe he was, she thought. Vanessa continued walking briskly towards the lock, past the small cottage to the grass verge, threw her hat and crop on the grass and sat looking out across the river stretching before her.

Stephen had sounded stressed when they spoke on the telephone and Vanessa had sensed immediately that there was something very wrong. Stephen was perfect, but married, with the last six months being punctuated with broken arrangements. Had Melanie found out? Vanessa tugged at the grass menacingly. It was not as if there were any children. She did not want any, Stephen had been told by her, but he did. She lay back on the grass tucking her hands behind her head. So what was the problem? She would produce dozens of babies, if that was what he wanted. She sighed. Must be the money, the house, the boat, the cars and the villa in Spain. All would be axed down the middle, or worse. Stephen liked his toys and would not give them up easily. Vanessa was beginning to feel comfortable, as the sun's rays were getting stronger and the faint voices of the first picnickers reached her ears.

'Hello, Miss Vanessa. I though that was your horse tethered up by the gate.'

Vanessa jumped visibly, shielding her eyes from the sun. 'George, you startled me.'

He laughed, 'Sorry, but old Charger was looking a bit restless. Knew you'd be around here somewhere.'

Vanessa wrestled with her jacket sleeve; she had left her watch behind and for a few minutes had dozed off. 'George,' she said, picking herself up, 'what's the time?'

With the last turn of the wheel the lock gates opened and George glanced at his watch, 'It's ten-thirty, missy.'

Vanessa grabbed her hat and crop and sped past George shouting 'thanks' and headed back across the narrow causeway, pushing past the many day trippers arriving with their children and hampers. Back at the mill gate she untethered Charger, mounted and raced across the valley towards the house at full gallop. She pulled over in front of the paddock, dismounting almost in full flight, handed the reins to the groom and ran into the house.

Lady Caroline had espied Vanessa's arrival through the drawing room window and, determined to confront her about her behaviour the previous evening, greeted her in the hall.

'Vanessa, I would like to speak to you this minute.' Vanessa hurried across the hall to the stairs, ignoring her mother's plea. 'Vanessa, stop this instant!'

The very last thing Vanessa wanted was a lecture on her outburst at the dinner party. 'No time, mummy, I'm late.'

Why did Stephen want to meet her so early? 'Be there at noon,' he had said. That was no request, that was an order. Vanessa did not like being told what to do, she was her own person and very adept at getting her own way. She climbed out of her riding gear and straight under a cool shower. She had 40 minutes to be there.

The red Alfa Romeo Spider pulled into the Compleat Angler at ten minutes after twelve and, not wishing to appear in a hurry, Vanessa ambled down the drive and into the garden. Suitably dressed in a white Ralph Lauren suit, she sat strategically placed to view the comings and goings of all the hotel guests. Stephen had not yet arrived.

'Miss Baron, can I get you a drink?' the waiter was quick to notice her arrival.

'No thank you, Tom, I'll wait.'

The Compleat Angler was always busy, set beside a picturesque bend in the Thames. A favourite haunt of the affluent and well-heeled members of both the town and country set and famous for its wonderful food and fine wines. This was Vanessa and Stephen's very special place. This was where their affair began 18 months ago, at the wedding reception of her old school-friend Sarah. From the first glance across the packed church to the frenzied love affair that followed, nothing and nobody else mattered to Vanessa. Stephen was her destiny, she loved him completely, but despaired at the situation she had allowed herself to be in. Usually, she discarded men like empty cigarette packets, but Stephen occupied her every thought and action; she was not in control of her life.

She watched a deliriously happy couple breeze past her on their way to the river, champagne picnic in hand. She eyed them enviously as they naughtily touched and teased each other when climbing into the punt that would carry them off on a romantic afternoon. All manner of craft were slowly cruising the river that day, ferrying people to and fro, creating an atmosphere of peace and tranquillity.

At 12.45 Stephen still had not arrived, as Vanessa looked around anxiously searching the crowd that had gathered in the garden. She stood up, angry at her weakness in allowing him so much grace and proceeded to wend her way through the occupied tables and out to the car park. She picked up pace, her head held high. That was the last time Stephen would stand her up. He would have to make a decision, her or Melanie. Vanessa climbed back into the Spider and drove out of the hotel in the direction of home. As she turned left into Pound Lane, Stephen roared down the High Street. She did not see him, but he spotted the red Alfa and quickly turned the Mercedes around.

Once into the Henley Road Vanessa put her foot down. She always drove too fast, especially where Stephen was concerned. One mile out of Marlow she caught sight of the Mercedes coming up fast behind her. She pressed the accelerator harder while quickly glancing again in the rearview mirror at Stephen gesturing for her to stop, his blonde hair blowing in the wind. He flashed his headlights, she ignored him. The Mercedes swung out into the righthand lane and tried to overtake the Alfa, but an oncoming vehicle made him pull back. Vanessa gained a little ground getting closer to home, as Stephen pulled out again, this time overtaking Vanessa, waving his left arm furiously for her to stop. She overtook him as he slowed down, when he raised both arms up in dismay, but continued the chase, determined to stop her. Past Medmenham and just before Mill End he dangerously overtook Vanessa, forcing her to stop sharply. He got out of the Mercedes and approached her still sitting behind the wheel.

'What the hell do you think you're doing?' he yelled, leaning on the side of the Alfa. Vanessa looked straight ahead, not uttering a word. 'OK, so I was late, but I have to talk to you.' Vanessa raised her eyes at Stephen, then straight ahead again. 'I'm sorry, is that what you want to hear? I did not intend being late.' Reluctantly Vanessa agreed and both vehicles pulled into the Marina, where they strolled slowly towards the lock, looking for a quiet spot to sit.

'Melanie knows about our affair,' he blurted out.

'How?'

'I'm not sure, gossip maybe, the Health Club. I – I mean we have hardly been discreet. Vanessa, I stand to lose everything.'

'What are you trying to say, Stephen?'

'I think we should be more careful, not be quite so open.'

Vanessa cut in, foreseeing her life with Stephen crumbling. 'How careful would you like?' She had to be positive about this. 'How much time do you need, Stephen? You've had eighteen months of my life, now where are we going to?'

'Vanessa, please.'

'No, Stephen, I will not hide behind walls just to keep Melanie at bay. Walk out. You say you love me, so walk out. What are you afraid of?'

Stephen took Vanessa's hand in his. She pulled away. 'I don't want to hurt you, darling, I don't want you involved.'

There was no logical way Stephen could convince Vanessa that there was a right way or a right time.

'I've waited long enough, file for a divorce immediately,' she stammered.

'Now just a minute, I have always said that we will be together, but you must let me do things my way.' Stephen was being very serious. 'You can't always have what you want when you want it, Vanessa. Life is not like that in the real world.'

Vanessa was flustered and angry. 'What do you mean?'

'You know very well what I mean. You have always had exactly what you wanted, now you are going to have to wait.'

Vanessa jumped to her feet. 'I can't wait, I want it now, Stephen, all of it, you and me together. I don't care about Melanie.'

They stood facing each other. 'Well, you should,' he said quietly.

'What!' she gazed into his eyes, unsure of what he meant.

'I said you should. She is still my wife, Vanessa. I would not do it to you.' Stephen watched the pain on Vanessa's face. She did not answer. 'I think we should have a break, darling. Please let me have some time to work things out.'

She did not even look back, she just kept on walking, then running until she reached the car and drove the last mile back to the house, barely able to see through her tears.

There was a stillness about the house, peaceful. Vanessa poured herself a large Cinzano and lemonade and strolled out on to the patio. Even Banjo their Labrador was not there to greet her. She sat down, kicking off her shoes and stretched out on the lounger. Stephen would call later, she thought. He would give her time to settle down and everything would be all right again. It was not the first time she had stormed out of an argument and it was always about Melanie. Vanessa convinced herself that she was right every time and Stephen was wrong. He always gave into her and so the affair continued.

Vanessa was alerted to a scuffling of feet behind her and a cold wet nose on her arm, dirty paws everywhere: at least Banjo was pleased to see her. She wrestled with the dog's total disregard for *haute couture*, pushing him repeatedly away as Sir Richard and

Lady Caroline returned from an afternoon walk through the valley. Vanessa could hear her father's booming voice on the telephone coming from the study as Banjo leapt away from her in the direction of the drawing room. Lady Caroline approached the patio through the French doors. 'Out, you filthy creature,' she shouted, ushering the dog towards the kitchen. On seeing Vanessa alone and unoccupied, she returned to the patio.

'Vanessa, there is something imperative that we must talk about.'

'I know what you are going to say, mummy, but I had every good reason to stop Jeremy's advances, he was drunk.'

'No, Vanessa, that's not the point.'

'If I spoiled your evening I'm sorry. Rupert will vouch for me. Jeremy's behaviour was appalling.'

'Your behaviour was also appalling. Vanessa.' Lady Caroline was becoming visibly angry.

'I am not interested in Jeremy, or Rufus, or Simon, or anybody else you care to push in front of me. mummy. I will choose who I want to see, not you.'

'Like Stephen Preston, I presume.'

Vanessa was stunned. She had no idea that her mother knew of her association with Stephen. 'Where did you hear that?' she replied defiantly.

'Who told me is irrelevant. I want to know if it is true.' Lady Caroline searched for a reaction.

'I know him,' Vanessa replied.

'I understand that you have been seen out with him on numerous occasions, Vanessa. Now why have we not met this young man?'

'He travels a lot.'

Lady Caroline was feeling her way very carefully. 'I believe he is an auctioneer,' she paused, 'Is he constantly out of the country?'

Vanessa was feeling uncomfortable; somebody had informed her mother very well. 'Don't be silly, mummy.'

'I want you to tell me, Vanessa. Now what is going on?'

Irritated at being put on the spot, she nervously replied, 'Stephen is a friend, somebody I like a lot. We share the same interests, meet up at the same functions and share the same friends.'

'Do you sleep with him?' The question was direct.

'That is none of your business!'

'Answer me!' Vanessa had never seen her mother so angry. Why was it so important she know?

'Stephen loves me and some day soon we will be married,' Vanessa blurted out without thinking.

'Am I to assume that is yes?' Lady Caroline was raging. 'You stupid child! I don't suppose I need to tell you that he is married, do I?'

Vanessa could not let her mother get the better of her. 'He is getting a divorce, mummy.'

'No, he is not, Vanessa.' Lady Caroline bellowed back at her. 'You are the talk of the village. I cannot hold my head up anywhere I go for fear of hearing our family name spread like muck in the field. Stephen Preston is not getting divorced.'

'Yes, he is,' Vanessa cried. 'Melanie has her own interests, they hardly do anything together.'

'Is that what he told you?'

Vanessa was feeling physically sick, never before had she endured such an argument with her mother. 'Yes!' she screamed, 'Stay out of my life! What has it got to do with you anyway?'

Lady Caroline's hand cracked across Vanessa's cheek, almost felling her to the ground – the first time that her mother had raised her hand in anger. 'Melanie Preston is pregnant and you, my daughter, are acting like a slut.'

Sick of Vanessa's selfish, intolerable behaviour, Lady Caroline lunged at her daughter, who steadied herself and cried, 'It's not true! You are lying.'

'It is true. Ask him, if he is gallant enough to tell you the truth.'

Sir Richard thundered through the drawing room on to the patio, 'What in heaven's name is going on?' he stammered.

Vanessa pushed past her father full of confusion and despair. She did not believe what her mother had said. Stephen would tell her it was not true, he would not lie to her. Later, not now, she would telephone, he would know that she had been crying.

Vanessa was in her room when she heard Rupert's Lotus roar into the drive. She hurriedly pulled on her jeans and a sweater and descended the stairs to the kitchen, to find him shovelling food into his mouth like an open pit. He kicked the refrigerator door closed and turned to Vanessa aghast.

'Christ, what happened?'

'It's a long story. Can we go to the Stag and Huntsman for a drink?'

'Sure, give me a minute,' Rupert gently turned Vanessa's face to one side. 'Preston packs a mighty punch, eh?' he joked.

She almost whispered, 'It was not Stephen.'

'Who did it then?'

'Mummy,' she mouthed.

'Mother!' Rupert shouted.

'Shut up, Rupert, please. Let's go please, now.'

The pair crept through the hall and out into the night air. 'Shit, mother? You've got to be kidding me, Vanessa. What did you do? Set fire to the aviary?'

As they walked away from the house a taxi pulled into the drive and a very tanned Piers poked his head out of the cab window. 'Hey, where are we going?'

'Stag and Huntsman,' Rupert replied.

'Mine's a special, be there in a minute. Boy, have I got some stories for you. Wow! What a holiday.' Piers dragged his case out of the taxi and ran into the house.

With Vanessa's jacket collar pulled up high around her face, they reached the pub. Rupert ducked his tall frame through the door behind Vanessa, to find the lounge was packed, but the snug was empty. This quaint old inn with its beamed ceilings and open fireplaces served the best ales for miles around and housed many a clandestine family meeting of the three Baron offspring. Vanessa threw off her jacket and sat wearily in the bay seat and ordered a large brandy.

'Oh oh, things must be bad.' Rupert started to take Vanessa's mood a little more seriously. 'Hungry?'

Vanessa began her tale of woe, of her meeting with Stephen, the argument and the fight with mother. Life had never been so bad; she looked and felt ghastly.

'Forget him, you're wasting your time with Preston, Vanessa. You're not his first and won't be his last affair.' Rupert was getting tired of Vanessa's love life. 'It's a mess and so are you. Take a good look at yourself.'

She searched in vain for some sympathy. 'But I want him, Rupert, I need him.'

'You want what you can't have. Now smarten up and get yourself a job, an interest, do something, Vanessa. Don't waste your life.'

The door of the pub flew open, and there, modelling his latest acquisition, was Piers.

Rupert laughed, 'You look like a poof.'

Piers waggled his bum and ran his hands through a sun-bleached mop of hair. 'Feel this,' he said, offering his jacket sleeve. 'What do you think?'

'Crap!' Rupert said.

Piers hopped over a barstool and grabbed his pint. 'Did I have a good time? Now where would you like me to start?' Piers was oblivious to the situation he had just walked into. After securing a degree, he had taken a well-earned sabbatical before law school. His quest for 'pussy', sophisticated debauchery, stylish ambience and 'much more pussy' had quite obviously been a success judging by his cock-a-hoop banter that Rupert was enjoying so much. Vanessa had all but dissolved into her third brandy when Piers awoke to the fact that she was still there. 'And what, dear sister, have you been doing to make you look so lovely tonight?'

Piers' sarcasm did not touch Vanessa as Rupert hastily interrupted, not wanting to retreat into another hour of tears and fears. 'The Bonningtons were here last night.' Rupert glanced at Vanessa.

'Old Billabong,' Piers exclaimed, edging closer to Vanessa. 'Still got those sweaty hands?'

Vanessa raised her eyes at Piers, the corners of her mouth turning upwards, 'Worse.'

'How much worse?' Piers' eyes twinkled, for they all knew of Jeremy's unconquered prowess and uncontrollable stammer.

'A lot worse.' Vanessa drained her brandy.

'Don't do it to me, Vanessa. Tell Piers all, every little detail.'

She proceeded to tell Piers and an amused Rupert the story of the dinner party and of Mummy's desire for Jeremy as a son-in-law. 'Oh shit!' Piers exclaimed. The stuttered, nonsensical conversation and the ritual abuse of her right leg. 'What a wanker,' Piers added.

'That's not far from the truth,' Vanessa mused.

Piers was astounded, 'What, he got his dick out?' Vanessa nodded. Piers fidgeted with anticipation. 'The frigging nerve! So what did you do?' he glanced at Rupert for confirmation, who filled him in with his side of the story. 'So tell me, will you, what did you do?'

Vanessa had barely said the words, when howls of laughter went up and she was beginning to tire of the conversation and the noise. Picking up her jacket, she attempted to leave, but Piers stopped her. 'Wait, wait just a minute,' they both sat staring across the table at her like a couple of schoolboys, 'How big was it?'

Exasperated she replied, 'Ooh, about the size of your big toe.'

Vanessa walked slowly back to the house, the sound of her brothers' singing still ringing in her ears. The brandy felt like a warm glow inside her, comforting against the cold wind. Rupert was her confidant and she loved him dearly. Piers, being younger, held no responsibility other than to himself, and they both were going away. Rupert had already established himself as a young lawyer in the city and spent every week in town and Piers was leaving to continue his studies. Vanessa would be left with mother

– she shuddered. On reaching the house, she checked to see if there had been any calls, there had not. Her heart sank with the realisation that maybe her mother was right. She would telephone his office first thing in the morning.

'Mr Preston will be out all day, Miss Baron.' Trying to break out of Auschwitz would have been easier that getting past Stephen's secretary, Irene. 'Yes, I will tell him you called. Goodbye.' The abrupt curtailing of conversation left Vanessa limply holding the receiver which she gently replaced. Stephen was always there on a Monday, unless travelling abroad.

She took breakfast and decided to stay around the house. Her parents were in the city for the day and so she could pace her day at leisure. By mid afternoon and feeling bored, she poured herself a large vodka and sat by the telephone. Her drinking was becoming a habit, but she needed some Dutch courage to telephone Stephen at home. She lifted the telephone and began to dial, but immediately replaced the receiver. If Melanie answered, what should she say? Who should she be? She waited then dialled again, but the answerphone intercepted the call and she hung up. Anxiety welled up inside her as she paced the drawing room carpet, then out into the garden; everything was too quiet. Restless, she jumped behind the wheel of the Jeep and tore out of the drive towards Turville, driving passed Stephen's house, to find the drive empty. The house looked quiet as she settled down behind the wheel, waiting, expecting to see some indication of life, but there was none. After what must have been an hour or more, she quietly pulled away from her lookout position and drove home.

The following morning, Vanessa went through the same ritual again. Even though Irene had told her that 'Mr Preston will be away for the remainder of the week.' Every day the same routine. Residents of Turville were beginning to recognise her and nodded 'good morning' as she passed through the village. At home, the atmosphere between herself and her mother was acrid; better by far to stay out of each other's way.

At the weekend, Rupert and Piers were back at home. Both were keen oarsmen and were out on the river from the crack of dawn to dusk. Sunday afternoon and weary from a week of uncertainties, Vanessa took up her lookout position again at Turville, this time hiding her conspicuous red car from view. At 5 p.m., Stephen's Mercedes swung into the drive and parked. Vanessa strained her neck to see Stephen jump out of the vehicle, rush around to the passenger side and open up the door. Vanessa wanted to heave, as they strolled into the house together, Stephen slipping his arm around Melanie's shoulder and planting a kiss on her cheek.

Vanessa arrived home in a state of fury, not knowing what to do or which way to turn. At a time like this, she missed her trusted friend Sarah, who was like a sister to her, sharing absolutely everything, including men. She thundered around the house trying to find something to occupy her thoughts, but nothing was going to appease her. She rustled up a salad in the kitchen and sat forking over the endive and cucumber that she did not really want, when Rupert and Piers arrived together, with Piers disappearing upstairs and Rupert, ravenous as ever, going straight into the kitchen. He manoeuvred around Vanessa, sensitive to her mood and after helping himself to a mountain of food sat down opposite her at the table. Neither one spoke. Rupert ploughed steadily through his platter of cold beef and roast potatoes, while Vanessa stared into space. Rupert eventually broke the silence. 'Had a good day, I see.'

Vanessa toyed with the cutlery, as Rupert got up and poured himself a beer, then sat down again, trying to peer under her eyelashes for recognition. He had forgotten the saga of the previous weekend, not dreaming that Stephen could still be the cause of the gloom. 'Who was the lucky guy this week?' he enquired.

Vanessa found her voice, 'Stephen and Melanie have been away this week and I hate him for it.'

Rupert paused for thought, placed his glass on the table and lost his temper. 'You senseless, selfish bitch!' He stood up, waving his arms in the air. 'You spoilt brat! You think of nobody but yourself. Everybody knows of your screwing around. Why can't you be a little more discreet about it?' Rupert was leaning hard over the kitchen table, as close to Vanessa as possible without touching her. 'Sometimes I am ashamed of you.' She shrank back in the chair. 'Can nobody make you understand what a prized cow you've become? God help the poor bastard that gets you, Vanessa, he's going to need it.' Rupert turned to leave the kitchen, but added, 'Everything you have heard about Preston is true. Good luck to him, he's better off without you.' Rupert slammed the door behind him, leaving Vanessa shocked beyond all belief. She decided there and then that the time had come to move on, build a new life and find that job she kept saying she wanted. She was educated, qualified and Sir Richard was well connected. Vanessa made a conscious decision to become a better person. In no way did she want her family to be ashamed of her.

Sir Richard was busy at his desk in the study when Vanessa poked her head around the corner of the door. 'Too busy to see me, daddy?'

'My darling girl, I am never too busy to see you.' He welcomed her with open arms.

'I want to talk to you seriously,' she said.

'Seriously? He sat her down gently on the Chesterfield. 'What could be so serious? You young things should be having a good time.'

'I love you daddy, but I have to get away from here,' she touched her father's hand, not wishing to hurt his feelings. 'I need a job.'

Sir Richard patted her hand. 'Not getting along too well with your mother,' he sighed. 'I knew it would happen sooner or later.'

'That's not the entire reason. I want a change of scene, meet new people and make some new friends.' Vanessa desperately wanted him to understand.

'Time to explore life, hum? Yes, well, I suppose so. I keep telling Caroline not to suffocate you, but she doesn't listen.'

Vanessa adored her father, to him she was still the ten-year-old child he used to play tag with, the little girl he let beat him at Monopoly, and now it was time for a new chapter to begin. 'I'll contact David Fielding straight away and see if he can come up with an apartment in town, then we can take it from there.' She beamed at her father and kissed him on the cheek. 'How does that sound?' he walked back to his desk.

'Fine, daddy, it sounds just fine. Thank you.'

'Be off with you now, we'll talk about this matter again later.'

The thought of living and working in London excited Vanessa. Before Sarah had married, the two girls spent much time in the city, socialising with the upwardly mobile set and she had forgotten what a good time they had had. During the past 18 months Stephen had taken up every ounce of her time and energy and she had become 'a prized cow' – oh, how those words had scarred her. She would try her best to block Stephen from her mind forever.

True to his word, Sir Richard had contacted David Fielding and arranged for Vanessa to view two apartments that week, one just off Sloane Square and the other in Pimlico. Lady Caroline, although outwardly relieved at her daughter's decision to move away from home, inwardly worried, as most mothers would do.

There was no doubt in Vanessa's mind that the two-bedroom apartment off Sloane Square was perfect and immediately made preparations to move. Once established, she would look for a job, although her allowance was perfectly adequate. She looked forward to the stimulation of work, where she could use her creative skills. Packed and ready to go, she bade her farewells and headed for the city.

3

November 1985.

Susy was settling in at Crawfords and Gill was enthusiastically moulding her the way she wanted. Trudy, on the other hand, was a hindrance, always late and uncooperative, a real shop window-dummy. It was just a matter of time before she departed.

Crawfords had many regular customers and there was much passing trade, especially during the summer months. Now, with the onset of winter, business was levelling out with new stock arriving daily. Gill allowed her girls to wear new lines during the day and from her clothes allowance, Susy had invested in one outfit. She was still unable to shed the weight required to pour herself into a size 12.

Susy did not miss market life at all. In fact, she had almost forgotten that she was ever there. How quickly the working pattern of her life had changed. All those years stuck in the same dead-end existence, she felt the world was now her oyster and just about anything was possible. Every morning the same exhilaration came over her as she left the station and strolled into work.

At the beginning of another week, Susy arrived to find Gill busy on the telephone. She raised her hand and smiled in acknowledgement as she walked through the door. 'Yes, that's it. Now this will go in tomorrow's paper?' Susy looked puzzled, '…and for one week, OK.' Gill put down the telephone. 'She's gone,' referring to Trudy.

'What, just like that?' Susy asked.

'Yep, just like that, the little bitch! Shouldn't have expected anything less. So it's you and me today, darlin'. Hope we get some luck quickly from the ad.'

The week was unusually busy and they worked well around one another. The advertisement had brought many enquiries, but only two unsuitable applicants. Gill was due to leave shortly on a buying trip and needed to replace Trudy as soon as possible. The telephone rang intermittently, each one enquiring about the position as sales assistant and out of six appointments made for that afternoon only two showed up. The first girl arrived and Gill escorted her off to the rear of the shop. She looked elegant enough, Susy thought and from the snippets of conversation she understood she had some experience in retailing. All looked promising, a new recruit, another pair of hands to share the workload. Susy was filled with optimism, but the look on Gill's face told a completely different story. For halfway through the interview, the girl opened up her handbag, took out a cigarette and lit up. Gill's fixed expression turned sour as she asked the obligatory question through a cloud of smoke. 'And how do you see your future in fashion?' Susy beat a hasty retreat, finding some mundane task to attend to elsewhere. She returned shortly, to feel the full effect of Gill's smouldering disposition filling the air. The girl was leaving. Rejected, cast off and very displeased, she dropped her half spent cigarette to the ground, treading it firmly into the woodblock floor with the ball of her foot and strode out of the shop. Gill watched her strut through the arcade, 'If I ever see that trollop before she sees me, I swear I'll burn her bush.'

Gill walked back through the shop, passing Susy who was busying herself at the rails. 'Coffee?' she barked. Susy nodded, not saying a word.

The day progressed and about 4 p.m. the second interviewee arrived. This one was different. Susy asked her to wait and alerted Gill to the shop floor. The girl was tall, graceful and well spoken; Gill was immediately impressed and the two women sat down to talk. As Susy passed them by on her way upstairs, she could not avoid hearing Gill's first question. 'Tell me,' she said, 'do you smoke?'

Her name was Polly Bartholomew, she was 22 and a model. A riding accident had curtailed her career on the catwalk, leaving her with a slight limp, which at best was virtually undetectable. A lot more therapy was needed before she could resume her career, if at all. Gill was delighted and hired her immediately.

Gill had no qualms about leaving the business in Susy's hands when she flew off to Europe on a buying trip. Susy for the first time held a position of some authority and found it difficult sometimes to stop calling the shots, just for the sheer hell of it.

Christmas was fast approaching and the shops looked glorious decked out in their Yuletide finery. Music tinkled from every corner, choirs sang, street entertainers amused, while chestnut sellers warmed their hands over hot coals. A magical time of year when Susy took charge of Christmas decorations, creating a brilliant arrangement of fun and fantasy and Polly uncorked many a bottle of wine – drinks were on the house.

While Susy had the working pattern of her life together, socially things were dull. Apart from the girls' night out for a drink and occasionally she and Polly would take in a movie, there was little else. Susy was also quick to grasp the fact that she did not fit in with Polly's fashionable friends. The diet was a slog and if she tasted another carrot juice she would vomit. Exercise, Polly kept telling her, and if ever there was a role model, she was working with it. Susy was lazy to exercise. After a long hard day at work, the last thing she wanted to do was throw her body around a gymnasium.

Polly talked incessantly about men and sex, the target of her lust being Sebastian. She would not rest until she had locked him in her groin and the obsession was overruling everything else. During one of these numerous conversations, when Polly did most of the talking, Susy interrupted her.

'Polly, next time you go to the gym, I'm coming with you.'
'Monday night. Do you want me to book you in?'

Susy almost winced in anticipation, 'Yes, but nothin' too heavy.'

Monday evening they took a brisk walk around to the spa. Once there they parted company, Polly to her more advanced aerobic class while Susy followed the crowd to an elementary class. They arranged to meet up in the pool later. Susy had invested in a black leotard, making her look quite slender in comparison to the assortment of bodies lining up. Looking around her this, she thought, was going to be a piece of cake. The aerobics teacher arrived looking slightly muscular, but with, as Polly would have said, great definition. The instructor glanced around at her class. The routine, she explained, was for novices, to prepare them for more strenuous exercise later on. They took up their positions behind the instructor and the music began. Just do what she does, Polly had said; follow the movements, get a rhythm going. Susy listened, watched and did what she was told. 'Legs apart and together, apart and together. Swing those arms and back,' the voice got louder. 'Forward and back, bounce up and down, turn, up and down.' The fat was sure flying as the music played on. Relentless, the teacher bellowed out instructions, 'Come on, ladies, you can do better than that.' Fifteen minutes into the routine and Susy was feeling decidedly puffed and very hot. A short break, she rested her hands on her hips and breathed deeply, looking around at the monstrous mounds of steaming flesh. No time for regret, the music recommenced and the instructor was checking each pupil as they bounced away, cajoling, criticising and now she was behind Susy, chanting instructions. Susy was doing her best to stay upright, when the voice sounded in her ear: 'Think of the flab, it makes us feel bad.'

'Fuck that!' Susy declared at the end of the session that was the hardest half-hour she had ever experienced.

Susy spotted Polly in the pool and swam over to her. 'How did you get on?' she asked.

'Who was that Nazi you put me in with?' Susy spurted out the words.

'They're all like that, Susy, that's what makes it work. I promise it will get a lot easier.' Polly giggled. Susy was unconvinced as Polly pushed away from the side of the pool. 'Come on, relax, race you to the end.'

Christmas week and Susy felt as though a London bus had hit her. Polly had persuaded her, with great difficulty, to keep up the sessions and her thighs were in shock. She could lift her arms no further than her shoulders and she hurt, felt sore and needed comfort in the shape of a cream bun.

Christmas Eve, the shop closed early and the girls went their separate ways. Gill was spending the holiday with her man at his brand new home in Barking. Polly was off to Henley on Thames and her family. Susy was spending the festive season at home with Eddy.

Uncle Bob and his wife were stopping over for the Christmas holidays. Susy was grateful for the help and got along well with her Auntie Joyce, even though she was a lush. As Susy approached the house, she could hear raucous laughter coming from inside. She turned the key in the lock and let herself in; sounded as if the party had already begun. Susy walked into the kitchen to find Eddy and Bob huddled over several empty cans of lager and Joyce nursing a glass of her favourite poison, sitting in the corner. Boxes of Christmas fare lay around on the floor still unopened. Joyce's pet Jack Russell, Micky, could just be seen peeping from his basket behind the kitchen door. Joyce was the first to notice Susy and swayed slightly as she stood to greet her.

'Hello, darlin', 'ow's my favourite girl, all right?' Joyce put her arm around Susy's shoulder, 'Shut up Micky, shut up.' She brandished her glass in the air, 'Get you a drink, sweetheart?' Susy watched her totter into the lounge in her pink tracksuit and fluffy slippers, then turned to Eddy and Bob.

Eddy nudged his brother's arm, 'What do ya think then, Miss Big Time. Market's not good enough for 'er now, look at the garb.'

'She's a little cracker. Come over 'ere, darlin' and give your Uncle Bob a cuddle.'

Bob looked dapper in his tweed jacket and cravat and crushed

Susy in his huge arms prickling his neat moustache on the side of her cheek. 'I want to 'ear all about it.'

Joyce returned, waving a vodka and tonic in the air as Susy struggled out of Bob's grasp. She made a grab for the glass and started to unpack the boxes of food. There was enough to feed them all for a week.

'Where's the turkey?' Susy asked, turning to Eddy.

'Don't worry, its comin'.'

'So's Christmas, who's bringin' it?' she was becoming agitated.

Eddy raised his voice, 'It'll be 'ere. Sit down babe, relax, enjoy yourself.'

Restless, Susy sat at the kitchen table, while Eddy and Bob remained motionless as Joyce replenished the drinks. She whispered in Susy's ear. 'Let's leave the boys to talk.' Micky snapped at Susy's ankles as Joyce led the way into the lounge. She sank back into an armchair adjacent to the Christmas tree, the flashing coloured lights playing games with her complexion. Susy lit the gas log fire and sat down on the sofa hoping that Christmas would come and go without too many problems. Joyce offered Susy a cigarette. 'You know, I can't understand your dad. I said, Eddy, you and Susy come to us for Christmas, seeing that it's a year now since your mum passed on and what with you now working up West, it seemed like a good idea.'

Susy was curious too, 'What did 'e say?'

'Well, sweetheart, he made some comment on how you both wanted to be 'ere, and...'

'Both?' Susy interrupted.

'Yes, darlin' and for Bob and me to just bring ourselves over and he would organise everything.'

'Did he?'

'And, well, you know your Uncle Bob, the lazy devil, anything for an easy life, said OK.' Joyce waited for a reaction. Several brandies down the line had not impaired her thinking. Susy sat silently gazing into the fire. What difference did it make, apart from the work, where they spent Christmas?

'Didn't ask you, did he pet?' Susy shook her head. Joyce shuffled out to the kitchen and returned with a plate of sandwiches, leaving the two men, who had still not moved from the table and closed the door behind her.

'Who's Norma?' Joyce was snooping.

'Norma Randle. Hasn't 'e told you about 'er yet?'

Joyce pressed on, 'And who's Dave and Linda?'

'Dave from the diner on the High Road. You know Dave.' Susy was puzzled. Why all the questions?

There was a rap on the front door. Susy jumped up, but Joyce pulled her back down again. She had barely begun her conversation. 'Let 'em get it.' There was movement coming from the kitchen. 'Made any plans for the holidays, pet? Aren't you goin' to any parties and what about boyfriends?' Again a loud rap on the door. 'You sit down and don't move.' Joyce held on to Susy's arm.

Both Eddy and Bob went to answer the door and from the shouting and cheering that followed, the turkey had arrived. When the noise subsided and Joyce could hear herself speak again, she turned to Susy and pointing in the direction of the kitchen said, 'Tomorrow, my lovely, he expects you to cook, serve and entertain six people, just like your poor mum did, God rest her soul. If I had known before today what that old bastard was doing, we would't 'ave come.'

Susy was angry, but not shocked; she knew how selfish and calculating Eddy could be. His ego was enormous, to the detriment of all around him. Clearly, Norma was invited for Christmas as one of the family and it was too late to change plans. Better make the best of a bad show.

Christmas morning Susy was up at eight o'clock, by her calculation the 24 lb bird had to be stuffed and in the oven by nine, for a three o'clock lunch. The house was still, nothing stirred except Micky, who raised one eye at her when she entered the kitchen. Still in her dressing gown, she make herself a coffee, then rolled her sleeves up ready to stuff the bird. But which end? With it trussed up, which end opened up, the neck or the parson's nose?

She stood back, then examined the bird closely, prodding and pulling every orifice. Maybe if she cut the twine she could get in. She had watched her mother prepare a turkey before, which looked easy. By now she was hopelessly tugging at the bird and with hurried determination snipped the twine, only to release the legs from the breast with a twang. Micky yelped with surprise, only to be shushed by Susy's towering form. She returned to the turkey spreadeagled in the baking tray and secured the legs with some string from the kitchen drawer, up-ended the bird and spooned in the stuffing, packing it down well.

'Good God,' Joyce exclaimed, looking over Susy's shoulder, 'it looks like a bleeding duck.'

'Give us a hand, Joyce. I'm getting in a terrible mess.'

Joyce tore the cigarette from her mouth and took over from Susy. 'Looks like you lost a hand up that turkey's backside, luvvy. I'll handle the bird, now you start the veggies.'

Christmas lunch got underway, while Eddy and Bob disappeared to the pub, promising to return sober and on time, while Susy and Joyce ploughed steadily through the preparations. They paused periodically for a Café Royal, and a chat about life with Norma Randle.

Two forty-five and everything was ready. Susy scrambled into a wool skirt and sweater, then raced downstairs into the dining room to check the table. Joyce had just placed the final cracker as she entered.

'Oh, don't you look a treat, give us a turn, pet. Well, if you're not snapped up by next Christmas I'll give up the fags.'

Susy flashed a huge grin. 'You're on.'

'Oh luvvy and so's the Queen.' Joyce turned the television on. 'There she is, God bless 'er, what a lady! Shame old Charlie's spoken for sweetheart, but Andy's still on the loose,' she winked at Susy, 'Think big darlin', think big.'

Dave and Linda were the first to arrive laden with brightly coloured packages and bottles of champagne. Susy ushered them both into the lounge. 'Where's the boss?' shouted Dave, pretending to search for Eddy behind the door and back of the sofa. 'Ha, still down the pub I'll bet.'

Susy left Joyce to make polite conversation with Dave and Linda, returning just in time to catch the first drop of bubbly cascading from the bottle. Eddy and Bob could be heard before they were seen, walking up the drive, late as usual, with Norma trailing behind. They burst into the house full of Christmas cheer, whooping and hollering at one another like a pack of hounds. Joyce remained detached from the frenzied 'hello's' and 'how ya doin's' and eyed Norma with disdain, as the fur coat peeled off to reveal a glittery fuzzball of angora and sequins that vied favourably with the Christmas decorations. Eddy enthusiastically introduced Norma to Joyce, who held out her hand like a wet kipper. No words were uttered, but a mutual dislike was evident. Bob began to furiously rub his hands together over the fire, 'Where's the grub? I'm starving.'

No time was wasted getting everybody seated at the table. Susy and Joyce made a good team ferrying in piping hot dishes from the kitchen in relays. With everyone seated and wearing their silly hats lunch began. Susy could breath a sigh of relief for lunch was perfect, thanks to Joyce. There had been no hiccups and everybody tucked in heartily. The wine flowed and tongues loosened. The men went back a long way and talked merrily about their capers. The wheeling and dealing and brushes with the Old Bill. Linda giggled incessantly like a hyena over her Dave's antics, a sure sign that the lioness would devour her lion in the sack later. Joyce smiled to herself as Norma, her back to the fire, began to swelter in her fluffy sweater. She hoped the sequins would melt, making her look more of a trash bag than she already was. Eddy gushed all over her, kneading her shoulder like a lump of dough, patted, groped, indulged his passion, until, 'A toast.' Eddy stood, glass in hand, 'To the chef,' he raised his glass to Joyce, 'the best turkey I've ever 'ad.' The company raised their glasses. 'To Joyce and to family and friends, cheers.'

'Cheers.'

Susy sat silently through the toast and as Eddy sat down, she raised her glass, 'Happy Christmas, mum.' Eddy lifted his glass half-heartedly and Norma flinched uncomfortably in her chair.

'Feeling hot, Norma?' Joyce piped up, 'thought you could stand the heat, darlin'?'

'At least I can feel something,' Norma retorted, 'I've got blood running through my veins.'

'Oh yeah! Pity it'll never reach your tits, luv.' Joyce strode out to the kitchen with Susy close behind, leaving Eddy to keep the peace.

They both rattled back into the dining room with dishes and the Christmas pudding decorated with holly. Joyce placed it in front of Eddy, who freely poured brandy with one hand, while fumbling for a light with the other. Joyce leaned over Norma's shoulder and whispered, 'Take a deep breath darlin', you should be able to light this in one.' Norma lashed out at Joyce, missing her by inches, as Bob intervened just in time. 'Leave it out, girls, it's Christmas. Give it a rest.'

Feeling full to overflowing, they all stumbled into the lounge and crash landed on the soft furnishings. Bob and Dave made themselves comfortable and if it was not for Linda's squeaky voice they would have dropped off easily. There was a rustle of ripped paper as Linda handed out the presents, to exclamations of delight.

'Ooo Dave, it's lovely,' Linda said, holding the silk negligée against her body.

Dave eyed her through an alcoholic haze. 'Dig deeper, darlin'.'

'Socks!' Bob shouted from the armchair.

Eddy slapped Bob on the back as he opened his box of Havana cigars, 'Thanks, mate.'

Joyce was content to sit back and watch while she finished her cigarette. She knew what she was getting from Bob, for she had been out to buy it the week before. Saves taking it back to Marks next week, she told him.

Susy had stockpiles of her favourite Chanel perfume, enough to see her through the year, a sweater from Bob and Joyce and chocolates from Dave and Linda. Rummaging through the piles of wrapping paper, she found a box from Eddy and eagerly tore off the paper, flipping the top open and there, to her complete surprise, lay a gold Rolex watch. She took the watch from the box and snapped it around her wrist. Eddy had surpassed himself; it was exactly what she wanted.

'It's just great, thanks a lot.' She planted a kiss on his cheek. Eddy placed his arm around her shoulder, for all eyes were now on Norma, who was sitting demurely on the edge of the sofa, nursing a large box from Eddy on her lap. She began to slowly tear off the wrapping paper, which fell to the floor, revealing a box, which she took out and placed on the coffee table before her. In silence she opened the box to discover a smaller box and yet another and another. Linda was at her side almost salivating in anticipation, until Norma finally held a small black box in her hand.

'Open it!' Linda screeched, almost grabbing the gift from her hands. Breathing deeply, Norma stood next to Eddy, her vast bosoms rising and falling like a pair of well-oiled pistons. Eddy lit up a cigar.

'OK, darlin', open it, they're all waiting.'

The silence was agonising, but in unison they all chanted, 'Open it.'

Norma slowly pulled back the lid and gasped in amazement at the dazzling diamond and sapphire ring staring up at her. She clutched at her throat, seemingly short of air and turned to Eddy. 'Oh darlin', I'm overcome,' she croaked, 'It's the most beautiful ring I've ever seen.'

Eddy shrugged like a proud peacock, Linda fell back on to the sofa stunned, while Susy and Joyce remained unmoved.

Dave finally broke the deathly hush that had descended on the party. 'Right little bobby dazzler you've got there, Norma. Whose arm did you have to break to get that, Eddy?'

Eddy, puffing away on his cigar, took the box from Norma's grasp, plucked the ring from inside, took her left hand in his and pushed the ring on to the third finger. He cleared his throat: 'This, my friends, is my future intended wife and I wanted you all 'ere to witness the event.'

Bob and Dave both shook hands with Eddy. 'You sly old fox,' shouted Bob, ruffling Eddy's bald patch.

'Crafty codger, keeping us in the dark,' yelled Dave from the drinks trolley, as he uncorked a bottle of bubbly.

Norma flaunted the engagement ring under Linda's nose, who hovered over the gem like a thieving magpie, but Susy and Joyce showed no interest whatsoever in the future Mrs Eddy Stevens.

'Going to congratulate your new mum, darlin'?' Susy was not amused. 'You'd better get used to the idea, pet. Life's goin' to change a lot round 'ere and soon.'

'I've got a life to lead, too, Joyce.'

'Got to 'ave it out with Eddy, then, sweetheart, get the picture straight. Make your own decisions now. Don't you wait for somebody else to make them for you.'

All Susy's life Eddy had been the strongest influence on her. Standing on her own two feet was long overdue; she had to face up to him or die.

A mountain of dirty pots and pans greeted Susy that Boxing Day morning, ashtrays full of spent cigarette butts, stale cigar smoke still hanging in the air. She threw open the kitchen window and filled her lungs with the fresh morning air, then took a good look around. Every conceivable utensil was sitting either in the kitchen sink, or on the kitchen table. A clean cup and saucer was not to be found anywhere. Eddy sauntered into the kitchen behind her.

'What's all this mess? 'Ave you forgotten we've got guests upstairs?' Susy ignored him. 'They don't want to come down 'ere and see all this. Clean it up.'

Furious, Susy seized the opportunity for a show down.

'I want to talk to you,' she shouted.

Eddy was taken aback at her directness, 'OK, babe, what's up?'

'All my life you have controlled me, you build me up, then you let me down. You don't ask me what I want, you dish out what you want.'

'Now you listen 'ere, Susy.'

'No, you listen to me. You taught me to respect you, now 'ow 'bout you respecting me. My wants and needs are more than an expensive peace offering, this is my home, too. You don't discuss anything with me up front, you tell me afterwards. What kind of dad are you?' She took a deep breath, 'And don't expect me to be a slave to your tart.'

'You're pushing me, Susy.'

'Oh I 'aven't started yet. I'm not a kid anymore, I'm a grown woman and I am taking control of my life from now on. You want to keep me sweet just in case you're on your own again, well start thinking again. I'm not sharing my life with that tramp upstairs. If she's movin' in, I'm movin' out. Got it? This is my decision.' Eddy lurched towards Susy. 'Don't you even think about it,' she warned. 'Now get that lump out of bed and tell her to start acting like a wife. There's a lot of cleaning up to do down 'ere, I'm goin' out.'

She stormed out of the kitchen grabbing her jacket on the way, only to find Joyce eavesdropping in the hall. She gave a silent cheer as she passed her by. 'You're on your way, darlin'.'

Susy slammed the front door behind her, climbed behind the wheel of her car and drove away from the house. Where was she going? She did not know or care. She suddenly felt free, free to please herself, be herself and nobody was going to stop her.

4

Vanessa had secured a position as a media assistant in a large advertising company in Mayfair and had her eyes ruthlessly on the top job, in the shortest possible time. Her creative talent had already been noticed and in two months she was well on her way to promotion.

The apartment off Sloane Square was comfortable, in which she had added a few personal items to an otherwise impeccable décor. The split level layout and high ceilings gave a feeling of space and light, with the French windows of the lounge leading out on to a balcony that overlooked a pretty square.

Socially, life was gathering pace. She had pushed Stephen to the back of her mind and had started partying again, making the transition from country deb to city socialite a total success.

The city was slowly getting back to normal again after a lengthy Christmas break, but mid winter and the weather had taken a turn for the worse.

Vanessa awoke to what was an important day at the office, only to find a foot of snow on the streets and a biting wind battering against the windowpane. The virgin white blanket of snow covering the square was not even dented, as she heard the muted sound of a lone vehicle crunching a path slowly down Sloane Street. There was nobody about. Picking up her mobile telephone, a tired voice answered after several rings. 'Erik, are you up yet?'

'Oh, I'm never down at this time of the day, darling. What's the problem?'

'Be serious, Erik, look outside.' She could hear Erik struggle out of bed and pad over to the window.

'Oh, disaster,' he screamed. 'Yanni, get up sweetie, you've got to dig the car out.' He picked up the telephone again. 'Vanessa, those Krauts will be waiting on the doorstep. What are we going to do? Two months' work flushed down the toilet?'

'Stop flapping, Erik. They want this job as much as we do. Can you pick me up on the way?'

'What! A pack of huskies won't get me there.'

'Erik, be a man, be here.'

'I wish, I wish.'

One and a half hours later Erik and Yanni arrived at Vanessa's apartment. The hazardous journey took another 40 minutes and sure enough the German delegation were waiting on the doorstep.

They both had worked hard on the prospective account, pitching against another two companies. Proving that they were the best in the business their presentation package was looking very good. Once assembled and in the confines of a warm conference room, Erik began to relax.

'Gentlemen, firstly I would like to introduce you to my assistant, Miss Vanessa Baron who has worked diligently on our project.' Firm handshakes followed. 'Please be seated.' Erik was in his element performing to a captive audience and apart from the occasional flick of the wrist, his performance was impeccably professional. With Vanessa's assistance, Erik launched straight into the illustrated layout of the new BMW Seven Series brochure. Page after page was meticulously explained, with Vanessa eyeing the Germans for any reaction. They grunted and nodded acknowledgement of the data they knew by heart, but Erik was giving them the hard sell. This account was worth millions, if secured. Erik turned to Vanessa who, on cue, rose and crossed the room to the video. She could feel their eyes burning the backs of her legs as she bent down to activate the machine. She turned quickly to face the meeting. 'Gentlemen, may I present a 60-second documented video which, as you will see, speaks for itself.' She stood aside, while Erik lowered the blinds. The video was polished and slick and required no further explanation. With polite arrogance the two Germans left the conference room, the portfolio in their possession, leaving Erik and Vanessa to await the decision of their hierarchy. When they were out of range, Erik glanced at his watch, the time noon.

'Time for a large one, luv.'

The snow continued all day, with council trucks creeping slowly around the city, trying unsuccessfully to keep the roads clear. More than half the agency staff had failed to show up for work and by three o'clock Vanessa packed, ready to leave.

'Bye, Erik,' she shouted, passing his door.

Erik emerged from his office, coffee mug in hand, 'Going, where are you going?'

'Home.'

'But how?'

'Walking.'

'Crazy girl, wait for us.' She waved her hand and stepped inside the elevator.

'See you tomorrow.' She waved.

Vanessa pulled the fur-lined hood of her coat over her head and descended the steps of the agency carefully and out into the street. The wind, still bitterly cold, was whisking flurries of snow across the square, which she found exhilarating. She joined the many red-faced pedestrians battling their way forward, wrapped in yards of scarves and carrying broken umbrellas, and trudged in the direction of Hyde Park Corner. Before too long she was in Sloane Street, rosy cheeked and feeling invigorated by the walk. She continued, treading lightly, the snow still falling in swirls around her and approached the traffic lights with Pont Street, but quickly the sequence changed to green. Vanessa waited, stepping from one foot to another, the cold beginning to creep into her toes. She looked up as the lights turned to red again; if she hurried she could make it to the other side. She stepped out climbing over mounds of snow and into the street. Her calculations had been wrong as a vehicle swung around the corner and, glancing up in a moment of panic, she lost her footing and tumbled into the road. The vehicle braked, but could not stop and slid towards her, getting closer and closer. Terrified, for there was nothing she could do, she covered her head with her arms and screamed. Lying prostrate in the middle of the road, her heart pounding in her chest, she knew at least she was still alive and on opening her eyes saw a front bumper hovering over her shoulder and two faces looking down at her.

'Are you all right down there?'

The realisation that she was intact provoked uncontrollable nervous laughter. 'All right? Oh yes, I'm perfectly all right down here.'

Two strong pairs of arms lifted Vanessa to her feet and supported by one young man she stood up. Her ankle felt badly sprained as she tried to take a step forward. The other rescuer retrieved the contents of her handbag that lay scattered across the street.

'We must get you home – that ankle needs looking at,' said one young man, his dark hair heavy with snow.

'I'll be fine, really, I live just across the square.' Vanessa tried to take another step forward, but stumbled into the railings, which broke her fall.

'Oh no you're not. Quick, Oliver, open the car door.'

They both heaved Vanessa on to the back seat of the vehicle, one pushing, the other pulling. In agony, she was grateful for the lift, but the ankle was beginning to swell and the pain was excruciating. Two grinning faces looked back at her from the front seats. 'I'm Oliver and this is Toby, and you are?' Vanessa whispered her name, 'OK, Vanessa, where to?'

Directing them around the corner to Cadogan Place, her good samaritans lifted her from the car and into the apartment. They placed her on the sofa and attempted to take off the boot. She yelped in agony.

'There's only one thing for it,' Toby said, peeling off his coat. 'We'll have to cut it off.'

Vanessa cried out in pain, 'No, please!'

Oliver was already in the kitchen and returned with a large pair of kitchen scissors, 'You might have broken it, Vanessa. Now hold still.'

She pushed Oliver's hand away as he attempted to insert the blade into the top of the boot. The slightest movement was stabbing at her foot. 'Who's your doctor?' Toby asked, grabbing the telephone book.

'Dr Paterson,' she whispered. 'Be careful, Oliver.'

Oliver was down to the ankle, but could not get the boot off, when Toby abandoned the call. They both carefully wiggled the boot in a vain attempt to free the foot, when they realised her screaming had stopped. Oliver looked up at Vanessa's ashen face, 'My God, she's passed out,' he said panicking. Toby was up on his feet putting his coat back on.'We'd better get her to a hospital – where's the nearest one?'

With the slashed boot flapping around her ankle, the two friends wrapped Vanessa in a duvet and carried her like a corpse out to the car. Still snowing, driving was hazardous and on reaching Westminster Hospital, Toby raced into the casualty department for help. They both watched the stretcher disappear through the swing doors.

'Name?' the large West Indian nurse asked.

'Er, Toby.'

'Not your name, da young lady's name.'

'Oh, um, Vanessa.'

'Yes – Vanessa who?'

They both looked at each other and shrugged.

'You must know da lady's name now, boys?'

Oliver went to the counter, tugging Toby's arm as he went. 'Well, you see,' he paused for thought, 'we found her.'

'I see den, you found her where?'

'No, no,' Toby interrupted, 'she was lying in the road.'

The nurse rolled her eyes, 'You mean dare was an accident?'

Toby looked at Oliver for support, 'No, well, actually yes, she slipped on the ice.'

'Ah, ah, and where were you, den?'

'We were driving the car.' Oliver knew as soon as the words tumbled from his mouth that he had made a terrible mistake.

Standing back, the nurse rolled her eyes once again from one to the other, 'Did you report dis accident, then?'

Toby was beginning to think that their cavalier act of mercy was turning into a charge for manslaughter. 'There wasn't an accident,' he shouted.

With clenched teeth, Oliver placed both hands on the counter and growled. 'Now listen sister, there's a frigging arctic storm out there, so hear me loud and clear. There was no accident and no dead bodies.'

'Alleluia,' Toby chanted. Oliver slapped his arm around Toby's shoulder. 'We was sent from heaven above to rescue this poor unfortunate girl from certain death.'

Toby clasped at his chest, 'Yes um sister.' The nurse proceeded to shuffle her papers, 'And if she lives, this day will not have been in vain.'

'Glory, glory.' They both chanted. 'For tomorrow is another blessed day, when you can ask her yourself, sister.'

The nurse picked up her pen and looked Oliver straight in the eye. 'Now, will you two honkies leave your names and addresses, so da Lord knows where to find you, brother?'

The following morning, Vanessa arrived back at the apartment plastered to the knee and on crutches. The X-rays had shown a fracture to the ankle, which would keep her inactive for several weeks. She propped herself up on the sofa and dialled Erik.

'All morning I've been trying to reach you, Vanessa. Who's bed have you just climbed out of?'

Erik balked at the news. 'Don't tell me, you've broken your right arm and I have got to do all this work myself?'

'No Erik, it's my right leg and you will not have to do all the work yourself, but I won't be in the office for a couple of days – I'm on crutches.' Vanessa toyed with the note Oliver and Toby had left at the hospital, while telling Erik what she could remember of the previous evening.

'Greedy bitch, not satisfied with one. So tell me, what are they like?'

'I can't really say, Erik, young,'

'Handsome and virile?'

'Well cute, but definitely not your type.'

'Huh, more's the pity.'

The different levels in the apartment were going to prove difficult during the next few weeks. The cast weighed heavily and getting around was no easy task, as Vanessa was already learning. She swung into the kitchen on her crutches to make some tea, a simple job, accomplished with ease. Tina would be in to clean and shop the following day and anything else could be delivered. She felt confident that everything was under control, or so it seemed. The journey back to the lounge was proving impossible, the tea went everywhere. Trying again, moving the mug from the counter to the table, then from the table to the bookshelf, the leg was beginning to ache, she had to sit down and rest. The final manoeuvre from the bookshelf to the coffee table was doubtful, but determined not to be beaten, she sank into the armchair exhausted. Help was needed and she took her address book from her bag. Which one of her friends should she rally first?

Lucinda finally succumbed to Vanessa's cry for help and promised to arrive at around seven o'clock with a Chinese takeaway and a video. Good, solid, dependable Lucinda, fashion editor of a popular glossy, was now engaged to a crazy photographer, forsaking her wild immoral past and she looked forward to an evening with the girls.

When Vanessa awoke it was dark. She leant over and switched on a sidelight and glanced at her watch, six o'clock. She had been asleep for more than two hours. Feeling stiff and dishevelled, she pulled herself up off the sofa and made her way upstairs.

Bathing was hazardous, one slip could prove catastrophic if tackled without due care. She reclined into the warm water, resting the fractured right ankle on the tap and wondered how she was going to get safely downstairs again.

The buzzer heralded Lucinda's arrival. Vanessa was ravenous and swung open the apartment door to find her hiding behind an enormous bunch of lilies, followed closely by a girlfriend she had not met before, stacked high with paper carriers containing supper.

'Vanessa, darling,' short kisses smacked the air in greeting. 'You poor thing, sit down.' Lucinda breezed passed her towards the kitchen. 'This is Polly,' she said, almost as an afterthought. Polly nodded hello at Vanessa while following Lucinda into the kitchen, who wafted back into the lounge carrying the bowl of flowers. 'Where do you want them, darling?' Vanessa hardly had time to catch her breath. 'Over here?' Clucking around the lounge like a mother hen, Vanessa was quite happy to let Lucinda take control and in no time at all, a feast of spring rolls, crispy duck, sea bass and boiled rice appeared piping hot from the microwave. During the course of the evening, it transpired that Lucinda and Polly had met some two years ago at the Models Ball and struck up a friendship. Polly's family home at Henley-on-Thames being only a mere five miles from Hambledon, also prompted conversation of mutual friends.

'I'm having a party Saturday night, please come,' Polly said, anxious to cement the new friendship with Vanessa. With visions of a couch potato springing to mind, Vanessa hesitated. 'But how?' she remarked, looking down at the leg.

'Don't worry about a thing, I'll arrange transport.'

Retrieving the coats from the closet, 'Simply got to go, darling,' Lucinda gushed, 'Douglas will think we've been abducted.'

Susy threw herself headlong into keeping fit. She had taken out full membership at the spa and attended four times a week. At 5 feet 8 inches, she weighed in at 10 stone 2 lb, two stone had to be shed before she reached her target.

Norma had moved in and Eddy had hardly spoken to Susy since their confrontation at Christmas. The atmosphere was cold, almost hostile at times and Susy could not wait to move out. Every evening on her return home, she would retire to her room and scan the newspapers for accommodation, but her salary belied her aspirations for a decent flat. At best, all she had viewed were cramped bedsitters masquerading as studios. 'Share,' Gill had suggested, pointing out all the advantages, an alternative she had not considered.

Saturday was Polly's 23rd birthday and the party she had planned was at home, in the apartment she shared with another couple and her cat Henry, in Thurloe Square. Susy was ecstatic at the invitation, although a little apprehensive at mixing with all those socialites, and saw the occasion as more of an initiation ceremony. How should she behave, what would she say, but most important what the hell should she wear?

With a borrowed jacket and trousers from Gill, Susy raced home after work on Saturday night to get ready. As she climbed into the suit, tucking the silk shirt down into the pants, the results of her workouts were evidently streamlining her silhouette. She zipped up the flies, slipped her arms into the jacket and with one last check in the mirror, adjusted the belt: she would have to do. Picking up her bag and neatly wrapped gift and with a bottle of wine tucked under her arm, she raced out of the house and into her car for the drive back across town.

All the snow had virtually disappeared and Susy had no difficulty in locating Thurloe Square. She parked and walked in the direction of the music. At the front door she climbed the steps and rang the bell. There was no reply and on ringing once again, a man's voice crackled over the intercom, 'Who's there?'

'It's Susy,' she replied.

'Enter, fair lady, enter.'

Susy climbed the stairs to the first floor and pushed open the door. The apartment was heaving with bodies as she edged her way through the throng. A waitress thrust a tray at her, 'Champagne, madam?'

'Can I take your coat, miss?' said the grinning black face, dressed in a dinner jacket and bow tie. She struggled out of her coat and with a glass of champagne in her hand, enquired the whereabouts of Polly.

'Miss Bartholomew is at the far side of the lounge, miss.'

How gracious he sounded. Susy was not accustomed to such manners and surged through the crowd of upper-crust toffs, feeling very much the underdog, when she spotted Polly jumping up and down above the sea of heads. 'Susy, Susy, over here, let me introduce you to some of my friends.' Giddy with excitement, but afraid to open her mouth, Susy was led by the hand across the room, to where some of Polly's friends were seated. The evening had only just began, but was already a blur. 'This is my brother, Paul, his girlfriend, Amanda, Julian, Tim and Lucinda.' Susy nodded to each one in turn, 'and this is Susy, from Crawfords and my sparring partner.'

Lucinda swung straight into conversation, 'Oh, fashion is such fun, don't you think, and how long have you been at Crawfords?' Susy was unsure of Lucinda's bombastic personality.

''Bout four months now,' she replied carefully.

'Oh, where do you come from, er, Susy, isn't it?'

'Bethnal Green.'

'I don't believe I know where that is?'

'It's in the East End.'

Lucinda tossed her head in the air, 'Really – I've never been there.'

'No, I don't suppose you 'ave,' Susy retorted.

There was a commotion coming from the other side of the room. 'Oh, my goodness,' Lucinda said, jumping to her feet, 'it's Vanessa.'

Polly and Lucinda quickly disappeared into the crowd to assist Vanessa's safe arrival, leaving Susy stranded.

'She's a bitch that one,' Julian said, touching Susy's arm. 'Take no notice, darling, she thinks we're from Fulham.'

'In fact,' Tim added, 'we're both from Whitechapel.'

'I'd never 'ave guessed,' Susy laughed, ''Ow did you manage it?'

'Practise, darling, years and years of it,' Julian said, grabbing another glass of champagne from a passing tray.

'Yes, but you both look the part, you look terrific, you know, the business.' Susy was eager to know more, 'What do you two do, then?'

Julian offered Susy a cigarette. 'Antiques, if I'm lucky.' Tim flipped the cap of his Dunhill lighter. 'And you?' she said, looking at Tim.

'Theatre costumier and I just love every minute of it.'

'Umm, brings it home with him, too.' Julian caught a glimpse of Lucinda returning, 'Behave, the bat's behind you.'

'Darling,' Tim gushed, 'everything all right?'

Lucinda picked up her glass of champagne. 'Where's Paul and Amanda? Gone, have they?'

Susy and the boys had not noticed them slink off during conversation to a quieter part of the room, and were quite thankful to see Lucinda stalk off through the ever-increasing crowd.

Polly was pleased Vanessa had decided to come and deposited her in a comfortable armchair, resting her leg on a footstool. At that precise moment, Lucinda arrived with a substantial platter of food and was fussing over Vanessa again, much to her irritation. 'Lucinda,' she stressed, 'I am not a complete invalid, now will you please stop mothering me.'

'Just trying to be of help, darling.'

Vanessa was not too happy being at bum level. Her usual mode of circulating was severely hampered by the burden of the cast. She was not the centre of attention to which she craved and Polly, who was busy playing hostess to her multitude of friends, returned periodically with a guest for her to savour.

The pace of the party was hotting up, with people bobbing around in unison to the music and the wine flowed by the gallon. Oliver noticed the plastercast first and side stepped around the armchair, 'You must be Vanessa?' Surprised, she looked up at the handsome face. He looked familiar, but for a few seconds she could not place him. 'Oliver, remember?' pointing to her leg, 'Westminster Hospital.'

'Yes, yes, I should have called to thank you.'

'Well, you can thank us now.' He disappeared to prise Toby away from a pair of breasts. 'Look who I have found, Toby.'

Looking a little the worse for wear, the party was not their first port of call that evening, Toby snapped his fingers. 'She lives. Waitress, three more over here.'

Oliver squatted down to Vanessa's level, 'You're looking a lot better tonight. How's the ankle?'

Any attention was most welcome. 'Uncomfortable. I feel so helpless.'

'I'm sure you will be up and active again in no time.'

Toby unsteadily handed round the glasses of champagne, slopping it everywhere. 'Going to be a bit of a handicap in the sack, eh, Vanessa?' Toby placed his hand on Oliver's shoulder for support. 'Could get a nasty whiplash from that.'

Oliver hastily interrupted, 'Don't be such a piss artist, Toby. Go and play with somebody else.'

Vanessa showed mild amusement at Toby's vulgarity as he tottered away to join the other dancers. 'Tomorrow,' Oliver said, 'he won't remember a thing.'

Susy had never enjoyed herself so much, any inhibitions she had were left at the door. She danced the night away, soaking up every wonderful moment, rubbing shoulders with them all. She had eaten and drunk her fill and spurred on by Julian and Tim, she rocked until she dropped.

The birthday cake arrived ablaze. With lights dimmed, everyone called for Polly to extinguish the fire and make a wish. 'Speech, speech!'

While Oliver was distracted and Vanessa was standing on one foot, she took advantage of the lull in activity to visit the bathroom. Walking carefully, she crossed the room angling her crutches so as not to whack anyone's ankles as she passed them by.

The bathroom was located off the landing, which she soon found, but the door was locked, causing her to wait for what seemed like a very long time. Performing a balancing act while taking a grip of her bladder the bathroom door flew open, knocking her completely off balance. She fell to the floor, losing control of her crutches, which clattered to the ground. Susy could only look on in horror, as she stooped down to assist Vanessa to her feet, wishing she had taken more care when forcing the bathroom door open.

'I'm sorry, luv, I didn't see you.'

'How could you possibly not see me?' Vanessa screamed.

'It was an accident, darlin', I wouldn't do it on purpose.'

Susy helped Vanessa to her feet, brushing her down.

Flustered, Vanessa glared at Susy, 'Leave me alone, you stupid girl.'

'I'm really very sorry. Can't I 'elp you?'

'Help me! Yes, just stay out of my way.' Vanessa hopped into the bathroom, leaving Susy standing helpless on the landing.

The party was thinning out. Julian and Tim had gone and the few people that remained were lolling about. Susy leaned up against the buffet table and nibbled the last remaining morsel of birthday cake left on her plate. She watched Vanessa struggle back into the room to be greeted by Oliver who helped her on with her coat, before leaving together.

Polly linked her arm into Susy's. 'I've hardly had time to speak to you all evening,' she whispered, 'I've done it.' Susy had no idea what she was talking about.

'Done what?' she asked.

'Sebastian.' She searched Susy's face for a reaction.

'No, you mean?'

'Yes, I mean, yes,' she said excitedly, drawing Susy's attention to the gallery bedroom.

The partygoers were bidding their farewells, the caterers were also packing up ready to leave and Polly insisted, 'Now you are not driving home, Susy.'

'But Polly I can't stay, where will I sleep?'

'Nonsense, I won't hear of it, you can sleep here and in the morning just let yourself out.'

Susy awoke just after noon. She could hardly lift her head from the pillow, for she had a monumental hangover. Stumbling into the bathroom, she found some aspirin in the cabinet, then crept into the kitchen to wash them down with a glass of orange juice. Half an hour later, she climbed behind the wheel of her car and began the journey home.

Eddy was standing in the hall, waiting for her arrival, when Susy put the key in the front door and let herself into the house.

'Where the fuck do you think you've bin?' he bellowed, the words hitting her like a sledgehammer.

'A party. I stopped.'

'A party, it's the middle of bleeding Sunday afternoon! You little cow, who've you bin shacking up with?' he pushed her up against the wall.

'Don't you believe anythin you 'ear?' She took a step towards the stairs.

'Oh no you don't,' he grabbed Susy by the arm and pushed her into the lounge. 'You're goin' to tell me exactly where you've bin. Now start talking.'

'I just told ya,' she shouted back.

Eddy punched her in the face and spat the words at her, 'You told me nothin'.'

Norma appeared behind Eddy, 'Take it easy, darlin'.'

Eddy spun around and confronted her, 'And you can shut it, too.'

Susy picked herself up off the floor, a trickle of blood appearing from the corner of her mouth. 'I stayed at Polly's,' she cried, for she had no strength to oppose him. 'You want me to lie?'

'You are lying,' he drew closer to her, prodding at her chest with his fist. 'Respect is what I want from you. You don't drive in 'ere in your fancy clothes, stinking of booze and tell me you just bin to a party.'

Susy swayed, sobbing uncontrollably, unable to speak. She held her arm up against the blows, she felt would rain down upon her again and again. 'Now you either do as I say, or you get out!' he hollered. 'Do I 'ave to say it again?'

Susy stumbled upstairs and fell face down on the bed and cried herself to sleep. Later that evening she phoned Polly, in a desperate cry for help. Then she placed the receiver back on its rest, took a case down from the wardrobe and packed.

For one week Susy slept on the sofa bed in Polly's lounge and every evening she viewed accommodation to rent all over town. On Sunday evening Polly's flatmates were due back from their holiday and Susy felt she would be encroaching on their privacy if she stayed.

Saturday evening, Susy waited for Polly to return from her dinner date with Sebastian. Curled up in an armchair, watching the late movie, with Henry purring contentedly on her lap, she had dozed off when they came in.

'Hey, you're still up. Had any luck?' Polly sat down on the floor opposite Susy.

'No, nothin'.'

At Polly's command Sebastian disappeared into the kitchen to make some coffee.

'I'll be out of 'ere tomorrow,' Susy said flatly.

Polly was appalled, 'And go where? Not back to that monster?'

'Listen Polly, you've bin very kind to me and I really appreciate it, but I've got to move on.'

Polly sat quietly looking into Susy's strained expression. 'Leave it to me, I'll find you somewhere. We'll start first thing in the morning.'

Susy was touched by the concern, after all she was not one of them. She was an outsider, a commoner, there were no loyalties, no affectionate brotherhood, no bloodlink, which is what she understood. So, why should somebody she barely knew reach out their hand in friendship? She had nothing to give in return. 'I owe you one, darlin'.'

Sunday morning Susy watched Polly and Sebastian detangle themselves at the front door. After their passionate goodbye, Polly bounded back into the kitchen looking radiant. Was obviously worth waiting for, Susy noted, as Polly swanned around the kitchen. 'Magic, pure magic,' she sighed.

After breakfast, Polly took her filofax from her bag and laid it open on the table, then prepared a list of the friends who just might be looking for a flatmate. Throughout the day they huddled over the telephone, not everyone was home and the ones that were showed little or no interest at all. Susy paced, agitated at the situation. Perhaps Joyce would take her in for a while, she was family. Polly would not hear of it: weakness of character going back, she said, the easy option. She was right, of course.

They sat silently side by side in front of the fire, watching flames flicker up the chimneystack. Polly had exhausted her supply of numerous friends and pondered on what to do next. 'I wonder,' she said out loud.

Almost hypnotised by the dancing flames, Susy watched Polly rise to her feet and return with a notepad. As she flicked through the pages, she said to herself, 'Vanessa ... hum, now this is a long shot, Susy, but we'll try.'

After the preliminary niceties, Susy listened intently to Polly's explanation of her dilemma and the predicament she had found herself in after escaping from a violent family situation. Vanessa appreciated the problem, as she remembered only too well the confrontation she herself had had with her mother, but did she really want another life going on under her roof? Polly explained that it would only be for a month, by which time Susy would undoubtedly have found a place of her own. Vanessa did have a spare bedroom and thought that maybe for a short time another pair of hands around the apartment might be of use to her, and any friend of Polly's would be welcome. Polly beamed from ear to ear, as she put the receiver down, 'You're in. I'll help you get ready and tell you all about it on the way.'

They pulled up outside the apartment in Cadogan Place and

rang the bell. Vanessa eventually let them in, with Polly leading the way up the stairs and Susy following with her suitcase. At the door there was the usual greeting, while Susy panting six paces behind, banged the suitcase to the floor.

'Vanessa, this is Susy,' Polly proclaimed.

Vanessa looked Susy icily up and down as Susy's eyes descended to the plaster cast, both remembering the clash the week before. 'We've met,' Vanessa said coldly.

'Oh, good.' Polly assumed, rightly, at the party.

Susy stood quite still and looked around her, trying to absorb the grandeur, the furnishings, the paintings, afraid to take a step forward. Vanessa hobbled over to the sofa and resumed her position.

'Well, come in,' she said. 'Polly, there's wine in the refrigerator and bring some glasses.'

Still afraid to touch anything, Susy sat on the edge of her chair sipping a chilled glass of Chardonnay, listening to classical music coming from every corner of the room, and noting the dining table set for two: Vanessa was expecting company. The bruising to Susy's face confirmed Polly's story, but Vanessa needed to know more about the 'friend' being dumped on her at such short notice. She drew Susy into the conversation, asked the right questions and learnt a little of what lay behind the young woman who was about to share her home.

'So you're a Cockney?'

'Born and bred,' Susy replied.

Polly sensed Vanessa's distaste for anything less than elite and promptly interjected, 'A rising star, Vanessa, wait and see.'

Vanessa was not convinced; what sat before her was nothing other than a down-stream market girl; a badly-spoken, uneducated peasant and she was beginning to regret the arrangement. On the other hand, Susy saw Vanessa as a rich, intelligent beauty, well travelled, well spoken and wanting for nothing. She feared that she was completely out of her depth and decided to adopt a low profile during the next few weeks. She fumbled in her bag for a cigarette while listening intently to the ongoing conversation, in which she was not included, and looked around for an ashtray.

'Polly will show you to your room,' Vanessa said, half smiling.

Gathering her belongings together, she followed Polly upstairs to her bedroom. The door opened up to reveal a bright spring-like room decorated with delicate pink and white striped wallpaper. Festoon blinds adorned the window and embroidered white bedlinen lay neatly over the bed, which was flanked by two bedside tables. On one wall hung a large mirror, which reflected more light from an opposing window.

'Oh!' Susy gasped, 'it's so lovely. How can I ever thank you, Polly?'

5

February 1986.

Every morning as she was rising Susy heard a taxi draw up outside the apartment, to transport Vanessa to the office. She would leave an hour later and return late, their paths rarely crossing. The arrangement seemed to be working, for the moment.

During the first week at Cadogan Place, Susy did not view a single apartment. Instead, she took in a session at the gym, followed by a leisurely hour or more at a local café or wine bar. She was indulging her newly found status and wallowed in her daily routine: shouting ''morning' to a rather surprised postman delivering the mail, followed by a short stroll along Sloane Street to the station, where she would chat for a while to the newspaper vendor, before hopping on a tube to work. Every evening Polly and Sebastian were, as she was led to believe, horizontal. Which apparently had struck her dumb, as neither Gill nor Susy could get any sense out of her whatsoever. Life was very sweet.

Susy overheard Vanessa on the telephone, making plans for the theatre with Oliver. Keeping this arrangement in mind, she planned to take full advantage of having the place to herself on Saturday evening.

Bags of shopping were placed firmly on the kitchen table, from which Susy took a bottle of wine. As she reached up into the kitchen cupboard for a glass, she thought how grand it would be to drink from a crystal goblet. The wine, of course, would naturally taste superb. She prepared a large green salad and placed the bowl to one side, brushed a haddock fillet with butter and poured herself another glass of wine. Susy knew nothing of classical music; rock and pop were more to her standing and flipping through Vanessa's CD collection meant very little to her. She turned each disc over in turn trying to comprehend the meaning of each piece. If I listen, maybe I'll learn something, she thought and placed a shiny metal disc into the machine. Beethoven blasted noisily through the speakers, filling the room with a shattering explosion of sound. Too harsh, she decided, putting the disc back in the case. Let's try another. The sound of Mozart delicately filled the air, conjuring up visions of crinolined ladies with their gentlemen swirling graciously around the ballroom floor. Susy found herself swaying to and fro. 'This is the business,' she said out loud, 'this is beautiful.' She danced around the furniture in time to the music, arms held high to the imaginary escort who was sweeping her off her feet and danced back into the kitchen.

Susy laid a table for one, lit a candle, dimmed the lights and turned up the music. She had watched Vanessa's decorum briefly and noted the manner in which she held herself. She picked up her glass lightly, pinkie finger poised and gently bumped the air to her absent dinner guest. 'Cheers, so nice of you to come,' she whispered coyly across the table. 'A little more salad, maybe?' She picked up her napkin and pressed the corners of her mouth. 'Another glass of wine, yes?' Susy poured herself another glass of wine and with that glided across the lounge floor head held high, shoulders back, as Polly had taught her. She reached the stereo, lowered her eyes only, not wishing to distort her stance, changed the CD, turned and glided back to the table. A little practice was all that was needed to act and talk just like Vanessa, but she lacked the funds to dress the part.

Susy sped up the flight of stairs to Vanessa's bedroom, clicked open the door and stepped inside. The opulent furnishings abounded, taffeta curtains neatly swagged and tasselled, silver trinkets adorning the dressing table. She picked up a photograph, hurriedly replacing it as her eyes darted around the room in every direction. She ran her fingers over everything, absorbing the very essence of quality and beauty as a blind man reads Braille. She opened the closet doors to behold rail after rail of silk, cashmere and leather. Grabbing a hanger, she held up a knee-length black silk jersey cocktail dress speckled with silver against her. 'Oh!' she sighed. Continuing through the racks, pulling out one garment after another for inspection, she slipped her arms into a Loewe jacket, sinking her hands into the soft leather, then took out a pair of Rossetti shoes from their box, as yet unworn and tried them on: they fitted. A veritable Pandora's box of goodies, but the climax of her indiscretion was a full length ivory evening dress, encrusted with seed pearls. Susy could not resist the temptation and stripping off, she stepped into the dress, pulling it on to her shoulders. Clinging to her like a second skin, she struggled with the zipper, then stood back in admiration, turning from one side to the other. 'Oh, Susy, you shall go to the ball.'

Still wearing Vanessa's evening gown Susy slipped back downstairs to the lounge as Mozart was just concluding his Jupiter symphony. Shuffling through the CDs she found Frank Sinatra, Aretha Franklin and Lena Horne, the tempo suiting her more decadent mood, as track after track reverberated through the apartment. The audience applauded and the drums rolled, on stage at the London Palladium. Susy knew all the words, cavorted to the music, swung her hips back and forth in Vanessa's fabulous dress. Lost in her imagination she was there out front, flirting with her fans and they all loved her. Knock 'em dead at Carnegie Hall and boy did they scream, she could hear them, feel the adoration. The vamp stomped her way across the arena of her fantasy until the final curtain, '– and I wish that he was trav'lin' my way, yeah.' A car door slammed and Susy could hear Vanessa's voice down in the street. She pressed her face up against the windowpane and panicked. 'Huh, she's back.' She swooped on the dining table, rushing the dirty crockery into the kitchen. Speeding back for the dirty ashtrays that Vanessa abhorred, fanning the air as she ran to disperse the smoke. She ran awkwardly up the stairs, the tightness of the dress restricting her movements. Inevitably something had to give as she struggled to undo the zipper, and she felt the stitching come away at the waist as she stepped out, hastily replacing the damaged dress back in the closet. Gathering her clothes from the bedroom floor, she tiptoed back to her room, closing the door just as Vanessa and Oliver entered the apartment. She was safe and prayed that Vanessa would not discover her folly.

There was no evidence that Oliver had stopped over. Apart from two empty coffee cups, the apartment was exactly as she had left it. Susy poured boiling water into the teapot, made two mugs of steaming hot tea and tapped lightly on Vanessa's bedroom door. She turned over wearily in bed as Susy popped her head around the door to find her alone.

'Yes, – What is it?'

'Cup of tea.'

'Thank you, no sugar.'

Returning with the tea Susy made up her mind to be nice, show some interest, converse. She placed the mug on the bedside table. 'Did you 'ave a nice time at the theatre?'

Vanessa did not remember telling Susy that she was going. 'Yes, wonderful. Do you ever go?'

'Not regular, my mum and I used to go to the East End clubs, the variety nights, but since she died I 'avn't bothered.'

'I'm sorry about your mother, Susy, I didn't know.'

Susy shrugged, 'that's life.' She was on her way out of the bedroom, when Vanessa called her back.

'If you're going out, could you get me a newspaper. *The Times* and something else. I'll leave it to you?'

Once dressed, Susy walked to Sloane Square to the newsagents, picking up the *Sunday Times*, *The People*, the *News of the World* and 40 Dunhill for herself. When she arrived back at the apartment, Vanessa was up and about. She had become quite agile on crutches, moving about with relative ease. Susy placed the newspapers on the dining room table. The quality of Vanessa's life was evident and Susy was also quick to learn that she was exceptionally talented, an actual storehouse of knowledge was just sitting there waiting to be tapped. How, in such a short space of time could Susy turn the situation to her advantage, be privy to her secret of success? They had barely spoken to one another in a week and in a short time she would be moving out, their paths destined never to cross again. Susy watched her pick up *The Sunday Times* and settle down in the armchair. Would she really be prepared to enlighten her on the finer things in life? In Susy's estimation the answer would be a resounding no. The telephone rang.

'Shall I get it?' Not expecting any calls that day, Susy picked up the receiver and said 'Hello.' Lucinda was checking up on Vanessa's progress and handing her the phone, Susy disappeared into the kitchen, opened the window and lit up a cigarette. She could hear Vanessa's conversation quite clearly. '... It's not for long, about three or four weeks.' Susy knew Lucinda would quiz her, 'Don't be silly darling, I hardly see her.' Susy blew a billow of smoke out of the kitchen window. 'New York,' she heard Vanessa say, 'just two days.' Vanessa started to giggle like a mischievous little girl. 'Not with this leg, darling, he's far too romantic.' What a nosy cow that Lucinda is, Susy thought. Doesn't anything pass her by? 'See you about six, then?' Susy threw her butt end out of the window, then returned to the lounge, to find Vanessa leafing through the *News of the World*. 'I didn't know papers like this existed,' she said.

''Course you did, you just wouldn't like anybody to see you buy one,' Susy explained. 'Help yourself, I'll see ya later.'

With absolutely nothing to do for the whole afternoon, Susy happily walked where her feet dictated. She marvelled at the splendour of the Victoria and Albert Museum, moving on through South Kensington to Chelsea and the Kings Road. Although quieter than a few years ago, colourful punks and trendies left over from yesteryear still roamed the famous street, with supermarkets and fashionable shops. With Sloane Square in view, Susy had walked full circle and finding a seat in a restaurant overlooking the square, ordered a glass of wine and the menu. She was not cooking tonight.

There was a momentary hush as Susy entered the apartment. 'Nice to see you again,' Lucinda said with a smile. Susy gave a slight nod of the head, the lounge was untidy and piles of newspapers, cups and glasses littered the place. 'Have you eaten?' Lucinda asked Susy, who knew full well there was not the remotest possibility of her running any errands.

'I 'ave,' she replied.

Vanessa cut in. 'We were just wondering what to do, Susy. I see no reason to go out when there is plenty of food in the refrigerator.'

'Quite right.' Susy said, glancing at Lucinda's doleful expression.

'Lucinda on the other hand, feels that we should go out, but with the leg still –.'

'I know Vanessa, you'd rather stay at 'ome.' Susy would settle the discussion. 'Now go on, Lucinda, get those pots and pans out and make your friend a nice supper. That's what she wants. You don't come into it.'

Susy left Lucinda rattling around in the kitchen cupboards for supplies, bowing out of the evening before she could be commanded elsewhere. As she turned to climb the stairs, was that a flicker of a smile she saw cross Vanessa's face, or was she still in pain?

The next three weeks sped by and Susy was becoming increasingly frustrated treading the streets in pursuit of a new home. Her time at Cadogan Place had expired and she feared that she would be intruding on Vanessa's generosity if she stayed a moment longer. The final ditch, a day off work and armed with a list of addresses, she set off.

The promotion to head the creative department had not come as a complete surprise to Vanessa; she had worked hard to secure the position and won. Messages of accolade greeted her when she walked into the office mid morning and sitting on her desk was a small gift with an accompanying card. She swung around in her chair and opened up the envelope from Oliver and inside the box a single orchid. How thoughtful, so simple and yet so beautiful. He was a gentleman, attentive, but not pushy, an old fashioned romantic. Vanessa was becoming exceedingly fond of him and the time had come to stop playing cat and mouse.

Susy bounded into the apartment after viewing the studio flat in North Kensington that the estate agent had said was as good as hers. She burst into the lounge unaware that Vanessa was entertaining guests. She excused herself and turned to walk away.

'Come in,' Vanessa said, ushering her forward, 'This is my house guest, Susy.'

'Not for much longer,' she replied, trying to contain her excitement, 'I think I've found somewhere.'

'This is wonderful news. When are you moving?' Vanessa asked.

'Saturday week, if that's all right with you?'

'Yes, well, as soon as it's available.'

Oliver handed Susy a glass of champagne and offered her his seat. 'And where is this flat, Susy?'

Sitting down, Susy turned to face Oliver. 'It's a studio in Kensington, but it's big enough for me.'

Vanessa was ignoring her guests and proceeded to introduce Erik, Yanni and Oliver's friend, Toby, 'Who I don't believe you have met before?'

Susy did not recall and would certainly have remembered meeting Toby, with his dark blond hair and piercing brown eyes.

'Well, hello,' he said suggestively, 'to the new flat owner,' and raised his glass. Erik's booming voice carried across the lounge. 'I remember so well, sweetie, my first flat.'

'How can you possibly remember post-war London Erik?' Yanni's astounded expression ruffled Erik's feathers. He continued, 'My first flat, darling, was just off the Bayswater Road in the early sixties,' he glared at Yanni. 'A blaze of colour and design, far ahead of its time and with a perpetual flow of friends and parties. Oh! How I look back with longing.'

'His misspent youth,' Yanni was chancing his luck.

'I can easily take you home, ducky, now wrap it up!'

Susy had met so many men of alternative gender in the past few weeks that she was worried if it was becoming compulsory. 'I bet you 'ad lots of fun though?'

'Fun!' Erik exclaimed, 'in the days when we had to go underground,' Yanni nodded in agreement, 'we never had so much fun; now it's got completely out of hand.'

Vanessa drew Susy's attention to the empty glasses. 'Could you?' she said.

'Sit, I'll get it,' Oliver said, placing his hand on Susy's shoulder.

Toby ambled around the room uninterested in the conversation, catching Susy's eye over the rim of his champagne flute several times and smiling. She flushed slightly, turning away, but kept his presence in the corner of her sight as he paced around the room, returning only to replenish his glass. Quite suddenly, he sat down next to her on the sofa, so close she could hear his breathing in her ear, forcing her to move up. 'Sorry' she said. 'My pleasure,' he replied. Susy felt a rush of excitement, causing her to speak out of turn. 'And what do you do?' she said quickly.

'Do – what do I do?' Toby thought.

'He rescues damsels in distress,' Vanessa laughed, waving her restored leg in the air.

'Hey! It's gone,' Susy declared, not noticing that the plaster cast had been removed. 'When did that 'appen?'

'This morning and not a moment too soon.'

Oliver returned with another bottle of champagne and Susy thought she would try again. 'So what do you do, Toby?'

Toby held out his glass for a refill, 'I work for an international finance house.'

'A high flyer,' Oliver added, filling his glass, 'especially after a few of these.'

'Yep and I travel a lot, too.'

He was very attractive, a master of seduction and his enigmatic smile had Susy captivated, and she wanted to know more.

'Time to go,' Oliver said, glancing at his watch, 'or we shall lose our table. Why don't you come along, Susy?'

'No thanks, it's your night, some other time maybe.' She watched them all file out of the apartment and walk down the stairs to the front door, hoping Toby would turn and look back. He did not.

Boxes of spring fashions were arriving at Crawfords by the hour. Susy and Polly were frantically getting the shop ship-shape before Gill arrived back from Milan. Working long into the evening, unpacking, checking and tagging the new range, getting home exhausted long after midnight. 'Ring Oliver, re flat', was the message left on Susy's dressing table, in Vanessa's handwriting. On Saturday she was due to move out. What flat could they be talking about?

Gill was impressed when she opened up the shop the following morning. 'Oh, you little darlings, what a sight for sore eyes. I couldn't have done better myself.'

'You owe us,' Polly shouted from the back of the shop.

'Ay you! Stop pinching my lines,' came Susy's voice from behind a screen.

'Girls, you both have done a great job.' At that moment a customer strolled into the shop, 'Now, when we get a chance, I want a word.'

The cards they had sent out produced a stream of regular customers into the shop to view the new spring range and it was not until the middle of the afternoon that they could sit down and relax. Gill flopped in a chair and lit up a cigarette.

'OK, now I hope you're both ready for this?' Gill spoke with extreme solemnity. 'There is only one other person who knows and I don't want it spread about, understood?' They both nodded their heads. 'I'm getting married,' she laughed.

Susy slapped her thigh in disbelief. 'She got us at it, Polly. Sneaky, what are you?' She wagged her finger at Gill and Polly threw herself around Gill's neck.

'Congratulations, but when?'

'Wait, I haven't finished yet – I'm pregnant.'

Polly snatched the cigarette from Gill's hand. 'That's the last one,' and stubbed the butt into the ashtray.

'Now let's be serious. It's due in October and I don't want to lose this little one, not like before,' Gill paused to reflect. 'This could be my last chance, girls. I've got to stop work, doctor's orders.'

'When?' Susy asked.

'In a word, now.'

'So what 'appens 'ere?'

'I have a meeting tonight with David and Estelle and will propose that Susy, you take my position as manageress and Polly, as your assistant. Your salaries increase accordingly and you will need more staff immediately. Susy, you're capable of running the show, darlin'. It will also mean you travelling to Europe to buy.'

Susy was speechless; the nearest she had got to Europe was a package holiday to Majorca in 1977.

'Wake up sweetheart, it's your big chance.'

Bounding back to reality, Susy asserted herself. 'I can. I know I can do it. Can't we, Polly?'

'Of course you can, Susy.'

The day had been so frenetic that Susy had completely forgotten to call Oliver until she was almost home, her head so full of impending responsibilities. She left the underground at full speed, almost breaking into a run as she turned the corner into Cadogan Place. She stepped out into the road, between two vehicles, glancing quickly behind her, nothing was coming, but she did not see the man as he crashed into her shoulder, almost spinning her around. 'Ay, watch where yer goin',' she shouted, watching the lone figure slink off into the darkness. Where the hell did he spring from? she thought. Once inside the apartment, Susy picked up the telephone and rang Oliver's number. After much clicking and tripping she connected. 'Oliver, it's Susy. Can you 'ear me, it's a very bad line?'

'Susy, hello, I'm in the car. I can hear you clearly.'

'I got a message to call you 'bout a flat?'

'That's right, there's a vacant flat for rent just off the New King's Road at Parson's Green. One bedroom. You should see it Susy, much better than a studio in Notting Hill.'

'But I've already accepted, Oliver.'

'It's up to you, don't let me sway you, but I think it was made for you.'

Susy thought for a moment. With a raise in salary a bigger flat might just be possible and looking did not cost anything, 'OK, Oliver, I'll see it.'

'Great, now can you hear me? Write this down: Flat 3, 42 Parson's Green. Meet me there Wednesday evening, say seven o'clock.'

'I got it.'

Vanessa walked into the flat as Susy put the telephone down. 'You look very pleased with yourself tonight?'

'Vanessa, I don't know where to start.'

'Let's try the beginning.'

In her euphoria Susy could not stop talking, following Vanessa around the apartment like a sheep. She began with her days on the stall in the Mile End Road, something Vanessa had not called for, to her departure from the East End. The job at Crawfords, where she met Polly and her desire to be a size 10. Vanessa was going out and stripped off in the bathroom to take a shower and Susy was right there with her, still talking. The promotion to manageress was the pinnacle of her present success, she had plans, ideas of her own and she was determined to make it the best fashion shop in town. Vanessa was by now applying her makeup, while Susy sat on the bed behind her.

'Well, I can understand your joy,' she finally said. 'Did you call Oliver?'

'Yep. He insists I see this flat in Parson's Green.'

'And are you going?'

'Wednesday night.'

'Good. Can you do me up, Susy?'

Susy slid the zipper up the back of Vanessa's gown with ease, remembering the ivory evening dress that she so foolishly ruined, as yet undetected. She turned to Vanessa, 'I want to thank you – please let me thank you for letting me stay 'ere in your beautiful 'ome. I want to repay you somehow.'

'Susy, it's not necessary.' Vanessa replied.

Pausing for thought, Susy hurriedly replied, 'I know, I'll take you to the new Covent Garden.'

'I have no idea where that is.'

'It's just down the road at Nine Elms. Please, Vanessa, let me take you there, show you my people. You'll love it, honest.'

Vanessa sighed, 'Do I have to? Anyway, what do they do there?'

'Do, don't be daft, it's the biggest market in the country, wall to wall flowers. It's beautiful. Please let me fill your home with flowers, just to say thanks? Go on!'

Knowing that there was no backing out of this arrangement Vanessa agreed.

'Wednesday morning five o'clock.'

'I have an 8.30 business meeting, Susy. I'll never make it on time.'

'You'll be there, I'll get you up and drop you off at the office on time.'

Grabbing her coat, Vanessa was about to fly out of the door in a frantic hurry.

'Cor, this must be some hot date you've got tonight, I've never seen anyone move so fast.'

'Susy, this is the one man I will not keep waiting.' Susy looked at her inquiringly. 'My father,' and Vanessa rushed out of the door.

She watched Vanessa run out across the road in search of a taxi, unable to appreciate the loving relationship she had with her father. There had been no word from home over the past few weeks, no consideration and no love. Susy had learnt to despise Eddy, she did not care if she never saw him again. Vanessa hailed a taxi on the corner and hopped inside. The girl's got a heart, Susy thought, shame she doesn't show it sometimes, but as she gazed down into the street, something stirred in the shadows. She backed away from the window; was the apartment being watched? Pulling the curtain discreetly away from the window, she peered down into the street again. Must be her imagination, there were always people moving around down there. She crossed the room and switched off the light, returning to the window. Her eyes searched the darkness and just out of the glare of the street light she saw him. The shadowy figure leant on the side of the railings for a few minutes, then took off and slipped silently out of sight. Susy nervously closed the drapes, telling herself that she was watching too many murder mysteries on television, but her streetwise upbringing breathed caution to her very soul. Was that the man who clipped her shoulder earlier? Better watch out.

Susy was busy throwing together a cottage pie for herself and Polly for tomorrow evening, when Vanessa arrived home. She looked into the kitchen to find Susy surrounded by every available utensil she had. 'Something smells good,' she said.

Susy brushed the hair from her forehead, she was hot. 'I'm no Moses man, but I try.'

Vanessa smiled, 'Don't you mean Mossiman?'

'Yeah, that's 'im.'

Concentrating on what she was doing, Susy forgot to mention the prowler, when she saw Vanessa disappear upstairs and close the door behind her. Too late, she would tell her tomorrow.

The girls said goodnight to Gill as she locked up the shop for the night, then walked on up James Street to the station. This was the first time Susy had invited Polly over for supper and as they walked they joked about the merits of cottage pie and a good bottle of plonk, unaware of the prying eyes watching their every move. They boarded the crowded train for the short journey home, hanging on to the overhead rail to squeeze inside. Susy felt the full weight of a body pressing against hers in the crush. The man slowly moving the bulge hard into the base of her spine. She could not move, the motion of the train agitating him as he angled his torso harder into hers. She felt his knees push the back of her thighs, and she managed to reach out and touch Polly's arm, gesturing behind her, but Polly's vision was obscured by his arm hanging on to the rail. At Knightsbridge the sea of commuters piled out of the train, the man disappearing into the crowd.

'Phew! Bloody pervert! Did you see 'im, Polly?'

Polly strained her neck to see through the swell, 'No. Not properly, but he had a navy Parka on.' She turned to Susy, 'Are you all right?'

'Yeah, bastard.'

Dinner was well underway when Vanessa returned from the office. Polly handed her a glass of wine as she collapsed into the chair. 'Hard day?' she asked.

Susy pushed a plate of cottage pie in front of her, 'Eat, you must be starving.'

'I've neglected everything and everybody to get this one out on time.'

Susy winked at Vanessa, 'Even Oliver?'

'You don't miss a thing do you, Susy?'

'Not much and he's a gentleman, treats you like a princess. Be nice Vanessa.'

'After tomorrow, I'll certainly have more time.'

'There you go then and by the way, we 'ave a prowler outside.'

'Don't be so ridiculous, Susy, this is Knightsbridge. A prowler indeed.'

'Twice I've seen 'im lurkin' out there.'

'Are you sure it's not your imagination, Susy?'

'No, it's too dark to see properly, but 'e's there all right, hiding in the shadows,' Susy waited for a reaction. 'I'm telling you Vanessa, just watch it.'

'All right Susy, don't shout, I hear you.'

'And you,' Susy said, pointing to Polly, 'are getting a taxi 'ome.' Polly touched her brow and saluted.

Vanessa looked long and hard at Susy. 'You've been here for over a month now and I have never seen a boyfriend?'

'That's 'cause there isn't one.'

'Nobody at all?'

'No,' Susy glanced at Vanessa. 'Don't look so shocked, some of us live without it.'

'But there must have been someone?' Vanessa was more than a little surprised.

Not wishing to continue along these lines, Susy started to clear the table. 'Did you enjoy the food?' then disappeared into the kitchen, not waiting for a quick reply. When she was out of earshot Vanessa turned to Polly only to be interrupted by Susy's spontaneous reappearance around the kitchen door, 'and before you can ask Vanessa, yes, I am still a virgin.' In a whisper Vanessa turned again to Polly, 'This is unheard of, how old is she?'

'Twenty five. She's had a rough time, though. Thank God she got away.'

Susy returned with a bowl of fruit and a selection of cheeses and sat down, the momentary silence being broken when she lifted her glass and proclaimed, ''ere's to the future, girls, and a good fuck.'

Vanessa was running through the last minute details of her breakfast meeting, when Susy rang for a taxi, which duly arrived to take Polly home. Vanessa had completely forgotten about their visit to the flower market as Susy politely reminded her.

'Five o'clock, bright and early.'

'Can we not make it another day?'

'No, there might not be another time. I'm moving at the weekend, remember?'

The alarm sounded at 4.45, when Susy slipped out of bed, tripped downstairs to the kitchen to brew a pot of tea, and then returned to Vanessa's bedroom door. Banging hard, she opened the door, switched on the lights and the radio, placed a mug of tea on the bedside table and left, saying, 'You've got fifteen minutes.'

Vanessa's limp body did not respond kindly to the abrupt intrusion of her beauty sleep. She turned over in bed and squinted at the clock. 'Oh, she meant it.' And flopped back on the pillow.

Ten minutes later Susy banged again on the bedroom door. 'Five minutes to go.'

Vanessa hung over the side of the bed, pulling on her stockings. 'I'm up,' she yelled.

Dawn was breaking over the city when Susy looked out of the apartment window. She had not been up this early in a long time and looked forward to seeing her old mates in the market and wondered if things had changed. Vanessa was now up and dressed, sleepily applying her makeup, when Susy ran up the stairs again and shouted, 'Aren't you ready yet?' Exasperated, Vanessa yelled back, 'Five minutes, I need five more minutes.'

'Right, I'll wait in the car.'

There was a chill in the air that early March morning as, sitting behind the wheel of her Metro, Susy rubbed her hands together and recalled how she used to heave box after box of produce on the van. Where is she? she thought, leaning out of the car window, the lights still blazing in the lounge. She climbed out of the car and ran up to the front door, giving several short sharp rings on the bell. Vanessa threw her coat over her shoulders, grabbed her attaché case and locked the apartment door behind her. Back behind the wheel and with the engine running, Susy thrust the car into first gear just as Vanessa fell into the passenger seat. Bumping along the Chelsea Bridge Road, Vanessa's long legs buckled almost up to her bust for comfort, protested. 'What have you got me doing at this ungodly hour of the morning?'

'Relax! Cheer up, Vanessa, this is the time when you're normally comin' in.'

Turning into the market, through the tollgates, they easily found a parking space. A variety of vans were being piled high with boxes of flowers. A little old lady walked by pulling a shopper filled with a profusion of daffodils sticking out of the top and the whole place was buzzing with activity. Walking through the doors into the market, Susy caught a glimpse of Vanessa's face. Clearly, the early morning light was not to blame, neither did her eyes deceive her. Angling her sight a little closer, Susy realised that Vanessa had only made up one eye. Her initial reaction was to turn back. 'Er, you're looking a bit pale this morning. Are you feelin' all right?'

'Of course, don't be silly.'

'We don't 'ave to go in if you really don't want to?'

Vanessa stopped momentarily, before striding out towards the market buildings again. The freshness of the morning air had woken her up. 'Nonsense, we're here and I'm feeling absolutely fine. Now which way do we go?'

The doors opened up to a blinding array of colour and a heady fragrance filled the air. Vanessa was impressed by the variety of flowers and stopped to talk to the traders as they walked from stall to stall. People looked curiously at her and she sensed that she was not their usual type of customer. After all, she was dressed for business, her business.

'Lookin' for anythin' in particular, darlin'?' a voice sounded from behind a weeping fig, causing Vanessa to jump.

'No, no, I'll call you if I need you,' she replied.

The trader emerged from behind the foliage and discreetly circled Vanessa, looking her up and down. Very nice, he thought, nice pair of pins.

A scream rang out across the market and everybody turned to find Susy cradled in the arms of a trader. 'Arnie, look what I've found. 'ardly recognised 'er, she's got so skinny.'

Arnie looked closely at Susy. 'Na, don't know 'er Gerry.' And turned away. Susy crept up behind Arnie and threw her arms around his neck. ''Ow are you, my old sunshine? Miss me?'

Arnie enveloped Susy in a bear hug. 'What kept you, sweetheart? You got too good for us now?' He stood back and had a good look at her. 'Don't they feed you where your livin'? Oy, Gerry, two bacon sarnies and coffee.'

Susy beckoned to Gerry. 'Make that three, Gerry.'

'Three?' he asked, looking round.

Susy led Vanessa back to the astounded traders. 'Eye, eye, what 'ave we got 'ere then?' Susy was not amused. 'Boys, this is Vanessa, a friend of mine.'

Vanessa held out her hand which Arnie eagerly held with both hands. 'Pleased to meet you, lady.'

Gerry took a closer look at Vanessa's face. 'Is it a new fashion darlin', the boatrace? Never seen nothin' like that before.'

Arnie slapped Gerry on the arm. 'Go on, 'op it – sarnies.'

Vanessa rustled through the display of flowers and foliage, leaving Susy to chat to her old friends. ''Ere, where did you find this one, darlin'?' he whispered.

'She's all right Arnie, believe me, I –'

'Your flowers are exquisite, Arnie,' Vanessa interrupted. 'I'm so pleased Susy brought me along.'

'Oh indeed they are, my lovely, but not as pretty as you.'

Vanessa managed a half smile at the little man, and Gerry arrived back with breakfast. Time was getting late and Vanessa began to pace, anxious not to miss the start of the meeting. Susy heartily tucked into the bacon butty that Vanessa declined, then ordered the lads to fill up the car. 'As much as you can get in, boys.'

'Opening up again?' Gerry said, piling boxes on to the trolley.

'I owe somebody a big favour.' Gerry nodded in Vanessa's direction and wheeled the trolley out to the car. 'Spot on.'

At eight o'clock Vanessa was already waiting and, wrenching the car into gear Susy hurried out of the market. The traffic was heavy and Vanessa was quiet, psyching herself into the right frame of mind to conduct a business meeting. Susy dared to interrupt.

'Be quiet, I'm thinking.'

'But, Vanessa.' The look said everything and her one beautifully made-up eye was flashing like a beacon. Susy kept very quiet. Pulling off Park Lane, she stopped outside the agency. With one swift movement Vanessa threw open the car door and got out, slamming the door hard behind her. Susy watched her hurry up the steps and sighed. At least she had tried.

'Good morning, Miss Baron, they are waiting for you.' As the elevator doors opened, she charged straight through them and into the boardroom, walking briskly to the front. She addressed a party of one woman and two men. Preparing her agenda, she looked up and smiled. 'Sorry I'm late. Let us waste no more time and get straight on with the programme.' She had no feedback from the three vacant faces staring straight at her, 'Is everything all right?'

'Yes yes, absolutely fine, please proceed,' came the reply.

One hour later the meeting adjourned. Everything had gone according to plan and Vanessa was ecstatic over the immediate acceptance of her proposed account. She would telephone Oliver at once and tell him the good news. This was certainly cause for celebration. On her way back to her office she stopped off at the ladies washroom, stood in front of the mirror and gasped at the half-painted face staring back at her. 'Ah!' She was furious, 'That little bitch! Why didn't she tell me?' She fumbled in her makeup bag to redo the damage. 'God, will I be glad to see the back of her.' She tossed her hair off her face and applied the mascara. 'Ungrateful little minx!' Back in her office and still raging, Vanessa lifted the telephone and called Crawfords. Susy answered as Vanessa screamed down the line, 'How could you, Susy?'

'Who is this?' Susy held the receiver away from her ear.

'Rushing me like that at five o'clock and what for, a bunch of flowers?'

'Vanessa.'

'Why didn't you tell me? I have just conducted a very important meeting looking like a clown.'

'I did try to tell you, but you wouldn't listen.'

'No you did not!'

Now Susy began to shout. 'You always think you're so right, Vanessa. You don't 'ear what anybody else 'as to say and sometimes, sometimes it just could be important. Now, did you get the account?'

There was silence at the other end of the line, before Vanessa condescended to speak. 'Yes.' She said flatly.

'So you looked like a clown and you still got the account? ... Vanessa, you've got a big problem, darlin'. When are you going to learn to laugh at yourself, instead of picking up the phone and crying over your cracked face? Laugh, it's funny. Life's not that serious, Coco. Then phone me up and tell me the good news.' Susy could hear the muffled sound of laughter as Vanessa held her hand over the mouthpiece.

'What did you call me?' she asked.

'I don't think I 'ave to repeat myself, but all I can say is, it's bin a long time comin'.'

Vanessa hung up.

For one week the excitement of moving entered into Susy's every conversation. Each time she opened her mouth it was to ask an opinion: what colour, what size or how many? The stockroom downstairs at Crawfords was rapidly becoming a storage room, for every day she would add another box or bag to the collection already there. On Friday she was due to sign the lease to the studio apartment in Kensington where, for the first time she would have a home of her own, answerable to nobody, where she could cook, entertain her friends or quite simply be herself. She could not wait, neither could Gill or Polly. Then there was Oliver; was the flat in Parson's Green really, as he put it, made for her? Susy was surprised and delighted that he thought of her at all. Now what should she do if she had to make a choice? At the end of the day, she told herself, the bottom line was down to how much. She needed more than just a roof over her head; she wanted to live, enjoy herself, buy clothes, go on holidays.

Gill had already left the shop. 'Polly, can you lock up, I'm meeting Oliver and I'm already late?'

'Want me to come with you for a second opinion?'

'Thanks, but I've got to make my own mind up.'

Susy applied lipstick, ran a brush through her hair and was out of the door. She walked towards the underground dodging late-night shoppers and, as usual, slipped quickly through the alley into James Street. The silent footsteps ten paces behind her kept well mingled with the pedestrians. On reaching the station she studied the best route, joined the queue at the ticket desk and handed the cashier a £5 note. 'Parson's Green' she said, then collected her ticket and change and made her way down to the platform. Like most other evenings the underground was very crowded. The hulk of a man stood back from view while Susy glanced back and forth down the line, until a fast approaching train rattled into the station and screeched to a halt. Suddenly there was a surge of bodies clambering for space, pouring themselves into the carriage. Susy managed to free her bag from the fray and standing in the gangway clung tightly to the overhead pulley. The hulk had sidled his way into the same carriage and watched just a few feet away. At South Kensington Susy changed platforms to pick up the District Line; she needed a Wimbledon train and the time was running very late. She started to hover, six minutes to the next train. Impatient, she began to pace and the man took a newspaper from his jacket pocket and proceeded to read concealed from view. Eventually the train arrived. Susy alighted and found a seat. The man dressed in dark clothing was very close, leaning against the glass partition and watching her through the reflection. At Parson's Green she brushed past him when the doors opened and ran down the steps and out of the station. She had the address written on a piece of paper which was tucked into her wallet, number 42. Hurrying along, she stopped a passerby for directions, then continued towards the green, dropping the piece of paper in her path. The time was after 7.30 and she was very late. Oliver would be angry, she thought. Walking down the wrong side of the green, she noticed that the number sequence was odd, so she turned and retracing her steps ran down the other side of the green. Puffed, she slowed down; night had fallen and the numbers were difficult to see. Then she noticed numbers 36, 38 and knew that she was on the right track, stopping outside number 42. The house was in darkness and looking around, Oliver was nowhere to be seen. What should she do? she thought looking along the street for his parked car. She returned to the house and walked up the steps to the front door – maybe he was inside. She knocked, listened, there was not a sound. Finding the entry button she buzzed Flat 3, but there was no answer. Annoyed, Susy stepped back to see if there was any movement at all inside the building. Oliver must have gone, she concluded, taking another step back and turning to walk away. The arm swung around her neck from behind like a vice, causing her to gasp for air and her stifled cry was clamped by the force of a hand across her mouth pulling her backwards, dragging her down into the shadows. She struggled frantically to free herself from his grasp, kicking aimlessly at his shins. He released his grip from her neck crashing a blow to the side of her head with his fist. She fell face down in the dirt and he picked up her head by the hair, his foot pressing down on her back. Susy could feel his head behind hers and she let out a small scream. 'Quiet, slag,' he said, brandishing a knife in front of her face before crashing her head violently to the ground again. He slit the back of her coat in two with the knife, viciously tearing at her clothing, shredding every layer until she was naked. Blinded by the blow to her face and too terrified to scream for her life, he lifted her buttocks high like a dog and thrust his cock into her hard, again and again, his full weight banging against her bleeding, tortured body. He clawed at her breasts and thighs relentlessly, until the dull groans of ejaculation made him withdraw. The pain like a knife caused Susy to cry out in agony, but with one blow of his fist she was knocked out cold. Her body lay mutilated and motionless as the rapist heaved himself up from the bloody scene, grabbing the knife in his right hand. A noise distracted him and he crouched low behind the wall hidden from view, until a couple passing by on the other side of the street stopped before walking by. He was not noticed and leaving his victim for dead, slunk off into the shadows.

Vanessa turned the key in the lock and opened the apartment door to an array of daffodils, tulips and crocuses. Every vase and jug was crammed to overspilling. She walked into the kitchen to find every available container filled with spring flowers. Everywhere she turned was a splash of colour, a breath of springtime. She threw down her coat and switched on the answerphone.

'Vanessa, hello … hello, damn these newfangled machines.

Can you hear me, my dear?' Vanessa smiled as the message ended – Sir Richard had never got used to talking to a machine.

'Hi, it's Oliver, I'll be a bit late. Forgot I was showing Susy the flat. See you about 8.30.'

'Like the bunch of flowers, Coco? 'Ope it brings a smile to your miserable face, but straight up, I'm pleased about the account. Have a drink on me tonight, darlin'.'

Vanessa had never met anyone quite like Susy before. Her brash, straight-talking lodger amused her, even insulted her. Coco indeed! She smiled to herself. She had better not repeat the slur to a living soul.

Oliver arrived punctually at 8.30, Dom Perignon under one arm and a bouquet of flowers under the other. 'Oh my God, Oliver, what am I going to do with them?' He stepped into the apartment and gazed in total amazement at the display of flowers. His seemingly paltry offering paled in comparison.

'I see I have some competition?' he inquired.

Vanessa took the bouquet in her arms and kissed Oliver on the cheek. 'They are wonderful, just wonderful, my darling. Sit down and I'll explain.' She propped the bouquet up in the kitchen sink and returned with two champagne flutes. 'This morning at five o'clock I was up and on my way to Covent Garden.' Oliver popped open the bottle of champagne. 'Susy, as you know is moving and –'

'Where is she?' he interrupted. 'We were supposed to meet up this evening and she didn't show.'

'Maybe she forgot. Anyway, the flowers were her idea of a parting gesture.'

Oliver nuzzled closer to Vanessa. 'So, there's no competition?' He brushed his mouth against her cheek, 'no pistols at dawn?' and sank his head into the nape of her neck. 'Umm, smells good, smells very good.'

Vanessa slid away from his advances. 'Well then my valiant knight, where are you taking this highly intelligent, newly-appointed creative director tonight?'

'To bed.'

'This very eligible woman of the world may want to eat first.'

Oliver jumped to his feet. 'Anything you want, anywhere you want.' The anticipation of a 30-minute dinner and eight hours in the sack overwhelmed him. They left immediately, destination the Caprice.

The atmosphere was cordial, the food exquisite, the clientele chic and the tinkling piano reminiscent of Casablanca. How clever of Oliver to choose Vanessa's favourite restaurant. While hardly stopping for breath, the champagne was doing its worst and Oliver, ever attentive, listened eagerly to every word his beautiful lady uttered. He took her hand. 'Vanessa, I cannot wait any longer, my darling. I have to make love to you before I go completely insane.'

She leant forward and whispered into his ear, gently nipping the earlobe with her teeth, 'Well, what are we waiting for?'

The apartment door was scarcely closed before the fire of lust burned down on Vanessa's lips, tongues lashing at each other as they peeled off their clothes on their way upstairs. They fell headlong on to the bed, making those hurried fumblings of their first time together. Oliver's hand rose slowly along Vanessa's thigh to the flesh above the stocking tops, while she ran her hand along the muscles of his back, across the taught buttocks to the heavy penis she cupped in her hand, massaging him gently as he caressed the fullness of her breasts with his mouth. Twisting and turning, flesh against flesh in frenzied love. He pushed her over, spreading her legs wide, and entered her. Vanessa arched her back in a gasp of ecstasy, the rhythmic movement came long and hard until the cries of orgasm subsided. He gently took her head in his hands placing soft kisses over her face, while she lay quietly soaking up the tenderness of his warm mouth against hers. Oliver said nothing, just continued to kiss her mouth, her eyes, and her ears. He lowered his head and sucked gently on her erect nipples, until she could feel him swell inside her again, the slow movement arousing an excitement in her loins. Vanessa pushed him over on to his back and pressed down hard on his penis, taking in all of him. Pulling her closer, enveloping her in his arms, they rocked slowly back and forth, he not letting go until her first shudders of orgasm began. Afterwards, they lay entwined together, Oliver watching his passion fall asleep.

'I love you,' he whispered, 'like never before.'

The elderly man tottered past the green, taking his Dachshund for a late night walk. He had left the noise of the pub behind him and was heading off home towards the New Kings Road. Reaching the corner he looked around for the dog and gave a whistle, but he did not appear. He turned back, calling as he went – the dog did not usually run off. 'Come on, boy.' The elderly man could hear whining, but still could not see the dog. 'Come on, where are you?' he shouted. Picking up pace to where the whining was coming from, the dog remained and did not move until the old man caught a glimpse of him hiding behind a pile of rubbish. He bent down, 'I can see you, now come here.' The dog became agitated and still whining ran circles around the rubbish. 'Have I got to fetch you?' he said, stepping forward, then staggered back in horror when his eyes fell on Susy's mangled body. 'Oh, dear me, it's a young lass, what do I do?' Distressed, he looked around for help. 'Good boy, now come here.' He picked up the dog and took a closer look at Susy's naked body lying there. There was no sign of life. Stepping out on to the pavement a car engine roared into action further along the green, attracting his attention. When the vehicle pulled out, lights blazing and travelled in his direction, the old man stepped out into the road, causing the driver to pull up abruptly.

'Please, a – a – please come.'

The driver could hear the old man having trouble with his words, 'What's up, mate?'

'Please,' he stammered, 'a young girl.'

'Where?'

'Here, over here, please hurry.' The driver got out of the car and followed the old man. 'There, see?' he pointed behind the wall.

'Jesus Christ! What bastard did that?'

Still holding on to his dog, the old man hung back while the driver stooped down for a closer look.

'Is she alive?' he asked.

'I don't know, old timer. Did you just find her?'

'My dog, he found her.'

The driver ran back to his car and contacted the police. Within five minutes they were on the scene.

A crowd had gathered, hoping to get a closer look, when the police pushed them back and cordoned off the area. An ambulance pulled up, sirens wailing, and medics piled out at breakneck speed to attend to Susy and take her off to hospital. A police officer turned to his superior. 'How do we stop this, sarge?'

'Difficult one, rape. She's a lucky girl, he didn't finish this one off. Let's hope she can remember something.'

'Any similarities to the one over at Hammersmith last month?'

'That's hard to say at the moment. We'll have to wait for the forensic report.'

The old man was still patiently waiting. 'Is she going to be all right? Will she live?'

'I certainly hope so,' the sergeant said. 'Are you the gentleman who found her?'

'Yes, Brownlow is my name, Derrick Brownlow. I live just over there.'

'All right, Mr Brownlow, we will want to take a statement from you when you're ready.'

'Oh I'll come now, officer, while it's still fresh in my mind. Poor little love, I don't know what's happening to the world.'

The medical team lifted Susy on to the stretcher and carefully into the ambulance and sped off to the Charing Cross Hospital.

Multiple contusions to the face and body, three broken ribs, lacerations to the abdomen and thighs and slashes to the lower back conducive to knife wounds. Susy lay heavily sedated in the hospital, but alive.

The nursing staff quietly got on with the job of checking Susy periodically, while the WPC sat patiently waiting for her to regain consciousness. Sergeant Moore arrived at the hospital to try and find out who the victim of this vicious attack was.

'Well, what have we got then?' he enquired.

'A Miss Susan Stevens, sir, early twenties, address, not quite sure about that, sir, but think the young lady lives in Cadogan Place, Knightsbridge. Just checking it out.'

The sergeant glanced at the medical report. 'Dear, dear, we have got to find this monster. Is she conscious yet?'

'No, but we are keeping a close eye.'

'Better inform family, husband, boyfriend, if there is any.'

Vanessa and Oliver were locked in a slumbering embrace when the telephone awoke them at 6.30. Vanessa untangled herself and sleepily reached for the receiver. 'Hello, who is this?'

'Excuse me, but does a Miss Susan Stevens reside there?'

'Yes, why, who are you?' Vanessa glanced at the clock. 'Isn't this a bit early for a social call?'

'Excuse me for telephoning so early, but this is Fulham Police Station. I'm afraid there has been an accident.'

Vanessa sat bolt upright in bed. 'What's happened?'

'Miss Stevens is in Charing Cross Hospital after an incident at Parson's Green last night.'

'I'll be right there, thank you.' Oliver by now was fully awake, when Vanessa jumped out of bed.

'Something terrible has happened. Tell me?'

'Get up Oliver.'

Vanessa was charging around the bedroom, pulling on her clothes.

'Where are we going?'

'That was the police, Susy's in hospital. They wouldn't call this early if it wasn't serious.'

Oliver was tucking his shirt into his pants. 'Where is she?'

Oliver dropped Vanessa at the hospital entrance and went in search of a parking space. She hurried through the main entrance and up to the desk. 'You have a Susy Stevens here, I believe?'

The nurse raised her eyes at Vanessa's impatience. 'Just one moment, please,' and calmly checked the list of patients.

'I understand that there was an accident last night. Now how long does it take to check it out?'

'Yes, we have a Susan Stevens admitted last night. Are you a relative?'

'No, I'm a friend. Now where do I find her?'

'Miss Stevens is not allowed any visitors at the moment.'

'Will you please tell me what happened?'

A ward sister, on hearing Vanessa's anger, approached the desk. 'Excuse me, can I help?'

'Will somebody please tell me what is going on?'

'Are you a friend of Miss Stevens?'

'Yes, I'm Vanessa Baron. She lives with me.'

'Come with me.' The sister led Vanessa down a long corridor to a wing of the hospital. As they walked, the sister explained. Miss Stevens was admitted last night after she was found unconscious in Parson's Green.

'Is she badly injured?'

'She is very lucky to be alive and has sustained multiple injuries.'

Vanessa and the nurse stood outside the door of the hospital room. 'Did they get the driver who knocked her down?' Vanessa asked.

'This was not a car accident, Miss Baron, this was a particularly vicious attack.'

Vanessa was visibly shaken. 'You mean rape?'

'You may go in for a few minutes, but I don't think you will get any response.'

Vanessa stood inside the room and the WPC got up and quietly left, leaving Vanessa with Susy's still form. She approached the bed very slowly, casting her eyes over the unrecognisable features, the battered, purple face that hid the now tightly-closed eyes. She stepped closer, nauseated by thoughts of what happened and softly spoke. 'Who did this to you ... what animal could do such a thing?' Vanessa stretched out her hand and held Susy's limp hand, choking back tears of anger and despair. There was no flicker of life, just the monotonous bleep of a monitor. 'Please don't die Susy, please don't leave us.'

The sister returned and eased Vanessa away from the bedside. 'The police officer would like to ask you a few questions Miss Baron.'

'Yes, of course, anything I can do.'

Vanessa, shocked and silent sat opposite the WPC who calmly proceeded to probe Susy's last known movements.

'Miss Baron, Miss Vanessa Baron?' Vanessa nodded. 'I understand Miss Stevens lives with you?'

'Yes, she does.'

'Is there anything you can tell me that will help us track down the person that has attacked Miss Stevens?' Vanessa stared vacantly into space. 'Miss Baron, any seemingly insignificant detail may lead us to the man before it happens again.'

'A prowler, she mentioned a prowler.'

'When was this?'

'Er, a few days ago, I don't remember exactly when.'

'Is that all, a prowler?'

'Outside the apartment, hiding in the shadows, she said.'

'Did you see this man?'

'No.'

'Miss Stevens was found in Parson's Green last night. Now maybe she was abducted elsewhere, assaulted and dumped there.'

Vanessa ran her hands nervously through her hair. 'No, she was meeting somebody there.'

'Do you know who she was meeting?'

Terrifying thoughts raced through Vanessa's mind as she almost choked on her words. 'She was meeting Oliver.'

'Her boyfriend?'

She felt a surge of fear run through her. Was it possible that Oliver could have done such a thing? 'No, my boyfriend,' she stammered. Vanessa looked up at the WPC for a denial of her thoughts.

'I'm sorry, but we have to cover every possibility.'

Vanessa continued. 'He, Oliver that is, was showing Susy an apartment.'

'In Parson's Green?' Vanessa nodded. 'At what time?'

'I'm not sure, around seven o'clock.'

'Can you be more precise?'

'No, I cannot,' Vanessa yelled. 'You'll have to ask him.'

'We have every intention of doing so, Miss Baron. Thank you for your help.'

Vanessa made her way through the corridor back to the hospital reception, where Oliver was waiting patiently for her to return. He jumped up to greet her. 'Vanessa, how is she?' she hurried passed him as if he was not there. 'Vanessa.' He ran after her. 'Hey, wait a minute, what's the hurry?' He nervously laughed. 'Is she all right ... what happened?' Oliver was running alongside her. 'Vanessa,' he grabbed her arm, turning her around. 'Speak to me. How's Susy?'

'Don't speak to me,' Vanessa thundered, pulling away from him.

'But I don't understand, Vanessa, is she dead?'

Vanessa stopped and turned in her tracks. 'As good as Oliver. She was raped, brutally battered and raped.'

'Oh God, no!' He held his arms out to comfort her.

'Where were you, Oliver, last night, before we met? Where were you?'

Oliver pulled Vanessa closer to him. 'I went to meet Susy at seven and waited. I waited for almost half an hour and she didn't show up, so I left, went home and the rest you know.'

'How do I know that you're telling me the truth?'

Oliver backed away. 'Oh no, you don't think I am capable of rape, do you? That's not how I get my kicks.'

Vanessa could hold back the tears no longer. 'I don't know, Oliver, I just don't know. It's so awful! She's unrecognisable.'

He put his arm around her shoulder. 'Come on, I'll take you home, then give a statement to the police.'

Oliver walked confidently into Fulham Police Station, thinking that the statement he was about to give would take ten minutes. He was ushered into an interview room where he waited for the detective superintendent to appear. The door opened and a lean, tired-looking man entered and sat down across the table from him, opened up a file and looked Oliver straight in the eyes.

'Good morning, I'm Detective Superintendent Pearce and I'm in charge of the Susan Stevens case. I understand that you have something to tell us?' The police officer's ice-cold stare made Oliver uneasy.

'Yes, I know Susy. I had arranged to meet her last night, but somehow we missed each other.'

'I see, sir. Well maybe we could start at the beginning.' The officer did not blink. 'Your full name, please?'

'Oliver Bryce Thomas.'

'Address?'

'3 Thurloe Square, SW7.'

'Age?'

'Thirty.'

The superintendent looked up and paused before speaking. 'Ready when you are.'

'There was a flat in Parson's Green that I wanted to show Susy and –.'

'How do you know Miss Stevens?'

'She is staying with a friend of mine.'

The officer looked at his pad. 'Miss Vanessa Baron?'

'That's right.'

'How long have you known Miss Baron?'

'About two months.'

'And Miss Stevens?'

'About the same time.'

'So you're dating Miss Baron and you're moving Miss Stevens to alternative accommodation?'

No, the arrangement was only temporary.'

'What arrangement?'

'Susy was staying with Vanessa for a short time, only while looking for somewhere else to live.'

'And you thought you'd help out. That's very nice of you, Mr Bryce Thomas.'

Oliver was ruffled, 'That's my job, superintendent – property.'

'Go on.'

'I went to the flat in Parson's Green at the time we agreed and waited for approximately half an hour, then left.'

'Were you alone?'

'Yes I was.'

'When did you make this appointment with Miss Stevens, Mr Bryce Thomas?'

'Er, a few days ago.'

'And did Miss Baron know about this?'

'Yes, she approved. Is that relevant, superintendent?'

'Just want the facts, sir. So, while you were waiting for Miss Stevens, what did you do?'

Oliver was tired of being questioned. 'I walked up and down the green and sat in the car.'

'Were there many people around?'

'Yes, a few.'

'See anybody, or anything unusual?'

'No, nothing at all.'

'So, when Miss Stevens didn't show, what did you do?'

'I went home, showered, changed and met Vanessa at her apartment.'

'And what time was that?'

'About eight-thirty.'

'I suppose Miss Baron can verify that?'

Oliver resented the question, 'Yes, she bloody well can.'

'And did you stay in for the evening?'

'We went out for dinner at the Caprice – check it out – then I stopped over until we got a call this morning about Susy.'

'Is there anything else you would like to add to what you have already told me?'

Oliver started to relax a little. 'I cannot think of a single thing.'

Detective Superintendent Pearce closed his file and stood up. 'Thank you for coming forward, sir, we do appreciate it.' They both walked out to the front desk. 'Ah, one thing I forgot to ask you, Mr Bryce Thomas. Where can we get hold of you during working hours, should it be necessary?'

Oliver handed the officer his business card and left. 'Umm, Bryce Thomas, Bailey and Bloom, Property Developers and Estate Agents ... fancy outfit, if I'm not mistaken.'

Joyce had knocked off early from her part-time job at the local newsagents. Bob would not be home for at least another hour, so she popped the kettle on for a cup of tea. Now then, she thought, lets see what's on the telly tonight. She poured the scalding water into the pot as she opened up the paper to the television page. Picking up the remote control she pressed a button and the television jumped into action. Flipping from channel to channel, she tried to tune into something interesting. The early evening news spewed forth much political rhetoric. 'Go on, Maggie, you tell 'em 'darlin.' Joyce reached for her cigarettes and lit up. 'Best bloody prime minister we've 'ad. Hey, you sit down, Taffy, you don't know what you're talkin' about.' Joyce continuously stirred her tea while turning the pages of the newspaper, the television blaring away in the background. Time was ticking away and Bob would be ravenous when he got home, so Joyce got up and reached into the kitchen cupboard. 'Ah,' she groaned, holding her aching back, 'must be getting old.'

'The body of a young woman was found last night at Parson's Green, West London. Susan Stevens, aged 25, who lives in Knightsbridge, was found by a passerby who was walking his dog.'

Joyce looked up from behind the refrigerator door. 'Can't be my Susy,' she said.

'Miss Stevens had been sexually assaulted and severely beaten whilst on her way to view an apartment.' A photograph of Susy flashed on to the screen. Joyce felt her stomach churn. 'It is. Oh, dear God! No! No! Not my girl!'

'She is now recovering in Charing Cross Hospital. The police, who say this was a particularly brutal attack, are asking anybody who was in the area between 7 and 9.30 last night to come forward.'

Joyce had her coat on and was out of the door at full speed.

Joyce charged through the hospital doors and up to the desk hot and flustered. 'I'm Mrs Stevens. You got my girl in 'ere. I want to see 'er.'

'Just a moment please.' Joyce drummed her fingers on the counter. 'Are you Susan Stevens' mother?'

'She doesn't 'ave a mother, darlin', I'm 'er Auntie Joyce.'

The nurse directed Joyce to Susy's room where the duty nurse let her slip quietly in. She stood beside the bed looking her up and down. 'Susy, sweetheart, it's me, Joyce, can you 'ear me pet?' Joyce brushed Susy's hair off her forehead, putting her face close to hers. 'Come on, precious, open those big beautiful eyes for your Auntie Joyce.' Susy flickered her eyelids in response; she could hear Joyce's words and tried to open her eyes, but the swollen flesh only allowed her a blurred glimpse. Susy turned her head slightly to the side and tried to speak. 'Shush now, my darlin', you're goin' to be all right,' Joyce whispered. 'You rest up now, nobody's goin' to hurt you again.' Joyce leant forward to kiss Susy's cheek and felt the deep slow sobs welling up inside her. 'There, there, go back to sleep, I'll see you tomorrow.' Joyce stood back, pulled the bed linen up under Susy's chin, as a mother tends her child, and slipped out as quietly as she came in.

Joyce marched back to the reception and accosted the nurse. 'Who's in charge 'ere?'

'It's Mrs Stevens, isn't it?'

'That's right and I want to see somebody straight away.'

'Please take a seat and I will see what I can do.'

Joyce sat down in a daze, wondering how and why it came to be that her Susy, a streetwise kid, who was as sharp as a razor and rarely missed a trick, could land up half dead in hospital.

'Mrs Stevens?'

Joyce's thoughts were interrupted by a doctor standing in front of her. 'I'm Dr Berkeley. Would you like to come with me?'

Joyce followed the doctor into an office and sat down. 'How bad is she, doctor?'

'She's been badly beaten up, but she will recover.'

'Was she raped?' Joyce almost gagged on the word.

'Yes, I'm afraid she was.'

Joyce became distressed. 'She's a good kid, doctor, smart, but innocent, you know what I mean. Didn't deserve that, no girl deserves to be abused like that.' Dr Berkeley allowed Joyce to talk. 'Isn't there enough easy girls out there on the street, to satisfy those bastards, eh? That they have to jump on a decent kid?'

'Mrs Stevens, I do understand your anguish.'

'Do you, doctor? Do you fellas really know what 'appens to a girl's body and mind? Don't let's forget the mind. It's just a physical jerk to them, doctor, hit and run, yeah, that's 'ow it is. How's my Susy going to cope the rest of 'er life?'

'Physically Susy will get better, but it will take a little time. Mentally she will most likely need some therapy. Now, let's take each stage as it come along, don't rush her. She will get all the help she needs.'

Joyce nodded as she wiped away a tear, 'Do they know who it could be?'

'The police will do everything possible to catch him. This sort of crime happens far too often. Let's hope there will be somebody out there who saw him.' Dr Berkeley sympathetically put his arm around Joyce's shoulder and they made their way out of the office. 'Why don't you have a chat with Detective Superintendent Pearce tomorrow? He will fill you in with the latest developments.'

Detective Superintendent Pearce did not relish another rape case, still smarting after reaching a dead end on the assault of a teenager six weeks ago. He hoped that he would nail the assailant this time.

'There's been another one then, Will?' Inspector Haines enquired as he entered the office.

'Yep, nasty one this time, carved her up a bit.'

The inspector shook his head and sighed, 'I think of my Laura every time one of these crops up.'

'How old is she now Frank – sixteen, seventeen?'

'She's twenty now and fearless. Never thinks it could happen to her and I pray it doesn't. Got any information from the young woman yet?'

'Not yet. WPC Phillips is at the hospital at the moment, so we hope to have something later, now that Miss Stevens is conscious.'

'OK, Will, got to get this one, next time he'll kill.'

'We'll catch him.'

As the inspector left, a WPC poked her head around the door. 'A Mrs Stevens to see you, sir, a relative of Susan Stevens.'

'Ah, yes, better send her in.'

Joyce bustled through the door armed and ready for action. 'Where were your boys, then, when my girl was bein' done over?'

'Now just a minute, Mrs Stevens.'

'Nowhere to be seen in a real emergency, are they? Yet they're too bloody fast if you let your meter run over five minutes.'

'Please sit down, Mrs Stevens, we'll talk about this calmly.'

Joyce sat down hard. 'You've got a lot to answer for. She could 'ave bin murdered.'

'Yes she could have, but she's alive, Mrs Stevens, and we will do everything possible to see him brought to justice. We are on your side, you know.'

Joyce quietened down. She had never felt easy in the presence of the Old Bill and fidgeted in her chair. 'What are you doin' 'bout it, then?'

'Please bear with us. Your daughter ...'

'She's my niece.'

'Your niece needs your support right now and hopefully we can piece together her life over the past few weeks and get some results.'

Joyce listened attentively to the superintendent; she wanted the rapist caught equally as much as the police. 'I'll 'elp if I can,' she offered, 'but she 'asn't 'bin 'ome since Eddy.'

''Eddy who?' the superintendent asked.

'Er dad, Eddy Stevens, threw 'er out.'

'When was this?'

''Bout a couple of months back.'

'OK, Mrs Stevens, let's have it all.'

WPC Phillips had waited patiently for Susy to respond to her questioning. Propped up in bed, but motionless, Susy moved her eyes when she heard the WPC's sympathetic words, 'Susy … Susy, I'm Jenny, I am here to help you, do you understand?' Susy nodded. 'Can you remember anything about the evening you were assaulted?' Susy did not respond. 'Please try to remember, Susy, however hard it might be.' Tears fell back on to the pillow as the police officer gently coaxed her to recall those terrifying moments again. 'Susy, I am right here and I am not going away. You are not alone in this, we are all here to help and protect you.'

Susy moved her head from side to side. 'I can't.'

'Try Susy, try very hard. Were you meeting somebody that evening?'

Casting her mind back, Susy recalled reaching the flat. 'Yes, but he didn't come.'

'Who had you arranged to meet?'

'Oliver, I was meeting Oliver.'

'Can you remember what time?'

'I was late and he was gone.'

'When Oliver didn't show up, what did you do, Susy?'

Distressed, Susy cried out, 'I can't, I can't remember.'

'Yes you can, take your time, we have all the time in the world.'

Choking words through the tears, she sobbed. 'I – I didn't see 'im.'

'Who, Susy? The man who hurt you?'

'Out of nowhere he came, from behind.'

'Did you see anything, anything at all?'

'I don't know, it was dark, I just don't know.' She was exhausted. 'Can we stop please?'

The WPC sat back in the chair. 'Yes we can, we'll talk again later.'

Susy closed her eyes, shutting out the world. The welcome quiet and blackness overcame her as she drifted into unconsciousness – she wished she was dead.

The following morning she awoke to a room filled with flowers. The nurse pumped the headrest up so that she could see them better. 'Aren't you a popular girl this morning?' Dazzled by the early-morning sun streaming through the window, Susy cast her eyes around the room. 'I want you up and out of that bed today, young lady. You've got a lot of living to do.'

Susy lay quiet and still, her body, mummified with dressings, ached from the slightest movement. She lifted her hand to her face and felt the abrasions, but determined to walk to the mirror, she lifted the bedlinen away from her, swung her legs out of bed and stood up, steadying herself as she slowly stepped forward, until she reached the washbasin. Afraid, she looked up into the mirror, not recognising the person she saw and gripping the sides of the basin vomited violently into the sink. The nurse caught her fall backwards and walked her gently back to a chair. 'That's a bit ambitious, Susy. Now you take one step at a time.'

Filled with anger and hatred, Susy found her voice. 'I want that bastard! I want to castrate him!'

The nurse listened to her ranting, while ripping the sheets from the bed. 'Will that make things even then, when you have done to him what he did to you?'

'Well, what else?' she raved.

'You concentrate on getting the right man, convict him and then lock him up for a very long time, so he can't get at anybody else.'

'But that's not enough.'

'As much as you'd like to see him hang right now, that's not the answer. Pity the poor guy. He may have been driven to commit such an act, he may be mentally sick.'

'He'll be mentally sick when I've finished with 'im. I'm the victim remember.'

The nurse stopped what she was doing. 'Anger and hate only poisons the mind, Susy. You're a tough girl, help the police catch him, talk about it, thrash it out of your system. You say to yourself, I'm not going to let this beat me, I'm one very special person who's got a life to live and enjoy. Pity the poor wretch that has violated you, but catch him.'

Susy looked down at her broken body. 'You'll mend,' the nurse said, reading her mind.

There was a tap on the door and Vanessa entered the room clutching a large box of chocolates and, beaming from ear to ear. 'Can I come in?' Susy watched her cross the room and looking up into her radiant face burst into tears.

'Oh Susy, please don't cry, we're all so pleased you're getting better, me, Gill and Polly.' Susy sobbed uncontrollably, tears tumbling down her cheeks. Vanessa wiped them away with a tissue and waited for the sobs to subside. 'I want you to know that when you are ready to leave hospital, you're coming home with me.'

'I don't know what to say, Vanessa.'

'Then say nothing, your room awaits you for as long as you like.' She thrust the chocolates under Susy's nose. 'And to hell with the diet, make a real pig of yourself.'

Susy took the velvet box in her hands, feeling the warmth and affection bestowed upon her as Vanessa stooped and kissed her on the cheek. 'I must fly now, the girls send their love and will see you later.' She got up to leave.

'He wasn't there Vanessa.' She turned to face Susy on reaching the door. 'Oliver ... if you think that it –'

'Nonsense, Susy, it never even crossed my mind.'

Detective Superintendent Pearce leant against the cabinet

nursing a mug of coffee. The forensic report was on his desk and informed him that, apart from the semen sample now being checked against the police list of suspects, there was very little to go on. Susan Stevens had been dumped on a pile of garbage bags; sifting through the lot it would be virtually impossible to determine if anything was left by the rapist. One thing for sure was that he carried a knife and the Super was certain that he would not hesitate to use it again. Robbery was not the motive of the attack, no money or jewellery was missing. What he was dealing with was a dangerous homicidal maniac and concluded that he must have been disturbed.

'WPC Phillips still around?' he asked the officer on the desk.

'She's just left for the hospital, sir.'

'Let me know the minute she gets back, will you?'

WPC Phillips was prepared for a long session with Susy; she had to convince her to open up and talk. As she entered the hospital room she was surprised to see Susy sitting up in a chair. 'How are you feeling today, Susy?'

Susy watched the WPC pull up a chair next to her. 'All right, I think.'

With a sympathetic voice and a kindly face the police officer was a woman who understood, and Susy felt comfortable in her presence. 'Are you ready to talk, Susy?'

'I'm goin' to try.'

'That's very good.' The first hurdle accomplished with ease, taking the next step would be difficult. 'Take as much time as you like, starting at the beginning again.'

Susy did not utter a word for several minutes, fighting off the emotional hurt she felt inside, until finally she found the courage to speak. Covering her tracks from the shop to the station. Oliver's insistence at her seeing the flat, the excitement, being late and getting lost. Jenny noted every word and encouraged Susy to delve into the depths of the attack.

'Were you followed, Susy?'

'I don't know, there were lots of people on the train.'

So far Susy's movements had been established and Jenny pressed on carefully. 'Was there anybody around, on the street, on the green? Did you see anything at all unusual?'

Talking was difficult. 'I got lost. I didn't see anybody funny.'

Jenny moved closer, clasping Susy's hands in her hands. 'Now think hard. Tell me what happened next?'

Tormented, she began to sob. 'No Jenny, please don't make me.'

'You must try, Susy. Do you want this man caught?'

'Yes! Oh yes!'

'Do you hate this man for what he did to you?'

'I want to kill him.'

'Then think, Susy, think hard. What did he look like, what did you see?'

Susy took a deep breath. 'He was big, thick set, but he was behind me, Jenny.'

'I know, my love, but did you catch a glimpse of his face, something, anything?'

Susy gulped down deep breaths recalling the horror of the attack.

'A ring, a big ring.'

'Good girl, come on Susy.'

She was holding on to Jenny with all her strength, staring into the distance, breathing erratically. 'Thick hair, he had thick hair.'

'You're going to get him, Susy.'

'He hit me, he hit me hard, he stamped on my back.' Susy screamed out in pain. 'Bastard! You fucking bastard! I'll get you!' She stared Jenny in the eyes with tears streaming down her swollen face. 'He took my honour, I feel dirty ... It was the first time, Jenny, nobody ever touched me before.' She clung on to Jenny secure in the knowledge that she was fighting for her.

'We'll get him, Susy, we'll get him.'

WPC Phillips arrived back at the station weary, angry at the irreparable damage inflicted on an innocent girl and was greeting by Detective Superintendent Pearce.

'How did it go, Jenny?'

'He's thick set and wears a large ring.'

'Is that all? Didn't she get a look at him?'

Jenny shook her head. 'No, that's all. I guess we're lucky she's alive to tell us anything.'

The information was insufficient, the task ahead of them awesome. 'Humm,' he mumbled, 'I think we can discount Mr Oliver Bryce Thomas, seems he was where he said he was. Feed all this into the computer and see what we can come up with. In the meantime, keep an eye on Miss Stevens. I don't think I can take another hammering from Auntie Joyce.'

6

April 1986.

'Lucinda, where did you put the smoked salmon?'

'Window ledge,' she shouted, walking into the kitchen. 'I cannot understand you, Vanessa. What do you think you are doing letting this – this girl live with you?'

'You're such a snob, Lucinda. I feel some responsibility towards her.'

'Responsibility?'

'Yes, and if it wasn't for Oliver and I she probably would not be in this mess.'

'But she's so common.'

'Let me be the judge of that. Lucinda. Anyway, she amuses me and right now she needs a friend.'

'Well, I never thought you would lower your sights, Vanessa.'

'I'm not, Lucinda. Now will you please finish the vol-au-vents. You're beginning to irritate me.'

A gathering of kindred spirits was marking Susy's first week back at work. Vanessa had organised the soirée along with Polly and Gill; Lucinda was there for the ride. They sat cross-legged on the floor, making light conversation, the cackle of hens chomping their way through picks and dips and uncorked more than a bottle of wine.

'No, no more for me,' Gill gasped, patting her tummy lightly. 'Give junior a chance.'

Lucinda, who was already showing signs of inebriation, sloshed the wine generously into half-empty glasses. 'Don't be absolute bores, my darlings. A drop of wine never harmed anybody.'

'How exciting, Gill. When is the baby due?' Vanessa asked.

Gill crossed her fingers for good luck. 'October twenty-eighth, God willing.'

'Huh! Another bloody Scorpio,' Lucinda exclaimed. 'Got a sting in their dicks, you know, and what's more they keep stabbing you with it.'

Vanessa viewed the remark with disquiet. 'What on earth is the matter with you tonight, Lucinda?' Scolded, Lucinda leant back on a cushion and sulked and Vanessa turned again to Gill. 'And when is the wedding?'

'May first. Civil ceremony, you know, quiet, just family.'

Polly interrupted. 'The dress is just fabulous, Vanessa.'

'Going to need letting out a bit though,' Gill added.

'Susy and I peeked in on the first fitting, didn't we?'

Susy sat quietly, content to let her friends do the talking. Outwardly she appeared back to normal, the only visible trace of the attack being a small scar above her right eyebrow, but inside the fun had gone out of her life, she was subdued. Polly shook Lucinda's arm. 'Are you still with us?' Her speech was slurred and almost incoherent.

'Of course I am. What do you think I'm drunk?'

'Don't go to sleep, Lucinda, ' Polly insisted. 'Gill was about to tell us about her wedding dress.'

'Ha!' Lucinda laughed. 'Going to make an honourable woman out of you, Gill?'

Vanessa attempted to take the glass out of Lucinda's hand, which she waved in the air. 'No, Vanessa, I need it.'

'I have never seen you like this, Lucinda. Douglas will be furious, you know how he hates you drinking.'

'I don't give a toss about Douglas.' They all glanced at one another in disbelief. 'You're all so bloody happy with your men. Why hasn't anybody bothered to ask me when I'm getting married?' Lucinda waited for a reaction, 'Well go on, ask me.'

Vanessa was quick to respond, 'Christmas, darling. Now why all this fuss? We all know when.'

Lucinda began to wail. 'Douglas says he's not sure, he wants a break. Oh, Vanessa, he doesn't love me anymore.'

Susy moved closer to Lucinda, placing her arm around her shoulder. 'Course he loves you darlin', he's just got the jitters.'

Lucinda pushed Susy away. 'Leave me alone, what do you know?'

But Susy was undeterred. 'Some people don't say what they mean when they get nervous, Lucinda. They're running scared.'

'Not my Douglas.'

'Why should 'e be different from anybody else? Marriage should be for life and he doesn't want to make a mistake.'

'She's right, darlin',' Gill chirped in. 'Anyway, it's better you sort it now than later.'

The wailing continued with Vanessa helping her to her feet. 'Dear God, Lucinda, you'd better lie down and sleep it off.'

Gill whispered in Susy's ear, 'Think it's time I went darlin'. You take no notice of this one,' pointing to the crestfallen Lucinda, being hauled on to the landing. 'You concentrate on getting it together. As from Monday you're on your own, running the show and you're going to be just great, let nobody tell you different, OK.'

'I want to prove you right, Gill.'

'You put all this horror behind you, you can't change what's happened, but you can prove to tarts like 'er upstairs that you're as good if not better … Are you ready, Polly?'

Susy threw herself back into work; the challenge of management was just what she needed to remain sane. Polly's endearing manner was supportive in every way and with two extra salesgirls employed to fill the void left by the reshuffle, Crawfords was busy.

Detective Superintendent Pearce had exhausted his investigation, nationwide media coverage had not turned up anything positive. All information gathered was recorded and filed away; the case was left open as so many before. Was another innocent girl going to fall prey to an assault, he thought? Even lose their right to a full life before science came up with a sure shot remedy to stop their attackers reabusing.

Susy's memory had drawn a blank. Although being pressed by WPC Phillips she could remember no more. She had also declined the therapy that was suggested to aid recovery, and dismissed any further questioning, anxious to put the whole sordid affair behind her and start rebuilding her life.

Vanessa was in demand professionally, her creative expertise accompanied by her self confident drive assured a continued rise to the top. Oliver was besotted.

A social whirlwind began blowing a gale through Cadogan Place as Oliver, who by now was virtually a resident, was well connected in the area of café society. Susy inevitably got caught up in the draught. Tina was now employed full time, keeping the apartment orderly before the next onslaught of revellers descended, of which there were many.

The month of May and the country was buzzing with excitement over the forthcoming Royal Wedding. The Queen's son Andrew had at last found a bride, Miss Sarah Ferguson, daughter of Major Ferguson, the Prince of Wales's polo team captain. This fine chestnut filly had ridden into the young prince's life and stolen his heart. There was bound to be much celebration, with the summer season about to begin and Ascot little less than two weeks away. The general consensus hoped that Miss Ferguson would relieve herself of a few unwanted pounds before the ceremony.

Susy was packing a small case when Vanessa arrived back at the apartment late and alone. 'Where are you going?'

'I told you, Milan.'

Vanessa had been so busy, she had forgotten. 'Ah, *bella Italia*. You're going to just love it, Susy.'

'I won't see it. I'm only there for three days working.'

'That doesn't matter, Susy. The Italians have such great style and the language is so beautiful it positively sings.'

Susy zipped up her case. 'I suppose you speak Italian?'

'*Si, certo.*'

'Aye, what does that mean?'

'Yes, of course, *parlo Italiano.*'

'I wish I could be like you. Like you know somethin' about everythin'.'

'There is absolutely no reason why you cannot start learning. It's never too late to start.'

'Help me then?'

'I don't have the time, Susy.'

'Then tell me what to do. I want to learn, be smart. I can look good, but I don't sound good.'

Vanessa laughed. 'You have got a long way to go.'

'Don't be a bitch, Vanessa. Don't you laugh at me.'

Vanessa sat Susy down on the sofa. 'OK, Miss Susan Stevens, you have been to hell and back, nobody would ever doubt that, especially me, but you can start with what comes out of your mouth. I do not want to hear you swear now, or at any other time. You find yourself a good speech therapist and take classes. Are you listening to me?' Susy nodded. 'Then you read everything and anything. How can you have an intelligent conversation with an empty head?'

'I'll try real hard.'

'Then indulge in some social sport like riding or tennis. Expand your interests. I'll guide you, but it's all down to you.'

Susy picked up Vanessa's *Times* and began to read, trying to absorb every word. 'Consortium, what does that mean?'

'Susy, there are three dictionaries on the bookshelf, look it up.' Vanessa was tired after a hectic day and did not intend shouting. A breakfast meeting tomorrow called for an early night. 'Good night,' she said, climbing the stairs.

'You'd better watch your back, Vanessa, I'm coming up fast behind you.'

Vanessa was on the telephone when Oliver entered her office. She beckoned for him to come in. '... but that's just a new angle on an old theme, Jack.' Oliver leant over the desk and kissed her full on the lips, '…ummm. Yes, I'm still with you … we have to get the clients to approve this ad … we are stretching a very small budget, Jack, and it's got to be perfect. I'll call you back this afternoon.'

Oliver swung Vanessa around in the chair and lifted her towards him, sinking his hands into her buttocks. 'What you need right now is–'

'Is you.' She threw her arms around his neck. 'But I'm so busy, darling. How will I get through all this work?'

'And how will I live through this afternoon without you?' He pressed his mouth hard against hers. 'I want to have you here and now.'

'Oliver stop,' she panted, 'someone may come in.'

'Here and now, Vanessa, to hell with the accounts.'

The door swung open and Erik stood watching them lying across the desk, 'Oh darling, see you've got your lunch box packed.'

They both jumped to attention. 'Erik, excuse us,' Vanessa said.

'Don't apologise, luv, I only wish I was in the same position. Take it you don't need another one for lunch?'

'Oliver, I haven't a minute to spare, really. I am up to my eyes, but I have to speak to you about the weekend.'

'Sure. Fire away.'

'Both my brothers are at home this weekend and I thought it would be nice if we joined the family.'

'Well, that's fine with me.'

'Good, that's settled then. I will telephone daddy and tell him we will be there.'

'Your father may not approve of me, my darling. Does this, I mean, will this mean I'm under observation?'

'Probably, but you need not worry about daddy, he's an old darling. Just watch out for mummy. Now, go please, let me work.'

Oliver backed off towards the door. 'Speak to you later?' he said, the telephone interrupting the conversation.

'Yes, my darling.'

'About seven?'
'Yes! Bye.'
'Love you.'
Vanessa picked up the impatient telephone, 'Love you too,' she whispered.

With the hood down Vanessa drove the Spider out of the city towards the motorway and Hambledon. Oliver had bowed to her wish to drive and sat white-knuckled as the speedometer passed 90 mph. As they sped through the countryside on that beautiful June morning, the wind whipping through their hair, Vanessa could not remember being happier. She had dismissed Stephen from her mind completely. Oliver was what she wanted now and she was about to show him off to her family.

Hand in hand, Vanessa led Oliver through the house and out into the garden, where they could see Sir Richard taking morning coffee alone. Banjo leapt to his feet and scampered across the lawn announcing their arrival as Vanessa approached into the open arms of her father.

'Vanessa, my dear, how good it is to see you.'
'And you. How I've missed you, daddy.'
'And this must be Oliver?'
Oliver stepped forward and held out his hand. 'Oliver Bryce Thomas, sir. I am very pleased to meet you.'
'Well, let's not stand on ceremony. Come, sit down, Marie will bring some more coffee.'

Lady Caroline had witnessed the arrival from an upstairs window, taking a small pair of binoculars from a dresser, to have a closer look at the trio sunning themselves on the lawn before joining them. She sharpened the focus and studied Oliver's fine features – the strong jawline, broad shoulders and well-dressed posture. Handsome, she thought, lowering the binoculars, and whom might she have plucked this one from?

Engrossed in conversation as if they had known each other for years, Sir Richard and Oliver were oblivious to Vanessa's discerning glance, watching her mother walk slowly towards them from the house. Oliver promptly offered his seat as she reached the table.

'Good morning,' she said, kissing Vanessa on the cheek, 'you're looking wonderful as ever, darling.'

'Mummy, I would like you to meet Oliver.'

Lady Caroline's swift appraisal was noted as Oliver politely introduced himself.

'My dear, Oliver knows Rufus Fielding. Now, what a coincidence.'

'Indeed, a family connection no less, how fortunate and a charming young man,' she added gleefully.

'The Fieldings have been good friends of ours for more years than I care to remember, Oliver,' Sir Richard chuckled.

'And Rufus is getting married in September.'

Was there no stopping her? They had only just arrived and already Vanessa could sense that the tone of the conversation was not conducive to a harmonious weekend. A quick change of course was required immediately.

'Oliver, would you like to see the valley before lunch?'

'Ready when you are.'

They made hasty excuses, then cut a dash across the lawn in the direction of the stables. Sir Richard watched them race off. 'Ha, ha, such energy, these young people have.'

They saddled up and galloped off across the fields towards the gently rolling Chiltern Hills that stretched out before them, stopping periodically to gaze at the lush green countryside, before moving on. The midday sun, unusually hot for June, beat down upon them while they rode on up and over the hills to a clearing, where they dismounted, tethered the horses, then fell face up in the long grass. They lay motionless, side by side, the warm breeze wafting over them.

'Listen, Oliver.'

'I'm listening.'

'Do you hear it?'

'I don't hear anything, Vanessa.'

'Exactly.' She placed her hands behind her head, lifting her face towards the sun and closed her eyes – total peace. Oliver turned over on to his stomach and playfully tickled Vanessa's face with a blade of grass, his eyes caressing her every feature.

'What are you thinking?' he asked.

'Just how much I love it here.'

'I thought you enjoyed your life in London?'

'I do, but here I can escape into another world and nothing else matters.'

Oliver was silent, the only sound was the rustle of the leaves on the trees and the hum of a bee hovering from flower to flower. Vanessa opened her eyes to find Oliver peering closely at her neck.

'What are you looking at?' she asked.

'Tut, it's nothing,' he said, moving her head from side to side, an expression of concern creeping over his face.

'What's the matter with my neck? Have I been bitten?'

'No, no, nothing so simple.' Vanessa touched her neck searching for any abnormalities. 'Did you ever get kicked by a horse?'

Sitting up she felt her neck and jaw with both hands. 'No, never.'

'Ah!' he exclaimed quite seriously. 'Now, why haven't I noticed that before.' He leant back out of arms' reach, 'A double chin.'

Vanessa lunged at him, 'Oliver, you rat!' But he was on his feet and running. He yelled back at her, 'I'll still love you when you're old.'

Vanessa stumbled after him shouting, 'You'll never reach old age if I catch up with you!'

Oliver raced across the valley with Vanessa, who was the better rider, close behind. They galloped across the fields at full speed towards the house, she taking a short cut to arrive at the stables ahead of him. Exhausted, but happy, they strolled back into the house past Rupert's Lotus, which was parked in the drive, and out to the pool. Rupert dived into the water and glided towards them, surfacing at their feet. He shielded his eyes with his hand and flashed a grin at the two figures silhouetted against the glare of the sun.

'Rupert, there's somebody I'd like you to meet.'

Rupert pulled himself out of the pool and reached for a robe. After informal introductions, he enquired if this was Oliver's first visit to the area. 'I see my sister has taken you on a hack already. Where did you go, up to the ridge?'

'Oliver is an excellent rider,' Vanessa interrupted.

'But there's a lot of room for improvement,' came Oliver's modest reply.

'Well, tomorrow you will get the chance to row,' Rupert said with a laugh.

''Rupert, I want him back in one piece.'

Oliver laughed nervously as Rupert slapped him on the back. 'Fine athletic figure, look at those muscles.' He grabbed Oliver by the arm, 'They could pull a barge. By the way, where is Piers?'

'You know what a bad timekeeper he is, Rupert, he will probably turn up tomorrow.'

Rupert had some calls to make and disappeared into the house.

'I'm so hot in these clothes, Oliver. Let's change and take a swim.'

'Thank God, Vanessa, I thought you would never ask.'

Dinner, although informal, was served in the oak room. Sir Richard was in jovial mood and took great pleasure in entertaining Oliver with tales of his youth. Oliver warmed to the man and enthusiastically spurred him on, punctuated by Lady Caroline's version of events. Dinner had passed amiably, Piers' absence had barely been noticed as they left the table amid much laughter and made their way into the drawing room. Vanessa was elated at the bonhomie and several times during the course of dinner, caught her mother's approving glance across the table.

The evening was warm, almost oppressive when Oliver and Vanessa decided to take their drinks and sit by the pool.

'You family's delightful, Vanessa, especially your mother. Not the big bad wolf I had expected.'

'That is because your family is well connected, darling.'

'I was unaware that she knew my family?'

'She doesn't, but you gave her enough information to start the ball rolling. Right now I expect she will be on the telephone checking you out.'

'I don't believe you.'

Vanessa put down her drink and reached for Oliver's hand. 'Follow me,' she said.

The pair crept back up to the house and positioned themselves outside the drawing room window, where Lady Caroline was alone and on the telephone. From their crouching position, they peered up and in through the open window, catching snippets of her conversation.

'…just for the weekend, he seems quite charming … was he married, or divorced? … Oh, what a blessing, who do you know them through? … Ah yes, the Charringtons, of course…'

Vanessa and Oliver ducked down out of sight when her mother turned around to face the window. 'What did I tell you, Oliver?' Vanessa whispered, peering once again through the window.

'…Oh Veronica, would you, darling? I would be so grateful … yes, as soon as possible. Goodbye.'

They crouched again under the drawing room window astounded to hear her dial again.

'Belinda darling, Caroline … yes, it has been a long time.'

Piers had spotted the eavesdropping couple and startled them with his presence. 'Can't you think of anything better to do?'

'Shush!' Vanessa uttered, before the three of them collapsed into the herbaceous border. Lady Caroline's hand reached through the open window, while they cowered below and pulled it to. With lowered voices, Piers offered a grubby hand.

'You must be Oliver.' They shook hands. 'What the hell do you two think you're doing?'

Vanessa stood up and brushed herself down. 'Just trying to prove a point to Oliver.'

'Ah, mother up to her usual tricks again?'

'You know, Piers, where mummy is concerned, nothing is sacred. By the morning she will have a complete dossier on the Bryce Thomases.'

'I suppose I should be flattered,' Oliver said, as the three tiptoed away.

'Flattered is a nice way of putting "a total invasion of privacy",' Vanessa added.

'Don't be too hard on her, Vanessa. Apart from those bloody birds, it's her only passion.'

'Oliver has not had the pleasure yet, Piers.'

'There is absolutely no doubt that you will, Oliver.' Back at the house Piers excused himself. 'See you in the morning.'

Oliver yelled up the stairs, 'Early start?'

'Yep, eight o'clock, be ready.'

Oliver turned to Vanessa as Piers disappeared from sight. 'Alone at last. Is there anywhere we can lose ourselves in this house?'

With a twinkle in her eye Vanessa replied, 'I'm not sure I know exactly what you mean, my darling?'

Oliver placed his arm firmly around her neck and they walked slowly towards the lounge. 'You cannot be expected to act like a nun, Vanessa.'

'That's a disparaging thought. Mummy, I'll have you know, has centurions posted at every strategic point. In fact, I'm not so sure that she isn't masquerading herself.'

The study door clicked as they passed, betraying the surveillance operation Lady Caroline had promised herself. Curiosity, or downright nosiness had got the better hand, so with an air of sincerity and in a loud voice, Oliver decided to play the game.

'I think I'll have an early night, Vanessa,' and lightly kissed her on the lips. 'Don't want to let the side down in the morning,' and winked. 'See you at lunch.'

'Yes, my darling, goodnight.'

The study door silently closed and Vanessa went into the lounge, switched on a video and settled into an armchair. Not before too long, she felt her mother's presence behind her. She turned, 'Going to join me, mummy?'

'No, darling, I think I will retire, it's very late.' Vanessa continued watching the movie. 'Has Oliver gone to bed?'

Without taking her eyes from the screen she replied, 'Yes, half an hour ago.'

'He appears to be a nice young man. I think you may have chosen well this time, Vanessa.'

'I'm sure you will tell me if I haven't.'

'Yes, well I'm only thinking of your future, darling. After all, it is in your father's and my interest that you marry well.'

'Mummy, can we please discuss this at some other time. As you said, it's very late and I would like to watch the end of the movie.'

Lady Caroline pecked Vanessa on the cheek and retired for the night.

Soon after, Vanessa uncurled herself from the armchair, switched off the video and padded barefoot through the house to her bedroom on the second floor. She opened the door and reached for the light switch when Oliver took her hand, sweeping her up into his arms and carried her to the bed. Not a word was spoken as he slowly removed her dress, letting the silk slip silently to the floor. She pulled him closer to her, feeling the fullness of his penis pressing against her belly; how she ached for him to be inside her. He gently laid her naked body beneath him, lightly running his hands over her neck and breasts, down the contours of her buttocks to the crevice between her thighs. Rhythmical movement slow and long, her soft cries of joy were hushed by his mouth over hers. When he felt her climax he thrust his manhood hard into her until the soft warm afterglow of passion subsided. Oliver stayed until his love fell asleep, then slipped quietly back to his room.

Vanessa awoke to the sun streaming through a crack in the curtains. Must be much later than she thought. Stepping out of bed, she put on a silk dressing gown and threw back the drapes to see Sir Richard walking the dog across the lawn. 'Good morning,' she shouted from the window. Her father stopped in his tracks and shouted back to her.

'Good morning. Time you were up, it's a beautiful day.'

'What time is it?'

'Noon.'

Vanessa stretched, shaking off the last vestiges of sleep. Why rush? She had only just opened her eyes and the boys were bound to be late back from rowing. She lay back in the tub and smiled to herself, recalling last night. What an opportunist Oliver was, waiting patiently for her to return to her room. It could so easily have been her mother entering her bedroom, only to be flung through the air by a naked Oliver. She laughed, then ducked under the water and resurfaced. She hoped Oliver would have realised his mistake before he got her knickers off.

Boisterous voices thundered through the house – they were back and early. Vanessa jumped out of the bath and hurriedly threw a towel around her. By the time she had dressed and arrived at the poolside, Rupert, Piers and Oliver were huddled over their beers discussing the mastery of the stroke. They apparently had enjoyed a successful morning on the river.

'Weight is an advantage,' Rupert said seriously. 'The man who throws his full power behind the sweep of the oar can't fail, although it has been known for a skilful lightweight to win races.'

'Technique is what it's all about and with the right training, Oliver, you can make it,' Piers added.

'Isn't thirty a little late to take up the game?' Oliver asked.

Vanessa placed her hand on Oliver's shoulder, 'You're in your prime, my darling.'

They all sat back unaware of her presence up until then. Rupert remembered how Vanessa could sleep away a Sunday morning without difficulty. 'Have you just surfaced?'

'Certainly not, and what happened to "good morning"?'

Rupert looked at his watch, 'One-thirty is hardly good morning, Vanessa.'

'Did you have a good time?' she asked.

If Oliver felt remotely strained he did not appear to be fatigued. 'Absolutely bloody marvellous,' he replied.

'Does that mean they are going to steal you away from me every weekend?'

Rupert was forever irritated by his sister's possessiveness. 'Good God, Vanessa, let the man have some space. There stands the making of a great oarsman.'

'OK people, this is where I have to say *adieu*.' Piers was anxious to be on his way. 'It was great, but greater things lie smouldering in anticipation of Pier's pecker.'

'Oh piss off, Piers, you can be a pain in the arse sometimes.' It was unusual for Rupert to be so touchy. Pier's crass remarks were normally greeted with some degree of amusement.

'Going so soon?' shouted Sir Richard, hurrying to join them by the pool.

'Sorry, Pa.'

'But you've only just arrived, my boy.'

'I'm already late.'

'Oh dear, dear, I was hoping to have a few words. Always in a hurry, I never speak to him nowadays.' He turned to Rupert and Oliver. 'Well now, how was the rowing this morning? Joined the team yet, Oliver?'

'Not yet, sir.'

'I remember my young days rowing for Eton College. Cut quite a dash in my blues, not unlike Rupert here, seems hard to envisage now, I know, time putting on a little weight around the waistline, ha! I had a little more hair too, then, ha ha! So tell me, Oliver, will we be seeing you rowing for the club, with Rupert and Piers?'

'I don't know that I could come up to their standard.' Oliver's self-effacing reply brought a thunderous response from Sir Richard.

'Nonsense, fine figure of a man.'

'But I would like to think that given the time to practise, I could be as good.'

'Ah! Bravo.'

'That is if my stupid sister gives the man a chance.' That unprovoked gibe at Vanessa was not taken lightly.

'Come now, Rupert,' Sir Richard retorted, 'that is not the way to speak to your sister.'

Rupert stormed off, much to his father's disgust.

'It's not important, daddy, there is something bothering Rupert. He has been on edge most of the weekend.'

'Seemed perfectly all right to me. What's the matter with the boy?'

'Please, daddy, let him go.'

Lady Caroline, on hearing raised voices, joined the group still seated by the pool. 'Ah, there you are. Have Rupert and Piers gone?'

'Well if they're not here Caroline, they must have gone.' Sir Richard was clearly bothered by the outburst.

'Mummy, why don't you show Oliver the rose garden.'

'What a good idea, Vanessa.' Oliver already standing, escorted Lady Caroline away from the poolside. 'I do so adore roses, Oliver, one of the marvels of nature, don't you agree?'

'Why, yes indeed.'

'Throughout time the rose has been a symbol of love and chivalry. Sacred to Aphrodite as well as the Yorks and Lancasters, who fought the wars of the roses, but, of course, I do not need to remind you of that.' She led him through the multitude of shrubs and climbers so meticulously kept by the gardener. The place was a horticulturist's dream. Oliver paid attention, listened with great interest, while Lady Caroline extolled the virtues of every bloom. He noted the subtle variations of colour, inhaled the heady fragrance as they passed by, until he could detect the twittering of birds. They were heading towards the aviary, the confines of which he was not going to escape.

Oliver stood back in amazement at the landscaped garden surrounding the large aviary, which housed a host of chirping budgerigars. Not being a bird lover and content just to watch the little creatures flutter from perch to perch, he had the unnerving feeling that he was about to be thrust right under their flight path.

Lady Caroline was as excited as a mother who had just borne a child.

'Now what do you think of my little darlings, Oliver? Every one reared right here under this roof?'

'They are charming little creatures,' he said apprehensively.

'See how they fly. Come, step inside, they won't hurt you, they are such friendly little birds.'

Oliver stepped hesitantly inside the door of the aviary, not wishing to offend, but keeping his back firmly against the wire, while trying to remain calm. Immediately a bird flew on to Lady Caroline's finger, 'This, Oliver, is a White Opaline Lacewing. Isn't she pretty?' Oliver did not speak, to him the budgerigar was the size of an eagle. She held the bird up in front of his face, in a sinister way that perplexed him. Could she know of his fear of birds? Oliver broke out into a cold sweat, his ashen complexion shining with perspiration. Taking his arm, she led him further into the aviary. 'They need room to fly, Oliver, feel free, as in their natural habitat. So I had an extended flight channel built on to make them feel unrestricted.' Had she not noticed his terror as a bird landed on his shoulder? He took a deep breath and prayed that the ordeal would soon be over. She lifted the tiny creature from Oliver's shoulder. 'Ah, a White Winged Sky Blue. There there, come to mummy.' Oliver had taken root where he stood and was virtually speechless. From a small child he had been terrified of birds. Lady Caroline had done her homework well and now she had him right where she wanted him. 'Budgerigars are not unlike us, Oliver, their lives are governed by companionship.' He gripped the wire meshing behind him as she got closer.

'I'm – I'm sure that's true,' he stammered.

'They find a mate, feather a nest, then ... need I say more?'

Jesus he thought, still riveted to the ground, am I dreaming?

'You're quite a performer I understand, Oliver?'

'What, who told you that?'

She took a step closer, 'it's unimportant whom,' and placed her hand on his chest.

'Now wait,' he said, grabbing her arm, 'I don't know what you think you're doing, but this is not my scene.' A flutter of wings pinned him against the netting once again, as she placed both her hands on his shoulders. She was calm, in control of the situation.

'Vanessa is still a child, Oliver. I can give you so much more.'

Oliver tried to make a dash, 'Let me out of here.' But Lady Caroline barred the exit with her body and clasping his hand to her bosom said, 'Don't be a foolish young man. She will dump you when she's finished with you. Can't you see that?'

He grasped both her hands in his and held them up against the wire meshing. 'You're a jealous woman who's trying to capture the pleasures of youth through the life of your beautiful daughter.'

Lady Caroline's eyes were aflame, 'You lie.'

'Oh no, I happen to love Vanessa and nothing in this world would allow me to give you that satisfaction.' She stumbled as he pushed her out of the way and opened the door.

'You'll regret it,' she yelled after him.

Oliver wiped his brow with the back of his hand and walked briskly back to the pool, where Sir Richard and Vanessa were still seated. The thought had never crossed his mind that Lady Caroline was anything but a caring, if somewhat overprotective mother. He was surprised, even shocked at his misjudgement of character.

'I am very impressed with your rose garden, sir.'

'Yes, splendid isn't it? Caroline takes great pride in her flowers. Show you the aviary did she?'

'Yes, in fact, I couldn't drag her away.'

'Confounded birds, as if we haven't got enough in the garden. Still, that's what she wanted and she certainly spends a lot of time there.'

'I'm sure she does.'

'What?'

'I am sure they require a lot of attention.'

'Yes, that they do.'

Vanessa, feeling the sun's rays burning her skin, plunged headlong into the pool. 'Come on in, it's lovely,' she shouted to Oliver.

'Go on with you,' her father said, struggling to his feet. 'It's time I took a stroll.' He straightened his back, adjusted his Panama and with the aid of his walking cane, walked steadily off in the direction of the rose garden.

Oliver dived into the cool revitalising water and frolicked with Vanessa like a couple of kids. He lifted her clean out of the water and down into his arms.

'When did I last tell you how much I love you?' he asked, as they trod water, arms entwined around each other.

'Something's happened?' Vanessa queried.

'What makes you say that?'

'Has mummy been suggesting...'

'Suggesting that I marry her daughter? Well maybe.'

Vanessa laughed, 'Oh, she's impossible.'

'She just can't wait to be a grandmother.'

'Did she say that?'

'Well not exactly, but I knew what she meant.'

'I'm not ready, Oliver, so you'll just have to wait.'

He kissed her long and hard. 'I'm an impatient man, I won't wait forever.'

Shadows began to creep across the garden and the glow of the evening sun fell slowly from the sky. Oliver threw their bags into the boot of the Spider as Lady Caroline joined Sir Richard and Vanessa in the hall.

'Is everybody about to leave us, Richard dear?'

Clearly they were. Vanessa embraced her father, 'Bye, daddy.'

Oliver bounded back into the house, his eyes meeting Lady Caroline's steady gaze. She was poised, courteous and almost demure as she took a step towards Oliver and held out her hand. 'Goodbye,' he said, 'I am very pleased to have met you and you, sir.' He heartily shook Sir Richard by the hand.

'Anytime young man, anytime.'

As Oliver drove the Spider away from Hambledon, Vanessa snuggled closer to him and squeezed his arm. 'I think you made quite an impression, my darling.'

* * *

The apartment in town was in darkness when they returned. Vanessa opened the door, switched on the lights and was startled to find Susy sitting quietly alone. By the reddened tear-stained face and piles of spent cigarette butts in the ashtray, she had obviously been there for some time. Oliver quickly disappeared with the baggage, leaving Vanessa to calm the storm. She rushed to her side.

'What on earth is wrong, Susy?'

'Nothing,' she sniffed.

'Don't tell me nothing, look at you. how long have you been sitting here in the dark?' Susy did not answer, just blew hard into a tissue. Vanessa took hold of both shoulders and searched for a clue through the torrent of tears streaming down her face.

'You are obviously not all right. No horrid men out there prowling around, are there?'

'No, nothin' like that.'

'Thank goodness, we can breathe easy. Then please speak to me. You must let it all out, Susy. How can I help you if I don't know what's going on in your head?'

Susy nodded, pulling Vanessa closer to her, resting her head on her shoulder. 'I'm alone, Vanessa, I don't 'ave anybody or anythin' in my life.' Vanessa allowed her to continue through the tears. 'I 'ave no love, nobody to care for me, only me on my own. I need to 'ave somebody to look out for me. Is that a lot to ask for?'

Vanessa stroked her hair and gave her a hug. 'Some day, somebody.'

'No, you don't understand me. You take for granted what I have to fight for. Oliver loves only you, your family care for you. Loving doesn't cost anything and you can't go out and buy it like another dress. Do you know just how lucky you are? I can pack my entire life into a suitcase. I feel lost and on my own. What can I do to stop the pain, Vanessa?'

There was no answer, nothing that would mend the hurt. Susy felt wounded and deserted; this was not a myth, but a fact of life.

Vanessa did not have a single word that would make it all come right, no magic wand to wave. At least the burden of torment and despair had been eased, if not resolved. Helping her upstairs to her room, Vanessa tucked her up in bed and switched off the light. At the door she turned back and watched her friend lying face down, her long hair spread out over the pillow.

'Life will get better,' she said softly.

7

Polly brushed the cat from her lap, the atmosphere was far too hot. 'Go find a cool corner, Henry.' She picked up the telephone that was persistently ringing.

'Polly, it's Vanessa. This is a very quick call, darling. I'm on my way out.'

'So how was the weekend?'

'Wonderful, but I haven't time to talk about it right now.'

'What's happening, why the panic?'

'Royal Ascot. Oliver's company have a box every year. Please say that you and Seb will come – Ladies Day the nineteenth?'

'Try and keep me away. But I'm not with Seb any more.'

'So bring somebody else.'

Polly was interested to know exactly who was going.

'Well apart from Oliver and me, there's Lucinda and Douglas.'

'Together again?'

'Temporarily, I'm sure. Nicky Bloom and his wife Rachel, Peter Bailey and Ursula.'

'Not Ursula Stone?'

'The very same. Now, where was I, oh yes, Susy, Toby and some business associate of Oliver's.'

'Vanessa, I'm coming on my own, there might be some big fish to net. What are you wearing?'

'Polly, we will talk about our outfits later. I must dash, 'bye.'

On Wednesday evening the fashion parade began at home. Susy had two outfits to choose from, a navy and white silk dress, the body of which wrapped around her contours like a second skin, gathered into a boot button fastening on the hip, unrevealing, but very flattering, topped by a large navy and white hat. The other, a green and white polka dot crêpe de chine dress, which was slinky and sexy, and a matching loose jacket, topped by a large white hat. The decision was crucial as Vanessa burst through the door laden with shiny designer bags over each shoulder.

'Help, I cannot make a decision,' Susy yelled.

'Wait just one moment,' Vanessa slumped into a chair, 'get me a drink, please.'

'I've just put the kettle on.'

'Not a cup of tea, a real drink, a large vodka and tonic.' Vanessa kicked off her shoes. 'I have had to move mountains today, just for one measly day out of the office and Polly, oh, she must have rung me six times. Should I wear the yellow or the blue, or maybe the green and gold. Gold! I said. Where do you think you are going Buckingham Palace?'

'Vanessa.'

'Really, as if it's all I have to do and as for Lucinda, she's turning into a boring lush.'

'I think I'm having a bad influence on you, darlin'. It's either that or this heatwave.'

Vanessa did not hear, she was watching the nine o'clock news. 'Come here quickly.' Rushing back into the lounge, they sat side by side in front of the television set.

'The Queen was accompanied by Miss Sarah Ferguson, who wore a white, raw silk flared calf-length dress, with broad green and navy blue chevrons on the bodice.'

'Flaming Nora, Vanessa.'

'Her hair is tucked under a navy pillbox hat, with navy blue and white shoes.'

'Blimey oh Riley! She looks like a pedestrian crossing.'

'Be quiet, Susy, I'm looking at the fashions.'

'Where's your sense of humour, Vanessa? If that's the competition, we're laughin' 'darlin.'

Vanessa was amused. 'You're absolutely right. Let's make some snap decisions. Go and get changed.'

Vanessa sat with her feet on the coffee table, sipping a vodka and tonic, awaiting Susy's entrance at the top of the stairs. She emerged wearing the green and white polka dot dress and jacket.

'All right, now walk towards me and turn around ... very nice, next one.' Still sipping her drink, she waited for the second outfit to appear at the top of the stairs. Vanessa beckoned her forward and made her twirl. 'Ah, Mademoiselle, *très elegant, parfait,* or, in your language darling, knockout.'

There was a flurry of activity in the apartment during the morning, with the telephone ringing incessantly while they tried to get dressed. The limousine was due to arrive at ten o'clock sharp and Vanessa was determined not to be late. Pinning on her hat as the doorbell rang, 'Can you get it?' she yelled from her bedroom.

Susy raced to the entryphone and buzzed Oliver up to the apartment and unlocked the door. Apart from the final coat of lipstick, she was ready, but Vanessa was still putting the final touches to her ensemble. Oliver tapped on the door as he entered.

'Are you girls ready yet?' He kissed Susy on the cheek. 'You're looking perfectly lovely Susy.' She raised her voice upstairs, 'We're leaving.'

Making a grand entrance, no matter what the occasion was Vanessa's forte. She opened the bedroom door and floated towards them, her lightly-tanned skin wrapped in layers of the palest pink silk. The dress and matching jacket were topped by the largest hat that revealed not a wisp of hair and tantalisingly hooded the eyes.

'Sensational,' Oliver said, taking her hand. She's overdone it again, Susy thought. I hope it doesn't rain.

'Don't forget we're picking up Polly on the way, Oliver.'

'Vanessa, everything is under control. Now let's go, Larry is waiting in the car.'

Larry Walsh was a business friend of Oliver's from Houston,

Texas. The rotund little man's eyes lit up when Vanessa and Susy entered the limousine.

Larry shook Vanessa's hand rigorously. 'Larry Walsh, Mame, I've been hearing a lot of nice things about you.' Then he turned to Susy, 'Pleased to meet you too, little lady, love the hair.'

'Thurloe Square, driver.'

'Very good, sir.'

The car slowly turned out of Cadogan Place and cruised leisurely along Sloane Street towards Kensington.

Larry broke the silence. 'This is quite an occasion, Olli?'

'It's the start of the social calendar, Larry.'

'Oh, I love this little country of yours, all those lords and ladies and Princess Diana. Oh yeah, great piece of ass. We don't have anything like that back home, no siree, it's a very special place, little England.' Vanessa pressed a button to open the car window, as soon as Larry lit up a large cigar. Susy studied the larger than life character; he was uncannily like Eddy and she took an instant dislike to him. 'Now see you here,' he continued, 'you just don't know what you're getting, Susy. I mean, I could be talking to the Queen's cousin, or on the other hand, a refuse collector. Now, if I'm not mistaken, your daddy is a lord?'

'You're right Larry, he loves lording it.'

Oliver interrupted, 'Vanessa's father is Sir Richard Baron.'

'See, now what did I tell you ... hey, was that Harrods we just passed?'

Oliver smiled, 'We're not stopping Larry.'

'No no, ha! Remind me I got a lot of things to pick up for my Ellen.'

Polly was ready as they pulled up outside her apartment and Larry could not believe his eyes when Oliver ushered her into the car. 'Another beauty, Ollie. You sure know how to pick 'em, boy.'

Nicky and Rachel had already arrived, followed by Peter and Ursula, who greeted them all with a bottle of champagne in hand. 'Just in time, my friends,' Peter said, popping the cork, 'hold the first course.'

Rachel was scouting the Royal Enclosure when Vanessa approached her. 'How divine you look today, darling.'

Vanessa knew she was the cat who'd taken the cream and swallowed the compliment graciously. 'Can I introduce you to Polly and Susy?' she said.

Rachel barely noticed the girls as she angled her line of vision over their shoulders. 'What do you think of that Ursula?' she whispered. 'Can't think what Peter is doing with her.'

'I think I can,' Vanessa replied.

'But sex isn't everything, darling, you can't spend your entire life in bed. Why doesn't he take her out and buy her some decent clothes? She always looks so cheap and who's that man talking to Oliver, the American?'

'That's Larry Walsh. Be very careful Rachel, you could seriously burn your fingers. You know you're a pushover for men with big wallets.' She disappeared behind them.

'How much jewellery can one person wear?' Susy asked. Vanessa watched Rachel make Larry's acquaintance. 'Rachel,' she mused, 'has enough to decorate her entire car as well.'

The party was well under way when Toby arrived, all dressed up in his morning suit and alone. He appeared taller than Susy remembered and his hair was longer. She stood back as he mingled with their party, shielding her inquisitive eyes under the brim of her hat. Why could she not look him straight in the eye? Was she afraid that he would see more than she intended? And yet she so longed to be near him? Toby turned quickly around and caught her glance. 'How are you?' he said, touching her arm. 'I'm fine' she wanted to say as he passed her by, but not one word was forthcoming. She watched him, noted every gesture, listened to every word, when he laughed she laughed, but best of all she was there beside him, pulse racing. She only had to speak, say something for him to notice her. He picked up a plate of poached salmon and a glass of champagne and walked straight past her to the front of the box and looked out across the track. Somebody then thrust a plate into her hand.

'Are you still with us?'

'Sorry Polly, thanks.'

Ursula started jumping up and down. 'There she is.' She was peering through a pair of binoculars into the Royal Enclosure. 'Princess Diana.'

Larry leapt immediately to his feet, 'Oh boy, this I gotta see. Which one, honey?' They all hung over the barrier. 'The emerald suit with the black polka dots. See there, to the right.'

'Yep, I see her,' he grabbed Ursula's binoculars for a closer look, 'Well I'll be darned, there she goes.'

'And look, there's Fergie.'

'Looking better than yesterday I hope,' Rachel said sarcastically.

'You don't knock that little lady,' Larry said seriously, 'she's hooked herself a prince. Now how many girls have done that?'

Rachel condescended, 'I suppose so, well yes, of course, Larry, you're absolutely right.'

'You bet your ass I am, lady.'

Oliver and Toby were studying form and money was changing hands at an alarming pace. The horses were leaving the paddock and cantering towards the start and Susy had not got a clue. Peter put his arm around her shoulder. 'What do you fancy?' She looked at the race card in total confusion, 'I don't know anything about form.'

'Oh yes you do. Now what are we looking at, the two-thirty, "Bridesmaid" – just what I'm looking for.' Peter gave her a little squeeze.

'You're pissed,' she said, moving away.

'And you're pretty gorgeous. Has anybody ever told you that?'

Peter's breath reeked of booze and cigarettes. 'Don't push me, Mr.'

Vanessa stepped in to dissuade Peter from making a complete fool of himself. 'Keep it down, Peter,' she whispered.

'Sorry, sorry, I apologise.'

The horses were almost ready to go and frantic final decisions had to be made before the close of betting. 'Come here Ursula, my little filly, let Uncle Larry show you how it's done.'

Polly was huddled together with Oliver and Toby. Larry was flashing a wad of notes under Ursula's nose and Nicky, whose foolproof formula almost always let him down, was having a small coronary, pacified by Rachel, who really did not give a damn.

Susy was caught up in the excitement. 'Who do I choose, Vanessa?'

'Back the favourite if you're not sure.'

'Which one is it?'

'Cyrano de Bergerac. But not on the nose – each way.'

'OK, got it.'

'Be quick, they're about to go.'

All bets on, they were off, six furlongs and all eyes were on that bend. The binoculars poised, the commentary getting louder, the crowd cheered and the dust flew that sizzling afternoon. Rounding the bend, the crowd stood up and roared. Susy yelled with the best of them. 'Come on Cyrano, baby!' They kept coming, louder and faster and the crowd was frantic. Screaming, cheering, until they thundered past the winning post to a tumultuous finish.

Oliver was ecstatic, he had backed the winner, £50 on the nose, not bad at five to one. Second, Cyrano de Bergerac, eleven to four favourite and third Bridesmaid, five to one.

'Is Nicky all right?' Vanessa asked Rachel, while she fanned his face with the race card, 'He's looking awfully pale.'

'He lost a hundred pounds. That's a pair of shoes, Vanessa.'

'It's the luck of the game, Rachel. Can I get him a brandy?'

Nicky raised his head. 'Thank you, it's the heat, I'll be fine.'

Larry had successfully backed the first two races. 'I told you, little lady, stick by me, I'll teach you a thing or two.'

Oliver slapped him on the back. 'Well done, my friend, maybe you could help Nicky out?'

'Oh yeah, he's not looking too good.'

Oliver gave Peter a gentle slap round the face. 'Hey, Peter, you're not supposed to sleep through this.'

'Sorry, Oliver, I seem to be apologising to everybody today.'

With all the euphoria and commotion surrounding the race, nobody had noticed Toby's absence. He had slipped out, disappeared, gone walkabout and why not? He was not obliged to stay with the group. Anybody, regardless of class, could mingle, rub shoulders with their fellow man – Ascot was such a grand British occasion. Susy opened her race card and studied form for the three o'clock race and drew a blank. A horse was a horse, as far as she was concerned – four legs and a tail. It was overtly apparent that some sound advice was needed urgently. Larry appeared to be the kingpin, a veteran race goer no less and leaning over his shoulder, she listened intently to the expert advice he was giving Nicky. Her curiosity was distracted by Vanessa waving to somebody over the balcony.

'Down by the enclosure,' Vanessa pointed.

Susy's eyes searched the crowd, 'Who am I looking for?'

'Toby,' Vanessa waved again, 'See, over there with Polly.'

Toby was leading Polly by the hand into the enclosure and could not be distracted, disappearing quickly into the crowd. Jealousy, tinged with revenge overwhelmed Susy as she saw her passion vanish from view. Vengeful thoughts consumed her mind. She would not be dismissed, or considered second-rate and she would have her day.

The three o'clock race came and went with the same frenzied excitement. Larry scored again. 'What a great day I'm having, Ollie. This is something I'm going to remember for a very long time.' Peter stirred and was back on his feet again, refreshed after a quiet snooze and called for Ursula.

Larry tweaked Ursula on the cheek, 'I've been keeping her warm for you, boy,' and patted her on the bottom, 'now run along, honey, and be a good girl now.'

The final race of the afternoon, The Gold Cup, was about to commence. The line-up was impressive as the riders cantered their horses towards the start. Toby was back, having lost his stake in the previous race. 'Are we too late?' he asked. He was hurriedly followed by Polly, her smiling countenance betraying traces of ownership already. She slipped her arm through Toby's and caught Susy's eye, who dropped her glance down on to the race card once again, her angry thoughts almost obliterating Larry's booming voice, shouting for hasty decisions.

'Longboat, Willie Carson!' Vanessa said.

Susy valued her judgement. 'Me, too,' she added quickly.

The starter gun fired and they were away, all eyes on the course. Excitement was reaching fever pitch when the riders approached the final bend. 'Come on, Eastern Mystic,' Oliver yelled. Nicky turned his back on the racecourse as the screaming and pounding of feet became unbearable. 'I can't look,' he said, grasping Susy's hand. 'Tell me when it's all over.'

Vanessa bounced up and down on her heels and Larry cheered. Peter, now wide awake, gripped Ursula's shoulders. Longboat was way out in front and a surefire bet to come in first.

'Get up you fool!' Rachel shouted to Nicky over the noise, 'your horse is going to win.' But Nicky was immovable.

Longboat thundered passed the winning post five lengths ahead of Eastern Mystic and Spicy Story was third. Larry was in jocular mood and furiously rubbed his hands together. 'Wow! Now that ain't bad, friends, that ain't bad at all.'

What a stupendous climax to end a wonderful day. They laughed, patted one another on the back, shook hands and embraced. Susy was so happy just to be there and wallow in such extravagance, but her heart sank when she looked up to see Polly locked in a clinch with Toby. Sneaky, devious Polly had known all along of Susy's desire to win the handsome Toby and yet she still pursued and won, flaunting her conquest for all to see. Susy fumed as she watched their lips part, and a voracious anger possessed her very soul. She would take her revenge when the time was right.

Rachel helped Nicky off the floor and sat him carefully in a chair; the day had not been entirely lost. He mopped his brow and the colour returned to his cheeks, when Larry handed him his winnings. 'Jesus, Nicky, you got to see a doctor about that.'

The journey back to town was long with Larry falling asleep for the entire trip and Vanessa snuggled up to Oliver, who suddenly realised they were a passenger short.

'Where's Polly?' he asked. Susy gazed vacantly out of the car window. 'With Toby,' she said flatly.

'I might have guessed,' he replied knowingly.

Susy continued to gaze out of the window. 'What happened to Lucinda and Douglas?' Vanessa shuffled around in her seat. 'I would have thought it was obvious, they almost certainly had another fight.'

The limousine pulled up outside the apartment, depositing Vanessa and Susy at the door, leaving Oliver to transport Larry, who was still sound asleep, back to his hotel.

'I had a great day, Oliver,' Susy said quietly, not wishing to disturb.

'A pleasure,' he replied.

Vanessa prised herself away from Oliver's grasp. 'Goodnight my darling, until tomorrow.'

'Claridges, driver.'

Polly begged Susy to allow her time off to go to Wimbledon with Toby, but Susy refused point blank, saying that the shop needed her more. The unusually hot weather had brought a surge of demanding customers and they were hard-pressed to keep the rails of shorts and minis filled, as the re-orders were always late in arriving.

Susy would never admit that she was jealous of Polly's relationship with Toby, but deep down she hated her for snatching what she thought was a chance at love from under her feet. Polly looked and behaved like an angel, but underneath she was clever and calculating and Susy was not going to let her get away with it. During the first week of Wimbledon she delegated much of the paperwork to Polly, keeping her cooped up in the backroom and away from the action. The floor assistants were constantly busy with customers, while Susy stayed close to the telephone. Her plan to keep Polly fully occupied had worked well; unfortunately she did not account for Toby putting in a personal appearance and was surprised when she looked up to see him standing in front of her, his tousled dark blond hair falling over his brow. Her heart jumped into her mouth.

'Hi Susy, Polly about?'

Knowing full well that Polly was obscured by piles of invoices and dazed by his dancing brown eyes, she replied. 'Um, she's at lunch.'

Toby glanced at his watch – three o'clock. 'Are you sure?' he said, looking put out.

'She must be in the pub.' And looking vaguely around the shop, 'She's not here.'

He paused momentarily for thought. 'I don't have time to spare, Susy. Please tell her I called by. Sorry, how rude of me,' he said, clasping her hand, 'How are you?'

'Fine,' she managed to say with a smile.

'You're looking better every time I see you, truly, you're in great shape.' He passed an admiring glance as she walked him to the door.

Watching him hurry away from the shop, she noted with some satisfaction that for the first time he had paid her a compliment. Now, all she had to do was discredit Polly and he would be hers, but how? She would find a way.

Polly was furious at not being told of Toby's visit. 'It was busy and it just slipped my mind,' was not what she wanted to hear. As Wimbledon fever took a grip, Susy showed muted interest at Polly's excitement of centre court tickets for the men's final, Sunday the sixth of July, coupled with Vanessa's arrangements for the Henley Ball on the Saturday evening. In fact, Vanessa had insisted that Toby and Polly stop over at Hambledon for the night before going on to Wimbledon the following day. Susy felt shut out, excluded from the social whirlwind that accompanied the busiest month of the year. She, too, would have loved to go to the Henley Ball, or sit at centre court, but an invitation was not forthcoming, or even mentioned. She began to question the friendship and sincerity she had forged with the girls. Was she still the misfit, the East End girl who, by chance, just happened to be there, hanging on by her fingertips to the edge of their prestigious circle? Were they so full of their own importance that nothing else mattered? The privileged, mannerless upper crust needed to be shown a piece of the bread and butter society. Susy had taken far more than her fair share of knocks in her young life. Now was the time for the tables to turn, heads to turn. She would be noticed, fulfil her goals. She had been kicked in the backside for the last time.

Susy walked out of Lillywhites laden with a complete tennis ensemble, her first lesson was booked for Tuesday evening. Vanessa was so preoccupied on the telephone when she returned to the apartment that she did not even notice her struggle upstairs with her shopping bags. The French windows were wide open to allow the slightest breeze to enter, for the evening was blisteringly hot. Three hundred and fifty tennis fans had been treated for sunburn.

Every evening during the second week of Wimbledon Susy shut herself away in her room to watch the tennis highlights on television. Peter, her coach, had instructed her to watch and learn, 'You are seeing the best there is'.

During the day Polly's blooming relationship with Toby crept into every conversation. Another gold-plated dick sent from heaven above to puncture her maiden form. Susy felt that she had a personal insight into Toby's anatomy. Every mole, orifice and pubic hair was mentally tagged and recorded. Polly fell in love too easily and Susy, like a lioness, watched and waited.

The weekend of the fifth and sixth of July, Susy had the apartment entirely to herself. She stocked up with food and holed up in her room. Nobody, in her estimation, would disturb her, even Lucinda was away, trying to salvage what was left of her relationship with Douglas. She switched on the answerphone and settled down in front of the television.

Martina Navratilova slammed Hana Mandlikova to a 7–6 6–3

victory. What a player, Susy thought, chomping her way through a bag of nuts and raisins. The undisputed queen of tennis and Wimbledon champion yet again. Sunday morning she slept late, rose and prepared a brunch of scrambled eggs on wholemeal bread, fresh orange juice and black coffee, which she ate off a tray in her room. Then she settled down to watch the men's final between Ivan Lendl and Boris Becker.

The centre court was packed as the camera panned across the spectators. Susy crept closer to the television hoping to catch a glimpse of her friends, but the screen switched to the on-court appearance of Becker and Lendl. A scorching hot day, Becker was ahead right from the start, taking the first two sets, 6–4 6–3. Then Susy spotted Vanessa fanning herself to stay cool, but where were Polly and Toby? The screen changed again, as the third set was about to commence. Becker thrashed Lendl game after game, the ball flying so fast across the net that Susy wondered if Lendl saw it coming. The enthusiasm she felt for her newly-found sport was exhausting. The camera switched back to the spectators again and there they all were, how could she possibly have missed them? The final set was won by Becker 7–5, a gruelling match that Becker won in just two hours and four minutes. Later that same evening Vanessa remarked to an astounded Susy, 'you missed an incredible match. Pity you couldn't come.'

On Monday morning the paperboy handed Susy her usual copy of the *Sun* on her way into work. 'Give me the *Daily Mail* and *The Times*, darlin'.' she said, fumbling in her bag for change.

'Oh, la-di-dah, going all posh on me sweetheart?'

'That's enough of your cheek, just give me the papers.' She disappeared into the subway.

Susy had remembered seeing a library in the Charing Cross Road and, although late, she got off the tube at Leicester Square and walked towards Trafalgar Square. Just as she approached the library entrance, the doors opened for business. She stepped up to a bespectacled librarian standing behind a large desk. 'How do I join, I want to read some books?'

The librarian looked her up and down. 'Do you reside or work in Westminster?' came his reply.

Should that make a difference, she thought, telling him where she worked.

'Then it's quite easy. Please fill out this form and I will give you a library card.'

Susy filled out the form and handed it back to the librarian, who in turn gave her a card.

'Is that it?' she asked.

'That's it.'

'Will it cost me anythin'?'

'Only if you don't bring your books back on time.'

Before leaving the library, she quickly looked up and down the shelves, her eye catching a card pinned to the noticeboard: SPEECH THERAPIST and a telephone number. Recalling an earlier conversation with Vanessa, she took the card from the board and placed it in her bag, then hurried on her way into work.

Polly and Vanessa were so wrapped up in their own lives that anything going on around them that was not connected, was not happening. Susy was well aware of this and could very easily keep one eye on them and one eye on what she was doing. Her upbringing had taught her to be alert and ahead of the game; only once had this indoctrination let her down and that was something she was coming to terms with. Each day a little stronger, more confident, more in control.

Susy began to utilise her time well; every moment of the day was accounted for. The papers were read first thing in the morning and, although not fully understood, she hoped that eventually something would sink in. Crawfords ran smoothly under her direction, David and Estelle were delighted at the increase in turnover, even with the added expenditure of extra staff. Two tennis lessons a week with Peter, her coach, and Mrs Potter, the speech therapist, assured her that she would speak exactly like the Queen by Christmas, even though the task seemed daunting.

The Royal Wedding was less than two weeks away and the

media had reached saturation status, following the Duke of York and his bride-to-be Miss Sarah Ferguson everywhere they went. There was also great speculation on the wedding dress, designed by Linda Chiriak. How the nation loved a wedding, as London's hotels began to fill up with visitors from all over the world. Larry was returning, with his wife Ellen. 'You guys sure know how to put on a show. Me and the little lady ain't missing out on this one, Ollie. Oh no, that we ain't.'

Café society was humming and Oliver's party of four were no exception. After picking Vanessa and Polly up from the apartment, he drove around the corner to Beauchamp Place, where they were meeting Toby for dinner. While Oliver parked the car, an apologetic waiter greeted the girls.

'Mister Toby will be a little late, Madam.'

'Nothing changes,' Polly said dryly.

They declined drinks, preferring to sit quietly at a corner table and wait for Oliver to arrive.

'Ah, Mr Bryce Thomas,' said the bustling waiter as Oliver entered the restaurant bar. 'Your table is ready, sir ... or maybe a drink at the bar first?'

'Take the ladies through to the table, Carlo.' The waiter led the way. 'I will be with you in a minute.'

The girls were ushered through the crowded restaurant, with its soft lighting and abundance of tropical plants, to their table on the lower floor. As they walked, they discreetly glanced at each table for that familiar face in the crowd – a celebrity maybe, even a royal – when Polly became quite alarmed.

'Vanessa, can we change seats, please?' she was already sidling around to the other side of the table.

'What's the matter?' Vanessa said in a lowered voice and sat down, 'Is there somebody you don't want to see? An old lover?' she queried.

Polly was pale and hesitant, but Vanessa pressed for an answer. 'Tell me quickly. Oliver will be here any moment.'

'Right behind me, look, table of four.' Vanessa glanced over

Polly's shoulder at two men, a blonde and a dusky-looking girl.

Snarling under her breath, waiting for Polly's hesitant answer, she asked again.

'I know the two men at that table. What I mean to say is that I have met them before.' Vanessa was very curious. 'The younger goodlooking man is called Daniel.'

'He looks nice, Polly. Where did you meet him?'

'At a club. It was an evening when I was as mad as hell with Seb and –'

'And so you spent the night with Daniel and now you regret it?'

'No, Vanessa, nothing like that. Daniel, the younger goodlooking man chatted to me, he seemed very nice, interested in what I did, interested in me.'

'Did you go out with him?'

'Please wait. See the other older man?'

Vanessa took a second glance at the two men seated behind Polly and said in a whisper. 'Yes, he's older, fatter, rather unattractive, I would say. Where does he fit in?'

'His name is also Daniel and he was with the younger man that evening, and when I left the club I gave Daniel my telephone number.'

'The younger man, is that right?' Vanessa looked hard at the four people apparently enjoying their evening. Curiously the blonde looked familiar to her, where had she seen her before?

'A few days later I had a call from Daniel suggesting that we meet up, so I gave him my address.'

'So you did go out with him, Polly?'

'No, Vanessa, please let me finish.'

Vanessa caught sight of Oliver crossing the restaurant floor, but he was stopped by a friend who caught his arm. 'Make it quick, Polly.'

'That evening, the evening I had arranged for Daniel to meet me at my apartment,' Polly was beginning to tremble, 'I opened the door to the other Daniel.'

'The older one? Polly how could you make such a mistake?'

'I am telling you what happened, Vanessa. He got his foot inside the door and closed it behind him. I tried to cover my surprise and offered him a drink, but he wasn't interested.'

'So what happened next?'

'Look at those shoulders, Vanessa, that short neck. He's as strong as an ox and I was very afraid, but tried not to show it. He took a step towards me and glanced around the apartment, then asked me if I was alone.' Polly was reliving every frightening moment. 'I told him I shared with another couple.'

'Were they in?'

'No, but I didn't tell him that. I wanted him out of the apartment and quick, so I asked him if we were going out.'

Oliver was on his way to the table, but caught the eye of the attractive blonde sitting at the table behind Polly. 'Sandy, how lovely to see you,' he said.

Polly continued. 'He said he wasn't taking me anywhere, all he wanted to do was fuck me.'

'An animal!' Vanessa was appalled. 'So what you're telling me is the younger man baited the beautiful lady and the older one got the prize. You didn't sleep with him Polly?'

'Give me some credit, Vanessa. He stood there like a bear waiting to pounce. I couldn't move a muscle, I was terrified, and every second seemed like an hour, as he stared right through me. I asked him to leave, but he continued to stare at me. God only knows what he was thinking to do, until he took a piece of paper with my address and telephone number on, tore it into pieces and threw it over my head, then left. I don't know what made him change his mind, but I am very grateful that he did.'

Oliver arrived at the table with the blonde in tow. 'I would like you to meet an old friend of mine. Vanessa, Polly this is Sandy Lawson.'

Vanessa eyed the attractive girl; there was something very familiar about her. 'Have we met before?' she asked.

'You're Vanessa Baron.' she replied. Vanessa was surprised. 'A friend of Lucinda Cory.'

'That's right,' Vanessa said. 'Where have we met before?'

'I was a beautician. Lucinda was a customer of mine before I joined the *Queen Elizabeth II*.'

'Yes, I remember. Where are you working now, Sandy?'

'Sturgis, Estate Agents. Oliver wouldn't employ me when I applied for a job with his company. Not enough experience, he said, but I'm going to show him just how good I can be, wait and see!'

Toby joined the table with many excuses for his late arrival.

'This is one very ambitious lady,' Oliver said. 'Why don't you pull up a chair and have a drink with us?'

'Thank you, but I really can't.'

'Where's your man tonight, Sandy?' Toby asked, looking round at her table.

'He's busy and this is a business dinner tonight, Toby.'

'Um, who's the dusky lady?' he whispered in Sandy's ear.

'That's Yasmin, a very old friend of mine.'

Still keeping his voice down Toby said, 'Sandy, Sandy, I haven't had an Indian beauty before.'

'Better forget it, Toby. She's unattached, but very moody and definitely not an easy lay.'

Polly was tense, not once looking around at the other table, as Oliver and Toby sat down and Sandy rejoined her table just as coffee was being served.

'That's an effervescent young woman.' Vanessa asked Oliver, 'Have you ever taken her out?'

'Not yet,' he laughed.

As the evening progressed Polly felt happier, safe having Toby's strong arm around her shoulders and when Sandy came over to say goodbye, she heaved a huge sigh of relief as she watched the two men disappear out of the restaurant.

Vanessa spent a great deal of time away from the apartment, leaving Susy on her own. She was perfectly happy with the arrangement, which allowed her plenty of time to pursue her own interests. She continued with tennis lessons which she found easy, but speech therapy was a very different story. Mrs Potter despaired at the diction emanating from Susy's mouth – there was no miracle cure for a lifetime of slack larynx.

Wednesday twenty-third of July, the day of the Royal Wedding, when Susy sat in front of the television and watched the ceremony from start to finish. How lucky can a girl get? she wondered – the Prince and a commoner. Timing – being in the right place at the right time that was the answer. Her thoughts were interrupted by the telephone ringing.

'Susy, is that you, sweetheart?'

'Joyce, how are you, my darling?'

'Thought I'd give you a ring, pet.' Joyce's voice crackled down the line. 'Did you watch the wedding?'

'What about the dress, eh! Wasn't it fabulous?'

'Thought you might 'ave bin there, seeing as you mix with all those toffs now. 'Aven't you got time to come and see me?'

'I have been a bit busy.'

'I know, you've found yourself a bloke?'

'No, not yet.'

'You will, sweetheart, might take a bit of time though. You feeling any better?'

'Stop worrying, I'm doing all right.'

Joyce raised her voice. 'So when are you comin' to see me then, or do I 'ave to come and fetch you?'

'I'll be there, next week, maybe.'

'You'd better, else there'll be trouble.' There was a long pause. 'Thought I should tell you, pet, Eddy got married.'

'I'm not surprised. When?'

'I'll tell you when I see you. All right, next week and don't you forget now.'

They hung up.

Sir Richard and Lady Caroline were staying at the Savoy after attending the Royal Wedding and Vanessa and Oliver had arranged to meet them later that evening in the hotel. They arrived promptly at the prearranged time, to find Lady Caroline in great distress.

'What's wrong, mummy?' Vanessa asked, with much concern.

'Thank God you're here, Vanessa, it's your father, I had to call a doctor.'

Her heart sank. 'How sick is he? Can I see him?'

'Not right now, darling, the doctor's with him.'

'But is he going to be all right, mummy? Please tell me it's nothing serious.'

'Can I help in any way?' Oliver asked Caroline.

'We must wait and see what the doctor says, Oliver.'

Vanessa was distraught. She could not imagine a world without her father, he was invincible, immortal, this could not be happening. The door opened and the doctor approached them. He looked first at Vanessa, then Lady Caroline.

'This is my daughter, Vanessa,' she said, anxious for the prognosis.

'Your husband is resting now and there is nothing too alarming to report,' he said, with a reassuring smile.

'But the pains doctor. Did he have a heart attack?' The strain was beginning to show.

'Sir Richard has angina, it's controllable with the right medication and he can look forward to many more years ahead of him.'

Oliver placed a comforting arm around Vanessa's shoulder, as she wiped away a tear. 'Poor daddy. Can I see him?'

'I think he has had enough excitement for one day,' the doctor said. 'Better that you let him rest now.' Oliver saw the doctor to the door.

'Mummy, I'm coming home for a few days.'

'Yes, darling, your father will love to have you there.'

'I'll go home immediately and pack.'

Oliver interrupted, 'What's the rush, Vanessa? Tomorrow will be soon enough.'

Lady Caroline maintained a stoic composure, revealing nothing of what she felt inside. 'I will let Rupert and Piers know first thing in the morning, Vanessa. Now I need to rest, too. It's been a very long day.'

The following day Vanessa left for Hambledon, where she planned to stay until she was satisfied that her father was comfortable. Oliver remained in town, keeping in telephone contact daily.

The planned holiday to Sardinia that coming weekend was cancelled. Sir Richard's untimely illness had set back Oliver's plan to propose to Vanessa. The romantic setting of the Costa Smeralda would certainly have sealed their destiny. They would go in September, meanwhile Oliver made social arrangements for the following week when Vanessa was due back in town.

Tuesday evening Vanessa drove back to London alone – she was cheerful. Her father was recovering well and when she entered the flat, Susy greeted her warmly.

'Hello, stranger, I feel I haven't seen you in weeks.' Susy was still in her tennis whites, having just returned from a lesson.

'Ah, tennis lessons, I see you've taken my advice.'

'I've got a dab backhand Vanessa.'

She was shuffling through her pile of mail. 'Remind me to give you a game sometime.'

'How's dad?' Susy asked.

'Much better thank you. I must admit I was very concerned, but he's back to his old self again. Any telephone messages?'

'Lots, I've written them all down.'

Vanessa cast her eye down the list of callers. She had left in such a hurry that she had not told anybody where she was. Erik would be furious, she must call him immediately. Susy handed her a large vodka and tonic as she got through to him. He was not at all pleased. 'Erik, I had no choice … but … I think we should continue this conversation in the morning … no, I do not, goodnight.' Vanessa slammed down the receiver as Susy raised her glass of Evian in the air. 'Cheers.'

Was there no peace Vanessa thought, picking up the telephone again. 'Hello!' she fumed down the line. 'Oliver, darling it's you! I've just had a heated discussion with Erik ... Yes, quick call, what is it? No, I haven't forgotten our dinner tomorrow night with Sandy Lawson ... You have invited Polly and Toby? Oliver, do you think that's wise after what I told you ... who's Sandy bringing ... all right then, if you're sure, bye.'

Vanessa was in the office at the crack of dawn the following morning, long before Susy had opened her eyes – one aspect of her life she did not relish. Susy overslept and arrived late at the shop, which was in the middle of the summer sale, to find the first delivery of the autumn range being unloaded off the van. She dumped her bag in the kitchen and helped the girls break open the cartons, hanging the new garments in the stockroom. The task took most of the morning before they could finally sit down and take a break. Polly looked worn out, not just from the morning's work. She was burning the midnight oil, drinking too much and not getting the eight hours sleep her body craved. In fact, she looked terrible, a complete mess. They sat hunched over mugs of coffee in silence, until Susy had to comment.

'When did you last get a good night's sleep, Polly?'

Polly was resting her head on her hand. 'What I do is none of your business.'

'Well, excuse me. I'm telling you as a friend, you look bloody awful. Those bags weren't there a month ago.'

'Shut up, Susy, you're beginning to sound just like my mother.'

Susy was not deterred. 'You and Toby must be at it all night.'

'Are you jealous?'

Polly had hit a nerve. 'You cow, is that why you did it, just to get one over me, is that it?' Polly did not answer. 'You knew I fancied him, so what did you do, wave your fanny in the air?' Polly laughed at Susy's anger. 'You find it funny, do you?'

'Susy, you're not his type. You're unsophisticated and very boring.'

Susy was hailed from the shop floor, as a customer required her attention. 'I'll make you eat your words, my friend.'

Polly sipped her coffee, satisfied at the swipe she had dealt Susy for all the degradation she had endured over the past few weeks, happy to see her smoulder and spit out words of jealousy. Polly always got what she wanted and she was prepared to do anything to hold on to Toby for as long as she needed him.

Polly pulled the *Daily Mail* from under Susy's bag and placed it on the table in front of her. She gasped as her eyes fell on the full-length picture of a young woman taking up half the front page. She frantically read the accompanying article, turning back the page to look at the picture again. 'Missing estate agent Sandy Lawson. 'This can't be true,' she said to herself as she re-read the article. 'Missing since Monday 28th July, when she left her office at 12.40 p.m. for a terrace house...' She read on. Her car was found abandoned at ten o'clock one and a half miles away. Polly grabbed the newspaper and hurried to the telephone. Vanessa was in a meeting and could not be disturbed, her PA informed her, so Polly left an urgent message for her to return her call. Toby was not due back from Germany until midday, but she dialled his number just in case. There was no reply. Polly panicked. Oliver was certain to be at his office, but he had just left and was not expected back until four o'clock. Polly banged the receiver down, her anguished expression causing Susy to comment. 'What's going on?'

Polly pointed to the headlines. 'We were supposed to have dinner with her tonight.' Susy turned the newspaper around and quickly scanned the article. 'I'm telling you Susy, it's definitely the same girl.'

'Are you sure about this?'

'I'm absolutely sure.'

'She'll turn up Polly. People go AWOL all the time, you wait and see.'

Polly sighed. 'No, Susy, my gut reaction tells me different.'

Polly hovered around the telephone for hours until finally Vanessa returned her call. From across the shopfloor Susy listened intently, while Polly relayed the newspaper article word for word.

Equally alarmed, Vanessa promised to call Oliver immediately, to see if they could obtain any further information. The atmosphere was heavy when Polly answered the telephone to Toby and, not wishing to hear the identical conversation again, left her alone.

Vanessa's mind was racing. Oliver had appeared unperturbed at the news. Yes, he had read the article and believed that there was no cause for concern. She was a smart girl, he said, quite able to look after herself and would turn up safe and well. He sounded irritated by Vanessa and Polly's paranoia, which he believed was a typical female over-reaction.

Five o'clock and Vanessa was on her way out of the office. Passing Erik to say goodnight, she saw a copy of the daily newspaper protruding from the wastepaper bin, and stopped briefly to read the front page.

'Another beauty bites the dust, sweetie.' Erik's foregone conclusion only fuelled Vanessa's active imagination. 'Did you know her?'

'I met her, Erik, she was a friend of Oliver's.' Vanessa stopped and thought about what she had just said. There was no evidence to suggest that she was dead. 'She is a friend of Oliver's.'

'Yes, duckie, of course she is.' Erik watched her tuck the newspaper under her arm and walk out of the office. He knew her so well, knew how her mind worked. She had doubted Oliver before and his dismissive attitude was intolerable, she would have to talk to him, clear the air – she did not like what she was thinking again.

After Susy had finished her session with Mrs Potter, she picked up a pizza on the way home and climbing the stairs to the apartment, could hear raised voices coming from inside. She opened the door, slipped inside and ducked just as an ashtray came hurtling towards her, shattering against the wall. Vanessa and Oliver were in the midst of a terrible fight. She clutched the pizza to her chest, shielding her body from missiles as Vanessa continued to pound Oliver with whatever she could get her hands on.

'You are being totally unreasonable,' he shouted.

'Am I?' she screamed back at him.

'I have never lied to you, Vanessa. Now why won't you believe me when I tell you I had nothing to do with Sandy's disappearance?' Vanessa was unappeasable.

'Where were you on Monday afternoon?'

Oliver could not believe the interrogation he was getting. 'I was on my way back from Norfolk. Now I have already told you that.'

'I want to know where you were and who you were with,' she bellowed. Susy was slowly moving away from the fray, when Vanessa turned to her. 'And how do I know that you were not connected to Susy's rape. Now answer me that?'

Susy was reluctantly becoming involved. 'Now 'old on a minute Vanessa. Oliver had nothing to do with it and you know it. Why do you always think you are so right and everybody else is wrong, or worse, a liar?'

Oliver was on his way out. 'And if that's what you think of me, then I certainly don't want to have anything more to do with you.'

Susy turned to Vanessa as Oliver reached the door. 'Don't be an idiot! Don't let him go, apologise.'

'I regret the day I ever met you, Oliver, you've brought me nothing but misery.' The door slammed behind him.

'Vanessa, that's not true.' But her words fell on deaf ears and Oliver had gone.

Susy sat down next to her. Vanessa's complexion was pale and she was distraught. 'What are we going to do with you?' she said, handing Vanessa a tissue. 'You've really blown it this time.' She looked deep into Vanessa's blue eyes. 'Shoe's on the other foot now, aye darling?'

'What am I going to do, Susy?'

She sighed, 'Let him cool down first, then you've got to eat a lot of humble pie.'

'Is it too late, do you think?'

'You're asking me, how should I know, I'm just an unsophisticated commoner.'

'I would value your unbiased opinion, Susy. Was I being unreasonable?'

'Unreasonable! Too right, Vanessa! If you want him back you're the one who's got to change, not him. You're a selfish, pig-headed woman. How could you say all those terrible things?'

'Anger, fear of the unknown, I don't know. Was I so awfully wrong?'

'You were and as for accusing him of having something to do with that Lawson girl, you've got to be out of your bleeding mind.'

8

The city thronged with visitors during August, banishing many a city dweller to the confines of the English countryside, or the Continent, seeking fun, sun and relaxation. Oliver was no exception; he had packed his bags and left town within days of encountering Vanessa's wrath. He had rejected her, casting her aside as if she did not exist. Polly tried to smooth things over, but Oliver was adamant. 'It's over, finished,' he said, and declined to discuss the matter further. Vanessa felt wretched and ran to the only person who loved her unconditionally.

Sir Richard and Lady Caroline were surprised to see Vanessa arrive at the house unannounced. She rushed into the ever-open arms of her father, feeling warmth and security shroud her, and broke down. He listened to her story of rejection, felt every pang of remorse as she told how she had loved and lost Oliver through her own stupidity. Sir Richard sat back in his chair.

'My dear girl, recognising your error must surely mean that you are half way to rectifying it. Use that pretty head of yours to solve emotional problems as smartly as you close any business deal, but with compassion. You are indeed at fault and only you can right that wrong.'

Vanessa's workload at the agency was light and nobody would miss her for a few days. 'Put everything on hold,' she told Erik over the telephone, 'they will just have to wait.'

The country house was quiet; Rupert now lived permanently in town and Piers was in France for the whole of August. Vanessa welcomed the peaceful hum of the countryside at high summer. Riding up to the ridge many times and throwing herself into the long grass, she recalled the time she and Oliver rode across the fields together. She felt the warm sun caress her body, as she lay stretched out by the pool. She felt peace and harmony where she could relax and try to unlock the complexities of her troubled mind. Her mother held her tongue and kept her distance. For it was only when Caroline's insufferable friends arrived for tea and idle gossip that Vanessa felt threatened, knowing her version of events most probably bore little resemblance to the truth and Vanessa did not stay around long enough to verify them. There were many uninterrupted moments when she could stroll with her father in the grounds, listen to his words of wisdom. He was her rock, her sanity, 'Be sympathetic,' he would say, 'Listen to others' points of view.' Vanessa knew she was intolerant, she had everything money and privilege had to offer, but nobody to share her life with. No money in the world could give her the one thing she wanted above anything else, love. She had held it in the palm of her hand, that old-fashioned, stomach-churning, heady, delirious sickness called love, and lost. She listened to her inner voice telling her what a child she had been to have ever doubted Oliver. She had destroyed something beautiful and, no matter how long it would take, she would win him back.

Sir Richard's health was stable and had benefited enormously from Vanessa's presence. As she prepared to leave, Rupert arrived on an unscheduled visit on his way back to town. Caroline was delighted and met him at the door, ushering him into the house and, as they walked into the lounge, Sir Richard and Vanessa were summoned to follow. Rupert looked somewhat strained, but happy. Although he and Vanessa lived in town, their paths seldom crossed and she was pleased to see him. Nervously Rupert began to speak.

'I am glad I have caught you all together. This is not just a passing visit, I have something important to tell you.'

Lady Caroline reached out and took Rupert's hand. 'I sense this is unpleasant, darling?'

'No, mother,' he laughed, 'not at all.'

Sir Richard was getting impatient. 'Well spill the beans, my boy.'

'Over the past few months my life has taken a sharp turn and I have not been the easiest of people to deal with.'

'I second that,' Vanessa added.

'Please allow me to explain. My relationship with Helena is over – she married Alex a month ago.'

Vanessa was shocked. 'Your partner? Rupert, didn't you suspect?'

'No, not until it was too late.'

Sir Richard was saddened. 'Bad show, Rupert, damn bad show.'

'Well, as you can imagine, it has put me in a very awkward situation and I have taken a conscious decision, after much deliberation, to leave the partnership.'

Caroline, still clutching Rupert's hand said, 'Are you sure you have made the right decision?'

'Quiet sure, mother.'

'But what …'

'Mummy, please let Rupert finish.'

'I have always joked about going to America, and because I am forced to make changes in my life, now is the right time to go.'

Rupert had always been too conservative, he never took chances. This was just what he needed to heave himself out of the rut he had carved for himself. Vanessa could not hide her approval.

'Helena has done you a huge favour, Rupert. When are you going?'

'Next week.'

'So soon?' Caroline cried.

'I'm sure Rupert knows what he is doing, my dear. Now how long are you planning on being away?' Sir Richard and Rupert walked slowly towards the patio.

'Not sure, Pa. Six months, a year, maybe.'

'Just what I would have done. Yes, make a clean break of it, nasty underhanded business. Vanessa's right, you know, not without her own problems too, but you Barons are survivors, you'll both come out on top. Just pacify your mother, for heaven's sake and write from time to time. Keep her off my back. You'll do that, my boy?' Sir Richard patted his son on the shoulder.

'Of course, Pa, that's the very least I could do.'

That evening Rupert and Vanessa sat in the kitchen over a bottle of wine, laughing and planning the rest of their lives, as they had done so many times before.

'Life will be different a year from now,' he said.

'No, well maybe, two years certainly.'

'Let's drink to that, Vanessa.'

Susy threw the ball into the air and swung the weight of her entire body behind the racket, crashing a perfect service across the net to Peter. She was light and fast on her feet, keeping pace with his speedy returns. They had been playing for almost an hour and she barely felt the strain. Back came the ball as she turned, wrists firm and slammed a backhander over the net. Peter missed.

'OK, Susy, that's it … Whoa, you're getting good, great backhand.'

'So you keep telling me.'

'And modest with it. Where do you find the strength?'

'I'm lifting weights, light ones. Don't want to look like a fella.'

'You, Susy? No, you're much too attractive.'

She zipped up her holdall and turned to walk away. 'Same time next week, Peter?'

Peter watched her cross the court and shouted after her, 'Hey, Susy, how about a drink?' She glanced behind her and smiled. 'It was just an idea.'

'Yeah, why not?' she shouted back.

'Wine bar, half an hour?'

'You're on.' She picked up pace, breaking into a run. Slow down, she could hear herself saying, he'll think you fancy him.

As Susy entered the wine bar, she could see Peter perched on a stool at the end of the bar. He was ruggedly goodlooking, athletic, but thinning hair gave him the appearance of being older than his years. He flashed a broad grin and waved, when he noticed her pushing her way through the crowd to join him.

'What would you like to drink?' he asked.

'A glass of white wine please, dry.'

Peter jostled for bar service, leaving Susy sitting at a corner table. She looked around at the other customers as she settled into her seat. Businessmen in suits stood in groups, eyeing dolly girls wearing too much makeup and skirts around their waists, hoping for a quick lay before going home to their mundane routine little lives. Two lovers sucking up to one another in a far corner, feeding crisps and peanuts into each other's mouths. The serious drinker leaning heavily on the bar alone, as the waiter uncorked a second, or possibly third bottle of wine. Peter angled his way through the crowd, holding two glasses above shoulder level and handed Susy her glass.

Tongue-tied, she searched for something to say.

'It's too noisy here, let's move,' Peter said, taking the glasses and walking to the far corner of the wine bar where they sat down again. They stared at one another, neither one speaking and then they both spoke in unison. 'Go ahead,' Peter said, swinging back in his chair.

'No, after you.' Susy hesitated. She found her voice. 'Peter, I want you to tell me the truth. Did I put enough spin on that drop shot, 'cause it bounced a bit high over the net?'

'Susy, we're off court now, let's just relax and enjoy a drink.' How stupid she felt, forcing him to talk shop. 'Tell me about yourself. What do you do, or are you a dark lady?'

'What do you mean by that?'

'Well, how do you manage to live in Cadogan Place?'

'You're straight to the point. No messing about with you, I can tell.'

Peter laughed, 'Just curious.'

'It's not my flat, I just have a room there. My girl friend's got a bit of money.'

'Yeah! I've seen her. Where do you fit in?'

'We're not hookers, if that's what you're thinking. Vanessa's father is a lord.'

'That's nice, but you still haven't answered my question.'

'I come from the East End. Can't you tell?'

Peter looked hard at Susy. 'Looks could fool a lot of us, but I bet you're the nicer person.' Susy felt herself flush.

'And what about you, where do you come from?'

'Vancouver. I came for a two-week vacation last summer and, as you can see, I'm still here.'

Now Susy was curious. 'What made you stay?'

'I guess I must like it here. You British don't really realise what you've got here. England's steeped in history, you can reach out and touch it everywhere you go. You must have been to Stratford on Avon?' Susy had not. Peter raised his arms in dismay. 'How about Stonehenge?' Susy shook her head. 'OK, a little closer to home, the Tower of London?'

Susy shrunk back in her seat. 'Not since I was a kid.'

'What have you been doing all your life?'

She felt ashamed of her ignorance; the person she hoped to portray had just been shot down in flames. 'I've had it tough, Peter, and a lot of people do.'

'That's true.' He downed his glass of wine. 'So what are you doing about it?' He did not give her time to answer. 'Another drink?'

Peter returned to the table with a bottle of wine in his hand and filled their glasses almost to the brim. 'I've got all evening,' he said. The combination of the wine and Peter's laidback manner allowed Susy to open up and talk. She felt relaxed and able to tell him things about herself that she had never even discussed with a girlfriend. Peter was a good listener, teased her, sympathised with her and gave her the confidence she needed to speak up.

'I haven't stopped talking,' Susy said. 'What time is it?'

'Time we had something to eat. Are you hungry?'

'I'm starving.'

'I know a great little Italian place, five minutes from here, makes a mean fettuccini.'

The waiter lit a candle, the flickering light illuminating their faces with a warm glow. They settled down and ordered. Peter had been right, the fettuccini was delicious as Susy abandoned her diet and threw herself headlong into dessert. What a lovely spontaneous evening they had spent together, a simple meal, a bottle of wine and good company. Susy averted her eyes from Peter's burning gaze.

'You're very beautiful.' She was silent as he placed his hand over hers. 'That's a compliment.' Susy pulled away. 'There must be a man in your life?'

'There's nobody, Peter, and that's the truth.'

Peter doubted her words. 'Somebody way back, there must have been?'

'Nobody that mattered.' She looked him straight in the eye.

'Somebody hurt you bad?'

'Yeah, something like that.'

Peter pushed the hair away from her face, brushing his hand across the tiny scar on her forehead. 'You want to talk about it?'

Susy fell silent again. Did she want to resurrect the memory she was trying so hard to forget? She looked up into Peter's face, he nodded reassuringly. There was a long pause before she spoke.

'I was raped.' Peter held her hand tightly. 'I don't expect you to understand how that feels.'

'I'm trying.'

Susy was dry eyed, enough tears had already been spilt, the hurt was fading, but the anger lingered on. 'I have to believe that they will find that bastard before he kills, like he tried to kill me.'

'You don't have to say any more,' he said softly, but Susy wanted to talk.

Peter listened in silent disbelief and held a lot of respect for the attitude she had adapted to her situation. The determination to succeed in the face of adversity was admirable. He was entranced when Susy smiled back at him. 'Thanks for listening,' she said, 'you don't know how much that means to me.'

Susy put the phone down declining Vanessa's invitation to dine with the girls – she had better things to do. 'But we never see you,' Vanessa had replied. Susy had tolerated the lamentable Lucinda for far too long, finding sympathy with the long suffering Douglas, who was now co-habiting with his personal assistant. Polly, too, had become wearisome, closeted in her affair with Toby, shutting out any intrusion into her private life. Susy watched from the sidelines and noted the change in Polly's character. She was becoming distinctly unattractive and, what's more, she was pleased.

Peter and Susy left the cinema arm in arm. He was becoming a buddy and she valued his friendship and advice above all others, but she was not ready for a relationship and he had to be content to wait in the wings.

Arriving back at the apartment, the sisterhood was breaking up. Susy breezed passed them saying a brief 'hello' on her way upstairs. When she was sure that they had left, she slipped down to the kitchen, only to find Vanessa crashed out on the sofa.

'Still up?'

'What a pain Lucinda has become, she is so morose, almost suicidal.'

'So you had a good evening, then?'

'And to think I have agreed to go to Sicily with her next week. I must be crazy.'

'You can always change your mind.'

'I can't, she has already booked.'

Susy smiled to herself. 'Goodnight.'

Vanessa peered over the top of the sofa at Susy ascending the stairs. 'Where have you been tonight?'

'Out and about.'

Vanessa was suspicious. 'You've been out with a man. I can tell?'

'Maybe I have.'

'What's he like? Where did you meet him?' She waited for a response. 'Why are you being so secretive, Susy, this is terribly exciting.'

Susy turned to Vanessa, when she reached the top of the stairs. 'I'll tell you all about it tomorrow,' and opened the bedroom door.

'You're so infuriating! What is wrong with right now?'

'Tomorrow, Vanessa.'

Vanessa's voice rang up the stairs. 'Joyce telephoned, she said something about lunch.'

Susy had completely forgotten, she would telephone Joyce in the morning.

A planned afternoon off to coincide with Susy's visit was just what Joyce needed to brighten up her day. Several weeks had passed since they last met and there was a lot to catch up on. Susy looked forward to seeing Joyce again, but apprehensive on returning to the East End, for news travelled fast and she did not want to bump into Eddy.

On leaving the apartment, Susy switched on the answerphone and gathered together her library books to be returned on her way into work. On opening the door the telephone rang, which she ignored, until the machine intercepted the call and the voice of a man was on the other end of the line.

'Susan Stevens, this is Detective Superintendent Pearce, sorry to find you not at home, would you please–'

'I'm here, this is Susan Stevens, what's happened?'

'Ah, Miss Stevens, I've caught you.'

'I was just leaving, have you got something to tell me?'

'No, not as yet, but we think there could be a possible connection with another case and we would like to see you again.'

Susy felt her stomach churn. This would mean reliving that night again, but maybe if she could help, unlock some hidden thoughts. 'When do you want to see me?'

'As soon as possible.'

She replaced the receiver. Rescheduling her lunch with David and Estelle would take her less than half an hour, they would understand.

WPC Phillips sat with Susy's open file in front of her. 'I'm sorry to put you through all this again, but we do have to follow up every clue, every angle.'

'I've told you everything I know. Has there been another one?'

'I'm sure you read the newspapers?' Susy nodded. 'We are investigating the disappearance of Sandy Lawson and seeing that the crime against you occurred less than two miles from where Miss Lawson disappeared, there is a possibility that we could be dealing with the same man.'

'But you know I didn't see him. What more can I tell you?'

'We have very little to go on, I know, but we must sift through all the evidence again. You never can tell, something may stand out, something we've missed.'

Casting her mind back, turning each step of that evening into a slow-motion picture show, mentally tearing every scene to shreds in the hope of coming up with something new. An hour or more passed by, but the end result was unchanged. Susy was exhausted. 'That's it,' she said.

'Thank you. That can't have been easy.'

'It helps, you know, talking about it, frees the mind, makes room for other things.'

'You've done well in such a short space of time. How's work, are you keeping busy?'

'Life's getting better every day.'

'And how's that glamorous friend of yours? Quite a little spitfire, I remember.

'Vanessa? She's putty underneath, once you get to know her, that is. Shame about her and Oliver, I really liked him.' The police officer was curious. 'She's a silly girl, threw it all away, you know.' Susy paused for thought.' Um, I ... er.'

'Is anything wrong?'

'Um, I'm not sure.'

'Have you remembered something?'

'I don't know if it's important.' Susy recalled the venom she had witnessed being hurled at Oliver the night he walked out on Vanessa. The unfounded accusations she found it impossible to control in her rage. 'She was really out of order,' Susy stated. 'A right little vixen. She and Oliver had a fight over this girl that's missing.' WPC Phillips was anxious to hear the full story. 'No, nobody's going to tell me that he was mixed up in this, nobody.'

Impatient to learn the truth she persisted. 'Did Oliver know Miss Lawson?'

Susy hesitated. 'I think so … yes, he did.'

'Why are you protecting him, Susy?'

''Cause he's a decent fella. How do you say, honourable?'

'Not everybody is how you see them, but I hope you are right.'

After establishing a connection, she was ushered into Detective Superintendent Pearce's office. He sat expressionless behind his desk and resumed the interview where WPC Phillips had left off.

In the early afternoon Susy arrived at Crawfords, looking pale and drawn. 'Where have you been?' Polly asked, as she charged passed her on her way to the backroom.

'Don't start, I'm not in the mood.' Susy rummaged through shelves and boxes, turning everything over.

'What are you looking for?'

'A cigarette, I'm dying for a cigarette.'

'But you gave up.'

She found a buckled packet in her rescue box. 'Not yet, I haven't,' and lit up, inhaling deeply.

Polly took a step back from the offensive fumes. 'You still haven't told me what happened?'

'Fulham Police Station.' Susy took another deep drag on the cigarette. 'Polly, I want you to do something.' From her serious expression, she instinctively knew that what Susy had to say was of great significance. 'I want you to contact Detective Superintendent Pearce at Fulham nick and tell him exactly what you told me about the two jerks that picked you up that night. You know, the ones with the same name.'

Polly was confused. 'Why should I do that?'

''Cause it's important, that's why. Does there have to be another reason?'

Feeling very uneasy at Susy's compelling tone, she answered. 'What has that got to do with you?'

'Just think about it, if that's not too difficult, before some other girl gets it in the back.'

Polly backed off. 'I won't do it, Susy. I'm afraid they will know it was me.'

'How will they know that? Or maybe you are telling me a story?'

'It's the truth, Susy, but I don't want to get involved.'

'Just as I thought, but who'd be the first one to scream if you lived to tell the tale?'

Polly ignored Susy's words, returning to the shop floor to tidy the already neat rails, escaping any further condemnation. The incident was not mentioned again.

Joyce flung open the front door and welcomed Susy with open arms. 'How's my girl?' They hugged each other tight.

'Hey, look at you, all poshed up. Where did you get that outfit?'

'Get away with you, this old thing ... come over 'ere and let me take a good look at you.' She felt odd standing in Joyce's front room, the garish décor almost blinding her with the sun streaming through the window on to the orange and green carpet. 'Lovely darlin', you're as good as any of them.'

The kettle whistled in the kitchen and Joyce returned with a tray of tea and sandwiches. They settled down on the settee, which nestled snugly into the bay window, the sound of noisy passersby drawing Susy's attention out into the street. She was back and asked herself why. Joyce poured the tea, handing Susy a cup. 'Have I got some stories to tell you,' she chortled, 'I don't know where to start ... cigarette?'

'I just quit, Joyce.'

'Wish I could, pet.'

Joyce waffled on, hardly giving Susy time to absorb one story before she was on to the next. Tittle-tattling about people Susy had never even heard of, pushing her knee in jest, waving her finger in disapprobation, followed by raucous laughter and endless bouts of chesty coughing. Joyce lit another cigarette with the butt of the last.

'Tell me about Eddy,' Susy asked.

'Married 'er, didn't 'e? Norma Randle, the old bag. I know 'e's your dad, darlin', but we all know where 'is brain is. As for 'er, she's feathered 'er nest, all right, I'd say. Clothes, holidays, 'e's even put the 'ouse up for sale. Bet that was 'er idea, got big ideas that one, about as big as her fanny.'

'Does he ever ask about me, Joyce?'

Joyce thought about Susy's question before answering. 'No, darlin', not now 'e's got somebody else to look after 'im. 'E always was a selfish bastard, so don't you go worrying your pretty 'ead about things like that now, you're well out of it ... Another pot of tea, pet, or something a bit stronger?' Joyce piled the crockery on to the tray and headed towards the kitchen.

'A G and T wouldn't go amiss, Joyce.'

'That's my girl.'

Joyce placed the tinkling glasses on the coffee table and settled back into the settee. 'Go on then, tell me all about it and don't you miss anything out.' Joyce listened intently to Susy's chatter, from her success in business to her grasp of high living. 'Keep at it, sweetheart, you'll go far.' She imitated her mastery of tennis and spoke fondly of her chum, Peter. 'I'm watching you, sneaky, you're not telling Joycie the full story.' Susy laughed at her inquisitive approach, diverting the conversation away from herself and straight into the frolics of Polly and Vanessa. The mood changed, doubt and fear crept into her dialogue, with the events leading up to Vanessa's disastrous fight with Oliver. 'Now wait, let's get this straight. Oliver knew this girl Sandy and made a date with 'er just before she disappeared, exactly the same way 'e made arrangements with you?'

'It's different, Joyce, you don't know all the facts.'

'How's it different, you tell me that?' Susy searched for an answer. 'I'll tell you what the facts are, sweetheart, you was lucky, this poor cow is long gone.'

'She could turn up, Joyce.'

'No darlin', let's look at it simply. A man doesn't pull a girl for a mate, especially if she's a looker and this girl's a looker. 'E'd nip in there 'imself.'

'But if the ugly one can't pull?'

'I've never known a man who can't pick up somethin', darlin', unless he's sexually retarded, believe me. It's more likely to be a woman. A jealous woman might set 'er up for fun, or gain.'

'She'd have to be one evil bitch, Joyce?'

'Sweetheart, you don't know what goes on out there. I know a few who wouldn't give it a second thought.'

'So you think it was a set up?'

Joyce moved closer to Susy. 'Listen darlin', she gets in 'er car, drives to an appointment, meets the man, then drives away, nothin' unusual, but maybe they'd arranged a little rendezvous.'

'What – her and this man?'

'Could be, or somebody else … and when they found 'er car, she and the keys had gone. It wasn't robbery, cause 'er bag was still there, so was she forced out of the car, eh? One mile, pet, from where they dumped you, remember. I 'ope you're listening to me.' Joyce lit up another cigarette and sat back into the settee again, an expression of profound concentration passed over her face.

'How do you know all this?' Susy asked.

'What else is there to do in that newsagents, but read the bloody papers.' Joyce drained her glass, placing it back on to the coffee table. 'You mark my words, somebody used and abused that little lady. Maybe they didn't mean to kill 'er, but if it was just sex they wanted, why didn't they go and pay for it? There's plenty of girls would do it, no matter what the old bugger looked like. No, there's more to it than that.'

'So somebody invented a fancy plan to lure the girl away for a kill, just for pleasure. Is that what you're saying?'

'You're getting the idea, pet.'

'And then they walk away unnoticed. Don't they have a name for that, Joyce? What the hell do they call them?'

'Serial killers, darlin'. They enjoy it like I like my fags and a tipple, then they get on with their lives, until the next time.'

What a prophetic conception. 'You're beginning to frighten me, Joyce. What kind of animals are these men?'

'Inadequate I'd say, or just plain evil.'

Silent inescapable recollections came flooding back into Susy's mind. Joyce had not intended to scare or distress her in any way, she only wanted to hammer home her thoughts and fears. Her ashen expression brought the conversation to an abrupt halt. This was to have been a happy afternoon, how insensitive had she been. Joyce placed both arms firmly around Susy's shoulders and pulled her close.

'My only worry is you, sweetheart. Take no notice of this old bag goin' off the deep end, you're the only one that matters and you're safe and well.' Joyce's trembling hand wiped away a tear from Susy's cheek.

'You should have had kids, Joyce, someone to love and look after.'

'I thought you knew, pet.' There was an element of surprise in her voice. 'But it was before you were born.'

'So there was one?'

'Yes, there was one, a little girl, she'd be about twenty-nine now, blonde curly hair.' A smile crept over Joyce's face. 'A right little tearaway.'

'I never knew, I swear. Nobody ever told me.'

The emotional pain had been immense, the loss incalculable, a catastrophe hidden, suppressed for more than 25 years. 'She ran out into the street, darlin', I couldn't catch 'er, then bang, a car hit her.' Joyce stifled a tear. 'My perfect little girl just lay there, there wasn't a mark on 'er, but I knew as I held 'er in my arms that she was gone, before the ambulance came.'

'Sorry,' Susy said very softly. 'I am so sorry, now I understand everything.'

'What's done is done. Now look at the pair of us gettin' all sentimental.'

Life was not always how it was perceived, the distorted expression giving way to a moment of tenderness. Joyce had overcome her grief, smothered her feelings and got on with living. The subject was taboo. 'Keep it quiet,' Susy could hear them all saying, taking for granted the strength needed to conquer such a tragedy. 'She'll have another,' but she did not. Fate had dealt her a cruel backhander and Susy had been gossiping for longer than she intended.

'I've got to go,' she said, squeezing Joyce's hand. 'We'll see each other again very soon, I promise.'

'Don't you forget to phone me, darlin'.' They made their way towards the front door. 'You've got no excuse now,' she said firmly, opening the door. 'I want weekly reports, do you 'ear, especially 'bout that Peter fella and what's more.'

'Yes, mum,' Susy said, turning to confront Joyce on the front porch, striking her dumb. 'It is all right if I call you that, Joycie?' and kissed her on the cheek, not waiting for a reply.

Just prior to her departure for Sicily, events of a sinister nature had been brought to Vanessa's notice. Oliver had been interrogated again and Toby had related the whole sorry story of his displeasure and concern. She was livid, blaming Susy for implicating him again and told her so in no uncertain terms. The atmosphere was frosty, vitriolic and Susy was pleased to see the back of her.

Having the apartment completely to herself, Susy meticulously planned the following seven days. A small dinner party, her first, was arranged, where she hoped her culinary expertise would catapult her to new heights in Toby's eyes. Polly, thinking that Peter had his feet well and truly under the table eagerly accepted. Susy mapped out her itinerary, faultlessly matching the correct wine to accompany each course, with the best crockery and crystal already lined up and sparkling in the kitchen. Satisfied that she had not forgotten anything, she set about preening herself. Flipping open Vanessa's address book, she noted the telephone number of her hairdresser and beautician and on Saturday morning, while leaving Polly in charge of the shop, she moved swiftly into gear. Everything in the kitchen was under control, the table, already laid, looked immaculate, before she closed the apartment door and made her way to the salon.

The next few hours were spent being deliciously pampered, every muscle responding to the nimble fingers of the masseuse, leaving her totally relaxed. Andre convinced her that her hair was too red, a darker, less fiery colour would be far more flattering. She consented, leaving the final decision to his good judgement. When finally she left the salon and walked along the Brompton Road, heads turned. Her dark chestnut hair shone like a mirror in contrast to her pale porcelain complexion. She looked and felt like a million dollars.

Peter was the first to arrive and blew a soft whistle as his eyes wandered up and down Susy's body. 'Wow!' he exclaimed.

She smiled. 'Well, are you just going to stand there gawking, or are you coming in?'

Peter walked gingerly through the door. 'Is this the same Susy I play ball with?'

She was already on her way into the kitchen. 'The one and the same,' she said, taking a bottle from the refrigerator. 'Champagne?'

'Sure, what's happened, something's different?' he noted.

She was pleased the transformation had been well received. The doorbell rang. 'Can you get that?'

She quickly glanced at herself in the mirror before Polly and Toby entered the apartment, leaving Peter to open the champagne. Polly was anxious to meet him and hardly noticed Susy's appearance as she walked through the door, with Toby prancing up the stairs behind her. He planted a kiss on Susy's cheek, then stood back to admire.

'Say, you're looking good.'

Feeling proud, serene and in control, she introduced her friends, then disappeared into the kitchen to organise the first course. Polly clearly approved of Peter, bubbling over with enthusiastic chatter, almost to the exclusion of Toby, who found himself wandering into the kitchen to talk to Susy. He crept up behind her as she placed the final touch to the starter, slipping his arm around her waist, making her jump. She reacted quickly with a thump to his chest, before realising her mistake, then laughed nervously, waving a fork at him.

'Don't do that again,' she said threatening, 'you might regret it.'

Toby raised both hands in defence. 'I surrender. Just feed this poor, starving knight and I shall be off.'

'Too right you will, now out of my kitchen.'

Toby stole a stuffed mushroom, popping it into his mouth, and made a fast exit back to the lounge.

Nothing was left to chance, every minute detail had been thoughtfully appraised and carried out, with Peter unwittingly playing host impeccably, flattering Polly greatly and indulging her fancy constantly. Toby was in splendid form, too, telling ghastly jokes that everybody felt obliged to laugh at, while through the flickering candlelight, he shared more than a moment of adulation with Susy. She had captured his mind and for the moment was content to let things take their course. Polly was an unspeakable flirt, playing up to Peter, knowing in her mind that he was accounted for, and she disappeared frequently to the bathroom to fix her makeup. Toby appeared unconcerned, disinterested, as he played footsie with Susy under the table, as yet an untried, untested piece of flesh. Peter watched with guarded interest, not wishing to disrupt an otherwise pleasurable evening. Coffee was served and as Polly fell back into her seat, Susy knew that she had achieved her goal. Polly was drunk and not a pretty sight; she was sober and the time had come to say goodnight.

After Polly and Toby had left, Susy kicked off her shoes, poured a large brandy for herself and Peter, then squatted on the floor at his feet.

'I've had such a lovely evening, Peter, thanks for coming. You're a real pal.' He sipped his brandy in silence. 'So, what did you think of my friends? Were they how you expected?'

Peter contemplated the question. 'They're fun, but not quite what I expected. How long have you known Polly?'

Susy felt mellow. 'Um, 'bout a year. She certainly knows how to have a good time, doesn't she?'

'Yep, that's for sure. Did you know she's a junkie?'

Susy was appalled at the suggestion. 'You must be mistaken, Polly a junkie,' she laughed, 'don't give me that.'

But Peter was very serious. 'I'm telling you, she's into something.'

Still fearful she continued, 'And I suppose you're going to tell me Toby is, too?'

Peter tried to relay some understanding. 'Susy, I've seen too many not to recognise them. Look at the eyes, watch those mood swings. Did you notice how many times they both left the table?'

'But Polly's always in the loo.'

'I just hope she knows what she's doing, she's a nice kid and pretty, too.'

It never crossed Susy's mind that Polly could be into drugs. Those dark, shadowy eyes, the aggressive behaviour. Was that why she was looking so worn out? 'What should I do, Peter? Should I let on I know?'

'You could tell her you suspect, but don't expect her to own up. She'll deny it, that's for sure.'

She did not really want to know the truth. 'And what about Toby?'

'They probably get high together and he'll be able to keep it up all night.' That's not what Susy wanted to hear and she could not hide her feelings. 'You got the hots for this guy?' Peter turned her face towards him. 'He's not for you, so better forget him.'

A defiant look answered Peter's question. Undeterred, brainwashed by Toby's unquestionable charm, Susy was more determined than ever to succeed.

* * *

Bleached blonde and bronzed, Vanessa banged her suitcase down and slammed the door behind her, disturbing Susy from her novel. 'Did you have a good time?' she asked.

'No!' she shouted, 'That crackpot should be certified.'

'Oh yeah.' Susy carried on reading, while Vanessa continued to rave on.

'What should have been a glorious seven days in the sun, turned into a nightmare and I can honestly say I'm pleased to be back. Trying to get that lump of flesh to move was an effort in itself. She didn't want to do anything, or go anywhere, except check up on that bearded louse, Douglas.' Vanessa stood over Susy, who put her book down. 'She criticised me for eating what I wanted, when I wanted, who I spoke to and what I said. I thought I would have to ask her permission to fart.'

'You should have gone off on your own.'

'Susy, I would have paid somebody to take her off my hands, but there were no offers, even the dwarf waiter was not interested.'

Susy returned to her book. 'So you won't be doing that again?'

'No, I certainly will not.' Vanessa shuffled through her mail. 'Have I missed anything this week?'

Susy knew exactly what Vanessa was referring to, but a little surprised considering her acrimonious departure. Oliver had not made contact. 'No, nothing,' she replied.

Vanessa looked back at Susy and grinned, 'And how's Peter, still around?'

She nodded, pulling her feet back along the sofa as Vanessa sat down beside her. 'Susy, I've been thinking. How would you and Polly like to run your own business?' She had Susy's undivided attention.

'What have you got in mind?'

'Your own boutique, but something rather special.'

She was curious. 'And where do you come in?'

'You're smart and have a good eye for style. I'll put up 50 per cent, you and Polly 25 per cent each.'

Susy was quick to respond. 'No deal.'

'Why not, Susy? It's a chance in a million. Are you going to be a saleswoman all your life? I can afford to expand my interests and I think you have the ability to make things work and, who knows, in ten years time, there could be a whole chain across the country.'

'I'll think about it.'

'Good, but make it snappy, before I change my mind.'

'Have you mentioned this to Polly?' Susy asked. Vanessa shook her head. 'Well, don't.'

'All right, this is between you and me.'

That night Susy did not sleep a wink, tossing and turning Vanessa's proposal over in her mind. How could she tell Vanessa that she would not embark on any business deal with Polly, and where would she find that kind of money, with almost no collateral? The following morning she arrived at the shop in a complete daze and had the telephone thrust in her direction. Polly interrupted her thoughts. 'He's really nice, Susy.'

'Who?' she replied

'Who?' Polly laughed, 'Peter. Toby got along with him so well, maybe you both.'

'Later, Polly, later.' She brushed passed her and took the telephone – another delay on a delivery.

That day and every day for the next week, Susy took a lunch hour, and wandered around the market window-shopping, pre-occupied with her own thoughts and ideas. Almost a year had passed since she first set foot in Covent Garden, and so much had happened that she felt she had always worked there. She stopped for a coffee at a café under the covered market and fought off the desire for a cigarette. Vanessa was talking big money. She did nothing by half. The problem was, how much? Susy knew she could do the job and well, but who could she tap for at least twenty grand?

Peter was on a two-week break home to see the folks, giving Susy ample opportunity to corner Vanessa. Friday night she arrived home fleetingly before taking off again for Hambledon.

'Vanessa, sit down, we've got to talk.'
'Can you make it quick, I'm so terribly late.'
'I've been giving this idea of yours a lot of thought.'
'And what have you decided?'
'I want to know more. Sell it to me.'
'Let me see, what can I tell you. A small exclusive boutique to start with.'
'Where?'
'Somewhere central.'
'You're talking a lot of money. You need storage space as well as floor space, can't be all ritzy fixtures and fittings. Keep it simple, so people can see what they're getting, good presentation sells.'

Vanessa stopped for one moment and looked Susy straight in the eye. 'And you want *me* to sell this idea to *you*?'

'OK then, what are we looking at – forty or fifty grand?'
'We would have to work the figures out.'
Susy was getting impatient. 'About?'
'Huh! Something along those lines.'
'That's what I thought.'
Vanessa was heading for the door. 'Anything else before I go?'
'No, that's all for now,' she replied.

Sunday afternoon, Susy had planned to visit Joyce. Bob was out for the entire day and they both had time on their hands. Joyce revelled in Susy's shadow, living every moment of her life with her. The idea for the boutique was contemplated and digested, with ideas and doubts, especially where Polly was concerned. Joyce had heard enough.

'Sweetheart, if you know she's doin' drugs, you don't 'ave anythin' to do with 'er, especially where business is concerned. I don't need to tell you where the money would disappear to, do I? Forget about Polly and concentrate on Vanessa – she's got the right connections and she's got the money. Is she a good business woman darlin'?'

'She's very successful, Joyce.'

'Can you trust 'er, 'cause she's not one of us?'

'Where business is concerned, I trust her. She's only interested in making money; she's not going to do a runner.'

'As long as she's not making one over you, darlin',' Joyce watched Susy intently. 'You'd 'ave to tie it up nice an' legit, protect your interests, keep it sweet.'

'The only way.'

Joyce hesitated for several minutes, then banged both her hands on the table. 'You've got the money, pet.'

Susy thought she had not heard right. 'Say that again,' she asked.

'I said, you've got the money. Twenty big ones, is that right?'

Astounded by the generous offer she was curious to know how Joyce had come by such a large sum of money.

'You don't ask, darlin'. Now listen, I put up the money, then you 'ave no bank charges and you pay me back soon as you can. This is between you and me, all right. In two years I get my money back and you get yourself a business. Do we have a deal?' Joyce held out her hand and beamed.

'It's a deal.'

Susy was impatient for Vanessa to return home on Sunday evening, but for no apparent reason she had decided to stop over another night at Hambledon, returning to London on Monday morning. The tension mounted and Susy paced the lounge floor in anticipation of her arrival that evening. She had thought of nothing else, mentally locating the premises, approved the décor, chosen the collection and banked her first million, and where was she? Looking out of the apartment window, she watched Vanessa park the car and, laden with bags, struggle across the street. Susy rushed into the kitchen, where a cigarette lay smouldering in an ashtray on the window ledge. She picked it up, inhaled deeply, then threw the butt out of the window, just as Vanessa kicked open the apartment door. 'Can you help me?' she cried. Susy was there in an instant, picking up the briefcase she had dropped, clutching it to her body, and watching her dump her bags on the floor.

'How was the weekend? Did you have a good time?' The enthusiastic enquiry aroused Vanessa's suspicious mind. 'And how was your father, well, I hope?'

'Everyone is very well, especially my father,' she replied, curious as to the sudden, but genuine concern. 'And you?'

'Interesting, very interesting.'

'Are you going to keep me in suspense, or do I have to guess?'

'I went back home to see Joyce, we had such a lot to talk about and she–'

'Susy, you can put the briefcase down.'

She could not contain the words any longer. 'Vanessa, I got the money, twenty big ones.'

Vanessa's eyes lit up. 'For the boutique?' Susy nodded. 'You are serious. Why didn't you call me as soon as you knew?'

'Because I wanted to see your face when I told you.'

'This is marvellous news, we'll start looking straight away. Tomorrow first thing, I'll make a few calls, get the ball rolling.'

Susy was ecstatic. 'I'm going to give this everything I've got. I really, really want this to work.'

'Then we will succeed; but be prepared for a lot of hard work.'

The following few weeks were fraught with setbacks and disappointments. Finding the ideal premises was not as easy as they had anticipated. Also keeping the whole operation under wraps until completion was proving difficult; Polly was suspicious.

Gill had given birth to a healthy, beautiful baby boy. Those last few weeks lying in a hospital bed were soon forgotten when she cradled her pride and joy in her arms. She called him Charlie and wasted no time in showing him off to her friends. Everybody at Crawfords, staff and customers alike, stopped what they were doing when she walked through the door, with Charlie strapped to her bosom. She was radiant and full of colourful chatter about the birth of her son, as if she were the only woman to have ever produced a child. Charlie had cemented the marriage and she had everything she ever wanted.

Susy waited for an opportunity to divulge her plans to Gill, sound her out, take full advantage of her many years in the business, but as soon as they were on their own, Gill focused her attention on Polly. 'What's that silly cow into?' she whispered.

'Is it that noticeable?' Susy remarked, glancing back at Polly serving a customer.

'I've never seen such a change in a person. Has she got a man around?' Susy nodded. 'Doesn't he notice? Why doesn't somebody tell her, you tell her?' Charlie was beginning to get restless.

Susy kept her voice lowered. 'She doesn't listen to anybody – you know how terrified she is of being on her own. She'll do anything to please her man.'

'Yeah, I suppose you're right. She's a big girl now and who are we to interfere?' she prepared to leave.

'Do you have to go? There's so much I want to talk about.'

'Yes darlin', but I'll stop by next week when we can have a good old chinwag.' They walked to the front of the shop, passing Polly on the way. 'What she needs is a hard slap – she's dead from the neck up.'

At the beginning of December Susy found the perfect location, just off the Brompton Road. Vanessa immediately put the wheels into motion and, if everything went according to plan, they would open in February. With Christmas less than a month away, Vanessa invited Susy to spend the holiday at Hambledon, which she eagerly accepted.

On Christmas Eve Susy stepped inside the house at Hambledon, placed her case beside her and looked in awe at the grand oak-panelled hall. There was a warm ambience, a strong feeling of stability and security emanating from the walls – this was a real home. 'I'll show you to your room,' Vanessa said, leading the way up the staircase to a guest bedroom on the second floor. As she climbed, Susy gazed at the paintings hanging majestically against the oak panels, touched the drapes, peeped over the landing to the cavernous hall which she had just left to Vanessa, who was holding open the bedroom door. 'Don't be long,' she said, 'dinner is in an hour.'

Susy descended the stairs, following the sounds of voices coming from the drawing room. She cautiously pushed open the door and entered to find Vanessa talking to her parents by the fireside. Sir Richard immediately rose to greet her with a warm handshake. 'So, you are Susy?' he said with a smile. 'It's a pleasure, my dear.'

'My pleasure, I'm sure,' Susy said, looking up into his kind face.

'And this is my wife, Caroline.' Susy stepped forward and offered her hand. The likeness was remarkable, a carbon copy. There was no doubt at all that this was Vanessa's mother.

'A glass of sherry, Susy?' Sir Richard motioned, bottle in hand.

Vanessa gestured for Susy to sit down, as Sir Richard handed her the glass of sherry. The quiet, comfortable drawing room, with a beautifully decorated Christmas tree twinkling in the corner, and a log fire crackling and sparkling cinders up the chimney, were a far cry from Christmases past. Susy sipped the sherry, feeling the warm nectar slide down the back of her throat.

Sir Richard broke the silence. 'Vanessa tells me you both have a little business venture on the go?'

'It's very exciting and is going to be a real challenge.'

'That it is. Vanessa has a good head on her shoulders. She takes after me in business and she will advise you well.'

'I've no doubt she will, sir.'

Vanessa interrupted, 'Susy has an exceptional eye for fashion, daddy. This is a partnership.'

'Dear dear, I hope you didn't misunderstand me, Susy?'

She laughed, hoping she was sounding proper. 'No, not at all.'

As usual, Lady Caroline sat back and observed, consuming every minute detail with relish. Susy felt intimidated by her silent stare, feeling her eyes piercing her mind as she spoke, stripping her down to the essentials.

'Any news of Rupert, mummy?'

'He's still in California, darling, having a grand time, by all accounts. I did so want him here for Christmas with all the family.'

Sir Richard intervened. 'It was just what he needed to get away, Caroline, what with all that ghastly business going on. He'll be back when he's good and ready. Anyway, Piers will be here tomorrow.'

'But it's hardly the same, Richard dear. We always spend Christmas together.'

Susy joined in the conversation. 'I think he'll love you a lot more when he gets back, then he really will appreciate a good home.'

'Do you really think so, Susy? I never looked at it that way.'

'You mark my words,' she added, 'he will never leave you again.'

Vanessa watched with great interest. How clever of Susy to find the right button to push and how loud those bells were ringing. Lady Caroline's face lit up. 'Tell me, Susy, or is it Susan? I don't think I can get used to calling you Susy.'

'Well, actually it's Susannah, but I never use it.'

'What a marvellous overture, "Susannah".' Vanessa was suitably impressed and judging by her mother's agreeable expression, so was she. 'Then I will call you Susannah.'

Dinner was served and they all followed Caroline into the oak room.

'Susannah,' Vanessa whispered as they were seated, 'you certainly scored yourself a Brownie point there. I had better keep a close eye on you.'

After an ample and very congenial dinner, the girls curled up in front of the fire, quietly gazing into the smouldering embers, intoxicated by the flickering light and alone in their thoughts. Susy angled her head to look into Vanessa's serene face, so still, so distant that she felt to speak would be an intrusion. Sensing her gaze, Vanessa turned and smiled, resting her head against the back of the armchair.

'Do you miss him?' Susy asked. Taking a sip of brandy, she did not reply. The emotional waters ran long and deep, and Oliver was constantly in her thoughts. '... If I ever added to your pain.'

'I miss him with all my heart, nothing seems quite the same without him. What happened wasn't anybody's fault, I just didn't handle the situation very well.'

'If it's meant to be, you'll find each other again – I really believe that.'

'I want to believe that too, Susy.'

A sense of melancholy veiled the conversation, what was needed was a sharp infusion of optimism. 'Just look at us a year ago,' Susy began. 'We wouldn't have thought twice about destroying each other, but today we are friends, partners even. Fate has a funny way of turning things around.' Vanessa was still downcast. 'Hey, remember when I knocked you flying at Polly's party? I didn't see your gammy leg and you got so angry.' Vanessa sniggered at her stupid behaviour. 'That's better, you know you've got quite a nice face when you smile.'

'I feel such an emotional mess, Susy. That was the night I met Oliver, too,' she cried.

Susy was not prepared to slip back into obscurity. 'So there you go, it's all in the stars. Things could be a lot worse; now pull yourself together and take a good look at me!'

On Christmas morning the house was buzzing with activity. Carols played, fires roared in every room and wonderful, delicious smells floated out of the kitchen, filling the air with unforeseen gastronomic pleasure. Rupert telephoned from Los Angeles, much to his mother's delight and Piers arrived noisily, with a buxom wench on his arm. 'Hi!' he said, raising his eyebrows at Susy as she descended the stairs and followed the crowd into the drawing room. Vanessa was handing out boxes of gaily-wrapped presents from beneath the Christmas tree, carefully selected gifts from London's choicest stores. Susy sat and watched; she was not forgotten, as box after box came her way. Mountains of paper and ribbon littered the floor, even Banjo had a gift, burying his nose under piles of empty boxes and barking at the frivolity. This was a happy home, filled with love and good will, a family united, not at war. Susy glanced around at Sir Richard's jolly face, his portly tummy jumping up and down as he laughed. Lady Caroline's hand slipped around her son's neck as she kissed him on the cheek, thanking him for the exquisite gift and Vanessa, how fortunate she was to have found such a friend. Vanessa watched Susy carefully when she took the small box in her hand and turned the card over. She looked up, 'For me?' she said. Vanessa smiled. She pulled the ribbon free and lifted the lid. Inside was a small suede pouch and a card. Susy turned the card around to read.

> Christmas 1986
> This key will open up the door
> to prosperity and what's more,
> if success is what you're after
> and I trust that we are partners,
> then I offer you my loyalty,
> after all, what are friends for?
> Vanessa.

Inside the pouch was a gold key to their first boutique. Susy stood up and hugged her friend. 'No matter what happens, I will treasure this gift for the rest of my life.'

Susy never wanted Christmas to end. They ate, drank, made merry, wore silly hats and played endless games. She donned warm woollies and wellingtons and trudged through the countryside, breathing in clean, fresh air. She shared jokes with the barman at the Stag and Huntsman and mucked out in the stables, much to Vanessa's distaste. Susy felt part of the family and looked back lovingly as they waved goodbye, turning the car out of the drive and back to the city.

9

There was no doubt in Susy's mind as to exactly what was required to kick-start their business venture into action. Apart from the odd hiccup, they were on course to open in the third week of February with a spring collection. She could not hide her enthusiasm from Peter, who promised on oath not to breathe a word to anyone until completion, and there was many an evening when they would stop and grab a pizza on the way home, chewing over ideas and Susy's aspirations to fame and fortune.

Vanessa arrived back from a week's holiday looking radiant. Apart from superb skiing in Gstaad, the *après-ski* had afforded her several nights of pelvic thrusting. At least for the moment her emotions were stable, as she swung right back into gear and took over at the helm.

Life was frantic and a pre-planned buying trip to Italy for the new shop was imminent. Vanessa, sensitive to the precarious position that Susy was putting herself into, covered for her whilst she was away. They were working well together, but there was only one thing they argued about and that was what to call the shop. Hours of deliberation were sunk into coming up with something simple.

'Why not call it Barons?' Vanessa said, to Susy's utter amazement. 'Sounds good and it's easy to remember.'

Susy cursed Vanessa's singlemindedness. 'Aren't you forgetting something, partner? We share the same common interest here and if Stevens isn't good enough for you, then neither is Barons!' And so the debate continued, right up to a week before the opening. With the signwriter awaiting his instructions, brush in hand, they finally agreed on 'The Coterie.' Short, simple and significant.

Polly greeted the news with a touch of envy. She had been so immersed in her own affairs that she had not noticed exactly what was going on and could not quite understand why they had not included her in their venture. However, she and Toby would attend the opening party, which was planned for the following Wednesday evening.

The invitations were in the post and replies were coming in fast. The only problem was Joyce, who flatly refused to show up. 'It's your party, darlin', nobody wants to see an old bag like me there,' she told Susy over the telephone. Outraged, Susy jumped in the car and raced across town, just in time to catch Joyce locking up the corner shop. She turned around with surprise. ''Ello my lovely, what are you doin' over 'ere?'

She bundled Joyce into the passenger seat and pulled away from the corner. 'I want words with you, Joyce Stevens. Suspicious of her petulant mood, she could tell that Susy was going to give her grief and was stopped before saying a word. 'Now you listen to me! I've worked my backside off getting this shop together.'

'Well.'

'Don't interrupt me. Day and night Vanessa and I have been making sure that everything is perfect.' Susy passed a quick glance at Joyce's sober expression. 'And it is perfect.'

'I'm very pleased to 'ear that, darlin'.'

'Only there's one thing missing. Opening night – you're going to be there.'

'I've told you pet a dozen times: no, and that's final.'

Susy screeched to a halt. 'OK, first thing in the morning I'll get on the blower and cancel the whole bloody lot. The advertising, the musicians, the guest list, the caterers and Vanessa won't be too happy, either.'

'You can't do that?'

'Oh yes I can, and I will.' Joyce pulled her jacket tighter around her bosom and huffed. 'Without you none of this would have been possible and I want so much for you to be there. Just for me, if nobody else.'

The boutique was light and airy, a simple uncluttered design to draw the eye into the shop, beckoning the customer through the door, where every rail could be seen at a glance and easy chairs were positioned for the weary shopper. Minimum fuss and maximum comfort and the interior decorators had completed on time.

The trio struck a chord as the first guests began to pour through the door. A clique of beautiful people arrogantly played to the camera, with each guest jostling for exposure, everyone expecting to see their face adorning the gossip columns tomorrow morning. Susy angled her way through the throng, searching for somebody she knew and wondered how her partner knew so many glamorous people.

'Where have you been?' Vanessa asked sharply. 'I can't handle all these people on my own.'

Dismissing any inadequacies she may have acquired on her way in, Vanessa threw Susy in at the deep end and left her to play hostess while she disappeared into the crowd. Peter hovered around at the entrance alone, catching Susy's eye, who prised her presence away from a guest and joined him. Plucking two fluted glasses of champagne from a silver salver, they found a quiet corner and toasted the triumphant success and prosperity of the new venture. As expected, Polly and Toby arrived late, propelling Susy into full flight.

'Now, just hold on a minute,' Peter insisted. 'Why not wait until they find you.'

The new fashion entrepreneurs mingled with the crowd, 'congratulations' being showered at every turn. Gill arrived with her husband. 'Wouldn't have missed this for the world,' she said. Erik and Yanni arrived, much to Susy's surprise and Lucinda also put in a brief appearance. But where was Joyce?

Confronted with Polly and Toby not far behind, Susy stood tall and proud and devoured every word of praise heaped upon her extraordinary achievement. 'It's stunning,' Polly said timidly, with more than just a hint of jealousy.

Toby pressed a kiss on Susy's cheek, almost knocking her over. 'Brilliant, utterly brilliant.' Polly's eyes momentarily dropped to the floor. 'I would not have believed and I don't mean this unkindly,' Toby sounded sincere, 'that you were capable of putting this together.'

A feat accomplished and acknowledgement of success, a virtuoso, Susy almost leapt into the air. 'Thank you,' she said demurely.

Throwing a pretentious smile back at Susy, Polly tugged at Toby's sleeve, almost pulling him off balance, 'Let's go,' she said quietly, turning away.

'Not yet, surely, it's far too early,' he protested, glancing back over his shoulder.

Susy stood perfectly still and held her breath. 'See you shortly,' he said, with a wink. Yes please, she said, under her breath.

A passing salver appeared before her and not looking down, she lifted a glass and watched Polly lead Toby out of the shop.

'Would there be anything else, madam?' the waitress said.

'Uh, no, thank you.'

'Very good then.'

Susy followed the voice. 'Wait! Hey, you! Stop! Turn around.' The lady with the salver about-turned. 'Joyce, what the hell are you doing?'

'You wanted me 'ere, pet, so 'ere I am.'

'Yes, but not like this. Look at you. How long have you been here?'

' 'Bout an hour, darlin'.'

'You're impossible. What am I going to do with you?' Susy marched her to the back of the shop.

'You were 'aving such a nice time with all those lovely people, I didn't want to spoil it for you and with you looking so pretty. Huh! If only your mum could see you now, darlin', she'd be so proud.'

Susy held on to Joyce very tightly, 'I thank God for you every day. You're the salt of this earth and I love you dearly for everything you've ever done for me, but I'm not standing for this.' They were disturbed by Vanessa's light tap on the open door.

'Somebody I would like you to meet, Susy.'

Joyce straightened Susy's crumpled dress and stood back. 'Go on, sweetheart, you show 'em what you're made of.' Susy stopped briefly and looked back at Joyce, in her starched hat and pinny, 'Go on, will you, and don't you ever look back, do you 'ear?'

The publicity drew much attention during those early days, bringing a steady stream of customers through the door. The Coterie was rapidly becoming *the* place to shop and Susy bowed to every request, indulged every eccentricity. She ran a slick, professional team, a tight ship, keeping costs to a minimum with Vanessa breathing hard down her neck.

Determined to beat him at his own game, Susy slammed an ace shot over the net at Peter, who was finding the strain increasingly difficult as the adrenaline ran high.

'Bravo!' the voice carried across the court. 'Nice shot.' They both stopped in their tracks and watched two figures walk towards them into the sunlight.

'Anybody you know?' Peter asked, shading his eyes from the blinding light as the two men drew closer.

'It's Toby and Oliver,' she said. 'I wonder what they are doing here.'

'I see she's giving you the runaround,' Toby remarked in jest, keeping his eyes firmly on Susy's strong, lissom physique.

'Yeah, she's pretty good now.'

Susy had not seen Oliver in months and greeted him warmly. 'I trust you are well?' he asked.

Curious to know if this was just a passing encounter or a deliberate diversion, Susy jumped at Toby's casual invitation to join them for a drink. Peter was not enthusiastic, being all steamed up and readily declined. 'We'll be there,' she hastily replied, refusing to pass up on such an opportunity, even if she had to go alone, and scowled at Peter.

They pushed a channel through the crowd to the bar and Oliver, always the gentleman, helped Susy into her seat. Scarcely having time to open his mouth to speak, when she bombarded him with a flurry of words and a continuous flow of rhetoric that rendered him dumb.

'So much has happened in the last few months that I don't know where to begin. Do you know how many properties we looked at? Well let me tell you – eighteen.' Oliver looked astounded. 'And the trouble I had with the builder.' In a short space of time, sagacity and an understanding of business had replaced the naivety that Oliver remembered. He was impressed and enchanted with the transformation. 'And where were you on the opening night?'

'I was out of town, Susy, otherwise I would have been delighted to be there.'

She held her breath, contemplating her next sentence. Oliver appeared receptive and at ease and she hoped that he would not take offence, as she found the confidence to speak out. 'She really misses you, Oliver. Vanessa didn't mean to say all those awful things, you've got to believe me.'

'I find it very difficult, Susy, to believe anything Vanessa's fanciful mind can conjure up.'

'But I'm telling you she's changed, I swear.'

Oliver did not wish to continue along those lines. 'That remains to be seen,' and quickly dismissed any further interrogation.

'You're looking positively radiant tonight. Life must be treating you very well. Tell me about Peter.'

Susy hesitated to reply when Toby placed the glasses on the table and sat down next to her, placing his arm around her shoulder and pulling her closer towards him.

'How's it going, Susy? Made a fortune yet?' She smiled back at him, revelling in the attention. 'Any time you want to invest some of that money, just let me know and I promise to double it, almost overnight.'

'Guaranteed?' she enthused.

'Cross my heart.'

Peter eyed Toby with caution. He did not like him any better than the last time they met. Slippery, was how he perceived him; here today and gone tomorrow, and he could not comprehend the fascination and esteem that Susy so rigorously held for him.

'How's Polly?' Peter asked sternly, breaking the spell.

Toby uneasily removed his arm from around Susy's shoulder. 'She's just fine. Looks as if she may have landed a new job.'

This was a surprise. Polly had not mentioned a change of occupation. 'Doing what?' Susy asked with interest.

'Organising fashion shows, or something like that. You'll have to ask her.'

She would, and was interested to know why Polly had not told her of any impending move from Crawfords. How odd, she thought, and hoped that she could put the change down to forgetfulness.

Oliver downed his beer and stood up. A previous appointment was waiting and he was sorry that he could not have stayed longer. Susy sadly watched him disappear out of the pub. 'He's such a lovely man, ' she said, 'I hope he finds Vanessa again.'

Toby laughed. 'Don't stop for breath, Susy. She's not the only pussy out there just waiting to be fleeced.' Peter flinched at the disrespect.

'I guess you know all about that, eh Toby?'

Still laughing, Toby continued, 'Don't tell me you don't know how it is, Peter? What man can resist a pretty face? Just look at Susy here and think what a fortunate man you are.'

Peter raised his voice in anger. 'And what am I supposed to make of that remark?'

'Well, you don't exactly come gift-wrapped, do you?'

Peter resented the remark and grabbed at Toby's throat, lifting him clean out of his seat and knocked the chair from under him.

'That's enough!' Susy yelled, pulling at Peter's arm, before he let go of Toby's collar.

'You be grateful there's a lady here, smartass! Else I might just be tempted to thrash you senseless!'

Without delay Susy bundled Peter out of the pub, leaving Toby pale and dishevelled. 'How could you do that, Peter?'

'How! The guy was insulting, you heard him.'

'The trouble with you is you take life too seriously,' she shouted. 'That's just his way of making fun.'

'Fun, oh yeah, he's funny all right. What the hell do you see in him?' Peter was over-heated and totally irrational in Susy's eyes. She was having none of his bloody-mindedness. She threw her bag over her shoulder, turned on her heel and stormed off in the direction of home.

Monday evening after an exhausting day, Susy arrived home to find Vanessa in and about to sit down to eat. She took an apple from the fruit basket and flopped down on the sofa, sinking her teeth into the firm flesh. 'Did Mrs Levine come back for the suit?' Vanessa shouted from the kitchen, showing an interest in her partner's day. 'She did, and what's more she bought the apricot silk dress and jacket and two pairs of shoes.' Vanessa appeared from the kitchen with a lightly sautéed escalope of veal and green salad on a tray and sat down at the dining table. 'How much did she spend?' she asked, before placing a forkful into her mouth. 'Fourteen hundred and fifty pounds.'

Susy watched the meticulous dissection of the escalope from her comfortable position on the sofa and asked casually if she also had a good day. 'Too many meetings,' was more or less the same reply to the usual question. A polite interchange of concern, which conveyed that all was well and running smoothly.

'Have you spoken to Polly recently?' Susy asked.

Vanessa looked up from her plate. Polly was the last person she had on her mind and felt guilty at her oversight, having not lifted the telephone in over two weeks. Throwing the apple core into the bin, Susy got up off the sofa and sat down opposite Vanessa at the dining table. Without looking up, Vanessa sensed that there was something in the air. 'What have you got to tell me?'

Without hesitation she related the snippet of gossip that Polly might be on the move, but with an enquiring glance Vanessa wondered how she had come by such information. The words tumbled from Susy's mouth, relating the chance meeting with Oliver and Toby at the weekend and what subsequently transpired over a drink at the local. Vanessa put down her knife and fork.

'He looked so handsome, Vanessa,' she waffled on, 'and he said how he would love to see you again. Let bygones by bygones, you know, and that maybe you could phone him?'

'I think you're telling me a story, Susy?'

'Honest, I'm telling you. He's such a catch and I know he still cares for you.'

They faced one another. 'How do you know? Did he tell you that? Or should I really make a fool out of myself by telephoning.' Vanessa was not convinced. 'If Oliver wants to speak to me, then why doesn't he pick up the phone and call me?'

'You are an obstinate cow, Vanessa. What have you got to lose if you still love each other? Somebody's got to give in.'

Vanessa raised her voice. 'I'm not calling him, Susy. Is that understood?'

Infuriated at her stubbornness, she conceded, 'And to think I told him you'd changed.'

Susy telephoned Crawfords and spoke to Polly, who took great pleasure in telling her that after two interviews she had been shortlisted, with one other, the final interview being scheduled for Friday. The job sounded demanding, paid extremely well, with the opportunity to work in Paris and New York. She was terribly excited and, if successful, would arrange for them all to dine out on her at Lorenzo's to celebrate. Susy genuinely wished her well.

The May bank holiday was approaching and Vanessa planned an open-house weekend at Hambledon – everyone was invited. The order of the day was informal – bring a swimming costume and rackets, if need be. Sir Richard enjoyed these weekends immensely. There was normally a sprinkling of pretty girls guaranteed to put a spring in his step. Not to mention the hot flushes Caroline seemed to be plagued with, when sitting around at poolside.

Erik and Yanni were the first to arrive, en route to their country cottage in Oxfordshire. They were met by Caroline at the door, who was only too delighted to conduct them around the house before any other guests arrived. Rarely had she listened to such exuberance over what she could only describe as quite normal décor, losing count of how many 'Oo's' and 'How divine's' she heard, before stepping out on to the forecourt, just as Vanessa rode up and dismounted.

'Good morning,' she said, peeling off her gloves and unstrapping her riding hat. 'I didn't expect you so early.'

'We've just had the grand tour,' Erik enthralled.

'And it's magnificent,' Yanni added.

'Then I hope you'll stay for lunch?'

'Well, we hadn't planned.'

'Nonsense, I insist, Erik.' Vanessa ushered them both back into the house. 'Now let me fix you a drink.'

Whilst she changed into something more suitable, Erik and Yanni sat quietly on the patio, nursing their drinks, but the peace and solitude was soon broken by laughing voices carrying across the lawn. Piers had arrived with a group of noisy young friends. 'Huh, my word, Erik,' Yanni muttered, watching the crowd cavorting towards the pool, 'we're staying the night!'

The sun was warm, although the wind was cool, but that did not deter the young people from stripping off and diving headlong into the pool. Sir Richard was alerted to the commotion from the study and made his way outside to greet them.

A buffet lunch was prepared and was being set out on large, white, linen-draped tables in the conservatory. Feeling refreshed, Vanessa bypassed all the activity and rejoined Erik and Yanni on the patio.

'How can you tear yourself away from all this, darling?'

'I sometimes ask myself the same question.'

'If it's ever put on the market,' Yanni enquired quite seriously, 'we want first refusal.'

Erik was incensed at his friend's absurd remark. 'Stupid boy, how could we ever afford it?'

'The estate has been in the family for generations, Yanni, and daddy would never ever consider selling it.'

Yanni was not to be deterred. 'But darling, things could change.'

'Don't take any notice of him, sweetie,' Erik butted in. 'Since he took that design course, he's got far too big for his knickers.'

'Cooey,' Caroline called out and waved, as she made her way towards the conservatory, 'Lunch.'

'What an extraordinary woman your mother is, Vanessa,' Erik remarked, walking across the lawn.

'Extraordinary?' Vanessa laughed, 'What makes you say that, Erik?'

'Her capacity for names and faces is quite remarkable.'

'Don't tell me, you've met somewhere before?'

'It appears she met my father some thirty years ago at a Masonic dinner.'

With profound regret Vanessa apologised for her mother's intrusion. 'I thought she would at least have left you alone.'

'Do you mean she's lying?'

'Not exactly. You see she will have obtained some scant information about you and what she is doing now is getting you to confirm it.'

Erik was flabbergasted, 'Well, excuse me, duckie, what a sneaky bitch!'

'I'm afraid you're right. The idle pastime of the rich and very bored.'

Susy shut the door of the boutique sharp at 5.30. Peter threw her holdall and rackets into the boot of the Golf, then they streaked off westward, down the M40 to Hambledon.

Pulling up outside the house, Susy was quick to notice Toby's silver Porsche parked among the many cars that lined the drive. Marie opened the door and directed them through the house to the conservatory, where Sir Richard was snoozing in a chair.

Pleasurable snorts and snuffles greeted them and not wishing to disturb, they tiptoed passed him and out into the garden.

The plop-plop of a ball being knocked across the net could be clearly heard, when they rounded the corner of the house to find Vanessa and Toby thrashing a game out on court. Peter stood behind Vanessa and caught the ball that she so foolishly missed.

'I could help you with that drop shot,' he said, bouncing the ball back to her. She had not noticed their arrival in her quest to beat her opponent and acknowledged them with relief and gratitude.

'How long have you been there?' she asked, catching her breath.

The game was surely over, when Toby picked up his sweater and walked past them, without so much as a 'hello'. Susy studied the figure as he continued to walk away. Could it be that he had arrived alone? 'Where's Polly?' she asked, not taking her eyes from Toby's back as he vanished into the house. Peter was demonstrating a different technique to aid Vanessa's faltering game of tennis. They did not hear, prompting Susy to asked again.

'Pool house,' Vanessa replied.

Entering the pool house, Polly caught sight of Susy in the reflection of the mirror. She appeared subdued, unwilling to talk, all wrapped up in a towelling robe, a wet bathing costume lying on the bench seat.

'Have you been here long?' Susy asked, over the drone of the dryer.

Polly switched the hair dryer off and ruffled her hair. 'About two hours.'

Leaning back against the wall, Susy tilted her head to one side and watched Polly apply mascara with an assertive upward movement. 'Are you staying the night?' she asked.

Polly threw the mascara into her makeup bag. 'Maybe,' she replied and applied a coat of lipstick.

From her cool disposition it was obvious that some form of contretemps had occurred. Polly silently unwrapped the bathrobe and stood naked in front of the mirror. She slipped on her pants and reached for her shirt, but not before Susy had noticed a large red mark at the top of her thigh.

Susy drew attention to the bruise. 'How did you do that?'

'Do what?' Polly said with surprise, professing not to have seen the mark before.

'You must have gone down with a wallop?'

Polly confirmed Susy's foregone conclusion, 'I slipped on the bathroom tiles and now he'll give me hell, accuse me of sleeping with somebody else.'

This seemed like a perfectly reasonable explanation, she thought. A bruise the size of a fried egg was surely not acquired during the act of copulation. Polly zipped up her jeans and stepped into her loafers.

'Don't look so worried, Susy. I can handle it.'

Together they left the pool house and walked back to the tennis court, where they found Sir Richard, who had just woken up from his nap. 'Must have dozed off. Is Piers still here? Where is everybody?'

'He's in the house, daddy, but I think some of his awful friends have gone,' Vanessa hailed from the tennis court, rounding off her game with Peter and joining her father at the conservatory door.

'What a pity I missed them,' he said disgruntled. 'I was rather enjoying their company.'

Taking his arm she led him into the drawing room. 'How about a large scotch on the rocks?' she asked.

'That seems like a very good idea,' he chuckled.

Nothing short of an earthquake could detach Caroline from her ladies bridge evening which, once a month, she religiously attended. Her friends and counterparts dispensed with social gatherings, such as open-house weekends, to indulge in a more intellectual form of entertainment, plus a small wager or two. Subsequently, Sir Richard could look forward to an uninterrupted evening with the younger set. He joined Toby in the lounge.

'So how's the world of high finance?' he asked.

'I'm doing very well, sir.'

'That's good. Can't be too careful who you're dealing with today, what with all the fraud cases coming to light. Just look at this Guinness scandal. Greed was their downfall, Toby, they didn't know when to stop. Let that be a lesson to you, for it could finish you off in the city.'

'I am fully aware of the pitfalls, Sir Richard and I intend keeping my nose clean.'

'That you must, otherwise you could end up with nothing. You bright young people have every opportunity to make good under this government. Grasp every opportunity as it comes your way and use it to your best advantage.'

'I have every intention of doing so, sir.'

Sir Richard gave an approving grunt. 'Are we on our own this evening?'

'No, but they all went down to the mill and should be back very soon.' He glanced out of the window, dusk was falling. 'Tell me, sir, what do you think will happen to Waite? Why did he go back to Beirut?'

A controversial question, Sir Richard was pleased that Toby appeared interested in the state of the world. 'Oh, some ludicrous notion that maybe he can solve the crises in the Middle East and get them all to sit down and talk. Bah! It's a festering pot of religious fanatics and Margaret is right not to make a deal with the kidnappers.'

'I think the lady has balls?'

A turn of phrase he wholeheartedly agreed with. 'She does, and what's more, they will hold him until they get exactly what they want, if they don't shoot the poor man first.'

'Do you ever see the situation being solved in the long term?'

Sir Richard considered the question. 'It's a dangerous world we are witnessing, my boy, and I only hope that it is not too late before there is blood shed, but I very much doubt it.'

Sounds of laughter filtered through the house and into the lounge. 'I thought I would find you both here,' Vanessa said, entering the room, followed closely by Polly and Susy.

Sir Richard rose to his feet. 'What happened to those two homosexuals?' he enquired.

'They have gone, daddy, and "gay" sounds so much nicer.'

'We used to call them nancy boys, my dear, but it's all the same, nonetheless.' Peter, hands in pocket, sauntered in behind them. 'Come in and take a seat. I haven't had a chance to talk to you yet.'

'I sure am impressed by your countryside,' Peter said. 'My family would be knocked out by its charm.'

'My family has lived in this house for generations, Peter, and the village is mentioned in the Domesday Book, 1086, drawn up by William the Conqueror.'

'A slice of history.'

'If you're really interested, tomorrow I can take you through the history of the parish.'

'Thank you. I would like that very much.'

Toby never missed an opportunity to insult. 'That's when your lot were living in wigwams, Peter.'

Sir Richard was quick to intervene. 'The Canadians have a fine history, Toby. There is a vast wealth of knowledge and opportunity between its vast shores and it helped liberate us during the war.'

'My father was there,' Peter added. 'Royal Canadian Army, Dieppe, August 1942 and he was lucky to get out with his life.'

'Ah! Poor devils,' Sir Richard sighed. 'They took a terrible hammering. The Nazis almost annihilated them.'

There was a momentary hush, then Peter broke the silence. 'But he survived and after the war moved to Vancouver, married, set up a flourishing salmon-tinning company and had four children.'

'That's the spirit I like to hear, my boy. And where do you come in line?'

'I have an elder brother and two sisters, but at twenty-eight, I'm still the kid brother.'

'A friendly rivalry, no doubt?'

'You got it.'

'So how do you occupy your time in Vancouver?' Toby asked, not wishing to be left out of the conversation.

'We favour an outdoor life. Being on the Pacific coast and with many inland lakes, there are all kinds of watersports, river rafting, fishing, of course. Try landing a thirty-pound salmon, Toby, it's real exciting!'

'Do you ride much?' Sir Richard interrupted.

'Whenever I can, sir, and we're not too far from ski country. The lifestyle is very attractive.'

Peter painted a vivid picture of fresh air and clean living. 'And what brought you here?' Sir Richard was curious. 'Can't have been the climate.'

'I love travelling, but I have stayed a little longer than I intended.'

'Do you hunt?' Toby asked, feeling certain that with so many diverse activities, Peter could not fail to be involved somehow in hunting. There had to be another side to the squeaky-clean-cut tennis coach.

'I can't say that I entirely agree with hunting, Toby.'

'Oh come on, Peter! It's well known that thousands of seals are clubbed to death every year and–'

'There is a cull, I agree,' Peter cut in, 'but the hunters are prohibited as to how many they can shoot and, let's get this straight, *shoot*, not *club* and on no account kill the pups. What you see here is media propaganda. But in England you have fox hunting, for sport?'

Sir Richard mumbled from his armchair. 'The British have always been keen hunters, fox hunting being just one of many inherited pastimes. Toby hunts, I believe, don't you, my boy?'

'I have been known to go out on a meet, but it's permissible, fair game.'

Peter protested loudly. 'As I understand it, you tear this creature apart as a prize, then throw the body to the hounds.'

'That is the tradition,' Toby replied coolly.

Peter was agitated. 'Then what about deer and pheasant hunting? Where do you draw the line?'

'OK, Peter, I think we take your point, although there are thousands that don't.'

Susy triumphantly moved the chequers across the Tavoli board. 'Six and a three, gotcha!' much to Vanessa's annoyance, marking up another victory for her partner. Polly tottered over to the refrigerator to replenish her empty glass of wine, saying, 'What do you think of Pier's new girlfriend? She's very quiet.'

'That's how he likes them, Polly, mute,' Vanessa replied, setting up the Tavoli board again. Polly returned to her chair and sitting down very hard spilled the full glass on to the floor.

'Oh, I wish I could hold my booze, girls. Am I being a real bore?' Neither one answered. The foregone conclusion required no comment. Polly stood up and, walking straight and tall, crossed the room towards the door. 'I think I'll have an an early night, my darlings,' closing the door quietly behind her.

They both agreed that Polly was looking better than she had in months and the new job would be good for her morale. Susy cupped the dice in her hands, shook them vigorously and watched them rattle across the board. Visions of weekend trips to Paris or New York and the opening of their second boutique crossed their minds and entered the conversation. Susy's turn to throw the dice, wagering a pair of sixes to make their dreams become a reality. They both peered down into the Tavoli board to see a five and seven come to rest.

'Never mind,' Vanessa said, 'we can't plan our future on the fall of the dice.' A foolish notion, indeed. A complacent attitude brought on by a game of chance was not the formula for a successful business, when Susy begged to differ.

'Six plus six is twelve, right?' Vanessa nodded. 'And five and seven is twelve, so we won.'

'Susy, that's cheating.'

'Yep, but it's the end result that matters, Vanessa.'

Peter was a night owl. Five hours' sleep was more than adequate and while the house slumbered, he prepared to settle down with a book that Sir Richard had loaned him from his extensive collection. At 1.30 a.m., he had to visit the bathroom, so placing the book on the bedside table, he donned his robe and slipped quietly out of the bedroom. He tiptoed along the landing, down three creaky steps to the bathroom overlooking the rose garden. As he stood in the dark, urinating into the basin, he tried to keep the flow to the side, suppressing the noisy torrent of water hitting the porcelain. He looked out across the fields to the silent, rolling hills, the hush of night, blanketed by a cobalt blue sky, giving way to a host of twinkling stars that decorated the heavens. He flushed the water closet, the swirling, gurgling action thundering through the pipes and into oblivion, hoping that he had not woken anyone. He stepped out on to the landing again, on his way back to his room, when raised voices caused him to stop and listen. The muffled sound of a woman's voice emanating from one of the bedrooms was quickly silenced as he crept across the floor. Not a sound could be heard, while he continued to walk the long landing, when the same muffled voice reached his ears, followed by a thud. Peter stopped and turned towards the offending door, only to hear Polly's faint laughter echo through the night. The thrill of a chase and the whoop of success as Toby scored a touch down. Peter smiled to himself on reaching the solitude of his bedroom; at least somebody was getting their oats tonight.

Susy got up at the crack of dawn, put on a tracksuit, plugged in her walkman and went out for a jog. The fresh morning air was invigorating as she set out along the track towards the village, with just the birds and Wolfgang Amadeus Mozart for company. Keeping at a steady pace she reached St Mary the Virgin as a few early-morning worshippers were entering the church for 8 a.m. Holy Communion. The village was otherwise still and she continued to pace along the road towards the mill. One day, she thought, while stopping to survey the beautiful green valley, I will buy a cottage here, in God's countryside, where peace and harmony rub shoulder to shoulder, as He intended. She moved on stopping again to take a long look at the river meandering upstream towards Marlow before setting off again back to the house.

Banjo leapt at Susy in play when she rounded the corner by the paddock, leaving Sir Richard to take his morning constitutional alone. She waved a hand in greeting, then raced toward and into the kitchen, where Marie handed her a glass of fresh orange juice.

'Anybody up?' she asked, after gulping down the juice.

'Everybody, except Miss Vanessa,' Marie replied.

How could anyone miss even one single solitary moment on such a beautiful morning? She joined Polly and Toby at the breakfast table, clearly sensing there was something wrong. An atmosphere of suspense hung in the air; anxious uncertainties, cluttering the mind with negative thoughts, were prevalent. After several minutes of silent eating and hostile glances, Susy decided to speak.

'What a terrific morning, isn't it?' There was no response as she took a sip of her coffee. 'Hasn't anyone been outside yet?' Barely an eyelid flickered in reply to her polite, benign question. 'Maybe I could give you a game later, Toby?' she said, trying to inject some enthusiasm into her voice. 'Show you just how good I really am.'

'We won't be here, Susy,' Toby said, rising from the table.

Polly was unaware of their early departure. 'I'm staying,' she said sharply.

'You can do whatever you like, but don't expect me to stick around,' he barked.

Vanessa entered into the conversation on sitting down at the table. 'There's a barbecue this afternoon and I would very much like you to join us, Toby.'

'As much as I appreciate your hospitality, Vanessa, I hope you will understand. I am afraid I have to go.' He turned and, without saying goodbye to anyone, left the house.

'Why is he so angry?' Susy asked, concluding that the fault must surely be Polly's. 'What did you do to make him go off like that?'

'Let him cool down,' Vanessa interrupted, before Polly could answer. 'Don't let it spoil the rest of the weekend.'

Susy attempted to leave the table, hoping to make him change his mind, succeed where others had failed. Polly tugged at her arm. 'Sit down, you're wasting your time. When Toby makes a decision, nobody can make him change his mind.'

The day had only just begun and already there was a feeling of despondency among friends. Vanessa's meticulously planned weekend would not be marred by such triviality as a lovers' spat and quickly dismissed the incident. 'Today, my dear friends, you are going to have the pleasure of meeting the Fieldings,' she sniggered. 'Just slip me a word later and let me know what you think of Rufus.'

Susy mentally stumbled through the minefield of names, people and events that surrounded Vanessa's life, trying to recall a Rufus. 'Is that the one with the small ... you know, the small–'

'Prick,' Vanessa said with perfect diction, exalting the Queen's english to new heights. 'You mean, small prick?' Susy gave a sideways nod. 'I haven't seen it, Susy. Neither do I want to. No, Rufus is mummy's idea of a perfect match. Unfortunately the idiot is available again, so just watch your backs, this one is no gentleman.'

The coals burned white hot as the barbecue got underway, hissing and spitting puffs of smoke into the air. There was a light breeze blowing when local faces began to appear and mingle informally with the hierarchy. The couple from the farm where Vanessa bought eggs and the publican were all familiar to Susy. Lady Caroline looked immaculate, over-dressed somewhat for a barbecue, welcoming her equally well presented and preserved counterparts into the garden. Peter appeared at Susy's side on the lawn having spent the morning with Sir Richard in the study, immersed in local history.

'Hi, how ya doing?'

Susy nodded in the direction of the guests. 'What do you think of the show?' she asked.

'I think it's great, almost vaudeville.'

'Where I come from, they would steal the clothes off your back if they though it would buy them class like this.'

'And so did their ancestors, Susy, only worse, they beheaded them, or burnt them at the stake if they were opposed. But time forgets. You see only what your eyes tell you. Now, let's get something to eat.'

Lady Caroline's voice carried well. Wherever you were in the garden, her dulcet tones could be heard loud and clear. Peter spent a great deal of time talking to the Fieldings. He found them interesting and well travelled, while Rufus took stock of the 'spare' females now shedding their clothes and diving into the pool. As the afternoon sun reached a high, Lucinda arrived with an unknown young man on her arm, much to Vanessa's surprise, followed by Erik and Yanni, who never turned down an invitation to dine. Polly pulled herself out of the pool and, finding a quiet corner, lay horizontal on the sun lounger to dry off. She closed her eyes, shutting out the buzz of voices and started to drift off, forgetting the harsh reality of the morning with the intense heat from the sun turning her skin a rosy pink.

'Mind if I join you?' came the loud masculine voice, his large frame towering above her, blocking out the sun.

'Oh, yes.'

'Is that "yes you mind"?'

'No, no,' Polly smiled. 'Please, do sit down.'

Rufus sat down on the adjoining lounger and offered his hand, 'Rufus Fielding.'

Polly sat up, covering her bosom from his gaze and introduced herself, making a hasty evaluation of the man she knew only by the reputation that preceded him. A well-built specimen, bald, with a heavy moustache, Vanessa had been kind in her assessment. Rufus raised his eyebrows above the sunglasses perched on the middle of a large nose.

'I don't believe I've had the pleasure?'

'No, we haven't met before,' Polly replied, inching away. 'Although I feel I know you.'

'Ah, Vanessa's been talking about me.'

'Actually, she did mention what a fine rugby player you are.'

'Rugby? No, she's got it all wrong, cricket's my game.'

Rufus unbuttoned his shirt and brushed his hand against the warm flesh of Polly's arm. 'Getting a bit of a burn, Polly?'

While retaining cover over her breasts, she turned over and tried to get up, only to be pulled down sharply next to him again.

Erik had noticed the malaise from the confines of the patio and alerted Vanessa's attention. 'Who is that grotesque man mauling Polly, sweetie?'

Dismayed at Polly's attempt to free herself from Rufus's grasp she replied, 'Oh dear, he really is a barbarian. I'll have to rescue her.'

Erik pushed her away with a sweep of his arm. 'Leave it to me, darling,' and walked straight up to them. 'I can't leave you alone for five minutes, can I?' he bellowed at Polly. She looked at Erik perplexed. 'And half naked! What do you think you are doing with this man?' Rufus jumped to attention.

'I'm so sorry, darling,' she replied, nuzzling up to his chest. 'Please forgive me.'

Pushing her away at arm's length he added, 'Go and put some clothes on immediately, before I am forced to thrash you.'

Polly ran across the lawn, leaving Rufus and Erik in a head-on clash. Obscured from view and with his back to the party, Erik seized the opportunity and thrust his hand hard into Rufus's crotch, squeezing and twisting the genitals until Erik felt the penis swell under his grasp.

'Yes,' he said with quiet confirmation, 'just as I thought, you shortsighted little turd.' The pain was evident as Rufus fought for composure. 'You dance both sides of the fence, don't you, duckie?' Rufus shook with fear while Erik released the pressure.

'Please, please I beg you,' he stammered.

Erik smiled as he fondled the erect penis. 'Oh, don't fear. I won't divulge your passion ... just be a sweetie pie now and come for daddy.' Erik did not let go, massaging the fullness of the erection through the fabric of the trousers.

Rufus managed to cough out the words, 'You are a bitch.'

'I know and don't you just love it?' Erik said supremely, feeling every contorted movement pump hard into his hand. Rufus gasped and grabbed at Erik's arm to stop, each contraction racking through his groin like fire. Once over, Erik released his grip, threw back his head in gratuitous satisfaction and walked away.

Susy cornered Sir Richard and sat like a child mesmerised by the numerous tales he had to tell. So much of her childhood she had been neglected that she wallowed in every story he told, even if he forgot and told the same tale again, as if it really mattered. He followed, more often than not, with a ditty or two, learnt many a year ago, which always brought a smile or chuckle of laughter.

Vanessa ordered tea to be served and a few guests found their way into the conservatory. A strong breeze was beginning to blow and the air had turned decidedly chilly. More composed, Polly joined Susy and Sir Richard in the conservatory, her cheeks quite flushed from the afternoon sun, while Peter was still talking to David Fielding. Lucinda, the crusader *d'amour*, had displaced or forgotten poor Douglas and was engrossed in carnal conversation with the very young and handsome man by her side.

There was a crack of lightning and the sky became dark, followed by a tumultuous rumble of thunder, shaking the very foundations of the house. With the first spots of rain, everyone ran for shelter and the heavens opened up to torrential rain, shattering plates and glasses left unattended to the ground in the wake. There was nothing to do except watch and wait for the storm to pass, when Vanessa saw two figures running across the lawn. She strained her eyes to see through the deluge as they drew closer. The driving rain lashing against the conservatory doors. 'Mummy!' she said out loud, watching Lady Caroline and Veronica stumble into view. Another crack of lightning rang out above them, causing Veronica to slip and fall headlong on to the soaking wet grass. 'Help me, Caroline!' she cried, holding out a hand. Caroline stooped to help her friend back on to her feet, they were saturated and together they struggled across the lawn. 'Daddy, what can we do?'

Sir Richard stood up and, leaning hard on his cane, peered out into the garden. 'It won't do for us all to get wet, Vanessa. Marie, quickly fetch some dry towels.' He switched on the outside lights, illuminating the pool. 'Ha, ha, come along, old girl.' He chuckled. Unamused Vanessa threw open the conservatory doors, in time for Caroline to hear his coarse comments. She was incensed by his sense of humour at a time of acute embarrassment. The driving rain continued to fall.

'Hurry, mummy, hurry!'

The two women had reached poolside, with the guests cheering them forward.

'Ha, ha, ha!' Sir Richard banged his cane to the ground, leaned back and laughed heartily.

Bedraggled and humiliated, without dignity and grace, Caroline aided her faltering friend. 'Laugh, will you?' she shouted, observing her husband's dishonourable behaviour. 'You wretched man!'

Veronica's makeup had dissolved and she was tottering precariously close to the pool, clinging on tightly to her friend, when a colossal clap of thunder broke above their heads. Veronica screamed and instantly lost her footing, tumbling feet first into the swimming pool, dragging Caroline with her. Vanessa looked on in horror.

'She can't swim,' she yelled, as all eyes turned towards the pool. Peter almost knocked everybody over in his haste and dived headlong into the water. Yanni also came out of nowhere and plunged straight in. Both men were fully dressed and they cut a channel through the water towards the floundering women, reaching the submerged bodies, bringing them spluttering, but safely to the surface, gently gliding them to the side and out of the pool. Vanessa held a large umbrella firmly extended and, holding on to her father's arm, hurried to the scene.

'She's not moving,' Veronica cried, distraught at her friend's lifeless body. 'Do something!'

Peter supported Caroline's neck and placed his mouth over

hers, breathing deeply into her lungs, but she still did not move. Again, he blew air into the motionless body, just as Sir Richard and Vanessa reached them.

'Is she dead?' Sir Richard asked, peering over Caroline's limp body. Vanessa fell at her mother's side, the wind lashing against them.

'Breathe, mummy! Please don't let us down, come on, breathe!'

Peter tried one more time and, like a fish out of water, Caroline coughed, took a breath and opened her eyes.

Sir Richard, leaning hard on his walking cane, struggled down on one knee for a closer look. 'Ha, ha!' He chortled, relieved and grateful. 'Caroline will do anything for attention.'

Peter looked up in amazement. 'But we could have lost her, sir.'

'There's a lot of life in the old girl yet, my boy, bring her inside.'

Calls of bravo and praise for the swiftness of thought and action greeted Peter and Yanni, when they brought Veronica and Caroline back into the house. An unexpected climax to the weekend that could so easily have turned into a tragedy.

As evening fell and most of the guests had left, Sir Richard called Peter and Yanni into the study and motioned for them to sit down.

'I cannot begin to express my gratitude at the way you both behaved this afternoon.'

'Any able-bodied person would have done the same, sir,' Peter replied.

'That may be so, but there was very little I myself could have done in an emergency, my own boys not being here.'

Yanni interrupted, 'The reserve team was close at hand.'

Sir Richard was thoughtful. 'I have been married for thirty-five years and know that Caroline will turn almost any situation to her advantage, but today, I feel remorse in my judgement of acquaintances and truly believe that without your help I would surely have lost her. I am forever in your debt.' And turning to Yanni. 'I am an old man, with old fashioned principles, stubborn, so as not to see the value of a good man beneath the façade. My fault entirely and I recant any jibe that I may have uttered at your expense.'

Yanni was moved by his words. 'Thank you, sir.'

Sir Richard stood up and walked towards them, placing an arm around each man's shoulder. 'Come now, Caroline would like to see you both before you leave.' They walked slowly through the house and up the wide staircase together. Once outside the bedroom on the first floor, Sir Richard quietly opened the door, then closed it. Caroline was peacefully sleeping; they did not disturb her.

Polly was packed and off to Paris on her first assignment, ecstatic over the new job which meant her spending more time away from London and Toby. He was not enamoured with the idea, mainly because the situation made her more financially independent and in control of her own life.

Susy locked up the shop for the night and strolled back in the direction of the apartment. She had the entire evening to herself. No tennis or Mrs Potter, and Vanessa was out for the evening – total solitude. She stopped off at the supermarket and, with her arms laden with shopping, she put the key in the apartment door. Sitting down with a glass of chilled wine, she opened the evening paper and read the events of the day. 'Maggie on course for a thumping third term'. What a lady! What an achiever, she thought, turning the page. 'All going the Tories' way, revealed the Mori Poll.' Could they possibly do it again? There was no opposition to speak of and both Labour and the SDP were beginning to play dirty, heaping vengeance on her leadership style, lost before they began.

Levering herself off the sofa, she placed a cassette in the deck and began to prepare a light supper, but was interrupted by the ring of the telephone. Not wishing to speak to anybody, she allowed the machine to intercept the call, but after Vanessa's recorded message had ended, the caller rang off. Unperturbed, she satisfied the griping pangs of hunger with an adequate salad and wholemeal roll and returned to the lounge, settled down on the sofa and curled up with a paperback.

Night had fallen when the telephone's rude, shrill tones woke Susy with a jump, causing the disoriented dreamer into a disconcerted scramble for the table lamp. With heart racing, she switched on the light and made a grab for the receiver. 'Hello?' she said to a dead line. Irritated by the intrusion, she lay back again and noted the time: ten o'clock. She had been asleep for two hours. When almost immediately the telephone rang again. Susy jumped on the machine.

'Hello, who's that?'

'Oh precious, that was quick. 'Ow are you, darlin'?'

'Joyce.' How good it was to hear her voice. 'Did you just call?'

'No, darlin', first time. Are you OK? You sound a bit flustered to me.'

Feeling more composed she replied, 'You woke me up. How are you?'

Joyce inhaled deeply on her cigarette. 'Mustn't grumble, darlin'. Got a bit of news. Thought I'd better tell you straight away. Are you sittin' down?'

'I'm lying down, Joyce. What is it?'

There was a pause. 'I've seen Eddy, sweetheart.' Susy did not answer. 'Yesterday, pet, 'e wants to see you.' She still did not answer. 'Seems 'e's in a spot of trouble with the business.'

'What's he want, Joyce, money? I hope you didn't tell him about our little arrangement?'

'Darlin', it would be more than my life's worth. I'm tellin' you, 'e knows nothin'.'

'Then he's up to something.'

'There'll be a good reason why. You know Eddy. It's up to you, pet.'

Disturbed by the request, Susy needed time to think and curtailed the conversation. 'Don't tell him we've spoken, Joyce. I'll get back to you.'

In the 15 months since leaving the East End, there had not been a single word from Eddy. Her mind raced as she stacked the dishwasher. What exactly did the old bastard want from her? Ever since her wrist turned green after the Rolex he gave her for Christmas proved to be a fake, she had finally realised what a fraudster he was. Maybe she should leave well alone and try to forget all about him, but on the other hand, meeting the devil again may very well put paid to an ugly chapter in her life. She was confused and put herself to bed before Vanessa returned from the theatre.

Thursday eleventh June, Polling Day. They left the apartment to register their votes before going on to business. They walked in silence, Vanessa sensing the heavy burden that Susy appeared to be shouldering.

'You're very quiet, Susy?'

'Yep.'

'Any problems at the shop?'

'No, everything's just fine.'

'Well something is bothering you. Do you want to talk?'

They placed their votes in the ballot box and walked outside. Before they had gone too far Vanessa felt compelled to speak.

'Talk to me, will you! You're like the living dead.'

'OK, so I've got a problem.'

'You don't say! Now what's so wrong. Can I help?'

Susy heaved a huge sigh, before relating the whole story.

'But I thought you had written him off?'

'I had, now he wants to see me.'

'Have you asked yourself why, after all this time?'

She had not thought of anything else. 'I know, I know, he probably wants something.'

Vanessa turned Susy around to face her. 'Now, listen to me,' she said with conviction. 'Whether you see him or not is entirely your business, but don't ever lose sight of what he did to you, and don't turn away from me when I'm talking to you. He beat you, Susy, then he threw you out of your home. You owe this man nothing.'

Susy walked on and hailed a taxi. 'You're right, of course, Vanessa,' and jumped inside, 'but maybe he needs a reminder.'

Later that evening Vanessa met Lucinda at a Conservative Party bash that was scheduled to go on well into the small hours of the morning. The campaign had been one of the roughest, toughest election battles since the war and as Vanessa arrived the adrenaline was running high, as yet another seat was gained to rapturous applause. The turnout of liquor-swilling yuppies who owed so much to Maggie was commendable, or was it just another excuse for a party? Vanessa descended the stairs and elbowed her way through the throng to the restaurant basement, where she found Lucinda buried under a swell of bodies rising and falling in time to the results now flowing in.

'How's it going?' she asked, over the din.

'Landslide, darling, they can't possibly catch us now.'

Vanessa looked around for the boyfriend. 'Are you alone, Lucinda?'

'Hardly, Vanessa, or hadn't you noticed?'

Another roar elevated the crowd to their feet; jostling for space and slopping drinks everywhere. The evening was hot and the place too crowded, with billowing, insufferable clouds of smoke wafting through the air and draping nauseating, suffocating fumes around Vanessa's head. 'Lucinda, can we move?' she said, beating the air with her hand. Disgruntled at being forced to leave her pitch, she followed Vanessa to a quieter corner, away from the hubbub. Vanessa leaned up against a pillar and gasped for air.

'I had no idea it would be so frenetic, what a crush!'

'Yes, but you've got to admit it's damned exciting.'

Vanessa preferred to think on that. 'If you say so.'

An air of jubilation rang out as the total number of seats exceeded 350. A runaway victory for the Tories, and the restaurant resounded to shouts and cheers as Vanessa attempted to distract Lucinda's attention.

'I really think I should be going,' she yelled in her ear.

'What! I can't hear you, darling, speak up!'

'I'm going,' she shouted, when a drunken couple pushed past them holding each other up. 'Four more years,' they chanted. 'Four more years.'

Lucinda enthusiastically spurred them on. 'This is great news! What a splendid evening.' The noise abated and a few people began to leave, united in victory and rewarded for months of diligent campaigning. 'Now, what did you say, darling?'

'I am going home, enjoy the rest of the night.'

'But it's hardly over yet, Vanessa,' she whinged. 'You really are becoming a bore.'

'Lucinda, it's two-thirty.' But as she spoke, Lucinda disappeared into the crowd.

Only then did she notice him sitting there, the profile, the dark hair falling softly over his forehead, the flash of white teeth as he laughed with a friend, over a joke, maybe. Vanessa's heart leapt violently, thumping so loud as to drown all other sounds. She stood alone, or so it seemed. Breathless, motionless, wanting desperately to reach out and touch him, feel his hand on hers, his mouth against her lips. She stepped forward. Did he know that she was there? Could he, would he, take her in his arms and forgive her? 'Oliver' she breathed, but no sound came forth. Still seated at a small table, almost obscured from view, with his newfound friends, Vanessa took another step forward. When the long willowy arm of a young woman slipped around Oliver's shoulder, pulling him closer, her thick, dark hair tumbling over her shoulders as she kissed his ear. A frivolous moment of mutual affection and he laughed, cupping her face in his hands and lightly kissed her forehead. Vanessa felt physically sick, a voyeur, a total stranger and tore her eyes away from the scene, but Oliver had noticed her standing there and called out her name. The beautiful young woman, seeing that her escort was distracted, turned her attention away from their party and towards Vanessa. Oliver stood up and politely gestured for Vanessa to sit down.

'Won't you join us?' he said.

Feeling foolish and incoherent Vanessa muttered. 'I er, um, I was just leaving, Oliver.'

He pulled out a chair. 'Please, Vanessa, I insist.'

The beautiful young woman sat back and watched Vanessa

closely, absorbing every small detail of the stammering intruder about to descend on their group.

'No, really, Oliver, it's very late and as you can see, I was just on my way out.'

He took her by the arm and guided her into a chair. 'It's been a long time. How are you?' he asked, with that captivating smile.

'Fine.' She heard herself trill, when there was nothing further from the truth. Oliver had lost none of his charm and dashing good looks. She only wished there could be a tiny flaw, something that she could beam into, a personality defect that would concentrate her mind and aid her failing conversation. 'And you?'

'I saw Susy,' he added. 'Maybe she forgot to tell you?'

'No no, she did not forget.'

Small talk, meaningless words hitting the air and disappearing into a huge vacuum, then silence. This was not how she had planned her comeback, this was a travesty of her innermost thoughts. Desperate for recognition, Vanessa looked deep into Oliver's eyes.

'Excuse me,' he said, with a smile, 'Vanessa, this is Julia.' The two women acknowledged one another cordially, a slight nod of the head being the only part of their anatomy that moved. She was stunning, Vanessa thought disheartened, when the raven-haired Julia slipped her arm possessively through Oliver's, smiling back across the table at Vanessa, who looked and felt decidedly uncomfortable. They were a party of six, none of whom looked familiar, all young and successful, judging by their attributes. A group of people who, with bilious complexions and hooded eyes, still found the energy to cavort and chant inarticulate melodies long into the night. Vanessa stood up, unable to stay a minute longer and witness the devouring of what she considered to be her man, her future. The whole scene was unbearable.

'Oliver, I really must leave you.'

After disentangling himself from Julia's grasp he spoke. 'You do seem determined to leave us, Vanessa. Are you going to Ascot next week?'

'Yes, couldn't possibly miss it,' she blatantly lied. 'And Wimbledon.'

'Then perhaps we will see you there?'

'Quite probably. Lovely to see you again.'

Leaving the party behind her and not once glancing back, Vanessa walked slowly away. The hurt and pain were suffocating. Choking back emotion, she failed to hear Lucinda call after her, on what must surely have been the longest walk of her life.

IT'S MAGGIES HATTRICK the newspapers stated the following morning. The Tories held 376 seats, an overall majority of 101. Susy closed the paper as two elegant young women entered the shop, followed by Peter, who was dressed smartly in a lightweight suit, shirt and tie, not his usual casual attire. She summoned her assistant to attend to the ladies, while she and Peter disappeared into the back room.

'Look at you,' she said, admiringly touching the cloth and searching out labels and looking him straight in the eye. 'You're up to something?'

'I am,' he said positively, not giving anything away.

Still maintaining eye contact, she posed a question. 'Where are you going?'

'Why should I be going anywhere?'

'Stop playing games with me, Peter, I've known you long enough.'

He held both hands up in defence of Susy's bark. 'OK, I confess. I've just landed a job at a sports centre in the Canaries.'

Instead of feeling elated at his good news, she felt saddened. 'When are you leaving?'

'September, for six months, maybe longer. Hey, don't look so serious.'

She placed both arms around his neck. 'I'm really going to miss you. It's going to be like having my right arm cut off.'

'Take some time out and come over for a holiday; get some winter sun?'

'How can I?' she shrugged, 'the business?'

Standing Susy at arm length, he reached into his jacket pocket and drew out an envelope.

'What's this?' she asked, with a curious side glance. 'Are you trying to butter me up?'

She toyed with the envelope, turning it over and over, while Peter laughed. 'All right, open it up. I give you my full permission.'

With one short sharp movement Susy ripped open the envelope and shook the contents out into her open palm: two centre court tickets for the men's final at Wimbledon. Shrieking with excitement, she threw her arms around his neck again and squeezed tightly.

'I guess I'm not so bad after all, eh?' he said choking.

'Thanks buddy, you're the best, the very best.'

As the week ended, Susy was riding on a high. Peter's forthcoming departure was not as depressing as she had initially thought, but rather the beginning of a beautiful and lasting friendship that would endure a lifetime. She bounded up the stairs to the apartment, picked up the telephone and dialled Joyce. Sunday afternoon, she was prepared to go home and meet Eddy face to face.

She wore a simple, yet elegantly tailored trouser suit and flat shoes. She clipped her long auburn hair off her face into a tousled chignon, applied a light makeup that enhanced her refined features and set out east – they were expecting her.

Susy drove passed familiar landmarks, spotted a few old faces, but nobody recognised her. Outside the house that she knew so well, she spent a few quiet moments contemplating the welcome she would receive once inside. She felt strangely detached from everything she perceived, a stranger on her own patch. Slamming the car door, she walked confidently up to the front door and rang the bell. A rumbling from the rear of the house, followed by heavy footsteps in the hall, brought Eddy to the fore. Opening the door wide, with a toothy grin, he looked slimmer than she remembered, not the formidably large character that was prone to massive bouts of anger. He stepped aside, allowing her a wide berth into the house. Susy's eyes followed the whole length of the hall, into the newly fitted kitchen and finally into the sitting room they had redecorated. The place stank of stale cigar smoke, mixed with the faint aroma of cheap perfume.

'Looking good, babe,' Eddy finally said, rubbing his hands furiously together. 'What's your poison, darlin'? G and T, vodka and orange, you always used to like that?' He waited for a reply. 'Or 'ow about a beer?'

'An orange juice will do.'

'Ow, come on babe, jivvy it up a bit.'

Susy sat down on the newly upholstered settee and could hear movement coming from upstairs. 'Where's Norma?' she asked, watching Eddy fussing over the drinks trolley.

'She'll be down in a minute. There you go, darlin', a nice screwdriver.' He handed over the drink and patted her on the knee, before sitting down next to her on the settee. 'So, 'ow's it goin', princess? Making lots of dosh?'

God forbid he should ask her where the money came from; Joyce would be burnt at the stake. 'I'm doing nicely, thank you.'

'Nicely eh!' he laughed. 'I should coco.' Leaning forward he produced a large cigar from a box on the coffee table and began the ritual of slipping and rolling the end between his lips, making it soggy. Eddy certainly had not lost any of the hallmarks symbolic of a successful car dealer, even if, as Joyce had intimated, business was bad. He blew a mouthful of smoke towards the ceiling, then gripped the phallic object between his teeth. 'Got a nice little place I 'ear, you and some fancy bird?'

'She's no bird, Eddy. She's a lady from a very good family.'

'As I understand it, you're running that smart dress shop for 'er near 'Arrods. What's it called, The Cat, Cit?'

'The Coterie,' she replied. 'You're well informed?'

'I 'ave my contacts, darlin' … I 'ope she's paying you well?' he chuckled.

Eddy quite obviously had no idea of the financial arrangement, for he would not have failed to let her know. Norma, looking every inch a charge-card's dream, careered towards her with open arms, placing a wet kiss on her cheek.

'Sweetheart, lovely to see you,' she gushed.

'Get yourself a drink and sit down, woman,' Eddy snapped. 'Me and Susy is 'aving a nice little chat.'

The scenario never changed: the pig-headed brute was about to lip-lash the fairer sex. Susy sensed the mood, felt the hackles rise along the ridge of her spine, but she was ready for him.

'You haven't asked me over here just for a chat,' she stated. 'Why don't you get straight to the point.'

Eddy was caught offguard by her directness and stiffened up against the back of the settee, while Norma drifted back across the room with a drink in her hand. 'What do you think of the new carpet, darlin'?'

A fiery flush of red radiated from under Eddy's shirt collar. 'Sit down and shut up, will you!' he yelled.

Without hesitation and clasping her glass to her bosom, Norma obeyed. Susy passed a cursory glance at them both. He was back in control and gently touched Susy's arm before continuing.

'Course there was a reason, babe. You're family, one of us.' A quick flick of his thumb on the cap of the cigarette lighter released a rush of gas that ignited a flame high into the air, as he attempted to rekindle the diminishing cigar.

'All right, so here I am. Now what have you got to ask me?'

Norma squirmed, 'Doesn't she sound proper, Eddy, just like a little lady.'

Turning sharply to Norma, Eddy reiterated his demand. ''Ow many times do I 'ave to tell you, woman, shut your bleeding mouth.' The spluttered blast of venom reduced Norma to a cowering weakling. 'Naw,' he began, shuffling up closer to Susy on the settee, 'I might just 'ave a little business deal that would interest you.'

Coming from Eddy, the mere suggestion reeked of impropriety. 'I'm all ears,' she replied.

'You know a few toffs where you are, don't you, babe? You know, moneyed people, Lords and the like.'

'And what if I do?'

'You've got your eyes open, you looks around and about when you goes to their places and see what they've got tucked away, know what I mean?'

The insinuation was blatantly clear. 'Like antiques and jewellery? Is that what you're talking about?'

'Yeah, yeah that's it, antiques.'

The thieving contemptuous bastard, she observed, studying the arrogant, opinionated expression on Eddy's face. 'You're asking me to screw my friends, so you can become a fat cat?'

'It's business, babe, you know the rules. Family comes first and I'm in a bit of a tight corner.'

Susy abruptly got up. 'Family, what family? You heap of garbage, I should have known better than to come over here again.' She picked up her bag and strode toward the front door, with Eddy and Norma close behind. 'I have picked myself up out of this trash pile and I intend making something out of my life.'

'You don't 'ave the brains, you stupid cow,' he shouted.

With eyes ablaze Susy turned on him. 'That's right, go on, try and make me feel inferior. Does it make you feel good?' She opened the front door, banging it hard against the wall. 'You're a liar and a cheat, Eddy Stevens, and you're not my father. I never had a father!'

'Go on, piss off!' he barked, waving a fist in the air.

'And I hope that you and that buzzard you live with burn in hell!'

What a blessed relief she felt as, pressing her foot down hard on the accelerator, she drove home. Home, she thought, is where you feel peace and love, where there is no conflict and everybody is worthy of consideration. When she encountered Vanessa in the kitchen on her return, she threw her arms around her neck and sobbed.

Vanessa had no plans for Ascot. Instead, she applied herself to the work at hand in the agency. June was turning out to be an exceptionally wet month and the entire sporting calendar looked like being a washout.

Erik placed a mug of steaming hot coffee on Vanessa's desk, while she stood and watched the rain fall through the office window and left her to her thoughts without saying a word. The encounter with Oliver had cut very deep and preoccupied too much of her time. Would he have detected the lies she so boldly told? The very idea disturbed her greatly, for he knew her so well. And what of Julia? Who was she and what did she do? He did not say. She was a beauty and young, so very young, she recalled. Picking up the mug of coffee, she wrapped her hands around the warm porcelain and sipped the bittersweet liquid. 'Ugh!' she exclaimed, replacing the mug on the desk, when would Erik remember that she did not take sugar? Continuing her vigil at the window, she watched the umbrellas bobbing along in the street below and the vehicles swishing around the square in an almost hypnotic formation, inducing a trance-like state. *I expect he's at Ascot today*, she brooded, *with Julia, no doubt, having an 'absolutely marvellous time'*, she could hear him saying. *I wonder if he ever thinks of me and remembers how beautiful life was? Anything less would be insufferable.* A knock on the door brought Vanessa sharply back to reality, as Polly's cheery face peered around the office door.

'Hello, I'm back,' she said with a smile, followed immediately by an office clerk waving a folder in his hand.

'Urgent, Miss Baron,' he said, banging it on her desk. The intercom sounded, making them both jump. Suddenly the office came to life. Vanessa depressed the button.

'Call on line two,' came a voice, loud and clear.

'Polly, I would love to chat, but as–'

'It will wait, Vanessa, but please keep Thursday evening free, I am taking you and Susy out for dinner.'

Vanessa opened her diary. 'Yes, wonderful. Thursday it is.'

'I have so much to tell you both. Paris was *très merveilleux*, *enchanté.*' She giggled, making her way out of the office. Vanessa instinctively knew that an amourette was at play, Polly was treading dangerous ground.

Vanessa and Susy met Polly as planned in the bar of the fashionable Lorenzo's restaurant, where they took aperitifs before descending the steps to the lower floor. Business was brisk, as usual, with neatly dressed waiters in their white shirts, black pants and dickey bows, paying homage to the rich and famous who frequented their tables. With timely precision and pen poised, the waiter reeled off the 'speciality of the day.' After much deliberation, Vanessa came to a decision. 'Sea bass,' she said, handing the menu back to the waiter.

'Me, too,' Susy echoed. As for Polly, the decision was never easy, with such a vast and varied selection to choose from. Invariably, the waiter broke the tip of his pencil scrubbing out the previous selection, only to repeat the same process again. Finally, she glanced up and smiled, settling decisively and quite simply for the vongole.

As the evening unfolded and after quaffing down several glasses of Sancerre it seemed Vanessa's judgement had been accurate, Polly had indeed indulged in a fling during her trip to Paris. Between hors d'oevres and dessert, she talked incessantly of nothing else, reducing Susy to a quivering mass of hysteria, with her expletives, followed by a hasty quip or two. Vanessa sighed. Why was Polly always so graphic about the penis, as if she was the only woman to have ever seen or touched one? Wasn't one penis much the same as another? Give or take an inch or two, in width also. We must not forget the one that's the size of a Campbell's tin of condensed soup – that is, if one could possibly contain it. Polly undoubtedly could. There she was, with amazing alacrity, filling in the finer details. Vanessa was bored and hailed the waiter to bring coffee, when she noticed the back of a balding head sitting at a table for two across the restaurant floor. He looks uncannily like Rufus, she thought, straining her eyes for a closer look, dining with a rather good-looking young man. Maybe she was mistaken, she thought, as coffee arrived with alarming speed and efficiency amid trills of laughter from her friends, and she turned away. Apparently Polly had attended Ascot the previous day with Toby, which made Vanessa prick up her ears.

'She showed no shame at all,' Polly giggled, 'and what's more, he ripped her dress in the process.'

'Who?' Vanessa interrupted. 'Who ripped whose dress?'

'Why – Nicky. Haven't you been listening?'

The two girls had been unaware of Vanessa's detachment from the conversation and began alternately to relate the incident again. There had been a row, not unusual where Rachel and Nicky were concerned, but whereas Nicky would normally turn a blind eye to Rachel's flirtations, he drew the line at open physical contact. The dress revealed more than was acceptable for a day at the races and Rachel not being averse to flaunting her bodily attributes, did just that and wrapped herself wholeheartedly around the left thigh of a rather stunned business associate, who found it almost impossible to discreetly shake her off.

'Was Oliver there?' Vanessa asked, anxious for any news.

Without elaborating Polly replied, 'Yes, he was there.'

Vanessa looked her straight in the eye. 'Was he alone?'

After a short pause Polly replied, 'No Vanessa, he was not alone.'

They both felt her heart sink as she lowered her eyes and silently stirred her coffee. Polly leaned forward and placed her hand on Vanessa's arm. 'She's nineteen, Vanessa. Pretty, but not very bright and she's not the only girl he dates. It's not serious, believe me.'

Vanessa proudly raised her head and smiled. 'I would know,' she said assuredly. 'Oliver would not be able to deceive me.'

Polly called for the bill, her treat, as promised, and promptly took out her cheque book, assessing the damage with relaxed formality. The following week she was off to New York on another assignment and Susy wondered cannily how long it would take for Toby to become thoroughly disgruntled with the situation. If he knew about Polly's indiscretion in Paris, that would definitely speed up the inevitable. With her objective firmly in sight and gripped by the impending demise of Polly's love affair, Susy threw her napkin on the table and prepared to leave. The waiter whisked away the salver on which Polly had deposited the cheque, coupled with a gratuity of ample proportions that protruded from beneath the chit.

'Thank you, Carlo,' she said graciously, 'the meal was excellent.'

Carlo, of slight build, with a vigorous moustache that compensated for the lack of hair, humbly clasped both hands together and bowed ever so slightly.

'*Grazie signorina, grazie*,' he replied, as they proceeded to walk away from the table. '*Molto, molto gentile.*'

In her quest for cultural growth, Susy felt compelled to ask, 'What did he say?' as they zigzagged their way through the tables.

'Ah!' Vanessa quietly replied, walking at Susy's shoulder. 'He said he has huge balls.'

'Go on.' Susy strained her eyes backward for a closer look at the waiter, who was still smiling in their direction, 'you're throwing me a line.'

'No, not at all, it's true.' Vanessa insisted. 'Ask Polly.'

The restaurant was still humming with waiters still running around in circles, not a table was unoccupied, when Vanessa remembered Rufus and glanced back, searching out the table where she though she saw him dining. How remiss of her to leave and not say hello, but he was nowhere to be seen, neither was he in the bar. Almost grateful for his absence, recalling Polly's recent brush with the insatiable beast, they left.

They walked slowly, arm in arm, still laughing and chatting down Pont Street, then across Sloane Street, to Cadogan Place, unaware that they were not walking alone. Behind them, at a calculated distance, was the solitary figure of a man, who watched them every step of the way. When they reached the steps of the apartment the glowing amber light on a Hackney carriage swung around the corner. Polly flagged the taxi down, said goodnight to her friends and sped off home.

10

Resourceful as she though she could be, Vanessa was counting the days until Tina returned from her holiday. With her bag slung over one shoulder, newspaper under her arm and clutching a large brown shopping bag from the supermarket, she struggled up the stairs to the apartment.

On hearing the door close, Susy shouted from her chair in front of the television. 'Quick, come here!' Vanessa set aside her bags and hurried to see what all the noise was about. 'Just look,' she chuckled, eyes still glued to the screen. 'This is our Royal Family making complete fools of themselves.'

They sat side by side watching the colourful caricatures roll and tumble in an effort to secure a point for their side. The larger than life tomatoes, bananas and potatoes raced to raucous cheers from their fellow competitors.

'Are you sure?' Vanessa queried, for the pantomime figures cavorting across the arena bore no resemblance at all to the Royal Family. 'What are you watching?'

'Sure I'm sure. *It's a Knockout*. See, there's Andrew and over there, look, there's Princess Anne.'

She was right, the indisputable faces of the young Royals having a whale of a time, romping mindlessly with celebrities from the world of entertainment.

'What fun!' Vanessa laughed, picking up the shopping bag and disappearing into the kitchen. 'What will they get up to next?'

Vanessa picked up a large pile of unopened mail from the kitchen table and made her way back into the lounge, planting herself firmly into an armchair where she proceeded to open them. Being of an inquisitive nature and not wanting to miss out on the smallest of details, Susy followed, slowly creeping up behind the chair to see precisely what she was looking at. Conscious of the prying eyes peering over her shoulder, Vanessa placed the literature face down on the coffee table and kindly requested that Susy bring her a glass of mineral water from the refrigerator. She obliged, returning swiftly with the frosty glass and placed it neatly on a coaster, next to a stack of property lists that Vanessa was avidly reading. Susy stood back, filled with consternation, gripped by the realisation that she could be homeless again, a nomad, a lost soul seeking refuge with anybody generous enough to take her in. Her life would fit comfortably into two large suitcases, for she owned not one stick of furniture. Was this Vanessa's callous way of telling her that the time was ripe for moving on? 'What do you think?' she said, pointing to the glossy photograph of a white-washed mews cottage with integral garage. Susy's half-smile and seemingly disinterested attitude brought a second, more intense glance from Vanessa as she shuffled through the remaining lists, discarding at great speed those that held no immediate interest. Finally, Vanessa selected three possibilities and without further reference, slipped them into her bag. Without a word, Susy watched her go upstairs to her room. This was intolerable behaviour, reminiscent of the selfishness that had plagued Vanessa for much of her life and which sadly looked as though it had returned. Susy paced the floor, angry at the dismissive attitude she had just witnessed. She knew that the lease on the apartment expired in December, which was time enough to make alternative arrangements, if necessary. She continued to pace, anxious to know the truth and keeping one eye on the bedroom door decided that Vanessa must be approached without further delay. When she reappeared, wearing a comfortable tracksuit and pumps, for a leisurely evening at home, Susy struck.

'Am I supposed to be a mindreader?' she stated, hands on hips.

Vanessa appeared surprised. 'I don't know what you're talking about.'

'The brochures, those property lists you are looking at. If you're thinking of moving, when do you think that might be?'

Amused by the outburst, Vanessa replied. 'Aren't you being a little hasty? I'm just having a nose around, to get the feel for the market.'

Susy paused. Maybe she had been a little premature, but her home was at stake and she was not prepared to be told at the eleventh hour to pack her bags. 'Please,' she said firmly, 'I want to know every step of the way what exactly is going on.'

'But–'

'No, but, this is my home as well, just in case you'd forgotten, and you will have the decency to keep me informed at all times. I need an anchor, Vanessa, something strong and secure. Please understand that and don't play games with me.'

The anguished expression revealed the depth of insecurity and need for a safe haven that Susy so desperately craved. How thoughtless and insensitive Vanessa felt, forgetting too easily the traumas of a battered past that piece by piece was being reconstructed so well and without recrimination. For a fleeting moment Susy had doubted their friendship needlessly; Vanessa understood.

While resuming her position on the sofa, Susy picked up the *Evening Standard* from the coffee table to select the evening's viewing, but in doing so she knocked a large, plain brown envelope to the floor that Vanessa had apparently missed. Retrieving the envelope from her reclining position, she threw it back on to the table, noticing that the letter was addressed to her. She sat up, turned it over, then tearing open one end reached inside and pulled out a photograph. There was no accompanying letter, no card, or compliment slip, just a photograph. She was puzzled by the contents, which was not the usual trash mail that regularly dropped through the letterbox; this was different and was specifically sent to her. Vanessa walked back into the lounge and flopped down in the armchair opposite her.

'What's that?' she asked, not really interested.

Without replying, Susy toyed with the envelope again. There was no mistake, the typed address was bold and clear, but the postmark was almost illegible. She looked again at the photograph, the silence attracting Vanessa's attention.

'Must be interesting?'

Susy looked up briefly, then down again at the photograph. 'What do you make of this?' she said quietly.

Taking the print from Susy's hand, Vanessa looked alarmed at what she saw. The black and white print, professionally executed, was of two women, two beautiful slender women, one blonde, one dark, faces semi-hidden from the camera, but suitably posed in the act of mutual oral sex.

'Oh my God, this is terrible,' Vanessa gasped in horror. 'Who do you think could have possibly sent this?'

Susy shrugged. 'I haven't a clue.'

'This is obscene literature. Somebody out there has a very sick mind. Let me have a look at the envelope.'

'That won't help,' she said, handing over the envelope. 'See, it doesn't give anything away.' Vanessa scrutinised every square inch. 'Do you think that whoever sent this is suggesting that this is you and me?'

'That is exactly what I think.'

Susy was disgusted. Trying to interpret the perverse, distorted mind of another human being was difficult enough when you knew whom you were dealing with. Vanessa made a hasty decision. 'Don't tell anyone about this, Susy.'

'Nobody? Why not? Better to be open about it. How will we ever find out who it is?'

'No, listen to me, he wants a reaction, whoever he is. Don't give him one. Let's wait and see what he does next.'

The day of the men's final was a scorcher. Pat Cash seeded eleventh, had knocked out Jimmy Conners in the semi-final to play Ivan Lendl, who was trying for the second time to secure the title. Susy was excited as she and Peter joined the throng on Centre Court and, holding her by the hand, he led the way through the hum of spectators settling down for the afternoon match.

The spectators roared as Cash, wearing a black and white headband, and Lendl appeared on court, their kit bags over their shoulders. Peter cheered, clapping enthusiastically, for he did so want Cash to win and Susy, being carried along on a surge of euphoria was alongside, applauding them both.

The game commenced with true grit and determination on both sides. Susy watched with admiration, the quiet concentration of service, the skill and speed of delivery and return. The stakes were high, reputations too, as Cash was clearly ahead after the first set. Susy braced herself as Peter hugged her tightly at the end of each game. 'Yeah!' he cried, pounding his fist on his knee, 'he's gonna do it!' With barely a moment to sit back and reflect, they were upon their feet again, Lendl more determined than ever to thrash life out of the Aussie who had shot up through the ranks to oppose him. Cash was steadfast, not losing a single service point during the second set and finished with six games to two. Susy had not noticed Toby and Oliver seated close by with Julia and an unknown young woman, but Toby had noticed her and watched her through the darkened lenses of his sunglasses. A natural beauty, radiant, sexy, he thought when she threw back her head and laughed at Peter's jokes. She was having a great time and Toby could not take his eyes from her. The third set began with all eyes on court. Cash was two sets up, Lendl had to do something. Fiercely hot, both men were tiring, but roused by his supporters, Lendl fought back, gaining ground. Peter was silent, fearful and visibly twitchy as they reached the tie break. A hush fell on court, as both players fought for the highest accolade of their profession. Cash pelted the ball across the net with vengeance; he had come so far and he was not going home empty-handed. 'He did it!' Peter yelled, leaping out of his seat, punching the air with both fists, joining Princess Diana and Mrs Thatcher in rapturous applause.

'Game, set and match, 7–6 6–2 7–5.' Pat Cash was the 1987 Wimbledon Champion and jumped into the crowd, over seats and people to reach his family. What a final!

A memorable day, far better than Susy had ever anticipated. Strolling slowly, arm in arm, through the grounds on their way out, nothing else appeared to matter and all thoughts of Toby and Oliver were furthermost from her mind. That was her misfortune, for their presence was still there, walking so close at hand, she could have reached out and touched them. Once through the gates, both parties being swept along by the swell, they took different directions.

While Susy was in Italy on a buying trip for the boutique, Vanessa took over the reins and managed the Coterie for a few days' light deviation. Bored, she yearned for something stimulating to occupy her mind and sat all morning on the telephone. Until, disturbed by a customer entering the shop, she summoned her very capable assistant to the floor.

'There's nothing to do,' she told Lucinda over the telephone. 'And she always told me that she was so busy. I can't think what she does with her time.'

Since the demise of her relationship with Douglas, Lucinda never missed an opportunity to lunch, dinner or party. 'Making up for lost time, darling,' she said enthusiastically, using her powers of persuasion to lure Vanessa away from the monotonous, tiresome routing of retailing. 'It's an emergency,' Vanessa told the stunned assistant, as she slipped her jacket on and made her way towards the door. 'I will be back shortly.' And left her to cope single-handedly during the lunch break.

In her absence the shop became frantically busy, not only with customers, but also with a steady stream of intrusive telephone messages that were hastily scribbled down on a note pad. Phone Erik, URGENT. His abrasive intonation cut short by the crash of the receiver at the other end. Followed by Harvey Nicholls perfumery department, who were 'Returning Miss Baron's call.' Back to the fitting room to assist a paying customer with a larger size and 'Yes, Madam, we do have the very same in blue.' In full flight, racing across the shop floor, to the rails and back again to a bare arm reaching out from behind the fitting-room curtain, when the telephone rang again. As feared, the caller was Susy, just checking that everything was running smoothly and the coffers were crammed to capacity. 'Where is she?' she finally asked of Vanessa, after several minutes elaborating on next season's collection. A simple straightforward question that one second's hesitation in replying betrayed Vanessa's absence. 'I'll call back,' Susy said firmly, not waiting for an answer. A car horn beeped outside the shop, attracting attention from inside. Peter was passing by and stopped to return Susy's sunglasses, which she frequently left in his car. For one and a half hours the distraught assistant coped magnificently, politely serving the customers with all the grace and favour of her training, to the thunderous race across the shop floor in answer to the incessant flow of incoming calls.

'Where the hell is she?' Susy bellowed down the line.

'She didn't say,' the assistant replied, biting her lip. 'But I'm sure she'll be back any minute.'

Enraged by her partner's irresponsible behaviour and the distance that prevented a right-royal dressing down, Susy hung up.

Within minutes Vanessa tottered through the door and planted herself securely behind the desk, where she proceeded to read the list of callers. A wave of alcohol distorted her line of vision, causing the words to rumba over the notepad in an uncontrollable formation. How ridiculous, she thought, drawing the notepad closer in order to focus. I only drank two glasses of wine, or was it three? Sitting back quietly, breathing deeply, the room began to roll gently when a crowd of shoppers materialised through the shop door. What should she do? Say she was frightfully sorry? But she felt a little drunk, how embarrassing, she chuckled, sitting motionless, like a dummy with hooded eyes. She hoped that nobody would notice her predicament, but she was wrong, when a simple transaction requiring her to total two items correctly went disastrously wrong. She overcharged the customer by £35, then insisted that the error was theirs. 'Silly me,' she finally agreed, handing over the goods full of abject apologies, 'it's been one of those days.'

Sobriety was not being maintained, she felt ghastly and, without much ado, she left the assistant to lock up for the night. Returning home, she pulled the bedroom curtains tightly across, blocking out the slightest sliver of light and put herself to bed.

Vanessa woke with a start, flickering her eyes open into the darkness and lifting her body off the bed and into the bathroom. Switching on the light, she screwed up her eyes with pain and she endeavoured to see the damage in the mirror. 'Ugh!' she groaned, poking out the rough tongue that felt like a doormat. Pressing an inch of toothpaste on to the brush, she proceeded to clean her teeth, at the same time fumbling in the cabinet for aspirin. At two o'clock she climbed back into bed, cursing the very name Lucinda Cory. How could she allow her to drink so much at lunchtime? Flopping back on the pillow like a corpse, she pulled the cover up under her chin and slowly dozed back to sleep.

The shrill piercing tone of the telephone broke the silence of the night. Vanessa's heart jumped violently as she stretched out her hand and lifted the receiver. 'Hello?' she said, feebly. There was no response, just a hollow void. She opened her eyes wide and said, 'Who's there?' but there was no voice, no sound of breathing, just complete silence. She turned over and sat up. 'Who is that?' she said loudly, expecting an answer, when seconds later the caller clicked off, leaving the monotonous pitch of a dead line ringing in her ears. Fully awake and angry at the intrusion of sleep that she needed so badly, she wondered who but a crank would call at such a time. Surely this could not be a wrong number? She shuddered, pulling the covers up and over her protectively, shutting her eyes tightly, willing sleep to envelop her quickly.

Early morning, long before Vanessa was due to leave for the shop, Susy telephoned from Italy, telling her, in no uncertain terms, exactly what she expected of her.

'You will be there all day, if necessary,' she scolded.

Still feeling queasy, Vanessa swallowed the lecture. She was quite content to sit from 10 a.m. to 5.30 p.m. and not move a muscle. She was not going anywhere.

Why had Lucinda insisted, cajoled, even pressurised Vanessa into accepting a date with a man she had never met before, and why had she agreed? It went totally against her better judgement. Must have been the alcohol, she decided, selecting a rather sombre outfit from her extensive wardrobe, to dampen the ardour of Lucinda's Swiss banking friend. He was bound to be boring, for she had never met one who was not. Perhaps, as Lucinda had enthused, this one was different.

At street level, Susy passed Vanessa who was on her way out.

'Business meeting?' she enquired coolly, noting the dark blue suit as Vanessa climbed behind the wheel of the car.

'How observant of you,' came the sarcastic reply. She started up the engine with a roar and, not wishing to promote conversation, swung the car out of the parking bay and drove off. How fortunate, the timing was perfect, one minute later and she would have been forced to lie and Susy, astute as she was, would never let go until she had the truth.

After an exciting and exhausting buying trip, Susy had paperwork to catch up on. She opened the French doors that let out on to the balcony, letting in the warm, evening air. She settled down at a small table, opened up a ledger and, surrounded by piles of invoices, buried herself within the pages. Ahead of target, the financial situation was looking decidedly rosy she thought, tapping happily away on the calculator. Apart from a natural ability to select a winning line, she always kept her eye open with certain customers in mind, for that 'special' ensemble. She did not wait for them to come to her, she went all out for them, flattered and pampered them. Even before the new garments were unpacked on the day of delivery, she would contact them all. 'It's perfect!' she would say enthusiastically. 'Especially for you,' which was true. The personal touch worked like a dream and they came running to her door, praised her good judgement and never left with only one purchase. Susy sat back, stretched her arms above her head and yawned. Satisfied, she closed the ledger and congratulated herself on an uninterrupted evening's work completed. Glancing at her watch, she had forgotten to call Joyce. She tapped in her number only to hear the intermittent bleep of a busy line. She would try again later.

A light breeze began to blow across the square, creating a chill throughout the apartment. Crossing the room to close the French windows, Susy stepped outside on to the balcony, where she could hear the swish of the traffic travelling down Sloane Street after a shower of rain. Looking down into the street below, her attention was drawn to the sound of a car door banging and Vanessa hurrying away. She stepped back into the apartment, secured the French doors, pulling the drapes closed. She was home early – to be precise, 9.30.

'I see you've been busy?' Vanessa remarked, observing the paperwork still lying on the table. 'How are we doing?'

'Great, just great,' Susy replied, picking up the ledger and walking over to the safe. 'How was your evening?'

Vanessa hoped that Susy did not want her to elaborate. Her evening with Lucinda's *bon ami*, the very eloquent, but snub-nosed Jean Claude had been staid, polite and humourless. He had talked incessantly about finance and extolled the merits of Gruyere cheese to a height that she could only have dreamt about. Then and only then, halfway into her *pot au chocolat*, did she feign an oncoming migraine. Unhappily she told a very concerned Jean Claude of her dilemma, but she would have to leave immediately. Sleep, solitude in a darkened room was the only remedy. She was most apologetic and an excellent actress.

Susy prepared the dining table meticulously, while in the kitchen Vanessa was putting the finishing touches to the baked lasagne. Joyce was coming to dinner and arrived on their doorstep very early. After pressing the wrong buzzer twice, she fumbled in her handbag for her glasses and the scrap of paper on which she had written the correct address. 'Flat 2 – Baron. Ah! Right, that's it.' she mumbled, pressing the button long and hard. She struggled up the flight of stairs, where Susy welcomed her with open arms, escorted her to a chair and handed her a large vodka and tonic. Joyce surveyed the room, the sweet smelling freesias placed on centre table, which mingled with the aroma of cooking coming from the kitchen, giving a warm and homely atmosphere. 'Hum, very nice,' Joyce mused, from her comfortable chair by the fireplace, which was decorated with a colourful display of dried flowers.

'You've gone to a lot of trouble, pet,' she said loudly.

'It's a pleasure,' Vanessa replied, placing a basket of bread on the table.

Susy uncorked a bottle of wine and checked the bubbling lasagne. 'Five minutes,' she said, slamming the oven door. 'I hope you're hungry?'

Susy plied Joyce with food and wine, while they talked avidly about business and of their long-term plans to combine fashion with fitness. A total package for the modern woman, from basic grooming to tomorrow's executive businesswoman. The whole concept was way above Joyce's head, finding the speed at which the young chose to operate difficult to comprehend. In six months plans for the Coterie were well on the way to becoming the most exclusive club for women in the country, and Joyce had helped make it happen. Nothing would ever be too much trouble where Joyce was concerned and after a very enjoyable meal, where they had demolished the lasagne completely, she eased back into an armchair with an after-dinner drink. Vanessa brought a cafetière and three cups on a tray and proceeded to pour coffee, while Susy discreetly took a large package from the safe. With a slight nod of the head, Vanessa disappeared upstairs, leaving them alone.

'Thanks, darling,' Susy said, wrapping her arm around Joyce's shoulder and pressed a kiss hard against her cheek. She almost upset her coffee cup when Susy placed the sealed package into her hand.

'What's this, then?' she asked.

Taking the cup and saucer from her hands and placing them carefully on the coffee table, Susy insisted that the bundle be opened immediately. With trembling fingers Joyce ripped open the end to find a wad of tens, twenties and fifty-pound notes stashed inside. She gasped, 'Huh, darlin', 'ow much is 'ere?'

'Five grand ... I owe you, Joycie.'

'Yes, sweetheart, but I didn't expect it so soon. Are you sure?'

'First instalment. I've got to honour our agreement.'

Joyce held Susy's face in her hands. 'You're a good gal and I loves you like I bore you myself, do you 'ear me? Nobody's ever goin' to hurt you again, else they've got me to contend with.'

'Attention, ladies!' All eyes ascended to the top of the stairs, where Vanessa stood clutching a multi-coloured silk dress to her body. She sauntered slowly towards them. 'What do you think, Joyce?' she said, circling the armchair.

'Oh, smashing darlin', go and try it on.'

Vanessa held the dress up in front of her, then searched for the swing ticket, which was attached to the sleeve. 'Oh, dear,' she tutted, 'it's not my size,' a look of disappointment creeping over her face, 'it's an eighteen.'

'Hey,' Susy exclaimed, nudging Joyce's arm, 'aren't you an eighteen?'

'Yes, darlin', but–'

'Then you had better try it on.'

'Oh, but I couldn't.'

Vanessa handed over the dress. 'Of course you can,' and directed her upstairs to change.

The impatient buzz of the intercom announced Polly's unexpected arrival. Looking pale and flustered, she was eager to talk, something was troubling her greatly. Vanessa rushed a cup of coffee into her hand and sat her down. Since returning from New York she had made up her mind to end her relationship with Toby. She had seen him only twice and on both occasions he had flatly refused to listen to her enthuse over her new job. He was stressed, she continued, working day and night on a deal that had gone disastrously wrong, and he blamed her for his failure. She was not there to support him when he needed her most. Polly paused for a moment; she was enjoying her work and had no intention of giving up. She was doing well and he despised her, loathed her success and when she told him that she was leaving for the winter couture collection in Paris, he flew into a monstrous rage. He had an important function that he demanded she attend; when she refused he hurled an ashtray across the room at her.

'I can't go back,' she despaired, 'I won't be bullied by his antics. It's over this time and I mean that, I've had enough.'

For a moment they had forgotten Joyce standing at the bottom of the stairs, wearing the silk dress that fitted her perfectly.

Susy got up. 'Who's a little cracker now?' she added, straightening the shoulders and smoothing out the skirt. 'Like it?'

Joyce touched the silk, the softness sliding beneath her coarse hands. 'It's just beautiful, darlin',' she said almost in a whisper.

'Then it's yours, a gift from Vanessa and me.'

Looking up with pride Joyce stood erect, her gravelly voice faltering as she began to speak. 'Thank you luvvies, thank you both very much.'

The commotion outside the boutique drew Susy to the front of the shop. 'What's happened?' she said to a man hurrying by. People were running, car horns blasting, the whole of Knightsbridge was alive with speculation. There had been a raid at the security deposit box offices, close to Harrods, and huge crowds were forming outside, screaming and shouting to get inside. Television cameras had just arrived, when the unruly crowd turned into a mob. Susy strained her neck for a better look, only to see Peter making his way towards her. 'Has anybody been hurt?' she asked, with concern.

'No, but there's an awful lot of angry people out there. It must have been one hell of a raid.'

Peter directed Susy back into the shop and closed the door

behind them, shutting out the din. A closer inspection of his receding hairline betrayed the glow of a suntan.

'You've been away,' she said. This was hard to deny, for he had only just flown into Heathrow and Susy was his first port of call. 'Where've you been?' she quickly asked, not giving him a chance to explain, 'You didn't tell me.' Peter begged to interrupt. 'OK, who is she?'

'Now just give me a break and I'll tell you,' he said firmly.

Peter had just returned from Lanzarote; apparently his services were required earlier than anticipated.

Susy bombarded him with questions. 'When are you leaving?'

He had returned only to collect his belongings and was departing at the weekend. There were no problems regarding the apartment, the tenancy was expiring and his students knew he was going. Everything tied in nicely and Susy was going to miss him terribly.

'Hey, cheer up, you know you're welcome any time.'

They embraced, squeezing the very life from each other, then he was gone.

Vanessa's secretary escorted Sir Richard into her office. 'Hold all calls,' Vanessa said, taking his arm and leading him over to a chair. This was a rare visit and an unexpected pleasure, for which she was honoured. 'What can I get you, daddy? Tea, coffee?'

'No, nothing, my dear, I am not staying long, but I couldn't pass your door and not say hello on my way to the Connaught.'

'Are you lunching?' she asked knowingly.

'I am, indeed, so I don't want to impair the appetite.'

The gastronomic skills of the Connaught's cuisine was one of Sir Richard's small pleasures in life. He waffled on about the traffic and the congestion in the capital. 'There's too many of us,' he stated, referring to the population explosion. 'No wonder we have galloping inflation.' Lady Caroline was well, but refused flatly to walk anywhere near the swimming pool, he chuckled, preferring to spend her time at coffee mornings and in the company of her little feathered friends. 'Bloody birds,' he said sharply, when there was a knock on the door.

'I didn't realise, excuse me,' Erik exclaimed, poking his head around the corner.

Vanessa beckoned him inside. 'You remember my father?'

How could Erik forget, living with a hero? Vanessa sat back and listened, while the two men became engrossed in conversation.

The Gulf crisis was a matter of grave concern, Sir Richard went on to say and Margaret had quite rightly stood up and urged other countries to send in mine sweepers to protect their tankers. A vast quantity of oil was being transported through these waterways, so why should the task be left to the USA, France and the UK? Erik agreed wholeheartedly, saying that the situation was a threat to the security of the western world. Sir Richard shuffled in his seat, commanding a more favourable position opposite Erik.

'I was born during the First World War, my boy, and served my country during the Second. I know only too well the implications and when you look at this man, Hess, the one that's just died, locked up for forty years. Just ask yourself, what's it all about and for what purpose?'

'Lucky to get away with his life.'

Sir Richard reflected, 'But what a life, better that he had perished with the rest.' He glanced at his watch. 'I shouldn't be here, my dear,' and struggled to his feet. 'Nice talking to you,' he held out his hand. 'Erik isn't it ... yes, well, we must do it again sometime.' Vanessa assisted her father to the door. 'I almost forgot, Vanessa. Rupert is coming home.'

'That's wonderful news, daddy. When?'

'Splendid. Next month, sometime. You had better ask your mother.'

They both watched him totter towards the elevator, raising his cane in farewell as the doors closed.

'He's such a lovely old boy,' Erik said with respect.

They stood idly gazing as the elevator's bright display light descended to the ground floor. A welcome few moments of inertia, induced by the hypnotic drone transmitting from the office floor. 'Call on line one,' came a voice from behind the desk, luring them both back into the realms of controlled chaos.

The first leaves of autumn were falling, creating a golden carpet throughout the city, tinged with a chilly wind that made flesh shiver and rush for cover. Vanessa was house-hunting, undeterred by oncoming winter, and insisted that Susy join her each time a property caught her eye. Treading the streets of London's more salubrious areas was enlightening, but disheartening, as one by one Vanessa rejected the most delightful cottages at a glance, dropping the specifications into the nearest litterbin without a second thought. 'I will know the moment I step inside,' she told her weary friend, who was hard pressed to keep up the pace.

'Why do you need me to come with you?' she asked angrily, thinking of a host of other things she would rather be doing.

'Because I need you, Susy.'

Vanessa was interested in nothing else and her routine never varied. Work, the occasional evening out with Lucinda and the driving obsession of becoming a property owner. In short, she was becoming a bore. Susy ran the boutique with proficient ease, still finding time to socialise. She kept up her sessions in the gym and since Peter was away, took up badminton, for which there was never a shortage of partners. Mrs Potter was pleased with her progress, although the lessons were taking a little longer than she initially thought to reach a standard of acceptability.

Polly returned from a business trip, keeping a hastily arranged date with Susy in the gym. They worked up a sweat, side by side, exchanging current news of interest and missed opportunities. Polly's repartee was side-cracking, as they both struggled for some degree of sensibility before busting a gut, or breaking a limb. She was having such a good time since breaking up with Toby that Susy felt confident to broach the subject of their long affair and extract the truth. Polly was euphoric, flying ten feet off the ground, when Susy came straight to the point.

'Heard from Toby?' she asked casually.

'Not for a month. Not a phone call, or message. It's like he doesn't exist.'

'How strange,' Susy agreed, 'but you did love him?'

'I guess I did at the beginning, but now he's shut me out, after I totally destroyed his ego.'

'What went wrong?'

Wistful thoughts delayed Polly's reply. 'I think I outgrew him. It happens. He always wanted to hold me back when I wanted to go forward. In the end we were travelling in opposite directions.'

Susy absorbed every word, storing every minute detail in her memory. 'Would you take him back?' This she had to know.

'No.' She was adamant. 'It's finally over. I can honestly say that it's all in the past.'

More than satisfied that this was the truth, Susy felt confident to pursue her ambition. The way was clear, direction certain. With her goal firmly in sight she was free to move on and move in where Polly had left off. Nobody would get hurt – her plan was perfect.

With her kit bag slung over her shoulder, Susy arrived home, picked up the piles of estate agents' mail from the hall table and ran upstairs. On putting the key in the apartment door, she noticed a postcard amongst the letters that was addressed to her. She kicked the door closed behind her, dumping her bag on the chair and proceeded to read the almost illegible handwriting on the back. Peter was fine, enjoying the work, island is barren, just like the moon, sorry I haven't written sooner, too busy, will call, love Peter. Susy placed the glossy bright blue postcard in prime position, under a magnet on the refrigerator door – at least he had written. Returning to the lounge, she picked up the kit bag, the contents of which were destined for the washing machine and walked back into the kitchen, smiling at Peter's postcard as she passed by. Her eyes rested on the pile of mail sitting on the worktop, as she stuffed the dirty laundry into the washing machine. There was nothing unusual about the stacks of mail that regularly fell through the letterbox, and yet she felt compelled to sift through it, running her fingers slowly over each one with considerable caution. Her pulse raced a little faster, breath came a little shorter, for amongst them, almost at the bottom of the pile, was a large brown envelope addressed to her, in the same bold typewritten print that she recalled so well. She stood for several minutes and gazed at the large, flat, sealed envelope, unable to rip it open. Neither did she hear Vanessa enter the apartment and walk right up behind her.

'What's wrong?' Vanessa asked, causing her to spin around with fright.

'You open it,' she said, thrusting the envelope into her hands.

Vanessa quickly tore open the end and pulled out the contents. The heavy silence confirmed Susy's worse fears. 'The same?' she asked anxiously.

'The very same,' Vanessa replied, 'only much worse.'

'Is there anything else?'

As anticipated, a second look revealed nothing. Vanessa paced the kitchen floor, not knowing quite what to do. 'Did you keep the other one, Susy?'

'It's in the drawer upstairs ... what should we do, call the police?'

Vanessa continued to pace slowly up and down, brushing her fingertips across her brow in deep concentration. 'Wait, let's think. When did you receive the other one?'

'I can't remember exactly when,' she answered, raising her voice. 'Six, maybe eight weeks ago.'

'July. That's a gap of two months ... why?'

Irritated by illogical mumbling, Susy hit back. 'Stop playing detective, will you, and let's do something about it.'

'Tell me, Susy. What have they got to go on? Absolutely nothing.'

'How do we know that? There might be some fingerprints on it. It's worth a try.'

Vanessa stormed out of the kitchen, with Susy hard on her heels. 'I very much doubt it.'

''This is my problem, you obstinate cow, and it's making me very nervous. I want to stop this jerk.'

'Susy, you are doing exactly what he wants, getting jumpy.'

With tortuous uncertainties she bellowed, 'So do nothing and then he'll forget all about it. Is that it?'

Undisturbed by the seething bout of neurosis Vanessa replied quietly, 'Yes, stay calm, do nothing and I promise you he'll go away.'

Ambiguous thoughts contaminated and clouded her worried mind. No words of reassurance could erase the shadow of foul play and yet, Susy bowed, somewhat reluctantly, to Vanessa's judgement.

Crossing the room she closed the drapes to the French windows and listened to Vanessa's conversation on the telephone.

'How exciting, when?' she heard her say, with eager anticipation. Responding with an intermittent, 'Um, um.' to the almost inaudible cackle at the other end of the line. She laughed with easy confidence, urging her friend to continue, words tripping over words, in a flurry of social chit-chat. When quite suddenly the mood changed and a profound and disturbing sense of gloom filtered through the air, leaving the eavesdropper with a taste of foreboding. Too late, as a shriek of laughter hit the ceiling. The chameleon was rising and falling as the conversation dictated and Vanessa was doing what she did best. 'Saturday the twenty-sixth, you will be there, won't you?' she impressed. Where, Susy wondered, staring Vanessa in the eye, anxious to know what was going on. 'At Hambledon, darling. I can't wait to see him too.' Who can't she wait to see? The suspense was gripping. 'It's been a whole year and I just know he will have had a wonderful time in America.' Susy searched her mind, quickly trying to piece together the snippet of conversation, until a picture began to form. 'I am so pleased, Rupert will be delighted to see you, bye, darling.' Vanessa replaced the receiver and with an arrogant expression, watched Susy slink back to the kitchen.

Polly stopped the car outside the Coterie, blasting the horn in an attempt to attract Susy's attention and waved furiously out of the car window. She looked up from behind the large desk at the rear of the shop and walked to the door. 'Come in for a coffee.'

'No time. Do you want to see a movie tonight?'

The traffic was beginning to pile up with impatient drivers lightly tooting their horns to move on.

'Yes, why not.'

'Eight o'clock, meet me at home.' Polly started to move away.

'Hey, what's on?' Susy yelled.

'*Fatal Attraction.*' How appropriate she thought, watching Polly drive away. Could she possibly be masquerading as a scriptwriter for MGM?

A quick change of clothes and a bite to eat was all there was time for. She switched on the answerphone, picked up her shoulder bag and was out of the apartment in good time. The drive to Thurloe Square would take precisely ten minutes, but on reaching the street she saw Vanessa emerging from a taxi, obviously in a great hurry.

'What's the rush?' she asked, as Vanessa paid the cabby.

'Give me two minutes and I'll be with you.'

'But I'm going to the cinema.'

'I know,' she said racing up the steps, 'me too, *Fatal Attraction*, I'll be right there.'

Susy unlocked the car door, climbed inside, switched on the radio and sat patiently waiting for Vanessa to reappear, humming and drumming her fingers on the steering wheel in time to the music. She checked her watch every 60 seconds, anticipating the entire evening to disappear inside of five minutes of the clock. Restless, she twiddled the tuner on the radio and readjusted the rear-view mirror. The street was quiet, just a light whistle of wind encircled the car, creating an eerie silence that sharpened the senses and awakened the mind. The front door banged and Vanessa hurried across the street in her direction, jumping into the passenger seat, as she turned the ignition, firing life into the old Metro. A dark-blue car parked several spaces behind started up the engine simultaneously, pulling away from the kerb with equal speed and trailed the Metro down Cadogan Place into Sloane Street. The traffic lights turned red at Knightsbridge, forcing Susy to pull up abruptly before turning left into the Brompton Road. The dark-blue car kept pace, the occupants incognito. Obscured from sight and suspicion, they continued to pursue the Metro down the Brompton Road, passing Harrods and the Oratory, where Susy took the slip road to the left, swinging the vehicle into Thurloe Square and parked. The dark-blue car purred slowly to a halt unnoticed, but within full view of the two girls running up the steps to Polly's front door. They rang the bell, then disappeared through the door. Polly was running late, a wearisome attribute, made worse by the pressure of work. Henry meowed around Susy's ankles, stepping over her feet and through her legs remembering an old friend; he was also starving. She scooped the great white bundle of fluff into her arms, when he headbutted her cheek, sinking his claws into her flesh, in a passionate plea for love and attention. Vanessa strolled into the living room, glancing around at the subtle shades of lavender and blue that blended well together. Polly had spent a considerable amount of money redecorating and the result was charming, aesthetic and feminine.

'Here, kitty kitty,' Polly called from the kitchen, hurriedly placing the cat's supper on the floor. Henry leapt from Susy's shoulder like a cloud off a breeze and scampered towards the evening's spread.

Prying eyes stared out of the dark-blue vehicle as it slowly circled the square, pulling up outside Polly's apartment. The driver nudged his mate's shoulder and pointed up to the first-floor window, where Vanessa could clearly be seen standing alone. They smiled smugly at each other and watched, until distracted, Vanessa turned and walked away, leaving the apartment in darkness. When they emerged out into the street, the dark-blue car had vanished.

The film was just beginning to a packed auditorium, when the usherette showed them to their seats. They edged past disgruntled people, rising and falling, holding on to coats and bags, anxious not to miss a single frame and settled down side by side, Susy in the middle, and watched as the plot unfolded.

'Isn't he gorgeous?' Polly whispered to Vanessa.

'What?' She had not heard and leant forward.

'Gorgeous. Michael Douglas?' Vanessa nodded. 'I wouldn't have to be asked twice, would you, Vanessa?'

'No, not even once,' she sniggered.

Ignoring the crossfire, Susy sat back into her seat trying to listen to the dialogue. Absorbing every small detail with loathing as the story thickened. Darkness shrouded her consciousness, for the special effects, like a malignant tumour, gobbled up all trace of virtue. The psychotic thriller was disturbing and destructive, causing her to gasp, as breathing became more spasmodic. Vanessa whispered across Susy's line of vision.

'Do you know who she reminds me of? Polly.'

'I don't give a toss who she reminds you of,' Susy said angrily. 'Shut up, or change places.'

Deeper and deeper they sank into their seats. Terrified, for each one could identify with some aspect of the story. The passion, hate, revenge and blood. Susy hid behind her hands, as the celluloid images became too real to bear. She did not see, but she heard the contorted voices, the unrelenting panting, screaming, choking and then silence, that welcome hush, when it was all over. With head bowed and hands still trembling, a single tear trickled down her cheek on to her shirt. She slowly looked up, wiping her face with her hand. She should never have agreed to go.

How quickly the weekend of the twenty-sixth had come around. Rupert was home and Vanessa intended to give him a rapturous welcome, inviting all her friends to Hambledon for the party. Susy felt unwell, the sore throat that had threatened to turn into a nasty bout of flu was getting steadily worse by the hour. On Saturday afternoon she telephoned Vanessa from the shop and apologised in advance for her absence.

Feed a cold, her mother had always said, so she did, pouring liberal quantities of hot soup down her throat as well as inhalants to unblock the nasal passages. She took an aspirin and had a hot bath. Stretching out under the bed covers, clasping a hot water bottle to her chest, she aimed the remote control at the television to see one repeat after another. How boring, she snuffled, flipping channels, the soporific effect of medication beginning to overcome her. Fuzzy-headed and full of self pity, she settled down, hypnotised by empty words coming from the television set that demanded no mental exertion and dozed off.

Rupert was looking slim, tanned and extremely well, as he mingled with family and close friends. Pleased to be home after having a tremendous time in America, he could now look forward to rebuilding his life. Lady Caroline fussed over him constantly and followed him everywhere.

Rupert was polite, flashing a wide refulgent smile at everyone. His dark hair, longer than usual, fell softly over one eye. He constantly brushed it out of the way with his hand.

'Rupert, we haven't had time to talk yet,' Vanessa said, having difficulty trying to hold his attention, when a friendly arm shunted him off to the other side of the room.

Cast aside, Vanessa looked around for someone to talk to and saw Piers heading in her direction. 'Hello,' she said with a smile, as he passed her by. Was there nobody willing to share a word or two?

'Vanessa?' came a small voice at waist height. She immediately looked down. 'It is Vanessa, isn't it?' She looked closer at the elderly lady. 'Miss Duffy, do you remember?' But Vanessa did not. 'I was Rupert's nanny.'

Good gracious, Vanessa thought, guiding the frail old lady to a chair. Mother had not forgotten anybody.

She had to be content to sit this party out, wait her turn. Watching Rupert circulate, enjoying immensely the attention being heaped upon him, she realised just how much she had missed him and how good she felt to have him home again. Miss Duffy talked incessantly at her, rambling on with one continuous sentence, recalling dates and events that she could not possibly remember. This once upstanding spinster and a staunch supporter of the Women's Institute helped shape the brother she loved so much and Vanessa hoped beyond hope that Rupert would not have forgotten.

Feeling worse not better, Susy climbed out of bed, struggled downstairs to the kitchen, put on the kettle and sat feeling mighty sorry for herself. Millions are spent on medical research and yet they could not find a cure for the common cold, just when she needed a remedy. She despaired and sneezed for a third time into a tissue. How she hated being sick, and what an inconvenience and total waste of time. The kettle boiled, shooting scalding hot vapours high into the air. She shuddered, pulling her dressing gown snugly up around her neck and poured the bubbling water out into the prepared mug of brandy, lemon juice and a teaspoonful of honey. After refilling the hot water bottle again and with the hot toddy firmly in her hand, she trudged back to the bedroom, collapsed into bed and hoped for a decent night's sleep.

Sir Richard sat majestically in the corner armchair, nursing a glass of claret and watched the buzz of activity surrounding his eldest son. He felt immense pride, looking on with affection and admiration. A year away had given him an air of self-confidence and a healthy physique. Rupert was fighting fit. 'A man amongst men,' he told Veronica.

Lady Caroline never faltered, orchestrating the party beautifully. There was never an empty glass, or a guest left unattended, bringing people together with all the charm and diplomacy of a professional hostess. She basked in the glory and appreciation her friends bestowed upon her; if not totally sincere, they could not question the hospitality and planning that fashioned a truly successful evening.

Polly found Vanessa locked into deep conversation with Piers when she arrived. Although they had met on several previous occasions she found him arrogant, brash, even immature, and not her type at all. She had not planned on staying long, an hour at most, when she bulldozed her way into the conversation.

'So sorry I'm late,' she said, smacking a kiss each side of

Vanessa's face, without so much as a whisper as to why she should be two hours late. 'Hello,' she said dispassionately to Piers, who acknowledged the greeting with equal consideration.

A salver appeared between them, bearing several glasses of red and white wine, from which Polly lifted a glass before the maid disappeared into the crowd.

'Hi!' came the voice from over her shoulder, causing Polly to turn round and gaze up into the bronzed face.

'Somebody I would like you to meet,' Vanessa said, taking Rupert's arm. 'This is my brother, Rupert.'

Polly's eyes lit up. No photograph could do justice to the real thing, and she hesitated before introducing herself, when Rupert took her hand. 'Polly, I'm delighted to meet you,' and was immediately swept off and into the crowd.

Still rooted to the floor, disappointed at the briefness of their encounter, she watched as Rupert was so abruptly torn from her grasp. 'Vanessa, I had no idea, he is so handsome.'

'Anybody can look good with a tan,' Piers remarked sarcastically, raising his voice.

'Piers, don't let yourself down, please,' Vanessa added wearily, his attitude being fuelled by disdain and envy. Polly was not at all surprised.

'I see Preston's back.' Shocked, Vanessa had no idea and felt the blood drain from her complexion.

'Back? Steven?' She asked enquiringly, 'Are you sure?'

'Quite sure. Haven't you seen him?'

Two years had passed since they last met, when he and Melanie were trying to salvage what was left of their marriage. The baby she was expecting must be 18 months old now.

'No, why should I have seen him?'

'I thought you might, that's all, now that he is divorced.'

Divorced! Somehow Vanessa felt that she would have known. They had been so close, why had nobody thought to tell her, she wondered, and when did all this happen?

'I don't believe you, Piers. Who told you this story?'

'It's no secret, Vanessa,' he laughed, 'Ask anybody.'
'And the child?'
'She lost it and they split up soon after that.'

Polly watched very carefully, sensing the confusion racing through Vanessa's mind as she tried to piece together the affair, recalling the agonising conversations of despair and humiliation she felt at the hands of her family.

'You'll find him in the Stag and Huntsman most evenings.'

Vanessa had heard enough, guiding Polly away from the lounge and into the kitchen, where Marie was busy preparing coffee.

'What do I do, Polly? Do I see him?'

'Only you can make that decision. But if you don't go, you may wonder for the rest of your life.'

Trying to lift the shadow of ambiguity was difficult, especially where Vanessa was concerned. Advice, however well intended, was not always received with equal understanding. Polly waited for a reaction, had she finally got through?

Susy tossed and turned for what appeared to be hours. One minute too hot, the next too cold. She propped herself up in bed and switched on the bedside lamp – 3.30. What should she do? The medication had not helped at all. She was still congested, breathing on half a lung and her head was as heavy as lead. She sat in an upright position, head tilted slightly back and allowed her system to drain; sleep would eventually follow. Comfortable and warm, she felt unconsciousness overcome her and reached for the bedside lamp, switching it off.

Nothing much stirred between four and five o'clock in the morning, when the two shadowy figures silently scaled the front portal at Cadogan Place. Cowering low so as not to be seen, or heard, they skilfully slipped over the balcony and crept along, their agile bodies barely making a sound. The French windows to the apartment were locked and the drapes pulled across, but they depressed the handle slowly, tampering with the lock. The only way in was to break the glass and they worked quickly and quietly, taping the windowpane well, before tapping the glass once. With a crack, the glass broke intact and not a fragment fell. Susy moved heavily over in bed, undisturbed, and sank into a deep sleep, while the intruders reached through the broken pane of glass, turned the key and slipped unnoticed into the apartment. They were professionals, polished and lethal. With one gesturing to the other without a word they each covered a section of the apartment alone. Nothing was left unturned; drawers and boxes were rifled, emptied, cupboards opened and furniture moved. Everything was searched for money, jewellery, credit cards, cheque books and anything small enough to handle. They had been in the apartment less than five minutes, when one of the burglars located the safe. Susy's breathing became laboured and she sat up half conscious, punching the pillows into a comfortable prop before settling down again. In the excitement, one of the burglars beckoned frantically to his mate. He needed help immediately, in order to open the safe, but he tripped foolishly, catching his foot on the table leg, causing the large pottery vase to tumble and fall, shattering into a thousand pieces on the parquet floor. Susy woke up with a jump, her heart pounding in her chest. Getting out of bed, she put on her robe and stepped nervously towards the bedroom door and switched on the upstairs lights, but the intruders had fled as skilfully as they had entered, leaving chaos. Susy could not believe her eyes walking around the apartment. Stepping over the debris, she searched and found her handbag, which was empty, tripping over cosmetics that were strewn across the floor. In a short space of time they had been thorough and, at a glance, Vanessa's collection of enamels and a pair of pearl earrings that were lying on the dining table were gone. She made her way over upturned furniture to the wall safe, which mercifully had not been opened.

The police officers walked around the apartment surveying the damage and made a few notes. There was not a lot they could do. 'Don't touch anything,' they said. 'the fingerprint boys will be here shortly.' Susy sat quietly hunched up on the bottom step of the stairs, her body aching from the heavy cold that was now well established. The fresh morning air wafting through the open

French door felt like an icy gale against her sensitive, clammy skin. She felt violated, angry and upset, wanting to lash out, scream out loud. How dare they invade her life, her home and her possessions, Vanessa's possessions. Sapped of all strength, she picked up the telephone and called Vanessa, knowing that Sunday morning was a bad time, but she had to let her know. Upstairs, she gathered the duvet from the bed and wrapped it around her shoulders, dragged a path into the kitchen, where she sat huddled over a hot mug of tea. How she craved a cigarette.

Vanessa raced through the door as the fingerprint boys were packing up. She stood back in horror, absorbing the destruction, not knowing which way to turn. 'Did you find anything?' she asked a police officer.

'Not a lot, miss. I'm afraid these lads knew exactly what they were doing.'

Susy switched off the vacuum, looking ghastly dressed in a thick tracksuit, with a scarf tucked underneath her chin.

'You mean there's nothing, no prints?'

'They wore woolly gloves,' the officer replied.

'How can you possibly tell that?' she asked in disbelief.

The officer picked up a piece of glass from the broken window. 'By the outline of the print on the glass, look, it's fuzzy. Sorry, miss, but we do have a heel print.'

'Is that all?' The officer nodded, shrugging his shoulders.

The remainder of the day was spent picking up the pieces, assessing the damage and counting their losses. The contents of the safe and Vanessa's jewellery would be transferred to the bank, cash kept to a minimum and an alarm system installed immediately.

11

On a pleasant evening and not being in any particular hurry, Susy decided to take the long route home. She locked the shop door, pulled her collar up around her neck and strode off down Beauchamp Place towards the Brompton Road window-shopping, stopping occasionally for a closer look, if something caught her eye. It was Friday night, when the traffic zoomed past at great speed, taking weekenders towards the Cromwell Road and the motorways. The rising affluent middle-classes fleeing the city to their country retreats, where they slept for two days to enable them to work harder in order to maintain two homes. That is if they did not die of a coronary in doing so. She turned left at the Michelin building and stopped for some time gazing into Joseph's window. What fun, she thought. Such style and co-ordination, an empire to be very envious of.

The light growl of a Porsche trailed Susy as she walked down Sloane Avenue. The driver lowered the window as he drew alongside, pulling the car over to the kerb.

'Hey, Susy,' the man's voice yelled from inside.

Surprised, she lowered her head to see who was driving, and her pulse began to race on seeing Toby smiling up at her.

'Where are you going?'

'Home.'

'Get in, I'll drop you off.' She climbed into the passenger seat. 'So how are you?'

'I'm fine, just fine,' she laughed nervously. 'And you?'

His eyes quickly glanced as she tossed her hair off her shoulders. 'Great, couldn't be better.' The Porsche roared into Sloane Square. 'How's Peter? Haven't seen him around lately.'

'He's in the Canaries, working.'

He laughed. 'Working eh! So has the little man got a real job at last?'

'You two should have tried to get along,' she impressed. 'He's a really nice person.'

Toby turned the car into Cadogan Place without replying and stopped outside the apartment. He slipped his arm around her shoulder, and she felt compelled to say something sensible, but the only thing that sprang to mind was Polly.

'I'm sorry about you and–'

'These things happen,' he quickly replied, stroking her hair.

Susy had rehearsed her role a hundred times should the opportunity present itself and now, as he pulled her closer to him, she was paralysed. Sensing her apprehension, he pulled back, brushing her face with his hand.

'I, I–' she began to say.

'Shush,' he said, quietly searching her face. 'You are exquisite, quite beautiful.' She flushed, lowering her eyes. 'Oh, really Susy, I mean exquisite.' Toby pulled her gently towards him, raising her face and softly enveloped her mouth with his. She felt her whole body respond to his touch, his mouth, his tongue. The long deep breaths as he released her and then kissed her again, harder and stronger, caressing her hair, her neck. She held on to Toby with all the strength that she could find, until finally he let her out of his grasp. For a moment there was silence, then he spoke, slowly and convincingly. 'I must see you again,' and kissed her gently on the cheek. 'I cannot lose what I have just found. Say yes, don't disappoint me.'

Susy held her breath for a moment. What she had wanted for so long, now wanted her. She could not believe what was happening as he held her in his arms again.

'I will not disappoint you, you have my word,' she said.

Toby held her tighter, running his hands through her long hair and pulling her head towards him, pressing his lips hard against hers in a passionate embrace. With his arm still around her shoulder, he sat back deep in thought.

'I'm going away for a couple of weeks.'

'When?'

'Tomorrow. LA and San Francisco, business and a little pleasure,' he smiled. 'I'll call as soon as I can.'

She sighed, two weeks seemed eternal. 'It's a long time.'

'I know, my darling, but when I return, we will make up for lost time, I promise.' He kissed her again. 'But now I have to leave you.' He started up the engine.

'Until then,' she said, climbing out of the car, feeling quite unsteady.

Later in bed, she lay back and relived every tender moment and hung on to every word that he had said. Her imagination allowed his hands to caress her body, as if he were there beside her. She took the pillow, encircling her arms around the soft fullness and squeezed, closing her eyes. She would tell no one, this was their secret, until he was hers and hers alone.

Vanessa felt nervous walking into the Stag and Huntsman with Rupert. Would Stephen be there as Piers had assured her? Rupert opened the door and followed her into the bar. Saturday evening and the place was crowded, with many local faces acknowledging their arrival, but no Stephen. She found a stool at a corner table and waited, while Rupert tried unsuccessfully to prize himself away from the counter. There was so much to talk about and to share with eager ears, who could only dream of such an adventure. Uproarious laughter filled the bar and pint mugs were raised in appreciation of a raunchy tale and there was so much more. For lowered heads huddled together like naughty schoolboys, listened while the soft rumblings of Rupert's lone voice brought the house down. Vanessa looked on and smiled, he had had a very good time, when Stephen walked straight up to the bar, attracted by all the noise and ordered a pint of special brew. He was alone and she was able to observe him unseen through the throng. Stephen looked gaunt and tired, his blond hair streaked with silver. He sipped his lager and glanced around the bar, but failed to catch her eye, then turned to join in the jollity. Time and circumstances had taken their toll, etched into every line and crevice on the once handsome face. Vanessa felt sorry, so very sorry for the pain she knew he had endured when they were together. Was this the man she had loved so desperately? The man she was willing to give her life to for ever? It now seemed such a long time ago. Fond memories were being destroyed by the harshness of reality as she prepared to leave. Rupert was having far too good a time without her.

'Can I buy you a drink, Vanessa?' Stephen's loud voice caught her off guard. 'A Cinzano and lemonade, if I remember rightly?'

Without speaking, Vanessa sat back down again and wondered what she should say after all this time. A rush of nervous confusion impeded any logical thinking. Would he talk of Melanie and the divorce, or would he just remember the good times they had shared? Or even worse, would they behave like complete strangers? She felt uneasy watching Stephen angle his way back to the table and looked up into his face. 'How are you?' she asked.

He hesitated, 'Well, and you?'

She nodded, 'Very well.'

'I hear you're quite a businesswoman now.' Piers had been talking. 'I always knew you were a capable woman, Vanessa. Lucky for you we split up.' He took a large gulp of lager.

'That wasn't necessary, Stephen.'

He stared into his lager, stonefaced and silent. Then looked up and smiled. 'You're right, my apologies.'

Stephen talked incessantly about business. How he had to close the Marlow office because of rising overheads, and how Irene's unflinching loyalty had enabled him to re-establish himself in a smaller office in Henley. 'I couldn't have done it without her,' he said, wringing his hands. He had also bought a small cottage outside Henley and was trying to be optimistic about the future.

'She took everything, Vanessa. Damn smart lawyer she found, bled me dry.'

She leant forward and took Stephen's hand. 'You don't have to explain, Stephen. Your pride has been shattered, you will rebuild your life, I know you only too well.'

Stephen glared at her with a piercing, almost fearful stare. 'Do you, do you really know?' He paused to reflect. 'And the child, our child – she got rid of it. Did you know that?'

Vanessa felt sick to her stomach. 'She had an abortion? Didn't she discuss it with you?'

Rupert appeared at the table, from which she dismissed him with a flash of her pale blue eyes.

'When did you find out about all this, Stephen?'

'Not until after the divorce. Melanie never wanted children and when things started to go wrong, well, a child would have complicated her plans.'

Vanessa's mind began to race. Stephen had behaved honourably and Melanie had been grossly underestimated. Clearly she had planned to ruin him, for life with Vanessa would have been full and rich, she knew that only too well, but by going back and playing her little game, he lost the lot.

'Stephen,' Vanessa said softly. 'Why didn't you call me? There would have been some way around the situation, surely?'

'She outsmarted me, Vanessa, and I was blind not to see it.'

Rupert was still propping up the bar, when the publican shouted, 'Time, Gentlemen, Please!' but Stephen continued to talk.

'There was so much between us that was good, Vanessa, and I would very much like to see you for dinner.'

'Of course,' she said sincerely. How could she refuse? 'Just call me anytime.'

Susy was frantic with worry, when she opened the newspaper to see the devastation in LA as the second earthquake rocked the city, registering 5.5 on the Richter scale. If only Toby had told her where he was staying, she could have attempted to call. Instead, two days had passed without a single word. He would be safe, alive and well and communication was undoubtedly limited, but as soon as possible, she knew he would call.

During the evening, Susy became increasingly restless, anxiously flapping the pages of a magazine over, absorbing nothing. Pacing the carpet, whilst changing television channels, catching the six, seven and nine o'clock news bulletins. He must be dead, she fretted, racing toward the telephone when it rang. 'No, Vanessa wasn't in,' she said sharply, hoping they would understand, jotting down a contact number on a notepad. She poured a glass of wine, settled into the armchair with a paperback and read the acknowledgements twice before throwing it across the room. The apartment door banged and Vanessa arrived home.

'Hello, anybody in?' she trilled cheerfully. 'Ah! There you are. Had a good day?'

Susy watched her drift across the lounge. 'Why are you so bloody happy tonight?'

'Does there have to be a reason, can't one just be happy? I've had an exceedingly good day, you obviously have not.'

Not wishing to arouse her suspicions and fall victim to a barrage of questions, Susy changed her tune, expelling gloom and taking on a more amiable demeanour.

'I know – you've been elected to the board?' she said lightly.

'Wouldn't that be nice,' Vanessa replied.

'OK, so you've met a new man?'

'Um no, well, maybe.'

'Yes or no, Vanessa, but never maybe. Who is it?'

Vanessa did not know how she felt about Stephen. She was happy to see him, of that there was no doubt. Alternatively, pity was not the basis on which to build a relationship. 'He's been crushed,' she said, relating details of the divorce.

'And all because of you,' Susy said knowingly.

Vanessa begged to differ. Stephen had made the decision, albeit wrong, while she stood aside. She would not take any responsibility for the outcome.

'So what are you going to do?' Susy asked, when confronted with the possibility of a forthcoming date.

'I really don't know.'

'You're impossible.'

'We have both changed an awful lot.'

'That you have, just look at yourself and your life. Men should be queuing up to get in here. Is there something wrong with every poor bugger who wants to get just a little closer?'

'You're no different.'

'You just leave me out of this and wake up to the fact that you're not getting any younger, you're wasting your time. Don't turn around when you're past your sell-by-date and say, "Oh! I wish", or "If only", because it will be too late. When Stephen calls, you see him.' Vanessa did not like to hear the truth. 'I'm telling you as a friend.'

For the past few minutes Susy had forgotten all about Toby, immersed in Vanessa's problems. So when the telephone rang, awakening her senses, she lunged forward.

'Hello,' she said, holding her breath. 'Hello ... hello?' A chasm of silence lingered down the line. Was there anybody there, could they hear her? 'Hello?' she said again, about to put the receiver down, when a faint voice called her name.

'Susy, is that you?'

'Yes yes, it's a terrible line.'

'It's Toby. How are you, my darling?'

'All right, really, but what about you? I've been so worried.'

'No need, we were diverted to San Francisco.'

Susy could barely hear his voice and fumbled in her bag for a pen. 'So where are you now ... can I call you back?'

'Hello, are you still there, Susy?' he shouted down the line.

'I'm here, give me your number.' The line went dead, but at least he had telephoned and was safe and well.

'Who was that?' Vanessa asked, walking back into the lounge.

'Er, wrong number.'

After a light lunch Vanessa and Polly emerged from the

restaurant feeling mellow, to walk the short distance across the square to where Polly had parked her car. They walked slowly, still talking, the autumn leaves swirling around their ankles. Polly had at first declined Vanessa's invitation to lunch, but not wanting to offend, or much more to the point, not wanting to miss an hour of idle gossip, she accepted.

Polly was working on her first London fashion show. From start to finish, this one was her baby. Nothing was left to chance, polished and professional, she planned a show to outstrip all others and with two weeks to go, every minute was accounted for. Lunch with Vanessa had been a pleasant interlude, but when she climbed back behind the wheel of her car, the afternoon schedule began.

When Vanessa waved Polly goodbye, her eyes crossed the street to a figure emerging from a parked Mercedes. He turned around, slamming the door, and walked in the same direction as her. She kept pace on the other side of the street, almost breaking into a run. He quickened his stride, then stopped, passing between two parked vehicles, pulling back as the traffic raced by. Vanessa stopped, heart pounding, her eyes never leaving him. Dressed in a business-like manner, briefcase in hand, Oliver appeared to be on his way to a business meeting. He darted in front of an oncoming car and got on the pavement a few paces in front of Vanessa, but he did not see her and turned right at the next corner. Stepping up lightly behind him, she too turned the corner, only to see him disappear through the entrance of a company headquarters, with an ensign flapping gently in the wind over the portal. Too late, a missed opportunity that may never occur again. She turned, head down and retraced her steps back to the agency.

The call sheet revealed that Stephen had telephoned at 1.35 p.m., leaving a number for her to return his call. Seated behind her desk, she swung the chair around and watched the fading afternoon light descend over the square through the office window. After several minutes of quiet contemplation, she picked up the receiver and dialled Stephen's number.

Vanessa sat at her dressing table, closely scrutinising her face in the mirror for fine lines, and meticulously applied makeup to an already faultless complexion. Susy was mistaken, she thought, for, in her opinion, she did not look a day older. In fact, she looked more self-assured, elegant and even younger. She picked up the atomiser and sprayed Calvin Klein's Obsession, Stephen's favourite, to her neck, cleavage and wrists and sat momentarily brushing her hair. Stephen sounded elated, almost grateful over the telephone when she agreed to meet him for lunch. The Compleat Angler, he insisted, at one o'clock in the bar. She rose from the dressing table, slid back the closet doors, selected a cashmere skirt and silk shirt from her wardrobe and changed. Her parents were away for the weekend and apart from the staff, the house was deserted. Reaching for the car keys, she threw her coat around her shoulders and left the house.

On that winding five-mile drive from Hambledon to Marlow, Vanessa recalled the heady days, two years previously, when she and Stephen played with each other's lives. The secret meetings and broken arrangements, the quickies in the back of the Mercedes, like a couple of kids. He had hated her with a passion for the chaos she caused him, the emotional demands and the refusal to understand his situation, only to love her with an equal passion that tore them apart. The thrill of the game – was that what their affair was all about? She slowed down at the small roundabout before crossing the bridge and dwelt on the prospect of life with Stephen. Did he need her now, as he professed, or did he just need somebody? She knew that she only had to say the word and he was hers, of that there was no doubt. She brought the car to a halt in the car park of the Compleat Angler and stepped out. As she proceeded to walk towards the hotel, somehow the setting did not hold the same magic. The excitement had vanished as she stepped back into yesterday, the love had gone and life had moved on. At the entrance she stopped, turned around and walked back towards the car. She felt no regrets while driving back over the bridge, just relief and freedom to pursue something she should have done months ago.

The week began on a downturn. Toby had not made contact again and Susy, anxious to know of his whereabouts, sank lower and lower. A huge cavernous void crept into her thinking, she felt alone, deserted by all, and emotionally imbalanced. Should he call now she must not appear too eager, or too forceful. She would stand back, let him lead, take the reins and she would willingly follow. Hours of idle daydreaming were interfering with work. Impaired concentration and a stubbornness to participate socially were beginning to irritate Vanessa, who was unexpectedly out every night. After a quiet evening at home alone, she took one of Vanessa's sleeping pills from her bedside table and went to bed.

While the city slumbered, all but the few who, by chance or design were out, a wind began to blow, gathering pace as it swept across the country. Warnings were not given and the gale became stronger and stronger. Battering the shoreline, lifting vessels clean out of the water and on to the land. Inland, trees still heavy with leaves began to sway, buckle and uproot. The hurricane-force gale engulfed the whole of the south and hurled a destructive path towards the capital. Vanessa was taking a nightcap at Lucinda's apartment, when a crash drew their attention outside. The wind whistled around the creaking building when they opened the door, uprooting anything that was not battened down. They looked on with horror, as branches broke off a tree and fell to the ground. Lamp posts leant over and scaffolding was ripped from buildings like matchsticks clattering all around. People were running, falling and holding on to anything stable, arms defenceless against the unyielding onslaught of debris. They struggled back inside, dodging slates being ripped from an adjacent building that projected against the front door. There was no way Vanessa could even attempt to leave the house.

The following morning was calm and peaceful when they stepped out into the street.

'Good Lord, Vanessa, this is England! How will we ever find a taxi, darling?'

How indeed, Vanessa thought, with trees strewn across the

streets and parks, their roots exposed, foliage scattered everywhere. They joined other pedestrians in pursuit of transport, each turning revealing even more destruction. Vanessa ducked under some fallen scaffolding, only to be rebuked by a police officer trying to keep the area clear. Two cars had been totally crushed, unrecognisably mangled together under piles of iron poles protruding from their shiny paintwork. Tormented, Lucinda could not remember where she had left her silver Peugeot and was convinced that the flattened vehicle they were observing was hers. Vanessa calmed her, by pointing back across the street to her brand new car that was parked exactly where she had left it and intact.

The quiet that hung over the city was frightening. Nature had wrought a powerful hand against mankind and won; the damage was incalculable.

Susy awoke cursing the electricity board for making her oversleep, but before going downstairs she banged hard on Vanessa's door. 'Get up, it's late!' she shouted, still feeling drowsy after a heavy night's sleep. Arms and legs cumbersome and awkward as she tried to move around, knowing how furious Vanessa would be rising at ten o'clock. No time for breakfast, just a hasty glass of orange juice thrown straight down the hatch. What was she doing? Had she not heard her call? Bags, keys, money, makeup that would have to wait, jacket, shoes, where had she left them? Up the stairs one more time and a final rap on Vanessa's door. Placing her ear to the door and listened, silence. She opened the door slowly and peered inside, to find the room empty and the bed unoccupied. Considering Vanessa's noticeable change in personality as she locked up the apartment, if a man was on the scene again, and it appeared that there was, then she most probably had dislocated her hip by now.

The hurricane had brought the city almost to a standstill. Trains were not running and the streets were deserted. The Coterie was open for business, but nobody was buying and, as her assistant had understandably not arrived for work, Susy closed the shop at three o'clock.

The sound of power saws carving up age-old trees was heartbreaking when Vanessa walked into the grounds at Hambleden. Rupert and Piers were both lending a helping hand to repair the damage reaped by the storm. Fences were down and part of the rose garden was flattened by an uprooted oak tree, narrowly missing the aviary. A bonfire smouldered in a far corner as the gardener piled another barrow-load of leaves and branches on to the heap. Sir Richard sat quietly on a chair, overseeing the attempt to bring some order back to his much loved garden, Vanessa by his side.

'Daddy, this is so awful.'

'Two hundred years those trees have stood there, my dear, many monarchs have come and gone, two world wars have been fought and still they stood there.' He paused to reflect. 'And in a single night the whole lot has been wiped out.'

Vanessa placed a reassuring arm around his shoulder, for the overwhelming despair exceeded any trace of anger. 'All is not lost, you'll see. We will make it beautiful again.'

Rupert handed Vanessa a rake and smiled. 'Seeing as you're here, why don't you make a start over by the tennis court.'

The team worked hard and methodically for the whole weekend until aching, but satisfied, they stood back and congratulated each other on their efforts. They were family, bound together by a crisis and a sense of responsibility, to defend the very foundation of their existence. Sir Richard and Caroline walked arm in arm around the grounds in stunned amazement, to see young trees already planted, soil turned, flower beds tidy and fences up, a *fait accompli*. To her chagrin, Vanessa noted for the first time the frailness of an ageing parent, overshadowed by a brood of adult siblings, at whose head Rupert's powerful presence could clearly be felt. He was supportive, without being intrusive. Strong, where failing health hampered rational decision-making. Taking command, with full consent and blessing, the reins of the family seat. Accountable for everyone's security, while establishing a new business. Vanessa felt confident and proud of her brother. From now on and for the foreseeable future, life for Rupert would be demanding and hectic.

The ledger flopped over with a bang, the Coterie's end of month figures were up and Susy placed the paperwork back into the safe and went into the kitchen to prepare supper. She hovered from the refrigerator to the cooker, the cooker to the table, deep in thought, evaluating her feelings and behaviour. Was the obsession with Toby a sign of impending insanity? Did she care enough to exclude all others from her life, or should she shelve the whole idea immediately? She longed to be loved, the idea of two persons sharing a spiritual, as well as bodily need to belong was foremost in her mind. Or was she just in love with love? Maybe the uncontrollable desire for emotional security stemmed from the deprivation of her childhood. Toby had not called for ten days and she began to question his intentions, when the telephone rang.

'I'll call you back, Polly, I'm eating.'

Polly. Now what would she say should an affair develop? 'It's all in the past,' she distinctly remembered her saying. That may well be, but should the door slam on an old flame, would the claws come out? A real friend would not do that, or would they? Susy's head began to pound, delusion and confusion hammered away at her intellect with a hatchet; she was behaving like an adolescent. Toby knew where to find her, should he want to. In the meantime, there were lots of other eligible men to explore and then he would have to wait in line. She picked up the telephone, flipped open her diary, tapped in a number and caught up with some friends.

The best part of the evening was spent on the telephone. She stretched, yawned and prepared to go to bed. Stacking the dishwasher, she turned the dial, which generated a gush of water over the dirty crockery, bolted the kitchen window and switched off the light. Padding over to the French windows, she brushed aside the drapes and secured the locks. It had become second nature since the burglary to check and double check everything, including the balcony. As usual all was quiet as she cast her eyes across the square, surrounded by streetlights and into the gardens left sparse by the hurricane, when she thought she spotted a figure looking up at the window. She turned away sharply, keeping her back firmly against the wall and held her breath, pulse racing. Was she mistaken? Who was out there, watching and waiting? She raced across the lounge floor and switched off the lights, returning to the window again, only to find the street empty. Was her imagination deceiving her as she breathed easy, feeling the tension leave her body? She checked all the doors and windows again, tripping over furniture as she thundered through the apartment in the dark. The apartment like a fortress was impregnable, she was safe and protected, except for the shrill, piercing ring of the telephone. Turning around, she paused before picking up the receiver and listened.

'...Susy?' The voice was familiar.

'Yes,' she replied weakly.

'That was some telephone call you were having earlier.'

'Toby,' she exclaimed, melting into the armchair. 'How are you? Where are you?'

He laughed, 'New York.' But before she could lecture him he added, 'I know, I should have called you sooner, but things got a bit out of hand here, you know how hard-hitting these Yanks can be.'

She had already forgiven him. 'When are you coming home?'

'I'll be there Thursday evening.' Four days, she was already counting. 'I have so much to tell you, my darling.' She sank lower into the cushions as he spoke. 'It's been such a long time, we'll celebrate.' The line crackled. 'Friday night, I'll pick you up about eight.'

Susy replaced the receiver radiant with joy, when three long sharp rings on the intercom announced Vanessa's arrival. Weary and dishevelled, Vanessa threw herself at the sofa, aching from head to toe, levering her shoes from her feet she lay prostrate nursing a bandaged thumb.

'You look like a skivvy,' Susy said, looking down at her rumpled body. 'What have you been doing?'

Vanessa rested her hand on her brow and sighed. 'Gardening.'

'You,' she sniggered, 'You who won't even wash up a cup.'

'Enough, Susy, I do not need your sarcasm tonight.' Vanessa grimaced as she tried unsuccessfully to get up, prompting Susy to lend a helping hand. 'Ow! Careful, can't you see I'm hurt.'

'I'll make you a hot drink.'

Vanessa protested, climbing the stairs. 'A hot bath and a good night's sleep is all I need right now.'

Susy double-checked the alarm system and again turned off the downstairs lights, before retiring to her room with a book.

After wallowing in a warm therapeutic bath of aromatic oils, Vanessa heaved her body out of the water, wrapped a fluffy towel around her aching limbs and dried off. Feeling drowsy, she slipped a silk nightgown over her head, the lightness barely touching her skin and climbed under the covers. Sleep could not come quickly enough.

Struggling to finish the final chapter of the book she was reading, her eyelids closing, causing a blurred, distorted jumble of words across her line of vision, Susy succumbed to sleep. Sinking back on to the pillow, breathing deeply, the book finally fell from her hands, coming to rest at her side.

During the early hours of the morning and deep in sleep, they were both disturbed by the sudden high-pitched ring of the telephone. Vanessa reached over, switched on the bedside light and lifted the receiver. Susy awoke with a jolt, her book still lying at her side and the bedside light still glaring down on her. Simultaneously, she lifted the extension, to hear Vanessa say 'Hello?' There was not a murmur at the other end of the line, only complete silence. Susy sat upright in bed fully awake. While Vanessa rolled over, rubbed her eyes and again said, 'Hello … who is it?'

'Talk, you bastard!' Susy screamed down the line, but there was still only silence, as they both waited impatiently for a response. 'Why don't you talk to me? Let's hear you, let's hear your perverted little voice.'

They listened intently to the hollow emptiness, willing their caller to stay on the line. Susy was up, clutching the telephone to her ear, angrily pacing up and down. She bellowed down the line again.

'Aye, wanker! Can't you get it up any other way?'

Disturbed by the intimidation, they both heard the beast groan, breathing heavily, in short agitated succession. Susy felt her scalp tighten and her pulse begin to race. Vanessa was out of bed and on her feet too, for the breathing got louder, coarser, until they were consumed by the grotesque sounds, unable to let go, when he found his voice.

'Slaaag!' the word reverberated down the line.

Susy screamed, dropping the receiver, grasping her ears to shut out the terrible word, shaking her head violently and convulsively. Vanessa burst into the bedroom and clutched Susy tightly in her arms, while she sobbed uncontrollably, replacing the receiver left dangling, to rest.

'It's all right, he's gone.'

Susy wiped away the tears with her fingertips. 'It was him. I know it was him.'

Vanessa stood back mystified by the comment. 'Who was it?' Convinced that the voice on the line was the man who attacked her, Susy could not be deterred from her thoughts. 'But how can you be sure, Susy? It could have been anyone.'

'I know. Nothing will make me change my mind.'

They sat quietly side by side on the edge of the bed, disturbed by the haunting fact that he was still out there and probably still offending.

'Tomorrow we will call the police.' Susy nodded in agreement. 'Give them the photographs, tell them everything. This has got to stop.'

12

Detective Superintendent Pearce looked closely at the photographs on his desk before glancing up at Susy and Vanessa. 'Is this all?' he asked sternly. They both nodded. He turned the envelope over to the identically typewritten address. 'And when did you receive them, Miss Stevens?'

Susy endeavoured to speak, curtailed by Vanessa's hasty interruption. 'I'm afraid I am to blame. You see I thought that if we waited they would stop.'

The superintendent directed the question again to Susy, adding, 'And when exactly did you receive the first photograph, Miss Stevens?'

'July.'

'And the other one?'

'September.'

'Are you sure?'

'Yes, positive.'

He placed the photographs to one side and quietly turned to Susy again. 'Now I want you to tell me about the telephone call. Think carefully, take your time.'

She paused, recalling the voice at the other end of the line. Vanessa, feeling every pang of agony, held her hand urging her on. 'It was the same voice.' Susy said uneasily. The superintendent then picked up the case file and turned to the contents. 'The same gruff voice.' He quickly read through her statement at the time of the rape. 'I know I'm not mistaken, I recognised him straight away.'

Looking Susy straight in the eye he asked, 'You never mentioned this in your statement. What did he say?'

Vanessa held Susy's hand tighter. 'He called me a slag. That's what he called me the night I was raped.'

'Is that it, nothing more?' Susy nodded her head.

'Do you think there is a connection?' Vanessa queried.

'With the photographs, possibly?' he answered, looking at them again. 'I would like to hold on to these, see if anything shows up. Now is there anything else you would like to add, Miss Stevens?'

In retrospect Susy had placed little or no importance to the voice, an error of judgement on her part. Foolishly, she had also listened to Vanessa's crass ideas of criminal behaviour. Was it too late before he carved up another life? Susy held nothing back.

'He's still watching me.'

'You think that or you–'

'I'm telling you, last night out on the street.'

'This is the first I've heard, Superintendent.'

'Let her finish, Miss Baron.'

Susy continued. 'Just like before, hiding in the shadows. He's close, sir, he's very close.'

Superintendent Pearce was convinced. 'We'll keep the apartment under surveillance and if either of you see or hear anything unusual, you will contact us immediately. Is that understood?'

Monday evening on her way home from the boutique, Susy scanned the street. If the police were out there, and she was sure they were, she did not see them. Just an animated welcome from Vanessa, who waved a postcard at her as she walked through the apartment door. Peter was arriving in London on Thursday for a long weekend and Susy immediately saw complications, with Toby due back the same day. For as much as she longed to see Peter, her bosom pal and confidant, her social itinerary must be impeccably timed.

'Umm, something smells good?' Susy remarked, after sifting through the rest of the mail.

'I've invited Polly over for supper,' Vanessa replied, spreading the grated cheese on top of the cottage pie, before placing the casserole under the grill.

Susy side-stepped over to the French windows, checking the street below, before closing the drapes – something Vanessa always forgot to do and a simple request that infuriated Susy almost every evening.

Polly arrived in a fluster, dragging her portfolio in one hand, bag in the other. The show had been fraught with problems and ironing them out was no mean task. She apologised profusely throughout supper for the incessant interruptions, over which she had little control. The design layout looked spectacular, the girls were impressed and the proposed sequence agenda without question was sensational. Polly had found her true vocation and London was about to witness a fashion extravaganza. 'I want you both there,' she enthused. They had no intention of missing a single twirl. 'I also need your help,' she pleaded, 'behind the scenes. I need as many pairs of hands as I can find.'

A unanimous decision, with Saturday afternoon being firmly marked out in both their diaries.

Surrounded by illustrations, Polly's dialogue was a perpetual flow of articulate and meticulously drafted ideas that rose amid the chaos. So absorbed was she in her new career that for the moment nothing else appeared to matter. Surprisingly also, men never entered the conversation. For two long hours, the girls listened with great admiration, gathering photographs and drawings together, placing them back in Polly's portfolio that lay open on the dining table. Susy stood back suddenly, as her eyes fell on a large brown envelope protruding from beneath the pile of illustrations. She held the corner between her thumb and forefinger and slowly pulled it free. She was ashen and speechless, then unexpectedly thrust the unopened envelope into Polly's hand.

Polly looked at them both in turn. 'Something's wrong?'

Vanessa shook her head, infuriated at Susy's insinuation. 'No, Polly, there's nothing wrong.' But Susy remained rigid, moving her eyes only, from the envelope to Polly's blank expressionless face. 'Nevertheless, I think you should open it.'

Polly ripped open the envelope, reached inside and pulled out a large glossy photograph, which she held at arm's length, looking over the top at the two pairs of eyes waiting for a reaction.

'You too?' Susy enquired, dry-mouthed with anticipation.

Placing the photograph right side up on the table for all to see she said, 'It's excellent, don't you think?'

The glossy fashion shot, taken at the Paris show, was superb. A group of fully-clothed models parading next season's day wear, was in no way what Susy had expected. She chuckled nervously, causing Vanessa to join in, the infectious cackle growing into raucous laughter. Polly looked on and giggled too, picking up the photograph again. What was so funny about a bunch of po-faced models in suits?

Later, over coffee, they confessed. The pornographic photographs were shocking and insulting and the phone call disturbing. Polly did not doubt for a second that Susy was not telling the truth, but there was one thing that she did not understand.

'Why has he come back?'

Susy quietly sipped her coffee contemplating the question she had asked herself so many times. 'I think he's a psychopath, Polly. He didn't finish the job.'

The week ahead promised to be memorable. Polly immersed herself in organising the show. Deadlines had to be met, tempers flew with amazing regularity, but with four days to go, they were finally on schedule.

Vanessa was busy at the desk when Erik appeared at the door. As he tried to speak, she raised a cautionary hand in order to expedite the work in hand. He looked harassed and eager to talk, sighed impatiently as she pushed the pen across the paper. She dotted the final fullstop and pressed the intercom button. The command received an immediate response from an office clerk, who bulldozed his way past Erik, grabbed the folder and left with equal speed. 'Yes,' she said, smiling at the morose figure standing in the doorway. The downtrodden, jowly, pallid fifty-something-year-old. 'Erik, you look dreadful.' He raised his eyebrows and sighed again.

'I have to talk, Vanessa, before I kill myself.'

'Yanni?'

'The bitch! Even that's too good a name for her.'

She picked up her bag, walked around to the front of her desk, grabbing Erik by the arm. 'Let's go. Tell me all about it over a drink.'

They walked arm in arm out of the agency and into a bustling wine bar, which was busy with lunchtime trade. Two bar stools became miraculously unoccupied, on which they firmly placed their bottoms and ordered a bottle of white wine. With acerbic connotations, Erik proceeded to pour out his heart. Yanni apparently had absconded with another man. She had suspected. A younger, more virile man, he was led to believe. 'All cock and no class.' Erik almost spat the words out. Over the hubbub of voices, she tried to listen as Erik prattled on, losing track of the conversation, with people fighting for bar service. She placed her empty glass on the counter, glancing up into the wall mirror behind the bar, while Erik quickly replenished her glass. In the reflection and seated only a few feet away, she caught the steady gaze of Oliver, who was looking straight at her. He did not move, neither did his eyes leave hers. Vanessa saw and heard nothing more, she wanted to reach out and touch him, feel his hand on hers, embrace him, if only for a fleeting moment.

'You're not listening to me, Vanessa,' came Erik's harsh words.

'Take him back,' she said without thinking.

'What! She'll have to grovel, darling, after what she's done.'

Erik's words trailed off in the clamour and commotion of people and conversation disappeared into unconsciousness. She turned again and searched the reflection, but Oliver had vanished, like an apparition into thin air. He was there and not a mirage, almost within her grasp and he wanted her. She knew in her heart that their souls were inextricably locked together as one. What should she do?

After a hectic day Vanessa stood under the shower, the invigorating jets of water pounding her flesh, and her thoughts turned to Oliver. With her mind's eye she traced the contours of his face, the strong handsome features and dark hair. How long had he been there watching her? Did he still love her as much as she loved him? Was destiny beckoning, drawing them closer, finally and completely together? She reached for a towel, stepping out of the shower, wrapped her wet hair up in a turban and padded back into the bedroom.

The front door of the apartment buzzed long and hard, impatient to be answered, bringing Susy hurriedly from the kitchen to find out who was there. Polly sounded desperate, the thump of her heavy footsteps coming up the stairs was cause for concern. Susy flung open the door just as Polly reached the landing, carrying a small holdall in one hand and Henry under her arm. 'Where have you been?' she shrieked, 'I've been trying to reach you for hours.'

Susy took the holdall from Polly's grasp and sat her down. 'Dear God!' Vanessa exclaimed, running down the stairs, 'What has happened?'

Between the sobs, Polly attempted to explain her dilemma, with Susy rushing a large brandy into her hand as Vanessa tried to calm her down. 'Slowly, Polly, I can't hear a thing.'

'Everything's gone,' she finally said. 'Absolutely everything. My jewellery, furniture, pictures, even my bed! They took my bed and cleared the wardrobe. Can you imagine? There's nothing left,' she sobbed.

Vanessa put her arm around her shoulder and tried to comfort her. 'Polly, I know it's not going to help right now, but everything is replaceable.'

'It's only things.' Susy said sympathetically. 'What's important is that you're all right.'

Polly rested her head in her hands. 'I don't know what to do. It couldn't have happened at a worse time.

The apartment would be cramped, but temporarily they would

manage. Polly had a bed to sleep in and clothes to put on her back and her beloved Henry was unharmed. Together they would not be defeated, the show most definitely would go on.

Ensuing chaos hampered normal living conditions, as the apartment rapidly resembled the foyer of a popular hotel. Exciting though it seemed there was neither leg room, nor counter space, for the kitchen was always occupied, as were the bathrooms. In truth, there was no room to swing a cat.

Susy could only presume that she and Toby would dine out that evening. Choosing a quiet moment during her working day to select a garment from the rails, discarding one after another as inappropriate for a first date, she ran her fingers down a line of neatly assembled garments until she stopped, pulling out a beautifully tailored, but short dress in blue, and held it up against her. Saucy, she would go as far as to say sexy, but would he approve? She did not want him to think that she was a floozy, and disappeared into a changing room to try it on. Perfect. She looked fashionable and elegant, he could take her anywhere.

Her assistant whispered at the door, 'Somebody to see you.'

Stepping quickly out of the dress and back into her suit, she stepped out on to the shop floor. 'Peter!' she exclaimed, with open arms. 'What a lovely surprise.'

With both arms tucked firmly under her armpits, Peter picked her up, swung her around, then landed her lightly back on to her feet. They laughed, thrilled to see one another again, when still holding both hands, Susy pushed away for a better look. Peter was bronzed, slimmer, his hair lighter from two months in the sun. 'Hey, you look great,' she said, eyeing him up and down. He patted his stomach and flexed well developed biceps which, astounded, she kneaded with both hands. Solid and fit, there was not an ounce of fat on him. They hugged each other again, all wrapped up in a warm affectionate embrace, before decamping to the backroom for a cup of coffee.

A flurry of words spilled from Susy's mouth before they even sat down, Peter barely having time to answer one question, before being led into another. He was enjoying the work immensely; working with such a professional team was both demanding and rewarding. His arrival late last night was the first break he had taken in two months. Impatient to burst forth into the social scene, he assumed Susy was also.

'We have four days ahead of us, Susy. Where are you taking me tonight?'

A transient, worried expression crossed Susy's face; the hesitant delayed response foretold her reply. 'I can't see you, Peter, I'm going out.'

Discarded, but not totally dejected, he suppressed the sudden urge to ask why. With only a short time at his disposal, he felt annoyed by Susy's terse reply. He had announced his arrival, so what was so damned important?

'Umm, got a date?' he reluctantly said with a smile.

She beamed, 'I've got so much to tell you.'

Peter leant back, knowing full well that he was going to hear everything, whether he wanted to or not.

'You have got to understand that I would never put you off for just anybody.'

He felt reassured by the change in attitude. 'I am very pleased to hear that – go on.'

'And we will spend time together over the next few days, I promise.'

'Great, that's fine with me.'

Susy searched her mind for a beginning, anxious to dispel any ambiguous thoughts of insincerity that may overshadow her joy. 'Right out of the blue,' she began to explain. 'You could have knocked me over.'

'Always when you least expect it.' Trying to smother his disappointment he managed to smile. 'This is going to be good, I can feel it.'

A pause, recalling a few priceless seconds of passion. 'I can still feel the warmth, Peter. Oh, I've waited so long, so very long, but then he had to go away on business.' Susy sighed, staring vacantly at the blank wall behind Peter's head, as if he were not there. 'Tonight is our first date and you are the only person I have told.'

Taking him into her confidence and leaving him suspended in mid air at the same time was not admissible. Peter leant heavily across the table and looked her straight in the eye. 'You're holding back. Now who is this lucky guy?' The tone was steadfast and to the point, causing her to skirt around the question.

'He did call me while he was away, if that's what you're thinking. Caught up in that terrible earthquake in LA.'

Peter slowly shook his head. 'Come on, Susy, stop throwing me one liners. Who is he?'

Still evading the truth and with stubborn faith she replied, 'He's free, free to see anybody he pleases and so am I.' Peter kept quiet and listened. 'His relationship with Polly ended weeks ago, you must remember that?' Peter's knuckles turned white with anger, but his expression remained unaltered. 'Please be happy for me,' she said softly. 'You are wrong about Toby and I care so much, I cannot let it go now. I want you to believe me when I tell you that he is a good and gentle person. Please be his friend for my sake?'

There was a tap on the door. 'Telephone, Susy.'

Immediately she disappeared into the shop, leaving Peter to wrestle with his thoughts. Her lilting voice confirmed the evening's arrangements. 'Eight o'clock,' he heard her say. 'And me too,' she giggled.

Peter rose to his feet and walked through the shop. 'Must go,' he said, heading for the door. 'Have a nice evening.'

The apartment was empty when Susy arrived home late, after an exacting American tourist had driven her demented for almost an hour and a half, trying to come to a decision. Tired, she needed a drink to steady her nerves and made straight for the drinks cabinet. She poured herself a large scotch and stood back, taking a deep breath. Friday, Tina's day to shop and clean and for the first time in three days, the apartment looked tidy.

With an hour to go, Susy had ample time to put herself together. She ran a bath with lots of bubbles, lay back and let the warm water soothe her frayed nerve endings. Her stomach churned with excitement, dancing with uncontrollable delight at the prospect of a night of unparalleled passion. She raised a leg out of the water, exposing a well pedicured foot. Scarlet polish gleamed like blood-red rubies as she wiggled her toes. The apartment door banged and the unmistakable voice of Polly resounded up the stairs. Polly, dear Polly, would she be hurt or offended, or even angry at her indiscretion? She did value her friendship so and some time she would have to be told, but this was not the right time. Climbing out of the bath Susy wrapped a towelling robe around her torso and padded back into her bedroom. She felt light-headed and frivolous, amused by the game she was playing. Her actions could only fan the fire of curiosity, when at eight o'clock she would disappear out of the apartment and into the night. Her deep rooted desire to belong, to love and to cherish, her very own secret, would be safe until the morning. With makeup applied, she pulled the dark-blue dress over her head, adjusted the fastener, clipped a large hooped earring to each ear and stepped into her shoes – she was ready.

There were hosts of people littering the lounge when Susy appeared on the landing. Silently, each pair of eyes followed her careful descent to the bottom of the stairs.

'Hurrah,' Polly cheered loudly and they all clapped. 'There's some lucky fellow out there tonight.'

The final preparations for Saturday's show were in full swing, with Polly drowning under people and paperwork. Susy turned to Vanessa, who nodded approval.

'You look lovely, Susy. Peter in town?' The look required no verbal confirmation as the intercom buzzed. 'Have a wonderful evening,' she said with a wink.

The sound of high heels tapped lightly across the tiled hall floor, until she reached the front door, which she threw open wide and there he was. Toby did not take the time to say hello, for he swept her up into his arms and holding her gently, but firmly, kissed her hard and passionately on the mouth, pressing her body into his groin. She felt him stir, before he broke away from her breathless and looked down into her glistening eyes. 'Hello,' he said and smiled.

'Welcome home,' Susy replied, straightening his tie.

'I know, I'm a mess, haven't had time to go home and change yet.'

They broke free from each other's grasp and hand in hand walked out into the street.

'I have a table booked for nine o'clock. Like Chinese food?' he said, opening the car door.

'Nothing better,' she replied.

Toby climbed in behind the wheel, 'But first I have to shower and change.'

'New car?' she observed, running her hands over the upholstery.

Toby started up the engine. 'Yep, like it? The other one burnt out – a bit like me.' They both laughed.

The white Mercedes Sport pulled away from Cadogan Place and headed in the direction of his mews cottage in South Kensington, with Peter's battered black Golf trailing close behind. Holding her hand as they drove along, Susy looked at Toby lovingly, not quite believing that she was there beside him and that it was not all a dream.

'You're quiet,' he said, glancing at her serene face.

'No, not really, just pleased to be here away from the madness.'

'What madness?'

The heaving mass of Polly's production team was news to Toby, as was the burglary. 'That's madness all right. Does she know?'

'About what?'

Toby turned to Susy and smiled. 'About us, darling. Did you tell her?'

'No, not yet.'

'And Vanessa.'

'No, they'll find out soon enough.'

The Mercedes swung into the mews and parked. With Peter keeping pace, not letting the car out of his sight, until the blaze of red rear lights went out. He switched the Golf's headlights off, slowly inching the car to the corner and stopped. Peter gripped the steering wheel, pulling himself forward for a better look, observing the right-hand door open and Toby climb out, slamming the door behind him. He walked to the other side of the vehicle and watched as Susy stepped out and into Toby's open arms. Peter felt a surge of revulsion consume him, a venomous loathing so extreme that made him snarl in fury. The two lovers locked in a clinch on the cobblestones, swayed and laughed, fooled around, before disappearing into the cottage. With the lights still off, Peter restarted the Golf and pointing the nose into the mews, let it freewheel silently to within a few metres of the Mercedes and waited.

Toby closed the front door behind them and patted Susy's bottom as she struggled up the narrow staircase in her slim skirt. Inside, the house was compact, functional, with large comfortable leather sofas and every conceivable piece of sound and vision equipment on the market – undoubtedly a man's domain. Toby took Susy's jacket and hung it in the closet.

'So, what do you think?' he said, pushing a button on his latest toy. 'Great sound.'

He loosened his tie crossing the room and lifting Susy into his arms threw her on to the sofa wilfully. She yelped in fun, beating his chest with her fists, but not before he had stolen a kiss.

Still sitting quietly behind the wheel of his Golf, Peter looked up sharply at the windows. Lights were blazing from every cottage as he glanced at each one in turn. 'Where the hell are they?' he mumbled to himself, opening the car door. 'Which one is it, for Chrissake?'

Toby ran his hands up and down Susy's long legs, searching out crevices and tantalising her. She was excited and submitted too easily, reaching down between his thighs to his penis, strong and hard. She wanted him, craved for his body next to hers, but he immediately got up.

'Tut tut, dinner first,' he said, walking away. 'Want a drink?'

Susy straightened up and reached into her bag for a lipstick. 'Yes, thank you,' she replied, repairing the damage.

'Help yourself, on the side by the window.'

Toby ripped the tie from his shirt and made his way into the bathroom.

Outside, Peter moved deeper into the shadows, out of sight, when he spotted Susy pouring a drink at a first floor window. She glanced down into the street, turned around and walked back into the room. Peter stood motionless, like a cat about to pounce, his eyes hardly blinking, fixed on that upstairs window.

There was a vast selection of CDs and after sorting through them, Susy made a selection, placed the disc into the machine and pushed the button. Back on the sofa, she drummed her fingers in time to the music and noted the time. They were running very late, perhaps the restaurant could deliver. She would telephone, or maybe she could conjure up something edible, without having to leave the comfort of the cottage. With that thought in mind, she proceeded to check out the kitchen, neat and tidy, not what she had expected. The refrigerator also revealed an assembly of limited, yet orderly assortment of supplies, when she heard Toby on the telephone. Clearly he was having an argument, raising his voice, almost shouting. She stepped back into the lounge and over to the window, peering out along the mews, noticing nothing.

Peter watched marking time, adrenaline running high. He had Susy firmly within his sight as she moved away from the window again, urging him slowly out of the shadows.

Books, books and even more books. Toby was an avid reader, for the shelves were stacked, but what did he like to read? Susy was curious. Lifting a book from the bookshelf she turned the page.

Toby was still dressed when he thundered back into the lounge. 'Sorry, my darling, business call.'

'No problem,' she said calmly. 'I'm sure they will deliver.'

'That's not a bad idea,' he replied, unbuttoning his shirt on the way into the bathroom. 'Not a bad idea at all.'

She could hear the water running in the bathroom and placed the book back on the shelf. Humming away to the music, she searched for something to look at. There were a few audio magazines, an old *Financial Times* and a pile of holiday brochures. She thumbed through them casually, paying little attention, when her eyes fell on a photograph album. She pulled the heavy album towards her and flipped open the cover. The glossy photographs of friends, some she knew, stared up at her – Polly, Toby and Polly, Polly and Vanessa, Ascot 1986, written in Polly's hand. Susy smiled, for she remembered the occasion well. Toby with Oliver and two pretty girls, she chuckled, turning the pages back. A wedding 1985, with Toby as best man. Summer 1985, Cape Ferrat, Toby obviously drunk, hanging over the shoulders of two brown beauties. She turned the pages to find more photographs of the same holiday. The beach bar, a barbecue, a toast to somebody's birthday. Back and forth she turned the pages, checking and rechecking. When looking closer at the photograph of the two bronzed girls and the hand on the raised glass of champagne, she became cold with fear, for there was no mistake. She dropped the album where she stood, her pulse began to pound and she felt dizzy and faint. This could not be true. She panicked, for she did not, could not believe what she had just seen. Toby called from the bedroom, 'Five minutes.' She looked up in the direction of the voice and swayed, looking down at the photograph again, but there sharp and clear, was the ring, that ring. Unmistakably, she knew where she had seen it before, imprinted on her memory for all time. Distinctive, large, square, third finger, left hand. Hyperventilating, she was terrified, desperate to get out, but her legs would not move. She knocked the glass to the floor, while fumbling for her bag, stumbling headlong on to the floor. She got up, spinning around, when she heard Toby appear in the doorway dressed in a robe.

'What's wrong?' he asked coolly.

Susy stood erect, trembling violently, as she looked at Toby, unable to speak.

'Speak to me, Susy,' he said, taking a step towards her.

She backed away, rigid with fear, incapable of moving a muscle. He looked around the room, spotting the open photograph album and walked over to the window. Without diverting his chilly gaze from Susy's petrified face, he pulled down the blinds.

Still waiting outside in the mews, Peter watched as Toby's figure moved across the first floor window, shutting out the world, obliterating all sound from within.

Terrified, she made a dash for the door, but Toby was quicker, blocking her exit with his arm across her chest. She pulled back, the touch of his hand on her body making her gulp back the vomit. There was no way out, no escape, she had no choice but to fight for her life.

'It was you!' she shouted. 'You who hurt me, scarred me for life!' Tears of rage fell down her cheeks.

Toby moved closer. 'Me, what are you talking about?

Susy stood defiant, eyes aflame. 'You bastard, it was you who raped me.'

With dead eyes, Toby held out both his arms and smiled. 'Come now, Susy, could I have done a thing like that?'

'The ring!' she shouted, pointing to the photograph album.

'Ring, what ring?' he shrugged.

She picked up the album and threw it at him. 'That ring.'

Without so much as a glance, Toby moved steadily closer. 'So I wore a ring. What's that got to do with you?'

Enraged by his brazen insolence she bawled, 'On the night I was raped, I saw that ring, your ring!' She picked up a metal statue and swung it above her head. Toby made a grab for her arm, wrenching her head backwards as he struggled to free the statue from her grasp.

'Who's going to believe you?' he growled, pulling his arm tighter.

She managed to release herself from his grip and stumbled across the room. Picking up the statue that had fallen by her side, she stood up and challenged him. 'I promised I would kill the bastard who did that to me and I will do time for you, you animal!'

Toby dived, catching Susy's foot hard in the crotch, and for an instant she was free.

Peter stood leaning up against a wall, watching a couple amble by with their dog, followed by the roar of a high powered sports car revving up the engine at the end of the mews. He was distracted and did not hear the thud of Toby backing into the window.

Like a bear, Toby lunged at Susy and missed. Quickly jumping to his feet he turned, back arched and roared. 'You slag! I should have finished you off then, it would have been so easy!'

In desperation, she threw the statue and screamed, shattering the glass which clattered across the cobble stones, to within inches of Peter's feet. He charged over to the front door and kicked it hard, again and again, until it split from the hinges and he could get inside. Peter scaled the stairs, three at a time, and with both hands grabbed Toby from behind, turning him around and punching him so hard that he lifted him clean into the air and across the room.

'Call the police!' he yelled to Susy, as she crawled away.

Toby came back at him, wild and bleeding, throwing punches into thin air. He was no match for Peter, who was fitter and stronger, but still he fought, lashing out in every direction. Susy found the telephone and hiding in a corner rang the police. They struggled, battering each other, when, with a final crack to the jaw, Peter knocked Toby out cold, leaving his crumpled body to lie unconscious in a bloody heap on the carpet. There was quiet, except for the soft whimpering coming from the corner of the room. Peter enticed Susy out, lifting her up and cradled her in his arms. 'Shush, it's all over,' he said, between her sobs. 'He won't ever bother you again.'

Nobody saw anything unusual when Peter and Susy walked into the apartment at Cadogan Place. Ruffled, but smiling, he guided her gently past the meeting that was in full swing, with barely a nod of recognition. Later, when the entourage had departed, they related the whole story to the girls, who listened in total silence and horror.

Saturday morning, the day of the fashion show, Polly was up and gone by the time Susy surfaced. After a remarkably good night's sleep, she threw back the covers, climbed out of bed and went downstairs to breakfast.

Vanessa was already up and reading the morning papers over a second cup of coffee, when she heard Susy about. 'Morning,' she said, without looking up. Susy appeared clutching a mug of coffee and sat down next to Vanessa at the dining table. 'Good morning,' she said cheerfully.

Vanessa put down the newspaper and with genuine concern asked, 'How are you this morning?'

'I never felt better,' she replied, much to Vanessa's surprise. 'Really, I feel, how should I put it, truly amazing.'

There certainly was a striking improvement overnight, as if a light had been switched on, a bright resplendent light and Vanessa could feel the glow.

'You buried him?' she said conclusively.

Susy nodded. 'Dead and buried. I'm free, Vanessa. Can't you see how wonderful that is?'

Vanessa leant forward and gave Susy a huge hug. 'Of course I can. I am so pleased for you.'

They knew the day had really begun when they received the first frantic phone call from Polly. Summoned from behind the scenes as rehearsals were about to commence, their attendance was required immediately. Polly's manners were usually impeccable, beyond reproach, rarely did one hear her ever curse or swear. However, under extreme pressure, what flowed from her mouth was reminiscent of a street fighters' brawl.

The girls ran up the steps of the hotel, to be immediately directed backstage, through dressers, makeup artists, hairdressers, lighting men and sound men as they searched for Polly. 'There she is,' Susy said, grabbing Vanessa's arm and pointing to where Polly was directing a mobile into position.

'Why the urgency?' Vanessa asked.

Polly breezed passed them both. 'Follow me,' she said, trotting off stage.

Once they had found a quiet corner, she addressed them

directly. 'I have a terrible dilemma,' she stressed, drawing in a deep breath. 'Flu, damn it.' She slapped her forehead. 'She was all right last night, you saw her?'

'Who?' they both chanted in unison.

'Lulu. She's out, flat on her back with a raging temperature. You have got to help me, girls.' Polly looked at each of them in turn. 'One of you is going on stage.' Acting like a woman possessed, a demon at large, the request sounded more like a command.

Vanessa backed down. 'Oh no, definitely not me.'

They both turned to Susy and smiled. 'I can't go up there. I don't know how. I might stumble and make a complete fool of myself. I'd let you down, Polly.'

'I'll show you how,' Polly replied calmly. 'You know how to walk.'

'Yes, but this is different, this is the real thing.'

Polly clasped her hands together and pleaded. 'Susy, we haven't got a great deal of time. We rehearse in ten minutes.' Her raised voice echoed across the stage, drawing everyone's attention.

'We're all behind you,' Vanessa encouraged. 'Go on, show them what you can do.'

Susy hesitated, stalling for time, contemplating the stage and the international set, whose attention she surely would hold. Could she take that walk? Would she help Polly, who appealed to her better nature?

'OK,' she said, having nothing to lose, 'I'll do it.'

Polly was ecstatic and wasting not a moment rushed Susy on to the catwalk. Bewildered, she lined up with the other models as the music began. Tall and graceful under Polly's instruction, she walked up and down, pivot and turn. 'Keep your head up, Susy, eyes ahead, and again.' The ballroom was grand, with magnificent chandeliers hanging overhead and Vanessa found a seat out front to watch as the elaborate last-minute preparations were being completed. Rehearsal over, the girls disappeared backstage to be groomed and painted, leaving the stage hands to place the final seats around the stage.

Pandemonium broke out behind the scenes, with models clamouring for attention, hairdryers humming and people screaming. Timing was crucial and time was running out fast. Clad in only a light dressing gown, Susy was having her hair dressed when she noticed Joyce's reflection in the mirror. She was standing right next to the hairdresser, handbag over her arm, admiring his creative abilities.

'Oh, very nice, it's a work of art,' she said dryly, standing back and peeping over his shoulder for a better look, and added, 'Don't suppose you could do somethin' with mine sweetheart ... when you've finished?'

Ignoring the request, the coiffeur completed his creation and with a haughty smile was off to attend to the next one.

'I'm really nervous, Joyce. What if I make a mistake.'

'So you make a mistake, pet. Now, how's about a nice cup of rosy?'

Polly appeared out of nowhere, barking instructions in every direction. 'Susy, wardrobe.' There were fifteen minutes to go.

Vanessa peeked through a curtain to see the ballroom filling up with affluent, stylish people. There was hardly an empty chair anywhere. Her eyes scanned the crowd searching for Rupert and Piers, who she knew were down there somewhere, when she spotted Gill, sitting three rows from the front. There looking remarkably like an aristocrat was Lucinda, sitting in prime position front row – well, where else? Being pushed and jostled behind the scenes and with only five minutes to go, Vanessa left the chaos backstage and joined the audience out front.

Nervous, but ready, Susy lined up with the other girls, as Polly stepped out on to the podium and took her position. The music began and one by one the girls filed out.

Pushing her way through the crowd, Vanessa remembered that Susy was fourth in line. She took a deep breath and watched her walk up to the end, unfasten the coat, hand on hip, turn and back, perfect. Now she could breathe easy.

Backstage they stripped, changed clothes and were out again.

Feeling more confident, and with her head held high, eyes to the front, she walked again. The changeovers were smooth and faultless.

Joyce watched from the wings and was clearly alarmed at the speed with which things happened, jumping out of the way as the near-naked models flew past her. Susy was among them, but she was damned if she could pick her out in the confusion.

Standing at the side and as close to the stage as was permissible, were Rupert and Piers. Their heads bent backwards as the new season's short flouncy skirts were being twirled above their mischievous faces. Vanessa caught sight of them and while the mannequins paraded, she made her way over to their side.

The show was received well, if the expression on buyers' faces was anything to go by. To say Polly was an artist and a genius was an understatement, but the best was yet to come. The finale was about to commence as Vanessa joined Rupert and Piers by the stage.

The tempo changed, with billows of dry ice clouding the back of the stage. Laser rays lightly sprinkled thousands of swirling droplets of colour on to the catwalk and the girls waited in the wings for their cue. Listening to Polly's words, who was still standing on the podium, at the precise moment they filed on. Piers whooped and hollered, while the audience stood up and applauded loudly. Vanessa bounced up and down and clapped furiously as the models passed slowly by. Dazzling, sensational, Polly's voice was almost drowned out by the noise. Susy was the last to emerge from the back of the stage and into the spotlight. She looked incredible, floating down the steps, the gossamer ballgown lightly lifting and falling each step she took. She turned and grinned at Vanessa, who cheered as she passed down the catwalk.

'Who is that girl?' Rupert asked.

'That's Susy,' Vanessa replied, watching her turn around and walk back.

'Have I met her before?' Vanessa caught Susy's eye again and cheered.

'No, Rupert, you haven't met her before. She's my business partner.'

Rupert watched Susy lead the other girls to the back of the stage, bringing the show to an end. He was enchanted, spellbound in fact. She was the most beautiful creature he had ever laid eyes on.

'I have to meet her, Vanessa. You must introduce me.'

Not that his curiosity had escaped her attention, she knew her brother only too well. He was smitten at first glance and from his impetuous expression, she would be compelled to fulfil his wishes.

'Very well, Rupert, you can meet her after the show.'

Joyce was still standing in the wings when Susy raised her arms in the air at the close of the show, revealing the exquisite ballgown she was wearing to full effect. Joyce looked on with immense pride listening to the applause and nudged the nearest elbow to her.

'Er, that's my girl out there you know … beautiful isn't she? … She's the best girl a mother could 'ave, believe me, I should know. I must be the luckiest woman in the world.'

The atmosphere was more relaxed when Vanessa arrived backstage. Susy was surrounded by a host of people, some of whom she knew. Gill was about to say goodbye, when Susy and Vanessa struggled through the crowd, pushing people out of the way, giving her a wide berth.

'Wasn't she a little cracker?' Gill said, pressing Vanessa's hand warmly.

'A star,' Vanessa replied.

'I had such a good time, girls.'

'And it showed,' they both replied.

'Did I look all right? Did I put a foot out of place?' She already knew the answer.

'You were absolutely bloody marvellous and you know it.'

The noise was intolerable when Polly joined the throng, deafened by three cheers, for she had superbly exceeded all expectations. Susy adjusted her makeup and was brushing her hair when Peter appeared beside her, planting a kiss on both cheeks.

'Um, what can I say, baby, you were just great!' He disappeared before she had a chance to speak, with a cute little blonde on his arm.

Vanessa took Susy to one side and spoke quietly, leading her away from the crowd to where Rupert was impatiently waiting.

'There is somebody who is very anxious to meet you.'

Rupert held out his hand and smiled. 'Hello,' he said, raising her hand to his lips. His voice was warm and sincere.

'Susy, may I introduce my brother, Rupert.'

'Enchanting,' he said, with all the finesse of an English gentleman. 'I am so very pleased to meet you.'

Rupert's smile was inviting, so much so that Susy forgot that anyone else was there. Vanessa backed away, turned around and bumped straight into Polly, who placed her hand on Vanessa's shoulder.

'Now don't think that you are getting away that easily, my friend.' Vanessa had no idea what she was talking about. 'Matchmaking, indeed. How could you stoop to such depths?'

They kept walking side by side, through the hotel, until they reached the bar. Polly opened the door, ushered Vanessa inside and quietly slipped away.

Vanessa stood at the end of the bar alone, until Oliver, sensing that she was there, looked up. He turned towards her and held out his hand, hoping that all the hurt and pain, the anguish and uncertainties, would disappear. Filled with unremitting love and desire, she reached out her hand and drawing closer fell into his embrace. Locked in each other's arms for several moments, no words were spoken, no explanation required – they had found each other again.

Epilogue

Toby Edward Jamison, aged 32 years, was married but separated from his wife of five years and had one child, a son, aged three. The wife, who still resided in the marital home near Oxford, filed for divorce after the alleged adultery took place with a local woman, during the summer of 1985.

A psychotic personality, subject to bouts of violent social behaviour, but a bright boy, some would say exceptional, from a modest background, brought up within a strict religious household, by his mother (divorced) and grandmother, there was no paternal guidance. An immense sexual drive, coupled with a tireless ambition to be rich, spurred him on. When things went wrong for Toby, business failed, he failed, then he would wreak vengeance on others, usually women. To destroy another life made him feel good, in supreme control and able to go on.

The cottage in South Kensington was rented from an old hunting friend, who was abroad on a two-year contract. Sympathetic to Toby's misfortune, he was only too pleased to have the cottage occupied in his absence; the situation was advantageous to both parties. Toby quickly added the luxury items associated with a man of means, blotting out all evidence of his past life. Creating the acceptable image of an affluent successful businessman, he cultivated new friendships and moved in the right circles. Nobody suspected, wrapped up in their own importance, the demon that lay within him, the dark side of the maniac who struck at the very heart of innocence and the vulnerable. A compulsive liar and cheat, he would sacrifice anything, or anybody, to reach his goals.

During the course of the investigation, the facts unfolded. Oliver had known Toby approximately two years. They met at his club, where Toby proved to be an outstanding squash player. Oliver was impressed and a friendship was formed, as they shared the same penchant for the finer things in life. Oliver found him amiable and entertaining, a fierce competitive spirit, although at times a little disjointed.

The evening that Oliver made arrangements with Susy to meet him in Parson's Green to view the apartment, was much the same as many other evenings. That particular evening Oliver picked Toby up in Sloane Square, unusual as Toby's office was in the city, but Oliver never questioned his movements. When Susy finally got through to Oliver on the car phone, their arrangements were overheard by Toby who was seated next to him.

Data previously ascertained that Susy had made a mistake in the time she had arranged to meet Oliver. Seven o'clock, he was on time. She arrived after 7.30, trailed by Toby from Crawfords, to where he brutally attacked and raped her, leaving her for dead. With his athletic physique, camouflaged by a hooded jacket, jeans and sneakers, he blended unnoticed among the commuters buried in their thoughts and newspapers, as they travelled home from work on the underground.

Investigations later proved that Susy was only one of many abused young women to fall prey to the hands of Toby Edward Jamison, but she was fortunate to escape with her life. Luckier than most. He usually travelled far to commit his hideous crimes, covering his tracks well, thus confusing the investigating teams, who had little to go on. His trip to California was a hoax, a diversion. In truth, he was in Hong Kong for seven days, working on a deal that if successful would make him a very wealthy man. His downfall was Susy. Why did he go back? If she had suspected he would surely have known, but he took the chance and played the game. The anonymous pornographic photographs were intended to terrify and force Susy into his protective arms, creating a false sense of security. For he was sure she would never point an accusing finger at him, if they had a relationship.

Peter was the only one who saw through the façade. He smelt the danger, feared for Susy as she unwittingly threw herself at Toby. The truth may well have been hidden forever, if the photograph album had been destroyed, but this oversight cost Toby his freedom.

On 24th March 1988, Toby Edward Jamison was tried and found guilty of the rape and attempted murder of Susan Stevens. The court recommended that the prisoner be detained indefinitely.